THE SHADOW OF THE FORCE

a novel by

NEVILLE JOHNSTON

GA Russell Publishing
Brockville, Ontario, Canada

Special Acknowledgments

To my lifelong friend, Toronto lawyer Fred Levitt, for his unfailing support and assistance, and my wife, Geri, who edited the manuscript of this novel over and over and over again, not only without flinching, but also with fervour and excitement at each reading.

Historical Personages and Other Characters

In this novel, there are references to actual historical personages, such as Catherine de' Medici, Diane de Poitiers and Gian Gastone de' Medici. Every attempt has been made to keep such references as historically true as reasonably possible. However, in the main, the actions and words ascribed to such historical personages are fictitious. All other characters are fictitious, and any resemblance to actual persons, living or dead, is purely coincidental.

Dedication:

To my dear wife, GERI,

my most Loyal Reader,

my most Trusted Critic,

my most Ardent Supporter,

and my most Faithful Friend

Table of Contents

CHAPTER ONE

IT SHOULD NEVER have happened. No. Not on Bay Street, the Wall Street of Toronto. Nor anywhere else, for that matter. And certainly not in the office of a lawyer as successful as Friedrich Bruni, aka Fred Bruni. The news hit the Toronto legal world like a sledge-hammer.

Yvonne Becker was Fred's secretary. A strawberry blonde, with sapphire eyes, a cute upturned nose, and full fleshy lips, she had been green behind the ears when she walked into Fred's fledgling law office in search of a job, about eighteen years years before this thing happened. Fred was then an ambitious young lawyer, who had just a few days before proudly affixed to the front door of his newly-rented office premises on Bay Street his charcoal-grey and silver steel sign bearing the engraved words:

FRIEDRICH BRUNI

BARRISTER AND SOLICITOR

In his own mind, the world was his oyster. All he had to do was to make the right moves, and he would pluck the pearls from their shells, one by one, until he amassed a fortune. He had advertised for a legal secretary, as they called the position back in those days. What Yvonne lacked in experience, she adequately compensated for in personality, intelligence, and good looks. Fred took a chance on her; hired her; and the relationship proved to be a perfect fit.

The day was now Monday, November 8, 1982. Yvonne, a real party animal, was young, single and carefree, and enjoyed playing the field. On weekends, it was party after party after party, and far too many Black Russians. Today, she dragged her tail into the office, like a she-cat limping back home after a night of carousing with the tomcats. She felt weak and fatigued, her head ached, and her mouth was as dry as the wallet of a beggarman. She looked at her watch; it was nine. Yup; she had done it again. She prided herself on always being on time. Fred had always teased her about her punctuality. He had often said that she would be two days too early for her own funeral. Her throat parched from thirst, she gripped tightly in her right hand the panacea for what ailed her, the tried-and-true prescription for her self-inflicted wounds; a Starbucks Grande Mocha Frappuccino with a double shot of Espresso. She dumped herself into her secretarial chair, and, muttering the words "First things first", voraciously gulped down the salvific beverage.

As she tossed the empty plastic cup into the wastebasket, her eyes wandered off in the direction of Fred's office. Strange, she thought; the lights were on in Fred's office. But Fred would normally wander in about ten; very rarely was he ever in by nine. She could have sworn that she had turned all lights off before she left on Friday. Surely, Fred is not in this early? She shrugged this off and began organizing for the day's work ahead. Her mind drifted to thoughts of Fred. She worshipped the ground he walked on. Fred sometimes razzed her for remaining a spinster for so long. "No man is good enough for you, Yvonne," he would say, with an impish smile. "Before you say yes to any man, I need to meet him, and give my approval or disapproval." She would usually respond with a guffaw, as she thought to herself "Yes; a spinster, but not a virgin! Besides, where in the world can I find a man like you, Fred Bruni!" But she was never bold enough to vocalize this declaration. She admitted to herself on numerous occasions that she had fallen for her boss, and all he had to do was give one ounce of encouragement and she would be his lapdog, or anything else he wanted her to be. Sometimes she wore tight-fitting sculpted sweaters, with nothing underneath, except, of course, her full-figured heaving breasts. And sometimes she made a point of raising the hem of her skirt to a revealing position above the knees, accentuating her shapely legs when she sat opposite him, with her legs crossed, one thigh on top of the other. And sometimes she would momentarily toss her head sideways, as she ran her fingers through her long, flowing strawberry blonde hair, or softly caressed her neck. But Fred would never bite the bait. He was always the true professional.

She picked up her steno pad, and headed for Fred's office to check Fred's calendar for today's appointments. As she entered, she saw Fred in his chair, slumped over, his head resting on his desk, as if fast asleep. He must have come in early and fallen asleep at his desk. She tip-toed over to the slouched body. She saw traces of a white foam on his lips. She shuddered. Her heart started to pound rapidly. This cannot be good, she gasped. What has happened to Fred? She reached for his shoulder, and tugged at him gently. Fred's body was completely listless. She stared into his wide-open eyes; the pupils were hugely dilated. He was as white as a sheet. By now, her heart was in her mouth. "Oh no!" she cried out. She felt as if the floor had suddenly opened and was swallowing up her whole world. Fred is dead.

She immediately ran out into the hallway, shouting for help. Within seconds, there were lawyers and secretaries from neighbouring offices gathered around her. "Fred is dead! Fred is dead!" she kept shouting, pointing back behind her, as tears streamed from her eyes. Instinctively, they all rushed into Fred's office, where they saw the gruesome scene. "Call 911!" someone shouted. "Too late," another wryly remarked, "the Grim Reaper has already left."

Within ten minutes, two EMTs arrived. They quickly took Fred's vital signs. They shook their heads from side to side; it was too late; Fred was indeed as dead as a doornail. Because of the circumstances of the death, especially the foaming at the mouth, they called in the Metropolitan Toronto Police and the Office of the Coroner. Fred's office was declared a crime scene and was soon cordoned off with the usual yellow-black tape. Even Yvonne was relegated to being a mere bystander, looking in from the outside of the crime scene.

Yvonne was beside herself. She stood there, shaking uncontrollably, bug-eyed, and awash in tears. Then the thought struck her; someone had to get hold of Fred's wife, Isolde, and break the bad news to her. "Poor Isolde," she kept saying to herself. Reluctantly, she decided that she was the one to tell Isolde. But it was best done face to face.

Trying as best she could to regain her composure, she tumbled into the elevator, and headed down to the underground parking garage, where her 1963 flamingo Volkswagen Cabriolet was parked, not far from the elevators. As she folded herself into the driver's seat, the tears were rushing in rivulets down her cheeks. So much for makeup, she thought, as her coral pink eyeshadow was daubed like paint all around her eyes. For a moment, she wondered if she should not have grabbed a cab instead of driving herself. Too late now. She had to get to the Bruni residence as fast as she could; there was no time to waste.

After years of tackling traffic from her apartment in Brampton to downtown Toronto, she now considered herself a whiz at beating to death the monster that masquerades under the name of 'rush-hour traffic'. She now had to make her way from Bay and King to the Bruni mansion in the Bridle Path, which meant that she would be going in the opposite direction to the bumper-to-bumper masses of steel slowly grinding their way southerly to the waiting offices of downtown Toronto. The fastest route was to go north on Don Valley Parkway, then north on Bayview and proceed to Post Road, and then make a right turn on to the Bridle Path, the most expensive residential district in Canada. This should take her no longer than thirty minutes. Yes, the Bridle Path, commonly known as *Millionaire's Row*. It had been only about three years earlier that Fred had purchased his mansion on Saddlers Court, for what he had thought was a real bargain; only $13,500,000. Yvonne had been there four or five times, always to deliver documents to Fred. She was familiar with the outside of the two-storey mansion, a sprawling structure, about twelve thousand square feet in living area, the wings resplendent with green ivy. She pulled into the sweeping speckled black and white cobble-stone driveway, which culminated into a circle, at the centre of which was an elaborate fountain, reminiscent of pictures she had seen of the Trevi Fountain in Rome. She could not help but think, as she had done on every other occasion that she had been there, how inconsequential a residence of such magnitude and opulence made her feel. But on this one occasion, there was another thought that haunted her. Now that Fred was dead, she would never ever have the opportunity of capturing his heart, and maybe, just maybe, changing places with Isolde in the mansion.

Her legs could barely sustain her as she climbed out of the cabriolet. Her knees were wobbly, shaking spontaneously from her body's neurological processing of the daunting task that she was about to perform. Courage, she whispered to herself. Must muster the courage necessary for the task. This is no time to succumb to weakness of mind. After all, she had already created an agenda to govern how she should, with the greatest degree of empathy, break the bad news to Isolde. She took a deep breath as she rang the doorbell. She waited. There was no response. She rang it again. Still no response. Isolde must be in a far end of the house. By and large, it would take a full five minutes at a minimum to walk from a distal end of the elaborate residence to the front entrance. God, please let Isolde be home. It would be far too painful to have to marshal the strength to do this all over again. She was about to ring the doorbell a third time, when the door opened.

"Yvonne," Isolde exclaimed, with a broad smile on her face. "How nice to see you. What brings you here? Is this not the most beautiful day? I just love when the leaves change colours in the fall; the endless shades of gold and crimson and orange and purple and brown. Don't you? Not a bad time to be out of the office, is it? I have not seen you in ages. How are you, Yvonne? Please come in and have a cup of coffee. And you must try my latest creation of butter tarts."

Yvonne choked, as she tried her best to hold back tears. Typical of a woman's modus operandi, she must above all control the agenda. It would not do to tell Isolde prematurely that her husband is dead. No; that would be too shocking. Isolde's barrage of questions had derailed her. Yvonne must quickly regroup. She must control the narrative. She had to do what she had to do in her own time. In exactly the manner in which she had planned it, step by step by step. So, which question should she answer first? The smile on Isolde's face was genuine. Ever since Yvonne had started working for Fred, Isolde had always been kind and courteous to her, unfailingly treating her as an equal, and not as a subordinate. There had never ever been a condescending sign of *noblesse oblige*. If only Isolde had known of Yvonne's feelings for Fred! Isolde cocked her head to one side, as she waited for Yvonne to answer.

"Is there something wrong, Yvonne?" asked Isolde, somewhat intuitively, as she took hold of Yvonne's hands and pulled her in for a quick embrace.

"I could use a cup of coffee," Yvonne responded, glumly. She avoided reference to the butter tarts. Screw the tarts, she thought. This was not the time nor place for tarts, as much as she was fully aware as to how proud Isolde was of her baking skills. Isolde was always experimenting with her recipes to make her sweet goods ever better and better. And she knew that Yvonne had always shown more than a passing interest in her creations. She had frequently used Fred as her emissary to deliver the prized products to Yvonne at the office.

"Then come into my parlour," Isolde insisted, as she put her right arm around Yvonne's shoulder and gracefully guided her into the kitchen. "Just make yourself comfortable, my dear".

Yvonne sat down at the kitchen table, ever mindful of what she still had to do, but not quite ready to do it. The silence in the air was suddenly ruptured by a wave of children's laughter which floated in from another area of the huge house.

"Emil and Sophie are playing video games," Isolde jovially commented, as she ground some Jamaican Blue Mountain coffee beans in a vintage manual coffee grinder. She always believed in grinding her own; 'brings out the real flavour', she would say, as she reinforced her belief in authenticity. "The world of electronics is consuming the lives of our children; to me, not necessarily a good thing. But it does keep them happy and occupied. Would you believe that Emil is now ten and Sophie eight? They are growing like weeds. Before we know it, they will cut the apron string; flee the coop, as they say." Yes, thought Yvonne. There is the other problem. All this time she had been concentrating on how Isolde would take the news of Fred's death; she had completely overlooked the children. How could anyone ever explain to Emil and Sophie that their daddy would never be coming home? Isolde now left it up to her Corning Ware coffee percolator to do its magic; to produce the best tasting coffee in the whole wide world.

Yvonne had still not done what she had come to do. She remained noticeably silent. Isolde was the one to break the silence. She sat down opposite Yvonne. She looked her directly in her eyes.

"I am sorry, Yvonne. I have been doing all the talking. You must find me a real chatter-box. How can I help you?" Before Yvonne could speak, Isolde intercepted with one more question. "You know, Fred slept at the office last night. He went in on Sunday evening; said he had some very urgent work to do for his major Swiss client; it was so late, he said he would just sleep in the office; would be home sometime today; he also wanted to let me know that he loves me. Have you been to the office this morning? Did you see Fred?"

At this, Yvonne broke down completely. She literally lost it. It's now or never, she decided, as the tears flowed torrentially down her face, drenching her blouse. Her heart was pounding so loudly she could have sworn that Isolde could hear it. Isolde perceived that there was a major problem.

"What's the matter, Yvonne. Is it Fred? Did he have an accident? Is he in the hospital?" She was now importunate in her efforts to get an answer from Yvonne. All this time, she had thought that Yvonne was there at the Saddlers Court mansion to deliver something from the office, or perhaps to seek help for a personal problem of hers. How could she, Isolde, have missed the point completely? How could she have been so totally blind?

"It's Fred," Yvonne finally blurted out.

"What has happened to Fred, Yvonne? You must tell me as soon as possible." Tears had now started to well in Isolde's eyes. Yvonne had to tell her the hard truth without any more delay. In a reversal of roles, she stood and wrapped her right arm around Isolde's shoulder.

"Fred will not be coming home," Yvonne whispered, her voice so painful it was hardly audible. "He is dead, Isolde."

Isolde blanched. Speechless, she stared blankly at Yvonne. She could not believe what she had just heard. The room started to swirl around her. Her husband is dead? Yvonne leaned forward to embrace her; to console her; to do whatever one needs to do under those circumstances. But Isolde pulled away.

"What happened to Fred, Yvonne?" she pleaded, in a high-pitched voice, her eyes wide open in shock.

"I do not know, Isolde. All I know is that I found him dead at his desk. He had been foaming from his mouth."

Isolde immediately got up. She was now in a state of frenzy. "I must go and see for myself," she said, as she started out of the kitchen, intending to grab her coat and rush to Fred's office.

"It's best that you remain here for the time being, Isolde. Fred's office has been declared a crime scene. The coroner has ordered an autopsy. He said to tell you that his office will be in touch with you shortly for you to go to the City Morgue and positively identify the body. In the meantime, there is nothing you can do."

Isolde was now beside herself. She was sobbing uncontrollably. Emil and Sophie heard her crying, and came into the kitchen to find out what was going on. Why was their mother in tears? But this was, of course, another problem. How would Isolde break the news to her young children that their beloved father would never again return to them? This was not the time nor place for doing so. She embraced Emil and Sophie in a family hug. She told them that she was not feeling well, but would be fine in a few minutes. They should go back to their game.

"I want you to know that I am always here for you, Isolde," Yvonne said, in a low, controlled voice. At least she would do the right thing for the woman whose husband she had coveted.

Without saying another word, Isolde picked up the phone in the kitchen, and dialed a number.

"Hi, Margot," she choked, still sobbing loudly. "No, I am not OK. Can you come over as soon as possible? Five minutes? Hurry, Margot. I have bad news."

Isolde turned to Yvonne. Margot, Fred's sister, who also lived in the Bridle Path, was on her way over. She will be here in five minutes. Isolde thanked Yvonne for making all that effort to convey the news to her personally. It was very much appreciated. Yvonne was a true friend; but this was now a time for family alone. Yvonne's mind somehow momentarily thought of that cup of Blue Mountain coffee that Isolde had so meticulously brewed for her. The aroma pervaded the air; sweet to the nostrils; but, at this point, like Yvonne, an unwelcome guest. The percolator slowly continued to do its work.

As Yvonne climbed into the cockpit of her timeworn little flamingo Cabriolet, she was thinking that not only did Isolde need to come to grips with the death of her husband, but she also had to cope with breaking the news to Fred's sister, Margot, and, last but not least, to the children, Emil and Sophie. In Yvonne's mind, these were Herculean tasks.

As she drove along Post Road toward Bayview, she could not help but note that the day which Isolde had described as "the most beautiful day" had in the twinkle of an eye turned into a bleak, dreary day, complete with the season's first drops of snow. Could it be that even Nature, feeling the loss of a great human being, was itself shedding a few tears?

Instinctively heading south on Bayview toward the Don Valley South, it suddenly dawned on Yvonne that, with Fred gone and his office having been declared a crime scene, once she was permitted access to the office, the only tasks she had to perform were to put a message on the phone that the office was closed until further notice; to post a notice to the same effect on the front door of the office; and to advise the general public by a classified ad to that effect in both The Toronto Star and The Globe and Mail. After that, she was, as a best-case scenario, on forced leave of absence. With Fred gone, she will have to take a few days to regain her composure and to contemplate her future. Her experience in Fred's employ had been nirvana. He had been a great boss; she had the general run of the office; and had been well paid. How could she ever replace that job? Where would she ever find a boss that could stand in Fred's shoes? She tried to shrug off these concerns; at least, for the time being. After all, tomorrow will just have to take care of itself.

"What a difference a day makes!" she uttered to herself, as the old Cabriolet sputtered and fumed down the Don Valley South. "Goddammit! Goddammit! Goddammit!" she cried. Her words broke the monotony of the worn and wailing windshield wipers, and the drab drone of the heating fan which was undoubtedly on the verge of dying.

CHAPTER TWO

TIME MOVED SLOWLY for Isolde, as she mourned the loss of her beloved husband. It was now eight days since his passing; and it was as if she had just received the news yesterday. Worst of all, she was not one iota closer to finding out the cause of death.

At least she had been able to break gently to Emil and Sophie that their father had gone on to serve in the mansion of "our Lord Jesus Christ as one of his angels". She was surprised as to how calmly they accepted the news; just as Fred would have expected of them. They did shed tears, but they never lost their composure. No doubt, they were cast in their father's own image. True Stoics.

Margot was a different kettle of fish. She completely lost it, and, notwithstanding Isolde's best efforts to comfort her, she was inconsolable. She and Fred had been joined at the hip. In the family of Alfonso and Kiki Bruni back in Bern, Switzerland, where Fred and Margot were born, they were the only children. Just two years apart in age, they were inseparable as they enjoyed their fairy-tale childhood. The family had left Switzerland for Canada when Fred was ten and Margot was eight, the same ages as Emil and Sophie are now. Being already fluent in English, they adapted very easily to their new lives in Canada. Fred became a lawyer, graduating *summa cum laude* from the University of Toronto Law School. Margot obtained a degree in Architecture. Fred married Isolde, also a lawyer, but who never practised law. Margot married an architect, Heinz Baumann. Strangely enough, Margot herself never pursued a career as an architect. Both Fred and Heinz quickly zoomed to the top of their respective professions. For each, the money flowed in copiously, as if from waterfalls, and there was no need for either Isolde or Margot to work. As Fred's practice blossomed and bloomed, his standard of living stayed one or two steps ahead of his income. He and Isolde enjoyed all the toys and pleasures of life, bar none. Their luxurious mansion on *Millionaire's Row*; Fred's 1980 silver Rolls-Royce Phantom; Isolde's 1981 fire-engine red Ferrari Berlinetta Boxer; their summer home in Muskoka Lakes, north of Toronto; their luxury condominium in Palm Beach, Florida; their fifty-seven-foot 1971 mahogany Chris-Craft Constellation boat *My Love Isolde* on Muskoka Lake; their ninety-five foot luxury yacht *Isle of Capri* on the Intercoastal Waterway in Florida; their memberships in the Granite Club, in the Toronto Cricket, Skating and Curling Club, in the Oakland Golf and Country Club, and in the Muskoka Fishing Club; their chalet in the Alpine town of St. Moritz in Switzerland; annual trips to Monaco; and the list goes on.

The lifestyle of Heinz and Margot was not much different from that of Fred and Isolde. While they tended to be more frugal with their spending, Heinz' highly successful architectural practice permitted him entry into the fabled *Millionaire's Row Club*. Apart from the strong filial bond between Fred and Margot, the financial success and rich lifestyle shared by both families drew them even closer together.

As soon as the coroner authorized the release of Fred's corpse to Isolde, she, with the assistance of Margot, planned Fred's funeral and burial. Fred and Margot had been raised in the Swiss Reformed Church. This was the branch of Protestantism that had emanated out of the Reformation in Switzerland in the sixteenth century, through its founder Huldryk Zwingli. It was only natural that, when the Bruni family relocated in Toronto, they would seek out a church such as the Lutheran Reformed Church of Switzerland, and that when Isolde entered the family fold, she would adopt that as her own church, notwithstanding that her father and mother had been, and she had been brought up as, ardent Roman Catholics. Faithful to her church, Isolde arranged for a relatively private funeral service in Fred's memory, restricted to family, close friends, Fred's business associates, and, of course, Fred's secretary, Yvonne. Immediately following the funeral service, the funeral cortege wound its way to Mount Pleasant Cemetery, where Fred's body was laid to rest.

The days gradually slid one into another, with Isolde being dragged along listlessly for the ride, as if being washed out to the sea of time by a tsunami. She compared her life without Fred to a flake of snow falling vibrantly from the sky, only to become absorbed, along with thousands of other snowflakes, to become a gargantuan snowdrift on the ground below. Got to take hold of myself, she resolved. How would Fred handle this? Yes; the first thing he would seek to find out is: What was the cause of death? As she pondered this question, it drove her into action. She had received the Death Certificate in the mail; but, what with the business of the funeral and burial arrangements, not to mention caring for the children, she had not taken the few minutes required to read it. She rummaged through a drawer in her desk in her office, and found it. The autopsy and the circumstances of Fred's death had led to a conclusion that the Immediate Cause of Death was **ASPHYXIATION;** the Underlying Cause of Death was **POISONING (NO TRACE OF THE POISONING AGENT FOUND);** and the Manner of Death was **SUICIDE.** What the hell? If the death was by poisoning, why could they not determine the type of poison? Why would Fred commit suicide, when he had everything to live for? Had he left a suicide note that she had not been told about? Why had they not spoken with her before coming to this conclusion of suicide? She would have told them that Fred had shown no sign of depression or other mental instability or any disease of the body. He had left the house on that Sunday afternoon to go to the office to do some urgent work. He had phoned her at about eleven to tell her that he would just stay in the office overnight. He sounded in a very upbeat mood. He had told her that he loved her; to tell the kids he loved them; and that he would see them all the next day. Why would a man like that commit suicide? Sure, the evidence of foaming at the mouth was suggestive of a poison; but even that symptom was consistent with other illnesses, such as rabies. In this modern day and age, would it not be a relatively easy thing to find traces of the poison, and identify the particular deadly agent?

She picked up the phone and called the Office of the Coroner. She asked for the coroner. Sorry, he was out of town, and would not be back for two weeks. Was there an assistant she could speak with? She asked the assistant why they could not determine the type pf poison used. He said that the autopsy had been very thorough; the pathologist had examined tissues from every organ in the body. Then how can they conclude that death had been caused by poisoning? Because the symptoms were consistent with poisoning. What symptoms? Foaming at the mouth; sudden unexplained death; no evidence of a gunshot wound; no evidence of a stabbing; no evidence of blunt force trauma; no evidence of asphyxiation; no evidence of a drowning; no evidence of a heart attack; no evidence of a stroke; no evidence of kidney failure; no evidence of anyone having entered the victim's office during the evening; the only logical conclusion is that death was suicide by poisoning. Why can the type of poison not be identified? There are poisons in numerous countries of the world that have escaped identification; it is an incomplete science. After spending about fifteen minutes on the phone with the assistant, Isolde ended the conversation in utter frustration. In her mind, one thing was for sure: Fred had not committed suicide. It was up to her to take the necessary steps to prove it. And the circumstances do not point to accidental death. In her mind, there was only one conclusion: Fred had been murdered. She would not rest until she had wholly unearthed the truth from its secret grave.

With Fred's remains buried, realism had now crept back into Isolde's life. Apart from being aware of the real estate assets in the Bridle Path, Muskoka, Jupiter Island, and St. Moritz; and the Muskoka boat *My Love Isolde* and the Intracoastal Waterway luxury yacht *Isle of Capri,* and the luxury cars, Fred's Rolls Royce and her Ferrari, she knew very little of the family's finances; Fred had kept that all bundled like secrets within the vault of his cranium, and, having complete trust and confidence in Fred, she had been content to leave all financial matters of the Bruni family completely in Fred's hands. Now here she is; completely destitute of information as to their true financial position. She has come to the stark realization that she knows zilch; *nichts,* as she would hear Fred say in German. Her instinct told her that it undoubtedly required a huge amount of money just to maintain the enormous assets and lifestyle that the Bruni family enjoyed. It was now incumbent on her, starting from scratch, to ascertain the full extent of their financial circumstances as soon as possible.

Isolde telephoned Bernard "Barney" Ratskeller, Fred's long-time friend and lawyer.

"Barney," she said, fighting to hold back the tears, "I saw you at Fred's funeral, but did not get an opportunity to chat with you."

"Isolde, I am so deeply sorry for your loss. Fred was a fine human being. We will all miss him so much."

"I need to come in and discuss Fred's estate with you. I recall Fred telling me that his last Will was prepared by you."

"Yes, Isolde. As a matter of fact, I have Fred's Will right here before me. I was waiting for the right time to call you to come in and see me. Can you come in at ten tomorrow morning?"

"Definitely, Barney. See you then."

Barney's law office was located in the same building as Fred's, just one floor above. As the elevator passed the floor of Fred's office, she had a sudden gut-wrenching feeling in her stomach; it was as if she was on the verge of vomiting. She remembered the numerous times that she had gone to Fred's office throughout their marriage, usually to collect Fred for a luncheon date. Now, to simply take the elevator past that floor made her feel sick to her stomach.

As she stepped into Barney's office, he got up to greet her, giving her a warm embrace. He looked sympathetically into her amber eyes, closest things he had ever seen to a cat's eyes, what with their yellow copper touches of tint splashed with hues of hazel and brown. The orbs of her eyes were wet with tears, as if to shield them from scrutiny. Once seated, she waited for him to lead the way. Strange, she thought; Fred had been a lawyer; and she was herself a lawyer; and here she was, hiring a lawyer. Lawyers must indeed rule the world and our lives, she thought. There is always some opening for lawyers. Whatever the client's lot in the vicissitudes of life, whatever the human condition, whether success or misfortune, the lawyer is always there, cap in hand, eager to collect a fee.

"My dear Isolde," Barney remarked, as he looked at the Will in front of him. "The Will is simple. As you know, Fred always wanted everything kept simple. You are named as the sole Executrix and Trustee, and, as would be expected, the whole estate is left to you."

"That's no surprise to me," Isolde remarked. "Did Fred provide you with a list of his assets?"

"Yes, as a matter of fact. I have it right here. His statement not only shows the assets, but also the estimated indebtedness registered against each asset."

"That's very helpful, Barney. I have no clue as to what we owe." She extended her hand for the statement of financial affairs. Barney handed the statement to her.

Isolde's face gradually grew grim as she read the statement, mouthing each liability as she read. "On the Bridle Path residence, mortgage of $10,000,000; on the Muskoka summer home, mortgage of $1,000,000; on the Florida condo, mortgage of $850,000; on the Rolls Royce, mortgage of $75,000; on my Ferrari, mortgage of $55,000; on *My Love Isolde*, mortgage of $40,000; on *Isle of Capri*, mortgage of $100,000. At least the St. Moritz chalet appears to be free and clear; thank God for small blessings! May I borrow a calculator?" Barney handed her a small calculator. She quickly tallied the figures.

"My God!" she exclaimed. "Debts of over $12,000,000! Barney, I have no real source of income. How will I be able to manage?"

Barney shrugged his shoulders. He had no magic elixir.

"You missed one item on the statement, Isolde. Fred listed a $1,000,000 policy of life insurance with Prudential Insurance Company of America. That also seems to be free and clear. We have to free up the death benefit as soon as possible. Have you got the Death Certificate?"

Isolde handed him the Death Certificate. He read the Manner of Death: **SUICIDE.** A frown crept onto his face. He explained to her that this may be a problem, as some insurance policies exclude suicide. He will have to read the insurance policy. He had his secretary make ten notarial copies of the Death Certificate and of the Will. He handed her the original and nine notarial copies of the Death Certificate, and nine Notarial Copies of the Will. Bothered by his statement that the life insurance policy may exclude suicide, Isolde explained to him that it was her firm opinion that Fred had not committed suicide; he had been murdered. In response to this, Barney simply raised his eyebrows. Although he did not say this to her, he was thinking that 'her opinion' really did not matter; she was not an expert.

"I will contact Prudential immediately. I will also read the policy. Hopefully, there is no exclusionary clause for suicide. If so, once I receive the Proof of Claim form, I will get you in to sign. You should have those funds within a week. At least, that will tide you over for now. Then you will have to consider selling some of the assets. We will broach that topic later."

Still reeling from the shock of what she had just learned, Isolde thanked Barney for his help. As she left his office, she shook her head and thought "What a fool I have been to have never questioned Fred about our finances!" Once inside the elevator, alone, she pursed her lips, closed her eyes, took a deep breath, and reprimanded herself, "My dear Isolde, you have been a real jack-ass!! Now smarten up! You have a mountain of work to do."

CHAPTER THREE

YVONNE was trying to adapt to her new life as an unemployed legal secretary; a temporary situation, she hoped. That morning when her phone rang, she had slept in late. She swore as she grabbed for the phone, buried under yesterday's underclothes.

"Hello," she mumbled.

"Good morning, Yvonne. I hope I didn't wake you up?" The voice was unmistakably Isolde's.

"Is that you Isolde? I have just been lazing around my apartment. How are you?"

"I am doing OK. I have seen better days; but I try to keep my chin up."

"What can I do for you, Isolde? How are Emil and Sophie?"

"The kids are fine. They miss their father; but I try to keep them occupied. I need your help, Yvonne. It's in relation to Fred's law practice. Can you meet me at Fred's office this afternoon?"

"Sure, Isolde. I will do anything I can to help. What time?"

"How about two?'

"Two is fine, Isolde. I still have a key. See you then."

When Isolde arrived at Fred's office, Yvonne was already there, sitting at her old desk in the reception area. She rose to greet Isolde. There was a quick embrace. Isolde pulled up a chair opposite Yvonne.

"You know, Yvonne, I have come to realize that I know nothing at all about Fred's law practice. I am starting out with a completely blank page. I know nothing; zero; zilch; nichts; niente; nada. I need to know everything there is to know about it. A crash course, so to speak. I need to rely on you, Yvonne. Of course, as there is no income, I cannot afford to pay you at your old rate. Would half your old salary do?"

This brings a faint smile to Yvonne's face, which does not reflect her true feeling. She feels a lump rise to her throat, as she cannot believe what she is hearing. Here is Isolde, awash with wealth, trying to nickel and dime her. The widow of the man she secretly loved needs her help; but is not willing to fully compensate her for it. Of course, at this time, any amount of money will surely help. She desperately needs a source of income.

"Thank you very much, Isolde. You are a real life-saver. Just tell me what you require of me."

"OK. Let's get down to work. Can you get me a steno pad and a pen?" Yvonne readily handed these items to her.

"Please tell me all that you can recall about Fred's law practice. Go slowly. Remember that I do not take shorthand." This evoked a laugh from Yvonne. Strange how ironically things turn out; the boss' wife was now taking dictation from her; a complete reversal of roles. But this was not the reversal of roles that Yvonne had obsessed over for so many years. Fred's death had made short shrift of her devious plans to lure him into bed, and to eventually take Isolde's place as the mistress of the Saddlers Court mansion and as the beneficiary of all the other trappings of wealth and prestige, real and imaginary, that went with it.

"Well, let me see. Fred had a very specialized law practice. He only practised Business Law; nothing else. But beyond that, he only represented Swiss clients. He never ever acted for Canadian clients, nor clients from any country except Switzerland. Contact with his Swiss clients was mainly by phone; and, also by e-mail, fax, and sometimes by snail-mail. His Swiss clients never came to the office; if there was anything to be signed, Fred would either sign on their behalf through Power of Attorney, or he would courier the documents to the clients in Switzerland, with instructions for signing before a Swiss lawyer. The only persons coming into Fred's office were lawyers on the opposite sides of his deals; lawyers whom he retained to do the more mundane stuff, such as real estate transactions and the like; accountants and other agents; and sales representatives in pursuit of Fred's business. That, in a nutshell, was the nature of Fred's law practice."

"Sounds like a 'dream law practice'. Every lawyer would have envied Fred for that, I suppose," Isolde commented, dryly. "Where can I find a list of all clients whom Fred represented over the past year?"

"It's all here, buried in the computer. I will print the client list for you." Within, a few minutes, Yvonne handed a client list to Isolde, which was surprisingly scant.

"Can you also print for me copies of the Clients' Trust Ledgers and the General Ledger over the past year?"

"Sure thing," Yvonne responded. Within a few minutes, copies were in Isolde's hands. Isolde was impressed with Yvonne's efficiency and speed. No wonder Fred had enjoyed working with her.

"Do you have Fred's Appointment Books for last year and this year?"

Yvonne went to a filing cabinet, and returned with the Appointment Book for 1981. "The Appointment book for 1982 is still on Fred's desk. Do you want me to fetch it for you?"

"No. that's fine. I will be working at Fred's desk. I have a task for you which will really test your memory, Yvonne. Apart from the period of approximately two weeks when Fred was away on business in Europe, I would like you to jot down for me all that you can recall as to Fred's activities during the sixty days immediately preceding his death. I need the name of everyone with whom he met, whether in his office, at another office, at lunch, or elsewhere. Also, the name of everyone who spoke on the phone with Fred, as best as you can recall. As for the period of approximately two weeks that he was in Europe, I would like you to relate everything you know, or have information about, Fred's activities in Europe. With whom did he meet? Where? When? Why? Can you do that for me?"

"I will certainly give it a good whirl," Yvonne replied.

"Thanks, Yvonne. Where do I find the files for Fred's clients over the past year?"

Yvonne pointed to a three-drawer filing cabinet in a corner of Fred's office.

"That's it? That small cabinet contains the files for all transactions over the past year or so?"

"That's it, Isolde. As I told you, Fred had a very specialized type of practice."

"Just one more thing, Yvonne. Do you have a copies of the Financial Statements for Fred's law practice for the last financial year?" Yvonne went into Fred's office and returned with the Financial Statements, which she copied for Isolde.

"OK, Yvonne. I will be in from 9 to 5 over the next day or so or so. Can you be here during those hours?"

"By all means, Isolde. Anything to help." Cheap bastard, Yvonne muttered under her breath, when Isolde's back was turned away from her. She wants all my time, but doesn't want to pay for it. What's happened to the Biblical adage *The labourer is worth of his hire?*

"I will write you a cheque tomorrow. For the indefinite future, you are still an employee of this law office."

Armed with the documents she had received from Yvonne, Isolde withdrew into Fred's office, and sat down behind his desk, ready to start on her quest for knowledge and information. She was faced with a task as Herculean as finding the Holy Grail. Yvonne remained at her own desk, already engaged in preparation of the memorandum re Fred's activities over the past sixty days, as had been requested by her new boss.

The first document reviewed by Isolde were the Financial Statements. They revealed that for the last Financial Year Fred had a net income of $2,567,425. Wow, she muttered under her breath. He sure had the income to support his lavish life-style. And the remarkable thing is that this income had been generated solely through clients in Switzerland.

Examining the Clients' Trust Ledger, she found that, as at the time of his death, Fred had active files, all opened separately, for what appeared to be forty-five different clients, but each client apparently represented by one trustee, namely, *VolksBankBern*, which, from the small amount of German she knew, she would guess as translating to 'The Peoples' Bank of Bern'. The indication that VolksBankBern was acting for different clients came from the files having been opened as follows: 'VolksBankBern in trust for Client #101', 'Volksbankbern in trust for Client #102', 'VolksBankBern in trust for Client #103', and so on. An examination of the General Ledger revealed that Fred rendered huge invoices to VolksBankBern, which threw light on the enormous net income accruing to Fred as shown in the Financial Statements of the previous year. Isolde made note of the contact information for VolksBankbern, which was located in the old City of Bern, Switzerland. That's odd, she thought; Fred had taken her to so many other cities of Europe—Paris, Barcelona, Berlin, Vienna, Moscow, Milan, Florence, Venice, Rome, Athens—but he had never taken her to the old City of Bern, where he had been born. And now she discovers that he had maintained for several years very close business ties with Bern, which housed his major client; and yet he had never taken her to Bern.

Isolde then tackled the individual files in the three-drawer filing cabinet in Fred's office. She scoured every document in each file. There was one common bond among all files; every file involved a purchase of, or a mortgage loan on, a very valuable asset in the Province of Ontario. There was not a single file which was for a sale of, or the borrowing of money on a mortgage, debenture or other security on, an asset in Ontario. Every file involved either the client purchasing, or loaning money on the security of, an asset in Ontario. Every invoice rendered by Fred to VolksBankBern showed Fred's fee calculated on the basis of a percentage of the amount of the transaction. It was always ten per cent; a purchase transaction involving a price of $1,000,000 resulted in Fred's fee being $100,000. Not bad compensation for Fred, Isolde thought to herself.

In reviewing the clients' files, Isolde found correspondence from VolksBankBern to Fred wherein the bank referred to 'our mutual client', which pretty well confirmed that the bank was acting in its capacity as a trustee only. There is one e-mail from the bank in which the client is referred to as 'our mutual client in Rome', but this was an anomaly. One other piece of interesting correspondence was a letter from Fred sent a few weeks before his last visit to Bern in which Fred suggested to VolksBankBern that perhaps he should know the identity of 'the mutual client', as he had to ensure that he was acting in accordance with the Laws of Canada and the Rules of the Law Society of Upper Canada. Isolde could find no response to this letter.

At this point it was five past five. Yvonne came in to see if there was anything more that she could do for Isolde.

"Not today, Yvonne. You may leave now. See you here in the morning. I am ready to wrap it up for today myself."

The next morning, both Isolde and Yvonne were back at the office, bright and early. The first order of business was to arrange with the firm's bank, The Toronto-Dominion Bank, that Isolde would, in her capacity as Executrix and Trustee of Fred's estate, have signing authority on the firm bank account. She dispatched Yvonne to the bank, with a Notarial Copy of the Will and a Notarial Copy of the Death Certificate. While Yvonne was at the bank, Isolde again reviewed the General Ledger, which showed a bank balance of $251,751. Yvonne was soon back with the required Signature Card, which Isolde readily signed. Yvonne was once again dispatched to the bank to deliver the signed Signature Card.

Isolde then resumed her detailed review of the General Ledger, the debit side of which was a treasure trove of information as to Fred's activities. One notable entry was a payment of $11,831.18 to SwissCan Travel Agency of Toronto made on October 15, 1982. She quickly located the invoice from SwissCan Travel, which gave a breakdown of the expenditures:

SWISSCAN TRAVEL AGENCY OF TORONTO
15 Yonge Street, Toronto, Ontario

Mr. Friedrich Bruni,

First Bank Building, Suite 810

30 Bay Street, Toronto, ON

Invoice: #5960 Date: October 15, 1982

Limousine (Bridle Path to Pearson International Airport) ....$ 115.00

Airfare (KLM from Toronto to Bern: Business Class) 3,469.59

Airfare (SwissAir from Bern to Florence: Business Class)...........................759.62

Hotel Accomodation (2 nights in Florence)..915.05

Airfare (Alitalia from Florence to Rome: Business Class) 439.15

Hotel Accomodation (4 nights in Rome)..1,875.00

Airfare (KLM from Rome to Paris: Business Class).....................................875.99

Airfare (Air France from Paris to Toronto: Business Class).........................3,266.78

Limousine (Pearson International. to Bridle Path) 115.00

TOTAL   *$11,831.18 (includes all applicable taxes)*

Strange, thought Isolde. Fred had been gone for about thirteen days. The SwissCan Travel invoice shows hotel accommodation in Florence for two nights, and hotel accommodation in Rome for four nights. Fred's client VolksBankBern is in Bern; but there is no record of Fred staying in a hotel in Bern. It appears that there is a complete vacuum for about eight days; and if you give and take a couple days for travel time, at least six days are unexplained as far as accommodation is concerned. And it all seems to centre on Bern. The $64,000 question is: Where did Fred stay for those six days in Bern?

Her mind drifted back to the day the limousine picked him up at the Bridle Path for the drive to Pearson International Airport. Come to think of it, he did appear somewhat irritable that day; one may even say that he was irascible; not his usual self, a sea of perfect calm. She had written it off to pressure at work; he had been spending a lot of time in the law office. In looking back at it, could it have been that he had been bearing some heavy burden that had become a significant yolk on his mind?

As Isolde's mind wandered back in time, Yvonne walked into the office.

"Look what the cat just dragged in." She held out Fred's wallet. The police had returned it, and Yvonne had signed for it.

"What took them so long?" Isolde asked, a curious smile on her face. She took the wallet, and immediately opened it up. She first of all checked how much money was in it. A paltry $35. "That's Fred!" Isolde exclaimed. "He never believed in carrying too much cash."

"I know what you mean," Yvonne remarked, wryly. "He was always hitting on me for petty cash." Both women laughed. Yvonne retreated to her desk in the reception area.

Isolde continued to flip mechanically through the other sections of the wallet. There is that picture of her and the kids that Fred loved so much. She remembered the day that Fred himself took that picture, with the fountain of the Bridle Path home in the background. He had been so pleased with it that he said it was "a keepsake that he would preserve forever." There were a number of credit cards, club membership cards, and the like. And then there was one of Fred's business cards. Not unusual to carry one's own business card, she surmised. She playfully flipped it through her fingers. She suddenly noticed a number written on the back of the business card. Hello. What have we here? It was Fred's handwriting, for sure. Bern 01-66-88-55. Is this a telephone number? she asks herself. All she knows about Bern is that Fred and Margot had been born there; that Fred's client VolksBankBern is located there; and that Bern is the de facto capital of Switzerland. It should be a journey of some interest to track down the owner of that telephone number in Bern. She tucks the business card away safely in her purse.

She went through each of Fred's desk drawers. She found a bottle of prescription pills, clearly labeled CAFERGOT. She had been very much aware of the fact that Fred had been prone to horrible migraines. She remembered how Fred would sometimes stand on his head in a desperate attempt to obtain any amount of relief during his migraine attacks. Fred's family doctor, Dr. Reuben Schmoltzer, had prescribed Cafergot, which is a brand of Ergotamine. Wherever Fred went, he carried his Cafergot pills with him. His fountain of relief, he called them. She instantly decided that she would get the pills chemically analyzed, just to rule them out as a possible source of poisoning. The only other item of any conceivable significance that she found in his desk drawers was a sheet of paper with a sketch on it. She looked closely at it. The sketch bore some sort of design; there were three crescents, all intersecting. What was this design? A crest? An emblem? What would Fred be doing with this? Had he been contemplating a ring with that design as a gift to her? This was indeed puzzling. She tucked it away in her purse.

As she was contemplating this pretty but unusual design, Yvonne walked in. She had completed the memorandum of her recollections as to Fred's activities over the period of sixty days preceding his death.

"I know that this is not much; but that is about all I can recall at this time," she said, apologetically, as she handed the typed memorandum to Isolde.

"Thanks, Yvonne. If you think of anything else, just let me know ASAP. Here is another thing you can do for me. Do you know the building superintendent?"

"Do I know the building superintendent!" Yvonne retorted, with an impish smile. "His name is Antoni Medlicoff. He's from somewhere in Eastern Europe, I believe. He is persistently asking me out on a date. "Please call me Tony", he keeps imploring me, in his strong Eastern

European accent. He has only one thing on his mind; to get me into bed. Now, mind you, he is not that bad looking! But he is just not my type. I go for men that wear the signs of success; not building supers!" Both women burst out in laughter; although Isolde was tempted to say 'You mean like Fred?' but restrained herself. At the same time, Yvonne was thinking to herself 'I mean like Fred'.

"Well, here is what I would like you to do. Go and see Medlicoff. By now he undoubtedly must be aware of Fred's death. I believe that there are security cameras posted throughout this building. I would like you to get access to reviewing the videos from the security cameras over the period of sixty days preceding Fred's death. I would like a report as to everyone that entered this law office during that period. Can you handle that?"

"No problem whatsoever, Isolde. I'll go see my good friend, Antoni. He will give me whatever I want," Yvonne responded, as she wiggled her voluptuous torso seductively. Both women again broke out in laughter.

While Yvonne was gone in search of Medlicoff and his videotapes, Isolde reviewed the memorandum that Yvonne had prepared for her as to Yvonne's recollections. The only entry that was of any real interest were two telephone calls that Fred had received in the week immediately preceding his business trip to Bern, Florence, and Rome. The first phone call had been from a caller who simply identified himself as "from VolksBankBern". Yvonne had transferred the call to Fred. The call lasted about fifteen minutes. What she had also observed was that immediately following that phone call, Fred was very upset. He had sat at his desk, just staring out the window at the skyscraper on the opposite side of the street. The second phone call was on the following day. The female voice asked for "Mr. Bruni", but the caller refused to identify herself. She simply said to "tell Mr. Bruni that it is Bern calling". When Fred got on the phone, he was laughing and chatting, as if the caller had been a very close friend.

Very helpful, Isolde observed. Somehow, Bern seems to appear more and more discernible in the picture that was being painted. She was starting to get the big picture. It was up to her to gradually fill in the details that make the masterpiece.

When Yvonne returned, she reported that Medlicoff was all too willing to show her the videotapes. He took her into a little back room, where he played the videotapes for her in the dark, while he sat closely by her side, as if ready to make a pass. But she kept the meeting on a strictly business basis, and slipped away as soon as she had what she wanted. The net upshot from the videotapes was that no-one outside of the ordinary had been captured on film entering Fred's office in the pertinent period.

After making arrangements for Yvonne to come into the office for an hour or so daily to check on things and deal with any emergencies, Isolde told Yvonne that she could leave for home, and that, as promised, Isolde would make sure that she receives pay cheques over the indefinite future. She would call her if she needed any special assistance.

Isolde felt that she had gone as far as she could in gaining information about Fred's office from Yvonne, the files and other records found in the office, and Medlicoff's security videotapes.

The morning of the following day found Isolde in the Yonge Street office of Julian Zimmermann, the manager of SwissCan Travel Agency of Toronto. She informed him of Fred's sudden passing; but he had previously received the news. "Fred is a fine human being," he said, offering his condolences, but, out of respect, referring to Fred as if he was still alive. Isolde told him that the purpose of her visit was to review with him all of his company's records relating to Fred's recent thirteen-day trip to Europe. He immediately located the file on his computer.

"To save time, Julian," Isolde began, "I already have the SwissCan Travel invoice. I would like to review with you the details of the items shown on the invoice. My intention is to try and outline as best I can Fred's complete itinerary during that thirteen-day timeframe."

"I will assist as best I can," Julian replied, obligingly.

"First of all, I note that your invoice was paid in advance on October 15, 1982," she continued.

"That's correct."

"The limousine picked him up at our home in the Bridle Path at seven in the evening of October 22. It would likely have been a one-hour drive to Pearson International?"

"That's a fair estimate."

"What time did the flight from Pearson International to Bern leave?"

"Estimated time of departure was eleven. It was an overnight flight."

"How long would the flight have been?"

"Approximately eight hours."

"So, Fred would have been in Bern on the morning of October 23?"

"Correct; assuming no delays."

"Your invoice shows no charge for a limousine from the Bern airport, nor any charge for hotel accommodation in Bern?"

"We did not book a hotel for him in Bern. He told me he had already made arrangements for his stay in Bern. I seem to recall that he said that he would be staying at a friend's home."

Yvonne raised her eyebrows at this response. Interesting; Fred had never mentioned to her that he stayed at a friend's home in Bern. But then, there was a lot that he had never mentioned to her.

"Did he happen to mention the name of the friend? Or the address of the friend's home?"

"No. there was no need for me to know that."

"The next item on your invoice is a charge for a SwissAir flight from Bern to Florence. Do you know the date on which he would have left Bern?"

"My records show October 29. The estimated time of departure was three in the afternoon."

"That means that he stayed in Bern for approximately six days?" Isolde asked, with a tinge of surprise in her voice.

"Presumably."

"What would the travel time have been from Bern to Florence?"

"Approximately one hour."

"So, he would have checked into his hotel in Florence on that same day. Your invoice shows a two-night stay at the Florence hotel. This would mean that he would have left Florence on October 31. Do you have a record of the estimated time of departure?"

"Estimated time of departure for the Alitalia flight from Florence was four in the afternoon. Travel time by air was approximately one and one-half hours."

"So, he would have arrived in Rome on the same day; October 31. And the invoice shows a charge for five days hotel accommodation in Rome. What date would he have left Rome?"

"He would have left Rome on November 3. The Air France flight would have left Rome at about eleven at night. Flight time would have been about two hours. He would have arrived at Charles De Gaulle Airport by about one the next morning. There he would have changed flights, boarding the Air France flight to Toronto within an hour. The flight from Charles De Gaulle to Pearson International would have been about eight hours. He would have been back in Toronto on the morning of November 4."

"So, the actual length of time that he was away after leaving Toronto on October 22 was thirteen days. I have a fair picture of that thirteen-day period. But what really baffles me is the gap relating to his stay in Bern. Of course, I understand that you are not able to throw much light on that. Thank you very much, Julian. You have been very helpful."

"My pleasure, Isolde. If I can be of any further help, just let me know."

As Isolde walked out of Julian's office, the real big question that bothered her was: Who was the friend in Bern that Fred had stayed with during his recent visit? She now knew from the records in Fred's office that his major client, if not his only client, was VolksBankBern, which was located in Bern. But that was in essence a business relationship; and Julian had specifically stated that Fred had told him that he would be staying with a friend while he was in Bern. Could it be that the note on the back of Fred's business card which she found in his wallet was a note of the Bern telephone number of this mysterious friend of Fred's? For the time being, she will just tuck that away in the back of her mind. She would dig deeper into the aspect of 'the friend in Bern' later. Today, the next item on her agenda was a visit with the Bruni family doctor, Dr.

Reuben ("Rube") Schmoltzer, whose office was located in the Medical Arts Building at the corner of St. George and Bloor West.

Rube Schmoltzer greeted her like an old friend. One of the attendees at Fred's funeral, he had expressed to Isolde his utter shock at Fred's sudden passing. She can still recall the puzzled look on his face, and his constant repeating of the question "How can this be? How can this be? How can this be?" when he had met with her just immediately preceding the funeral service.

Rube came out of his office to personally greet Isolde. Fred and Rube had been close friends for eons. They had met on the squash courts when both Fred and Rube were students in undergraduate courses at University of Toronto; Fred was majoring in Latin, and Rube in Science. Rube used to tease Fred by saying "What the hell are you going to do with a Latin diploma? That's just 'mickey mouse' stuff, man." Fred would in turn tell Rube that he, Rube, would end up just treating old folks' sores and babies' pukes. When Rube received his licence to practice medicine, Fred was one of his first patients; not that Fred had then needed any medical care, but he just wanted to support his good friend who had just put up his shingle on the front of a dilapidated building over at Ossington and Queen. From that lowly beginning, Rube climbed the ranks to a very prestigious office in the premier Medical Arts Building. Unlike Rube's slow start, Fred's legal career took off like a rocket on its way to the moon. But then Rube was a true survivor. His parents had been gassed and their bodies burnt to ashes in Auschwitz. Rube was only seven at the time, and, as an orphan, he had been placed in the Children's Camp at Auschwitz, awaiting a decision by Himmler's *Schutzstaffel,* or Protection Squad, more commonly known as the *SS,* as to his ultimate fate, he and about two hundred other Jewish children. Miraculously, the war ended in the nick of time. As a *DP,* the term then commonly used for a *displaced person,* he was sent to Toronto, where he was adopted by a Jewish family, Jacob and Zelda Schmoltzer, themselves survivors of the Holocaust. From then on, he never looked back.

"Hi, Isolde. How nice to see you; please come into my office. Would you like a cup of coffee?"

"Not today, Rube. I just need a few minutes of your time."

"Take as long as you wish, Isolde. I am here to help you as much as I can."

As soon as Isolde was seated, she pulled from her purse Fred's bottle of the Cafergot pills that Rube had prescribed for Fred's migraine attacks.

"Here are the last migraine pills that you had prescribed for Fred, Rube," she said, as she handed the bottle to him. His eyes dropped to the label.

"Yes; that's correct; Cafergot really helped Fred."

Isolde again reached into her purse, and pulled out a Notarial Copy of the Death Certificate. She handed it to Rube.

"Look at the Cause of death shown on the Death Certificate, Rube. It says that the Immediate Cause of Death was **ASPHYXIATION;** the Underlying Cause of Death was **POISONING (NO TRACE OF THE POISONING AGENT FOUND);** and the Manner of Death was **SUICIDE** What the hell are they talking about, Rube? Forgive my French, but this is pure crap! Can you explain it to me?"

Rube rolled his eyes as he read the Death Certificate.

"My dear Isolde, I am as confused about that as you are. First of all, if they cannot find a trace of the poisoning agent, how can they call it a death by poisoning? Also, Fred had no reason in the world to commit suicide. Did he leave a suicide note?"

"No note was found."

"Precisely," Rube exclaimed. "What would ever have led them to conclude that Fred died by suicide?"

"Rube," Isolde interjected, "is it possible to have the Cafergot pills chemically analyzed to determine if there is any trace of poison?"

"Definitely. I will contact the pharmaceutical manufacturer, and have them run some tests. Just leave the bottle with me. I will let you know the results as soon as I receive their report. They will of course have an invoice for you, as the chemical analysis is not covered by OHIP."

"I will gladly pay for it, Rube. Thanks for seeing me on such short notice."

"Anytime, Isolde. I am here for you. You should hear from me soon."

As Isolde climbed into her fire-engine red Ferrari on St. George Street, a small group of U of T male students happened to be passing by, and let out some howls and whistles. Isolde was not sure as to whether they were fascinated with the red Ferrari, or with her natural beauty, or both. Whatever it was, she accepted the compliments graciously. She demurely smiled at them, and sped away, as in her rearview mirror she watched them beaming victoriously at the amiable response they had received from the curvaceous, amber-eyed champagne blonde in the fire-red Ferrari.

When she got back to the mansion on Saddlers Court, there already was a voicemail waiting for her. It was from Barney Ratskeller.

"Isolde, it's Barney," the voicemail said. "I have some good news for you. The insurance policy does contain an exclusionary clause, but it does not exclude suicide committed more than two years after issuance of the policy. Fred's policy had been issued about six years before his death, and so the exclusionary clause does not apply. Prudential will pay you the full death benefit. I have the Proof of Claim form ready for you to sign. Just slip into my office and sign as soon as you can. You should receive the $1,000,000 within a week after signing. Ciao."

Isolde was ecstatic. "*Yes, Virginia, there is a Santa Claus,*" she shouted with joy. This would permit her to meet her foreseeable expenses, and, more importantly, fund the massive mission that she was about to undertake to unearth the truth about the cause of Fred's death; to prove that Fred's death was not a suicide, but in fact a murder. From the core of her inner being, she believed that Fred had been murdered. She swore that she would get to the bottom of it all, come hell or high water. She had to do this for herself, for Emil and Sophie, for Margot, and, above all, for Fred.

CHAPTER FOUR

EMIL AND SOPHIE were still at school. They would not be home for another couple of hours. Isolde would use this time to summarize what she knew so far, about Fred's law practice, about Fred's recent business trip to Europe, and about Fred's death.

In the beginning, she knew nothing about anything. She had to start completely from scratch. She could kick herself for not having taken any interest whatsoever in Fred's business life while he was alive. But what has been done is done. No purpose is served in crying over spilled milk.

What has she learned so far that would possibly be relevant to the questions in relation to Fred's law practice, Fred's recent business trip, and Fred's death?

She has learned that Fred's law practice was not what you would call the 'normal' law practice. In essence, there appeared to be only one client, VolksBankBern, notwithstanding that the bank appeared to be acting in a trust capacity, as confirmed by the reference in correspondence to 'our mutual client'. Through this one institution, Fred had received an annual income of millions of dollars, based on a flat percentage fee of ten per cent of the value of each transaction that went through Fred's office. The real question now to be determined is: What are the names of the actual clients for whom VolksBankBern was acting as trustee? Outside of the relationship, the question arose as to the details of Fred's apparent quest for more information about 'our mutual client'. Isolde needed to put those questions directly to VolksBankBern in Bern. She had gone as far as she could with her own investigation in Toronto. The answers to her questions about Fred's law practice must lie in Bern.

She has also found that there is a huge gap in information as to Fred's stay in Bern for approximately five days. He does not appear to have stayed in a hotel in Bern. And, as a matter of fact, the travel agent Julian Zimmerman had said that Fred had told him that Fred would be staying with a friend in Bern. Isolde was not aware of Fred having a friend in Bern with whom he would have stayed for about five days. And then there was the mysterious telephone number Bern 01-66-88-55 on the back of Fred's business card which she had found in his wallet. Whose telephone number was this? Could it have been that of the friend with whom he had stayed? The answers to these questions must also lie in Bern.

Although VolksBankBern is located in Bern, on his recent business trip Fred had visited Florence and Rome, in addition to Bern. What would have been the reason for Fred to go out of his way to visit Florence? And to visit Rome? Surely, these were not sight-seeing trips; both Fred and Isolde had made tourist visits to both Florence and Rome many times in the past. Why would he have visited these cities on a 'business' trip?

Finally, while it may or may not be of any relevance in relation to Fred's death, what was behind the enigmatic sketch that he had tucked away in one of his desk drawers? The sketch of the three intersecting crescents. It had to have had some meaning to Fred. For all the years that she had known him, he was never one to store meaningless trash.

There was only one way to find out the answers to the questions that perplexed her. She had to go to Bern, and possibly to Florence and Rome. She could not rest until she unearthed the answers to these burning questions.

She stared out the window from her office. It was snowing heavily. My God, she thought to herself, it seems to snow earlier and earlier every year. As the environmentalists say, it must be 'global warming'. Not the best time to visit Bern, Florence, and Rome; but she had to do it. She picked up the telephone, and dialed Margot's number.

"Hi, Margot. I need to ask another favour of you. This one is a biggie. I have to pick up the kids in about an hour. May I stop by to chat with you for a few minutes? Thanks, Margot. See you in about ten minutes."

In no time at all, Isolde was parked in Margot's driveway on the Bridle Path. Margot greeted her with a peck on the cheek.

"Got time for some coffee, Isolde?"

"Sorry, Margot. I don't want to be late for the kids. To cut to the chase, I have been investigating Fred's death. I have found out a lot; but there are still many unanswered questions. I need to fly to Bern, and then possibly go to Florence, and Rome. I don't have time to fill you in on all the facts I have learned so far. That will be a task for another day."

"You would like Emil and Sophie to stay with me, I suppose? Don't give it a second thought. The answer is yes. It will be my pleasure. When are you leaving? How long will you be gone?"

"I would like to hop on the next available flight to Bern. I don't know how long I will be in Bern. Three or four days, perhaps. Once finished in Bern, I may have to go to Florence; and then possibly to Rome. My best estimate as to how long I will be away is about fifteen days."

"As soon as you know when you will be leaving, just let me know. I will be ready to receive Emil and Sophie; they are such darling angels!"

"Thanks oodles, Margot. What would I ever do without you?"

"Knowing you, I am confident you would find a way." Both women laughed heartily at this comment.

Once Isolde arrived back home after picking up Emil and Sophie, she went on the computer and researched next available flights from Pearson International to Bern leaving within the next couple of days. Yes; here is a good one. KLM; leaving tomorrow Wednesday at seven in the evening, Toronto time; arriving in Bern eight hours later, which would make the ETA nine on Thursday morning, Bern time; one seat still available in Economy Class; can be booked online directly with KLM. She laughed to herself, as she uttered the word 'Economy'; Fred would never have booked 'Economy'; he always flew either 'First Class' or 'Business Class'. But times have changed, and she had to watch the expenses. The important thing was to get to Bern; to this, her comfort took second place. She immediately phoned Margot. Yes; that was fine with Margot. Does Isolde want her to pick the kids up at school, so that Isolde can get away without any bother? Isolde thanked Margot; but declined her offer to pick the kids up at school; she, Isolde, could handle that; she will drop the kids off at Margot's. Isolde then booked the flight. She also arranged for an airport limousine to pick her up at Saddlers Court.

As luck would have it, the next morning at about eleven, Rube phoned her. The pharmaceutical company that manufactured the Cafergot was located in Toronto. As a special favour to him, they had put a rush on the chemical analysis of all the pills left in the bottle. They confirmed that without a doubt the pills were as had been manufactured by them, and that there was not the slightest trace of any poison.

"Thank you very much, Rube. Please mail me a copy of their report and invoice. I will be leaving for Europe this evening, but I will pay the invoice as soon as I return. And if I am not speaking with you before Hannukah, Happy Hanukkah."

"And a Merry Christmas to you, Isolde. Have a good time in Europe."

If only Rube knew. It would be no holiday in Europe. It would be more of a 'business' trip. She could be off on a wild goose chase. One thing was for sure, she had her work cut out for her. Besides, it would be unthinkable that she would be off on a vacation while still grieving the death of her beloved husband. But it did not matter that Rube was not aware of what she was up to; and so, there was no need to explain to him. The news that Rube had given her as to the report of the pharmaceutical company was what you would call 'good news, bad news'. The good news was that the pills in the bottle labeled Cafergot were what they were represented to be; Cafergot, with no trace whatsoever of a poison. The bad news was that the actual Underlying Cause of Death and the Manner of Death were still up in the air.

As soon as she finished the telephone conversation with Rube, she immediately dialed Yvonne's phone number. Yvonne answered after the fifth ring. She must be bored out of her mind, thought Isolde.

"Hi, Yvonne. How goes it?"

"Frankly, Isolde, it sucks! I really miss my job. I miss Fred. I miss my regular duties in the legal world. I am bored stiff."

"I thought you should know that I will be out of the country over the next two weeks or so. I have to be in Bern, and perhaps a couple other cities. I would like you to continue to check on things at Fred's office on a daily basis. You know, like go through the mail; check telephone messages; put out any fires that may arise; that sort of thing."

"My pleasure, Isolde. If there is anything that I think you should deal with, how do I get hold of you?"

"As soon as I check into a hotel in Bern, I will let you know where I am staying and give you their phone number. I will contact you as soon as I am back in T.O. I will pay you then. OK?"

"No problem at all, Isolde. Have a good trip."

It snowed heavily that day. The snow, sitting in mounds on the ground outside and drooping down from the branches of the trees, had created a winter wonderland. Far too early for this kind of weather, thought Isolde. All I need is for my flight to be canceled because of bad weather. This reminded her to pack some warm clothes, as a Bern November would likely be chilly. Crappy time of the year for what she was undertaking; but she could not afford to delay her investigations.

She picked up the children at school, and brought them home.

"Mommy will be away for a little while," she told them. "There is something very important for me to do in Bern. You will be living with Aunt Margot while I am away. So, I want you to pack your suitcases with whatever you will need for about fifteen days."

"Bern," Emil repeated. "Is that not where Daddy was born? I heard him talk about it many times."

"You are correct, Emil. You have such a good memory. Be sure to pack all the games you will be wanting to play while you and Sophie are at Aunt Margot's."

It was not long before Emil and Sophie were at Margot's. Isolde stayed long enough for a cup of coffee. Then she hugged and kissed the children; told them to be good for their Aunt Margot; gave Margot a warm embrace; and was back at Saddlers Court, waiting, with her luggage, at the front door for the arrival of the airport limousine. The snow had not let up. I will be lucky to get out of Toronto tonight, she fretted. She was a woman on a mission. She had to get at it. She wanted nothing in the world to block her path. She must do what she had to do.

CHAPTER FIVE

ISOLDE DID NOT ARRIVE at Bern International Airport until eleven in the morning, Bern time. A snowstorm in Toronto, a rarity for this time of the year, had resulted in a loss of about two hours for de-icing the frozen wings of the huge Boeing 767, with passengers all on board, just sitting and waiting impatiently until the huge metal bird could become safely airborne. What a colossal loss of time, Isolde thought. But then, one has to thank God for small blessings; at least the flight was not cancelled. Now, after a sleepless night, thanks to an incessantly crying infant on board the plane, here she was in the Arrival Concourse of Bern International Airport, awaiting her luggage in the Luggage Pickup Area. During her wait, she booked into Best Western Plus Hotel Bern on Zeughausgasse for three nights. She chose this hotel because of its proximity to VolksBankBern, which she found out was located in the Old City (the *Altstadt*, as they call it in German). The *Alstadt* is the medieval city centre of Bern, surrounded on three sides by the arms of the River Aare. From there, it would only be a walk of about thirty minutes at the most to VolksBankBern, which was located at Bundesplatz 34. Once she gathered her luggage, she was transported to Best Western Plus Hotel Bern by the hotel's shuttle service. Arriving there at about noon, she made herself comfortable, as she dozed off in the hotel lobby, while her room was being readied for her. Eventually, her room, #205 on the second floor, was ready; and all she had to do was follow the bellhop. As soon as she entered her room and tipped the bellhop, she just flung her limp body across the bed, and immediately fell sound asleep.

The bongs from a nearby bell tower woke her up. She counted six of them. Six o'clock, she mumbled. She could not believe that she had slept for over five hours. She felt refreshed, except that now she felt her stomach writhing from pangs of hunger. She dialed Room Service. Good; they spoke English.

"This is Mrs. Bruni in Room 205. I would like to order dinner in my room, please. Yes; I would like the Swiss Steak; a couple Sister Schubert Rolls; the Swiss Berry Dessert. Do you have Jamaica Blue Mountain Coffee? Great; a small pot please; and a bottle of French Wine, preferably Beaujolais. How long will that be? Thirty minutes? Excellent."

While she waited for dinner, Isolde pulled out her steno pad and reviewed the notes she had made back at Fred's office. She had to come up with some sort of agenda for the tasks she had to undertake in Bern. She decided that she would start with a visit to Fred's major—and, most likely, only-- client, VolksBankBern. Apart from the relatively minute information she had been able to glean from the files in Fred's office, she knew precious little about this bank. From a practical perspective, all that she knew was that their address was Bundesplatz 34, which was a relatively short walk from the hotel. She would not phone them. She wanted to simply walk right in, and, hopefully, catch them off guard. She showed this as #1 on her agenda. After VolksBankBern, she would then investigate the mysterious Bern telephone number she had found on the back of Fred's business card in his wallet. She would be starting from scratch with this item; and she would just follow the slightest of leads, wherever those led her. This was #2 on her agenda. Having tabulated the essential tasks she had to undertake in Bern, she would just have to play it by ear as she went along. Just wing it, so to speak. Hopefully, the main items would spawn subitems, which would scatter like newly-birthed fish branching out in all different directions after being dropped from their mother's belly.

The thought struck her that she should advise both Margot and Yvonne as to the name of the hotel she was staying at in Bern, and the telephone number, notwithstanding that they both had her mobile phone number. She dialed Margot's number first. Margot answered the phone.

"Hi, Margot. I am in Bern. How are the kids?"

"They are just fine, Isolde. They are doing their homework. Just a minute; I will get them on the line."

"Hello, Mommy." It was Emil.

"Hi, my darling. How are you and Sophie doing?"

"Great, Mommy. When are you coming home? We miss you already."

"It will be a few more moons, honey. I am in Bern. I have a lot of work to do here. Are you also on the line, Sophie?"

"Yes, Mommy. I am here. We love you."

"I love you both. Are you being good for Aunt Margot?"

"Of course, Mommy," Emil piped up.

"Good. Go back to your homework. Love and kisses to you both. I need to speak with your Aunt Margot."

"I am here on the line, Isolde."

"Margot, I am checked in at Best Western Plus Hotel Bern. It's the one on Zeughausgasse. Have you got a pencil and paper? I will give you the phone number. But you can always reach me on my mobile phone." Once Margot was back with pencil and paper, Isolde gave her the phone number of the hotel.

"Thanks again for taking care of the kids. And please give my regards to Heinz."

"Take good care of yourself, Isolde. Remember, Bern can be a dangerous place, especially for a single woman. Be very careful."

The next phone call was to Yvonne at her apartment. Yvonne was not in. Isolde left a message on voicemail.

"Hi, Yvonne. This is Isolde phoning from Bern. I am staying at Best Western Plus Hotel Bern. It's on a street called Zeughausgasse. If you ever need to contact me, here is the hotel's telephone number. Bern 01-66-42-87. Please keep the home fires burning at the office. See you when I get back to Toronto."

There was a knock on the door. It was Room Service. The meal was scrumptious. It was just as she remembered from her many stays in St. Moritz. Even though she and Fred owned the chalet at St. Moritz, it had been the order of each day to dine out at one of the many quality restaurants that graced the town. "I am not going to have you spend your time here at the chalet cooking," Fred would say. "You need to relax and enjoy the wonderful meals that Switzerland has to offer. To do that, you must be exposed to the best chefs in the world, right here in Switzerland." If only Fred was here, she pined. O, I miss him so much!

After dinner, Isolde luxuriated for about two hours in the bathtub, making full use of the wide array of amenities offered by the hotel: the fine bath soap, the scented bath oils, the sudsy shampoo, and so on. She got out of the bathtub only after she noticed that the skin of her hands was starting to shrivel up. She jumped into the woolen pajamas she had brought with her, and curled up in bed, watching television. The best she could find was the old movie *An American in Paris*, a 1951 classic starring Gene Kelly and Leslie Caron. It was all in German, titled *Ein Amerikaner in Paris,* with English subtitles, which helped Isolde, as her grasp of the German language left much to be desired.

She had no idea as to what time she had fallen asleep that night. When she awoke to the tolls of the bell tower in the nearby square, it was six in the morning. The television was still on; but the station had signed off. She must get going. She had work to do. No time to waste.

Treating her intended visit to VolksBankBern as a business matter, she dressed accordingly. Her two-piece business suit was burnt orange, her shirt white and high-necked, and her shoes alabaster. She looked at herself in the mirror. Perfect, she thought. Her amber eyes twinkled, highlighted by her champagne blonde hair, cut in a long shaggy style and parted so that it drifts down past her captivating eyes. Naturally endowed with the eyes of a cat, she felt like a tiger ready to go on the prowl. And she assured herself that she would fit comfortably into any business environment; any boardroom; any executive office. Such a milieu would be her jungle. Watch out, VolksBankBern, here comes the tiger.

She had a light breakfast in the hotel's café. And then she exited onto Zeughausgasse, where she headed west, on her mission to try and accomplish #1 on her brief agenda. The cold air chilled her bones, and, for a brief stretch, she wished she had worn her coat. But she soon warmed up to it, accustomed as she was to the rigors of Canadian winters.

From Zeughausgasse, she went onto Schützengasschen, then Marktgasse, followed by Amthausgasse, and eventually Bundesplatz.

As she walked along this route, she looked in passing at the very old buildings, most of them relics from the Middle Ages. The City of Bern has to be complimented on the preservation of such vital parts of its long history.

Finally, she arrived at #34, the address of VolksBankBern. She was in shock. This was not the type of bank building to which she had been accustomed. Whenever she had thought of the headquarters of a bank, she had had visions of a skyscraper building such as Royal Bank Plaza on Bay Street, or The Toronto-Dominion Centre on Adelaide Street. The only aspect that commended the building in which VolksBankBern was located was its obvious antiquity. The sign that read **VOLKSBANKBERN** was almost undiscernible. Had it not been for the plaque which showed the number "34", she would have sworn that she had gone to the wrong place. If she was in the oldest section of Bern, then the building in which VolksBankBern was located must indeed be the oldest building in the Old City.

Moving ahead, Isolde tried to open the huge wooden door in order to gain entry; but the door was locked. She looked at her watch. It was now ten-fifteen. Nonplussed, she was wondering what to do. And then she noticed a small sign in German: **KLINGEN FÜR SERVICE**. Well, it was obvious even to someone who did not speak German that that was German for **RING FOR SERVICE**. She pressed the nearby button, and could hear the loud beep emanating from within the building. She waited. There was no response. She then pressed her full body weight against the button for about thirty seconds. She waited again. This time, the huge wooden door opened slowly, with the worst godawful squeak that one could ever imagine. In dire need of some WD-40 on the hinges, Isolde mused. An elderly white-haired man, dressed in a crumpled black suit, was standing there in front of her. He carried a huge hump on his back, clearly an imperfection of the spine, and, with her vivid imagination, Isolde could see standing before her in black and white a true clone of Victor Hugo's *Quasimodo,* the 'hunchback of Notre Dame'.

"Guten Morgen. Was is es?" he growled.

"Sorry," Isolde apologized. "I do not speak German."

"I said '*Good morning. What do you want?*' Can you understand that?" the old man barked, very impolitely.

Isolde was taken aback by the lack of civility in his manner and his words. This was not the way she had expected to have been greeted at VolksBankBern, or any other bank in the world, for that matter.

"I would like to see the manager of VolksBankBern."

"Do you have an appointment?"

"No; but tell him that I am Mrs. Isolde Bruni from Toronto, Canada. I am sure that he will want to speak with me."

With a swoop of his hand, the old man beckoned her to step inside. Without a word, he left her standing there in this large vapid anteroom, while he disappeared through a doorway like a ghost. As she looked around, she noted that there were no bank tellers in sight; nor any other bank employees for that matter, such as would be found in a typical bank processing documents and cash and the like. Red flags rose high in her head. She could see them clearly in her mind's eye. This was the strangest bank she had ever been to. Surely, this is no way to run a bank.

After about five minutes, another man appeared. He was a short man with a large paunch. But, unlike the clone of Victor Hugo's *Quasimodo* who had let her in, he was meticulously dressed in a grey business suit, a shirt of silk that was lily white, the cuffs held together by gold cuff links. He wore a wide smile, displaying two rows of gold teeth, which glistened to high heaven whenever they came in contact with a glint of light. His eyes were what you would call shifty, darting quickly from side to side.

"Good morning, Frau Bruni," he opened, taking both her hands into his, as if he was a one-man welcoming committee. He spoke with a very strong German accent. "I am Constantino Rapini, the manager of VolksBankBern. This is indeed a surprise. I am so sorry to hear about Fred." This almost floored her. How could he have heard that Fred was dead? Surely, Yvonne would have mentioned to her if she, Yvonne, had communicated the news of Fred's death to VolksBankBern. And if not communicated through Yvonne, then through whom?

"It is my pleasure to meet you, Mr. Rapini. I have a few questions to ask you in relation to Fred and his estate."

"By all means, Frau Bruni. Please step into my office."

Rapini's office was the absolute antithesis of the dour, old building that she had seen on the outside, and of the bare and drab anteroom that she had just left. It was the epitome of luxury. The walls were lined with crimson textured velvet wallpaper. The floor was marble, as white as alabaster. The lights were six miniature chandeliers, each made of gold and crystal. And the furnishings were Louis XIV antiques, the best that money could buy. What a difference a few steps make!

When they were seated on either side of Rapini's huge dark-mahogany antique desk, he leaned forward and asked condescendingly: "Now, Frau Bruni, how can I help you?"

She was silent for a minute or so, as she stared into his eyes. It was as if she was trying to fathom the depth of his soul through his eyes. She considered herself a pretty good judge of character; and she quite often trusted her instinct in this regard. He shifted uncomfortably before her. It must have been from the mesmerizing power of her cat's eyes.

"I see that you are aware of Fred's passing," she blandly observed, half-expecting him to offer the information as to how he came by that knowledge.

"News flies fast," he retorted, giving no indication whatsoever of how he learned of Fred's death. One strike against him, she ruled in her own mind. An honest, open person, with nothing to hide, would have readily volunteered the source of his information.

"Yes. It sure does," she commented, rather coldly. "I understand that VolksBankBern was Fred's major client, if not his only client. Do you know how the relationship started? How had it come about that Fred was introduced to VolksBankBern, and vice versa?" Rapini hesitated, as he pondered the question.

"I really cannot recall how it happened," he eventually started. "I think it had to do with Fred having some connection with Bern. As you know, he was born here. Besides, Fred had a good reputation as a lawyer. We are always seeking out the brightest and the best for our legal work." Another wrong answer. How could VolksBankBern have known anything about Fred's legal acumen when VolksBankBern was the first and only client that Fred ever had? Rapini was playing it cagily. This only whetted her appetite for getting more answers from him.

"I see," she said, offhandedly, in an effort to let him believe that she was buying the baloney that he was selling. "As you will recall, Fred was here on business shortly before he died. Do you know where Fred stayed while he was here in Bern?"

"No. I really do not pry into our lawyers' personal lives. If he stayed at a hotel, we gladly pick up the expenses. If he stayed elsewhere, that would have been his choice. A private matter."

"The records show that Fred had been in Bern for about five days. But there is no hotel bill for that period of time in Bern. How many times did Fred meet with you while he was here in Bern?"

"As best as I can recall, perhaps about four or five times; each time involving a meeting of about an hour or so. It could very well have been that each meeting was on a separate day. That would have explained the five-day stay here in Bern." Strike three! He is hiding something. He is trying to fudge the picture. To create a blur, so as to hide the truth. This is definitely not an honest man.

"And during those five days Fred never once mentioned to you what else he was doing in Bern? No hint at all? No boys' talk?" Rapini raised his eyebrows, and started a knowing smile, as if he had just had a revelation.

"Frau Bruni, now I understand what you are about. You want to find out if Fred had a mistress here in Bern. Is that not so? After all, Fred was a handsome man." Isolde was insulted by this crude comment. But she would continue to play his game; she needed more information, or lack thereof, from Rapini. Sometimes one can garner much more information from what a person does not say than from what he or she in fact says. As the saying goes, silence speaks stronger than words.

"You are dead right, Mr. Rapini. You can't blame a woman for being jealous, especially when married to a good-looking man such as Fred." By this answer, she made Rapini believe that she had bought his diversionary tactic, obviously intended to send her off on a wild goose chase. Chalk up another strike for the Isolde team.

"In reviewing Fred's files in his office, I found a reference to 'our mutual client'; I think it was in an e-mail from VolksBankBern to Fred. Who is 'our mutual client'? And was that reference to 'our mutual client' in relation to that particular file? Or were there a number of mutual clients?"

At these questions, Rapini cleared his throat, and his whole demeanour immediately changed. From his body language, Isolde was confident that she had touched a raw nerve. Very raw; as raw as the meat of a freshly slaughtered pig. She knew that she was on to something; something that made him extremely uncomfortable. He shriveled in his chair, as his beady eyes moved swiftly to the right, then to the left, then to the right, almost ad infinitum. It was as if he was, above all avoiding eye contact with her. Like a tiger stalking its prey, her cat's eyes stared intensely into his shifting eyes, as if into his soul. She waited interminably for an answer. Gotcha, Rapini. What's the matter? Can't you answer that simple question?

"I am sorry, Frau Bruni. But I cannot answer that question. Do you have any knowledge of the law?" he eventually queried.

"I was educated as a lawyer," she responded.

"Very well then. You undoubtedly are aware of the term 'undisclosed principal' in the law of agency?" he sneered.

"Yes; I am. That's where a principal hires an agent with strict instructions to never disclose the principal's identity."

"Very good," he said patronizingly, like a law school professor getting the correct answer from his student. "I am sure that you must also have heard of the obligation of secrecy that an attorney owes to his client?"

"Yes; but you are the manager of a bank; not an attorney."

"You are correct; but a bank owes its client an obligation of confidentiality. There is no real distinction between the obligation of secrecy in the lawyer/client relationship and the obligation of confidentiality in the banker/customer relationship." His shifty eyes now tried to focus on her. His message was loud and clear; his lips were sealed. They were frozen stiff, like an iceberg in the depths of hell, which could not be thawed by even the eternal flames of damnation. Thanks, Rapini. Another strike against you. She had hit upon a very sensitive nerve. There was much more to her question than meets the eye. For whatever reason, Rapini would not, or, more likely, could not, reveal the name of 'our mutual client'. This was obviously a major secret. This was a very important clue in moving her investigations forward. Who in God's name was 'our mutual client'?

"I fully understand," Isolde remarked, wistfully. Above all, she must let him believe that she is buying the bag of goods that he is selling. She must keep on appearing to be playing his game. He was in charge of all the rules, some of which he made up during the game. She sat there in silence, looking down at the floor, as she contemplated her next question. Rapini broke the silence.

"Is there anything else that I can do for you, Frau Bruni?" he asked, tartly.

Isolde raised her head, and looked directly at him; how well dressed he was, in his fine woolen suit. She looked at the colourful kerchief that he sported in the lapel pocket of his jacket. And, suddenly, she noticed it for the first time. On his lapel was a gold pin, which in itself was not noteworthy. But what was significant in her mind was the emblem engraved on the pin. She blanched, as if she had just seen a ghost. She had come accross that design before. It was the design on the sketch of the three intersecting crescents that she had found in Fred's desk drawer. The sketch that she had been so baffled about. The sketch that she had brought with her all the way from Toronto to Bern. The sketch which posed a mystery that she had resolved to solve.

"Mr. Rapini," she ventured, "I cannot help but admire the beautiful gold pin on your lapel. It fascinates me. I know that this may be somewhat personal. But are those three intersecting crescents engraved on it?" Rapini's face flushed at this question. He seemed to squirm in his chair. It was obviously a question that he would have preferred not to have to answer.

"It was a gift from my wife," he responded, with a spurious smile. "Yes; it's a beautiful design; but that's as far as it goes. It does appear to show some intersecting arcs. But there really is no significance to that. Is that all, Frau Bruni? I have a lot of work to do." He was already out of his chair, and, with a wave of his hand, was in the process of ushering her out of his office. Isolde had touched another raw nerve. Rapini did not want to talk about his pin of gold with the three intersecting crescents. He had abruptly terminated the meeting; it was his way of ducking the issue. What was he hiding? Before she knew it, she was traversing the large anteroom, led by Rapini, on her way out. Rapini opened the huge wooden front door, which creaked even louder than when the Quasimodo clone had let her in.

"Thanks, Mr. Rapini. I appreciate the fact that you took the time to see me, especially without an appointment."

"You are most welcome, Frau Bruni. Auf Wiedersehen, as we say here in Switzerland," he bade, with an undisguised air of relief.

"Auf Wiedersehen, Herr Rapini." At least Isolde knew that much German. She had heard Fred use that phrase umpteen times during their marriage, to say goodbye. Rapini had a broad smile on his face; but Isolde knew that deep down he had been discomforted by her questions. She thought she heard him mutter something in German as he hurried back to the luxurious den which he called his office. She could have sworn it sounded like "Dumme Schlampe!" *Dumb bitch!* For her, the hunt was on.

CHAPTER SIX

THE DAY AFTER Isolde met with Rapini at VolksBankBern, she went out for a brisk morning stroll. The temperature was about fifty Fahrenheit, which made her walk invigorating. As she wandered along the streets of the Old City, she thought carefully as to how she would tackle #2 on her agenda. She had to get to the bottom of the mysterious Bern telephone number on the back of Fred's business card which she had found in his wallet. She could easily dial the number; but what then? Whom would she ask to speak with? How should she identify herself? What questions should she ask? It would be likely more complex than she had imagined.

When she returned to the Best Western Plus, she found that there was a message for her at the Front Desk. It was from Yvonne. Yvonne wanted Isolde to phone her ASAP. She would await Isolde's call at her apartment. Back in Room 205, Isolde phoned Yvonne at home.

"Hello," Yvonne answered, in her familiar raspy, almost subdued, voice.

"Hi, Yvonne. It's Isolde. I got your message. What's up?"

"Hi, Isolde. I am so happy you called me back so quickly. You will find this hard to believe; but all of Fred's client files are gone." Isolde gasped. The plot thickens.

"What? Where have they gone? Who took them?"

"Two grim-faced men showed up at Fred's office late yesterday afternoon. They identified themselves as bailiffs. They showed me a Court Order requiring me to deliver into their possession all files relating to Fred's client VolksBankBern; and stating that refusal to obey the Court Order immediately would be deemed contempt of court, punishable by imprisonment for up to five years. I tried to reach you at your hotel, but you were not available. I had to obey the Court Order. They took all the VolksBankBern files with them."

"Absolutely incredible!" Isolde exclaimed, her voice weighted down by utter shock. "Why did you not call me then on my mobile phone?"

"I'm sorry, Isolde. But I misplaced your mobile number." Isolde gathered that Yvonne had phoned during the couple of hours that she, Isolde, had spent having dinner in the hotel's dining room.

Isolde's knowledge of the law immediately led to a strange feeling in the pit of her stomach. The law does not work that way. First of all, a court would not order delivery up of the files without ensuring that Isolde as Executrix of Fred's estate had an opportunity to respond; and Isolde had received no notice whatsoever of any court proceedings. Sure, the court could on a motion without notice freeze the files in Fred's office; but, certainly, would not order the files to leave the possession of the estate. She could smell a rat.

"Yvonne, do you have a copy of the Court Order?"

"Yes; they gave me a copy, only after I insisted on it."

"OK. I want you to contact lawyer Bernard Ratskeller. He was Fred's lawyer; do you know him?'

"Yes; I do. What should I tell him?"

"Tell him exactly what's happened. Fax him a copy of the Court Order. Tell him I would like him to check it out ASAP. Call me back as soon as you hear back from him. This is Saturday morning. He may be in his office. If he is not in his office, call him at his home."

"Thanks, Isolde. I will call him right away. I sure hope that I have not screwed things up."

"Don't worry about it, Yvonne. Let's hear what Barney has to say. I will wait right here in my room for your call."

As she hung up the phone, Isolde had all kinds of conspiracy theories racing through her head, as fast as horses in the homestretch of the Kentucky Derby. But she smelled a rat in Rapini. It was far too much of a coincidence that it had been only yesterday morning that she had met with Rapini. As she quite often said about unexpected events: *It's too coincidental to be a coincidence.* Within a couple hours, the phone rang. It was Yvonne. Mr. Ratskeller was in his office. He had examined the Court Order. It was a complete fake. "I have been duped," Yvonne blurted out. She sounded as if she was sobbing.

"Thanks, Yvonne. Don't be too hard on yourself. You did what any legal secretary would have done. The information is very helpful to me. At least I have some clue as to what I am dealing with."

"If there is anything else you would like me to do, just let me know, Isolde. I will try not to screw up again."

As she sat there by her window in Room 205 at Best Western Plus Hotel Bern, Isolde looked out at the scenery, the old weather-beaten buildings that had survived for so long, defying centuries of spoliation inflicted by the ravages of time, inclement weather, and horrible wars. These buildings had withstood all that both nature and man had thrown at them. And if these inanimate objects could conquer the inflictions of the ages, then, surely, she, possessing the intellect that they lacked, could be victorious in the Herculean quests that she had embarked upon. The ancient buildings strengthened her resolve to succeed. Her mind went back to Rapini. Rapini was an insidious rascal, she thought. He was a damned liar, who was hiding some deep secrets which dwelt within the dark recesses of his brain, like the Minotaur running loose within the confines of the Labyrinth. And, from what she had just learned from Yvonne, Rapini would stop at nothing in pursuing his ends. He was a dangerous man.

Once she collected her thoughts, she decided to move ahead with the first step in #2 of her agenda. Yes; the mysterious Bern phone number. She reached into her purse, and pulled out Fred's business card with the Bern phone number inscribed on the back. It was there, as plain as day. Bern 01-66-88-55. She slowly dialed the number. This was going to be tricky. She had to play it by ear. She waited as the phone rang a number of times. Finally, someone answered.

"Guten Morgen." *Good morning.* It was a pleasant female voice. Isolde drew a blank. What should she do now?

"Guten Morgen," the female voice repeated. "Is jemand da?" *Is someone there?*

"Hello," replied Isolde. "Do you speak English?"

"Whom would you like to speak with?" The question was asked somewhat impatiently, in impeccable English. Isolde did not want questions. She only sought answers.

"With whom am I speaking?" she finally mumbled.

"You phoned this number. Who are you, anyway?" The conversation was going nowhere fast.

"I am sorry. I must have the wrong number". Isolde then hung up the phone.

So, what had she learned? Firstly, there was a female at that phone number. Secondly, from the voice, likely a young woman in her thirties. Thirdly, the woman was fluent in both German and English. Fourthly, the woman did not give out information freely. This was a meagre start. She had to get the information as to who was at that phone number; and where did that person live? She thought of just phoning the telephone company in Bern, and putting the questions to them; but decided that that would likely be futile because of privacy laws. The best way to proceed would be to retain a private investigator in Bern; the good old 'private eye'. The kind that she had watched so many hundreds of times on TV, such as *Magnum, P.I.* But, where could she find a Magnum, P.I. in Bern? It struck her that divorce lawyers were always hiring private eyes to spy on their clients' spouses. Why not start there? She phoned the Front Desk.

"This is Frau Bruni in Room 205. Would you be so kind as to give me the names of two good Divorce Lawyers in Bern?"

"By all means, Frau Bruni. One moment, please." Within a couple of minutes, the Front Desk was back on the phone. "There is Gabriel Girtman, telephone number Bern 01-32-71-95; and there is Anna Lehmann; Bern 01-86-72-85."

"Very helpful. Thank you very much."

Isolde then phoned both law firms. Whom would they recommend as the best private investigator in Bern? The response was unanimous.

Joaquim Fankhauser; telephone number Bern 01-63-79-35. Bingo. He must be the best; very highly recommended by both law firms. She immediately dialed his number.

"Fankhauser." He answered on the first ring. Impressive. No fooling around. Right to the point.

"Mr. Fankhauser," Isolde started. 'My name is Isolde Bruni. I live in Toronto, Canada, but I am here in Bern; at Best Western Plus Hotel Bern on Zeughausgasse. You have been very highly recommended as a private investigator. May I meet with you ASAP?"

"Who recommended me?" he asked, somewhat surprisingly.

"Two law firms. Gabriel Girtman's and Anna Lehmann's."

"Oh, yes. Gabriel and Anna. I know them very well. Did they happen to mention to you that I am very expensive?" At this, she chuckled. He sure was forthright. No gilding of the lilies with him!

"No, they did not. But I am willing to pay handsomely for the best." She could not believe that she had said that.

"I am willing to meet with you over dinner. But I hate the food at Best Western Plus. Suppose we meet for dinner at the *Della Casa*. It's an old restaurant over on Schauplatzgasse. It dates back to the 1890's. The cuisine there is out of this world. You will get to savour real Swiss food, Frau Bruni."

"OK with me."

"How about seven? I will reserve a table."

"Good. I will see you there at seven. I look forward to meeting you."

She liked his manner. Direct. Businesslike. Honest. Pleasant. Lover of quality. Sounded like a true professional. She dressed appropriately for the dinner meeting. In a business suit, but with a touch of casual flare. She grabbed a cab, and was at the restaurant after a five-minute drive. As she walked in, her watch showed seven. She was right on time. She was immediately touched by the ambience of the *Della Casa*; the gas-lamp lighting; the delicate richness; the peaceful quiet, broken by only the soft, soothing sounds of the Overture from Mozart's famous opera, *Le Nozze di Figaro,* known in English as *The Marriage of Figaro.* The maître d' gave the perfunctory half-smile so characteristic of a maître d' toward new diners.

"My name is Isolde Bruni. I am meeting with Herr Joaquim Fankhauser," she told the maître d'. At the mention of the name Fankhauser, the maître d' visibly straightened up, expanding his smile into a broad, genuine smile.

"Yes, Frau Bruni. Follow me, please, Frau Bruni."

Fankhauser was already there, seated at the table for two. He rose to greet her. A man of good manners, she thought to herself.

"It is my immense pleasure to meet you, Frau Bruni. What would you like to drink?".

"Just call me Isolde. I will have a glass of red wine, thank you."

"And I am Joaquim." He then beckoned to the waiter. "A bottle of Früburgunder, please." He turned to Isolde. "I hope you don't mind that I took the liberty of choosing the wine. But I am sure you will enjoy it. Full-bodied; rich, dark colour; minimum acidity; and delightful aroma. From one of the wine valleys of Germany; I really cannot recall which one; but its famous for its first-class wines. Now, what brings you to the ancient city of Bern?"

As he spoke, her cat's eyes studied him very carefully. His English was impeccable. He was a tall man, perhaps about six feet three; much unlike Fred, whose height had been about five feet eight. His eyes were a cross between jade green and slate grey, depending on how you looked at them, and the angle at which the light hit them. Warm, compassionate eyes. His hair was chestnut brown, with small waves of curls. He had started to show grey at the temples. She would have guessed his age to be late thirties; perhaps thirty-eight.

"It's a long story. It all began about a month or so ago, with the sudden passing of my husband, Fred. Fred was a business lawyer, who had a very successful practice in Toronto. Fred's law practice was not the run-of-the-mill practice. It appeared, as I found out after his death, that he had essentially one client; VolksBankBern. It's centred here in Bern. You must have heard of it?" she paused for a few seconds, waiting for an answer. But Fankhauser simply said "Please go on."

"Fred had just recently returned from Europe. He had been here in Bern for about five days; then in Florence for a couple days; and then in Rome. I can understand Bern, because VolksBankBern is located here in Bern. But I cannot for the life of me understand what it was that took him to Florence and to Rome."

The wine arrives at their table. The waiter goes through the usual ritual of having Fankhauser approve the label, of opening the bottle, and of pouring a small amount in Fankhauser's glass for him to taste. Fankhauser approves the wine with a simple nod of his head. The waiter pours the two glasses. Fankhauser tells the waiter to not disturb them for about an hour; they will place their orders for dinner then. Isolde takes a sip of the wine. Yes, indeed; it has a wonderful taste, not to mention the colour and the bouquet. "Please continue, Isolde," Fankhauser says, without even touching his wine. He is all ears.

"Shortly after Fred's return to Toronto, he went to his law office to catch up on some work. It was a Sunday evening. He phoned me at about eleven to say that he would just bunk down in his office, as it was so late, and he still had more work to do. The next morning, he was found dead at his desk. It was Yvonne, his secretary, who found him. She said there was froth that had come from his mouth; poor girl." She took another sip of wine.

"The coroner had an autopsy performed. Take a look at the Death Certificate." She handed him a copy of the Death Certificate. "It indicates that the Immediate Cause of Death was **'ASPHYXIATION'**; that the Underlying Cause of Death was **'POISONING (NO TRACE OF THE POISONING AGENT FOUND)'**; and that the Manner of Death was **'SUICIDE'.** Can you believe all that crap? The truth is that Fred had no reason in the world to commit suicide. In my heart of hearts, I believe that Fred was murdered." She looked at Fankhauser for his reaction.

"Please go on, Isolde." He was listening intently. He wanted the whole story before making any comments. A true professional, Isolde thought.

"So, for the first time in our many years of marriage, I needed to learn about Fred's law practice. Prior to that, I had never enquired as to any aspect of Fred's law practice; as to what the nature of his practice was; as to who his clients were; as to how much he earned in his practice; and so on. I went into Fred's office and, with the assistance of Fred's legal secretary, delved into all the basics of Fred's law practice. That's when I discovered that Fred's only client was VolksBankBern. Mind you, they were acting in a trustee capacity, the principal being referred to as 'our mutual client'. Fred's fee was always a flat percentage of the value of the transaction, namely ten per cent. Fred's net income averaged between $2,000,000-$3,000,000 a year, all from VolksBankBern.

"I found that Fred had written to VolksBankBern shortly before his last business trip to Europe asking for disclosure as to the name of 'our mutual client'; but no evidence of such disclosure. My sixth sense told me that this question of the identity of 'our mutual client' had something to do with the reason for Fred's last business trip to Bern, Florence and Rome.

"In Fred's desk drawers, I found two items of interest. There was a bottle of Fred's prescription pills, Cafergot, which he took for his migraine headaches. I had the contents chemically tested. The pills were as represented on the bottle, pure Cafergot; absolutely no trace of any poisoning agent. I also found this sketch." She pulled the sketch of the three intersecting crescents from her purse, and showed it to Fankhauser. "I have no idea in the world as to why Fred would have a sketch of this type in his possession. It is a beautiful design; but it means nothing at all to me; totally beyond my comprehension. Seems to be some sort of emblem. Have you ever seen this design before?" Fankhauser looked at the sketch with interest. He shook his head from side to side. No; he had never seen it before.

"In Fred's General Ledger, there was an entry of payment of $11,831.18 to SwissCan Travel of Toronto in relation to expenses for Fred's last business trip to Europe; I found the invoice for these expenses." She pulled a copy of the invoice from her purse, and gave it to Fankhauser. "You will note that there are charges for hotel accommodation in Florence and Rome, but nothing for Fred's stay in Bern. I discussed this invoice and Fred's travel arrangements with the manager of SwissCan. It appears that Fred was in Bern for about five days. So where did Fred stay for those five days in Bern? The manager of SwissCan told me that he recalled Fred telling him that he would be staying with a friend in Bern. To add fuel to the fire, I found one of Fred's business cards in his wallet. On the back of the business card was a Bern telephone number." She handed the business card to Fankhauser. "I need to find out the identity of the person at that phone number. I need to speak with him or her. I need to fill in the details of the missing five days in Bern. This is where you come in. Can you help me?"

"Very interesting case," Fankhauser observed. "Yes; I should be able to provide you with the identity of the owner of that telephone number. That should be relatively easy. I have friends in high places at the Swiss telephone company. Do you want me to do more than that?" Isolde smiled, as she contemplated Fankhauser's question. She had confidence in him and his professionalism. He was already her closest ally in her quest for the truth. She needs to keep him on board.

"Joaquim, I have every confidence in you. I am usually a good judge of character. And I am willing to place my complete trust in you. I would like you to work with me in solving this bizarre case. Can I put you on a general retainer?"

"By all means, Isolde. May I suggest a money retainer of CHF15,000? That's 15,000 in Swiss francs. As we proceed, I will account to you for every penny of the money retainer utilized." That's quite a hefty amount, Isolde thought to herself. But she needed help; and he was recommended as the best.

"No problem. Just write down details of your bank account here in Bern. I will have my Toronto bank transfer CHF15,000 into your bank account ASAP."

"I look forward to working with you, Isolde."

"Oh, I forgot to tell you that I met with Constantino Rapini, the manager of VolksBankBern yesterday. To say the least, he was very secretive; tried to avoid all my questions; I concluded that he knows a lot; that he is hiding important facts from me. Not a man to be trusted. I should also mention that my eyes were drawn to a lapel pin that Rapini was wearing. It was a gold pin. And what do you think was the design on the face of that gold pin? The design was the same as shown on the sketch I found in Fred's desk drawer. Joaquim, it was as clear as day; the three intersecting crescents. Then, to my utter shock, I learned today that two men turned up at Fred's law office a few hours after my meeting with Rapini and presented Yvonne, Fred's legal secretary, with a Court Order requiring delivery to them of all Fred's clients' files, the only client, of course, being VolksBankBern. Yvonne turned over the files to them. It turns out that the Court Order was a complete fake. While it may be impossible for me to prove his involvement, I cannot help but believe that Rapini was behind this. He is a very dangerous man."

"I am glad you mentioned that, Isolde. Gives me an idea of the ruthlessness that we are dealing with. Whoever Rapini is in cahoots with, it appears that they will stop at nothing to achieve their aims. But we shall, I can promise you, get to the bottom of this. *The truth will out,* as the saying goes. For now, let's eat." He signaled to the waiter that they were ready to order. Yvonne had a warm fuzzy feeling. It was the same feeling she had experienced so many times as a child whenever her mother tucked her in her bed at nights; the same feeling she had enjoyed so many times as an adult whenever Fred gave her a tender, loving embrace. Her instinct told her that she would be safe with Fankhauser at her side. He had joined the ranks of her Lord Protectors. She was on the right track.

Once they placed the orders for dinner, Fankhauser poured some more wine, and then turned to look directly into Isolde's eyes. "Fascinating," he whispered. Isolde was taken aback.

"What is?" she questioned.

"Your eyes," Fankhauser responded, unabashedly. Isolde blushed. This is getting too personal, she surmised.

"What about my eyes?" she pursued.

"Cat's eyes. Has anyone ever told you that before?"

"Has anyone ever told me that I have 'cat's eyes'? The story of my life!" Isolde admitted, laughing out loud. "Is that good or bad?"

"Without a doubt, good! As I said, they are fascinating. That shade of amber is a rarity. They are penetrating eyes. When they look into another person's eyes, the subject cannot but feel that your eyes are penetrating his or her soul. No wonder Rapini was defenceless against you. God, Isolde, I sure wish I had your eyes!" Isolde accepted his words as a compliment, rolled her eyes, and chuckled.

CHAPTER SEVEN

THE NEXT MORNING, the sharp, crisp rings of the telephone brought Isolde back to life from a deep sleep in Room 205 at the Best Western Plus. As she scrambled to grab it, she glanced at the clock. It was nine-thirty. Who could be calling her so early on a Sunday morning? Was something else wrong back in Toronto?

"Good morning, Isolde." It was Fankhauser.

"Hi, Joaquim."

"Sorry if I woke you up. Just thought I should let you know ASAP the identity of the person behind the mysterious telephone number."

"No problem, Joaquim. I should be up anyway. I am all ears. Who is the mystery person?'

"The name of the mystery person is Lise Brunner. I will spell it for you: L-i-s-e B-r-u-n-n-e-r. Got that? It's her home telephone number. She resides at Spitalgasse 29. That's about twenty minutes by car from your hotel."

"Thank you very much, Joaquim. It's incredible how fast you work."

"May I ask what you intend to do, now that you have that information?"

"I intend to pay her a visit. I would like to hear from her directly as to what her relationship had been with Fred. Did Fred stay with her during the missing five days in Bern? Can she throw any light on Fred's death? So many questions I would like to ask her."

"My advice to you is to proceed cautiously. Experience tells me that expeditions of this type can be fraught with danger. And you must never forget that you are a woman alone in a strange city."

"Thanks for the advice, Joaquim. But I have to do this part on my own. I will let you know how it turns out. In any event, I have a feeling I will need your help down the road."

"Look forward to speaking with you further, Isolde. Have a good day."

Success, thought Isolde, as she placed the phone on the hook. Fankhauser was worth his weight in gold. She now had to plan her moves very carefully. She would come face to face with this mysterious woman of Bern, this Lise Brunner, who was the owner of the telephone number, and whose name Fred had never once mentioned. How would she, Isdolde, introduce herself? What probing questions should she ask? She definitely could not ask this Brunner woman outright "Were you sleeping with my husband?" or "Did you have anything to do with my husband's death?" She had to be subtle. She had to get this Brunner woman on her side. She had to befriend her. And then, very, very carefully pull out the information she needed, like a dentist extracting a number of teeth, one by one. What was the best time for her to undertake her surprise visit? It could be that the Brunner woman worked; and may not be at home during the hours of nine to five on workdays. And then, if she worked, time had to be allowed for the subject to prepare and eat dinner. Isolde decided that the best day on which to pay a call on Lise Brunner was that same day, Sunday; and that the best time would be in the early evening. The die was cast. She would visit the Brunner woman at her apartment at seven-thirty that evening.

By seven that evening, Isolde was busy dressing for her confrontation with this mystery woman. It would be inappropriate for her to power dress; she had to be someone that Lise could feel comfortable with, and so the 'power suit' was certainly not the way to go. Similarly, a tailored dress would just not do; even that could be too intimidating. She must dress down; the more casual the better. And so, she wore jeans; a rather dull blouse; Nike running shoes; and a faded Blue Jays baseball hat, with her champagne blonde hair in a pony tail, which protruded from the aperture at the back. Further, instead of enhancing her beauty cosmetically, she applied a minimum amount of makeup, so that she would appear as the rather dour-looking wife. If Lise had been 'the other woman" in Fred's life, it should make her feel better to know that Fred had good reason to opt for a dalliance with her. Strange sort of logic, but Isolde just had to work the odds.

Exiting the Best Western Plus, Isolde hopped into one of the cabs that played the waiting game outside the hotel.

"Spitalgasse 29," she commanded the driver. She felt her heart thumping louder and faster as they closed in on the destination. Steady girl, she said to herself; this is no time to panic. Finally, they were there, right in front of Lise Brunner's apartment building. She paid the cab driver; and slowly made her way into the front entrance of the building. She noticed the mail slots on the wall. Yes; there it was; **LISE BRUNNER 02.** That would be Apartment 2. She climbed the stairs, and was soon on the second floor. And there it was, to her left; Apartment 02, which housed the woman known as Lise Brunner. She took a deep breath, as she knocked on the door. Here goes nothing, she mumbled. The door opened almost instantaneously. Lise Brunner stared at Isolde, standing there before her.

"Was willst du?" she asked in German, rather abruptly. *What do you want?*

"Are you Lise Brunner?"

"Yes; I am Lise Brunner," Lise replied in perfect English.

"I am Isolde Bruni; Fred's wife. May I come in?" Lise blanched, as if she had seen a ghost. She was speechless. Isolde's heart was pounding so loudly she was concerned that Lise could hear it. Woman to woman, they each stood there, neither knowing what to do or say. Eventually, Isolde repeated her question. It seemed the simplest way to break the stony silence.

"Come in," Lise said, as she shrugged her shoulders rather resignedly. Well, Isolde thought; she had at least got that far. Here she was, now a guest in Lise's apartment. What will transpire next? Lise beckoned her to sit in an arm chair in the living room; Lise seated herself on a loveseat, upholstered in a dazzling array of large pink hydrangeas. Isolde's imagination momentarily took over, as she tried to picture Fred filling the void beside Lise on the colourful loveseat.

"Please accept my condolences on Fred's passing." This caught Isolde by surprise. How had Lise learned of Fred's death?

"How did you learn of Fred's death?" Isolde ventured to ask.

"Herr Rapini at VolksBankBern told me. You know, Fred did a lot of business with VolksBankBern. It was I who introduced Fred to the bank. Fred and I had been childhood friends. We had been neighbours when the Bruni family lived here in Bern. I knew that Fred and his family had moved to Canada. I had lost track of Fred, until one day, many years later, on the ski slopes at St. Moritz. I saw this man, whom I swore was Fred. I approached him and asked him if he was Fred Bruni; and he said he was. He told me that he had studied law in Ontario; and that, upon his call to the bar, he intended to set up practice on his own. He wanted to specialize in Business Law. Not long after, the opportunity arose; VolksBankBern needed an Ontario lawyer to handle their Ontario transactions. I introduced him to Herr Rapini, a friend of my family; and, in the blink of an eye, Fred was lawyer for the bank. A very rewarding relationship for Fred, I believe."

Isolde was amazed; in fact, stunned, and somewhat slighted. Fred had never once mentioned Lise's name to her. Imagine, the renewal of Fred's relationship with Lise had been rekindled at St. Moritz, most likely while Fred and Isolde were there together. And Fred's major client, if not his only client, came about as a referral from Lise. And yet Fred had never once in all those years mentioned the name Lise. The other aspect of Lise's response that got to her was the mention of the name of that creep, Rapini. As the old saying goes, *Birds of a feather flock together*; or the other old adage *You lie down with dogs, you get up with fleas*. If Lise was a friend of Rapini, then Lise could not be a good person. In fact, it would likely mean that Lise was a rotten egg.

"Did Fred ever mention my name to you?"

"Yes; many times. He told me from the outset that he was married; and that he loved you very much." Well, that was honest, thought Isolde. "And when the kids came along, Emil and Sophie, he would show me pictures of them. He was such a proud father. What beautiful kids!" Isolde smiled, and thanked her for the compliment. But there were deeper questions that needed to be answered.

"May I offer you a cup of coffee? Or tea? Or hot chocolate? We Swiss make the best chocolate in the world, you know. After all, this is the home of Nestlé. Or would you prefer some alcohol? Cognac? Wine? Beer? Anything at all?" Lise asked. Isolde's 'cat's eyes' were fixated on her. She had to decide whether Lise was using diversionary tactics, or whether she was just being hospitable. Her instinct told her that they were now both engaged in a game of épée fencing; that the épées were fully drawn; that the entire body was a valid target area; and that the offer of a drink was really a diversionary tactic to distract Isolde in order that Lise may plunge her épée into Isolde 's heart. Isolde resolved that she had to maintain her powers of concentration, her accuracy in the pursuit of her goal, and the speed with which she made her moves. She had to remember to play the game on a *no holds barred* basis. She had learned all this from the sport of fencing which she had pursued as an extra-curricular activity at the Women's Athletic Club at the University of Toronto. She had taken to the sport like a fish to water.

"If you have red wine, I will take a glass, thank you," Isolde politely responded. Lise poured two glasses of red wine from a decanter that was sitting on a nearby table. Handing one glass to Isolde, she held up the other glass, said "Prost", and, as Isolde also mouthed "Prost", downed her glass in one fell swoop. Isolde interpreted this as a sign of nervousness on Lise's part, notwithstanding the bold, complacent front that she had been putting on in their little game of fencing. Isolde immediately parried with a direct question.

"Were you having an affair with my husband?"

"Yes," was Lise's swift unrepentant response. Isolde flinched. She was taken aback. She had not anticipated such directness, such boldness; such honesty. "It had not started out that way," Lise continued, "but over time we developed a sexual attraction for each other." Nice parry, thought Isolde; designed to catch me off balance. Touché, Lise! Isolde's cat's eyes stared into Lise's almond-brown eyes, like a flame lighting up a dark room. As the French say, *Les yeux sont le miroir de l'âme,* which in English reads, *The eyes are the mirror of the soul.* Fankhauser was so right when he told Isolde that her cat's eyes are "penetrating". They are absorbing eyes; mesmerizing eyes, that make you squirm; eyes that suck you right in before you even realize it.

"Did Fred stay here with you on his last trip to Bern, a couple weeks or so before his death?"

"Yes," Lise was quick to respond. "He phoned me from the airport; said he had not been able to get a booking at a good hotel in Bern; could he stay here with me? Of course, I said yes." Isolde immediately recognized her answer as another counter-attack to ward off Isolde's épée with a counter-move. After all, Julian Zimmermann, the manager of SwissCan Travel, had told her that Fred had told him that there was no need to book a hotel in Bern as he would be staying with a friend. Further, Yvonne had reported that shortly before leaving for Europe Fred had received a telephone call from a woman in Bern. Although Lise was not aware of it, Isolde was gaining in points against her in their little game of fencing.

"How long did Fred stay with you on that visit?" Isolde queried.

"As I recall, it was only for two or three days," Lise replied. Isolde found this interesting. How could Lise forget that it was for about five days? Was she trying to downplay the length of Fred's stay at her apartment? Was this another parry in their game of fencing? Isolde had to strike quickly with her next question.

"I found correspondence from VolksBankBern to Fred in which the bank referred to 'our mutual client'. Do you have any idea as to the identity of the person or institution that was 'our mutual client'?" At this question, Lise sat up straight in her chair. She cleared a lump from her throat. She started fidgeting, playing with a ring that adorned the middle finger of her right hand. Isolde had struck a raw nerve. Good. That was an excellent attack, Isolde thought. She had caught Lise completely off guard. Lise suddenly seemed at a loss for words.

"I was never aware that there was a 'mutual client'," Lise responded eventually, once she had regained some degree of composure. But Isolde's eyes were now drawn to the ring with which Lise had been fidgeting. She stared at the ring. It was a sight to behold. The shank was likely of eighteen carat gold. Exquisitely worked into the head was a base of black onyx, inlaid with three pieces of mother of pearl. As her eyes zeroed in on the setting in the head, she almost fell off her chair. Each of the three pieces of mother of pearl was in the shape of a crescent, and all three crescents were intersecting. Her mind immediately floated back to the mysterious sketch which she had found in Fred's desk drawer, and to the gold lapel pin that had gleamed from the lapel of Rapini's jacket. There must be a common bond. There is obviously some deep secret, of which she must obtain disclosure.

"That is a beautiful ring," Isolde said, boldly. At this, Lise looked down at the ring, and attempted to cover it up with her other hand. "Are those three crescents I see in the crown?" Isolde's attack was swift.

"They are three semi-circles, anyway. An ex-boyfriend of mine gave it to me. The poor guy; he later died in a car accident. Was driving down a steep hill in the Alps; lost control on the icy surface. It was all over in a few seconds. I am sorry, Isolde; but you must leave now. I am expecting company in a few minutes." Touché for me, thought Isolde. She had just scored another major point. She had linked the design on the sketch from Fred's drawer with Lise; and Lise more closely with Rapini. The three intersecting crescents must represent something more than just adornment in jewelry. They must be part of a secret that both Rapini and Lise were going to great lengths to hide from her. Rapini had tried to deflect her attention away from the three intersecting crescents; he had referred to them as "arcs". Lise had also tried to divert her away from them; she had described them as "semi-circles". What's wrong with just calling them as they are; calling a spade a spade; calling them "crescents"? Isolde declared herself victor in the fencing match. Her visit with Lise was a success. It gave her the resolve to carry on, like the tiger she was, in search of her prey.

"Thanks for seeing me, Lise. I really appreciate your courtesy and hospitality. I just want you to know that I hold no hard feelings about your intimate relationship with Fred." In saying this, Isolde was putting the best foot forward. Deep down, she resented Lise for having screwed her husband. And, as for her dead husband, well…let's just say that it may be best at this stage to let sleeping dogs lie. She got up, shook Lise's extended hand, and headed for the door. As she approached the door, her eyes were somehow drawn to a framed colour photograph that sat on an ebony console table. It was a photograph of Fred, almost like a portrait painted by an artist. He wore his typical broad smile, which revealed the straightest rows of ivory teeth that one has ever seen, well positioned in a thickset jaw. His head was adorned with wavy, flowing chestnut hair, cropped short of the shoulders. His light brown eyes beamed through the narrow slits that were more pronounced whenever he engaged in his familiar smile. His handsome facial features would have made a good subject for any of the famous Roman sculptors, not excluding Michelangelo of Renaissance fame. As she stared at this beautiful picture of her dead husband sitting so prominently in his mistress' abode, she felt her legs quivering beneath her weight and a lightness in her stomach as if she was about to be sick. She dug the nails of her right hand into her left wrist, so painfully that she was tempted to scream.

"Where are you staying? Would you like me to call you a cab?" Lise asked.

"No. I am staying at Best Western Plus Hotel Bern over on Zeughausgasse. It's a stone's throw from here. I prefer to walk. It's beautiful out. Besides, I need the fresh air and exercise." With that, Isolde exited Lise's apartment, sauntered down the stairs, and slipped out of the apartment building, onto Spitalgasse. She walked about one hundred paces from the building, ensuring that she was out of sight; but stopping at a point from which she could have full view of persons entering the building. Shivering in the cool evening air, she stood there for a full hour, just waiting and watching. During that whole time, there was not a single person entering Lise's apartment building. There are two takeaways from this. Lise had been getting uncomfortable with the game of fencing, because Isolde had been hot on her trail; and Lise was a liar, and not to be trusted..

CHAPTER EIGHT

SITTING ALONE at a table for two in the dining room of the Best Western Plus Hotel Bern, Isolde jotted down some observations from her meeting with Lise. It was a pleasant atmosphere in the dining room. The lighting was soft, coming from small gas lamps on the walls, almost reminiscent of the nostalgic lighting so typical of Paris. In one corner of the dining room, a pianist was playing a medley of well-known nostalgic Liberace tunes, including *As Time Goes By, Strangers in the Night, Dixie,* and the ever-popular *Chopsticks.*

"No," she told the waiter, "I am not expecting anyone to join me. I will be dining alone. I would like to start with a Manhattan, please." As she waited for the cocktail, she read the menu. The waiter returned in a couple of minutes with the Manhattan.

"What would Madame like to order from the menu?"

She ordered a bowl of Bündner Gerstensuppe. It was one of her favourites. Fred had introduced her to it in St. Moritz. She recalled it being especially good with Swiss bread. Following the soup, she would like the Coq au Vin as the main course. And for dessert she would love some Swiss Chocolate Cake.

She then turned again to collecting her thoughts. Mentally, she reviewed every detail of her meeting with Lise; every bit of information that Lise had given her; and every bit of information that Lise had failed to give her. She recalled the body language that had emanated from Lise's reactions; and every thrust and parry that had occurred in their little game of épée fencing. There is so much that she had learned. But also, so much that she still had to learn. As she thought about it, there was very little that she knew about Lise. What was her history? Not just with Fred; but, delving more deeply, her family history? As with thoroughbred race horses, one can tell so much from a study of one's pedigree. Was Lise descended from a line of thoroughbreds? After all, she must have had some degree of influence. She had lined Fred up with VolksBankBern; and she was only a young woman. Her influence must have flowed from her parents, grandparents, and other ancestors. So, how had they become so influential? Had that influence been acquired through financial power? Or had it been through political power? Or had it been through social power? Or had it been through some nefarious means? If Isolde could grasp the true nature of the relationship between Lise and VolksBankBern, then that would likely go a long way toward providing the answers to some of the questions that had yet to be answered in her quest for the Holy Grail. She concluded that she once again needed help; she needed her knight in shing armour, aka Joaquim Fankhauser.

An impetuous woman, she lacked the patience to delay, once she has devised a plan. She literally gulped down the soup, the main course, and the dessert. She then requested the check, and paid it in an instant. Before long, she was back in Room 205, with the telephone in her hand. She held Fankhauser's business card in the other hand. Fankhauser's home telephone number appeared on the business card below his office telephone number. She dialed the home number, and Fankhauser answered on the first ring.

"Guten Abend," Fankhauser said. *Good evening.*

"Good evening, Joaquim. This is Isolde. Sorry to phone you at home. But I need to speak with you immediately."

"Hi, Isolde. In any event, my office is a room within my apartment. My business card shows one telephone number for my office, and another for the rest of my apartment. So, it really does not matter which number you call; it's all in my home. What can I do for you?"

"I met with Lise this evening. She admitted to having had an affair with Fred. She told me that she had been the one that had connected Fred with VolksBankBern. She was wearing a beautiful gold ring; the crown was black onyx, inlaid with mother of pearl. And you would not believe the design that the mother of pearl made?"

"Don't tell me; the design was the three intersecting crescents on Fred's sketch; the three intersecting crescents engraved on Rapini's gold lapel pin. Right?"

"Precisely. There are more monsters in the swamp than we had anticipated. I need to know more about Lise; her lineage; her family; her history; everything. Can you get on that immediately for me?"

"No problem, Isolde. Your wish is my command. I will try and get back to you within forty-eight hours. In the meantime, you should take a few hours to see some of the historic sites in Bern. There is just so much to see in the *Altstadt.*"

"Oh, Joaquim. Thank you very much. I feel so safe in your hands."

"Now don't get carried away. All I can promise is to do the best for you."

After a sound sleep that night, Isolde awoke bright and early, ready to set out on a site-seeing tour of Old Bern, as Fankhauser had recommended. She grabbed a bagel with cream cheese and a cup of coffee, and, armed with a brochure containing a list of the 'must-see' sites, she began a walking tour of the *Altstadt*. Fortunately, the sun was beaming down on the Old City, diminishing the effects of the frigid morning air on her body. Her first stop was at the *Münster Kirche*, the huge cathedral in the Old City, construction of which had started as far back as AD1421. It is the tallest cathedral in Switzerland, its tower rising to a height of three hundred and thirty feet above sea level. She climbed the tall tower, all the way to the top, and was rewarded with a spectacular view of the whole city of Bern. Next on her list was the *Zytglogge*, the medieval clock tower built in the early 13th century. The tower contains an astronomical clock and a huge bell, which results in the name *Zytglogge*, meaning 'time bell'. Not far from the *Zytglogge* is the *Bundeshaus*, the building that seats the Swiss House of Parliament. Finally, she did a foot tour of some of the numerous fountains in Bern, which has been dubbed *'the City of Fountains'*. This tour included the *Läuferbrunnen,* the Läufer fountain depicting the Runner; the *Kindlifresserbrunnen*, the Ogre Fountain, portraying the Ogre devouring children; the *Mosesbrunnen,* the Moses Fountain showing a statue of *Moses Holding the Ten Commandments*; the *Pfeiferbrunnen*, the Piper Fountain on Spitalgasse; the *Anna-Seiler-Brunnen*, the fountain on Marktgasse memorializing the founder of the first hospital in Bern;

and the *Zähringerbrunnen,* the fountain on Kramgasse constructed as a memorial to the founder of Bern. After she was 'fountained out', she dragged herself back to the quietude of her 'home away from home', Best Western Plus Hotel Bern, where she had a late lunch, and, armed with a bottle of Pinot Noir, retreated to the sanctuary of Room 205. Her mind was now temporarily freed from the thoughts of how to solve the mystery of Fred's untimely death. She opened the bottle of Pinot Noir, turned on the television, and watched *Play Misty for Me,* a psychological thriller of the early 1970's directed by and starring Clint Eastwood. The movie was the German version with English subtitles. She could not escape that warm and fuzzy feeling throughout her body; the same feeling she had had at dinner with Fankhauser at the *Della Casa.* She is in the hands of Fankhauser. There is nothing more for her to do until he reports on Lise's *history.* When that happens, she will then plan the next step forward. For the time being, she will relax, imbibe her Pinot Noir, and enjoy the movie rerun.

She did not have long to wait to hear back from Fankhauser. He was back to her at about seven that evening. His efficiency amazed her. When the telephone rang, she whispered to herself: "Oh, God, let it be Joaquim".

"Isolde, I have unearthed something about Lise that I thought you should know immediately. Have you ever heard of the 'Medicis'?"

"I remember the name 'Medici' from my university course in European history. I cannot remember the context, except that it seemed to come up in lectures on the Renaissance. Outside of that, I must confess to ignorance. Why do you ask, Joaquim?"

"I have found out that Lise has some ties to the Medicis. I have not been able to tie down the precise relationship; but I think that we have to sit up and take note whenever the Medicis are mentioned. Permit me to give you a little background in history. The Medici family was one of the most powerful families to have ever existed in Europe. They were from Tuscany, and were largely responsible for the flourishing success of Florence, where they were headquartered. They were dominant in Italy for over three hundred years; during the 15th, 16th and 17th centuries. They established their own bank, and were financially extremely successful. To their credit, they were great patrons of the arts; of any type of culture; art, sculpture, architecture, literature, music; you name it, and they were there. They took Leonardo da Vinci, Michelangelo, Raphael, and numerous others Renaissance men under their wings, and eased their paths to success. Even Galileo came under their influence. And just look at the intricate beauty of the *Boboli Gardens*, just across the River Arno, a stone's throw from the *Uffizi Gallery* in Old Florence. For their role in the Renaissance, the Medicis have left a huge boon to mankind. But there was another side to the Medici family. You likely have never heard of Giralomo Savonarola. He was an Italian religious reformer; a member of the Dominican Order of Priests. Savonarola happened to get on the wrong side of the Medicis. This was his undoing. He was tried and convicted of sedition, and a number of lesser charges. He was sentenced to be hanged. But it was not enough for he and his two companions to be hanged, they had to be burnt, in a huge bonfire. The Florentine artist Francesco Rosselli captured the horrible event in his magnificent painting *The Execution of Savonarola and Two Companions at Piazza della Signoria*. I think the painting hangs in *Galleria degli Uffizi*, which, coincidentally, is located at Piazza della Signoria; the same square in in Old Florence where Savonarola was made to meet his maker. The message from the Savonarola brutal spectacle was loud and clear: *Don't mess with the Medicis*. And then, you may have heard of Catherine de' Medici and her notorious *Chamber of Secrets,* her apothecary of poisons at Château de Blois just outside Paris. Heaven knows how those poisons had been meted out throughout Catherine's lifetime. One more thing. It should not be forgotten that the tremendous power of the Medici family also extended into Vatican City. Did you know that there had been no less than four members of the Medici family who had become Pope?"

"No," Isolde confessed, "I did not have the faintest idea."

"Well, that's the God's truth. Giovanni di Lorenzo de' Medici became Pope Leo X; Giulio di Giuliano de' Medici became Pope Clement VII; Giovanni Angelo de' Medici became Pope Pius IV; and Alessandro Ottaviano de' Medici became Pope Leo XI. So, you can see that the tentacles of the Medici family even extended into the Vatican. How about that for power?"

"Absolutely incredible!" Isolde gasped.

"So; where does that take us? The first takeaway is that we may be dealing with extreme power; and remember the old saying; I think the British historian Lord Acton coined it; *Power tends to corrupt; absolute power corrupts absolutely*. If Lise is a member of the powerful Medici family, we may be dealing with a force so great that we are like the poor people of Pompei in the deadly path of the molten lava rushing down from Mount Vesuvius. In other words, the road ahead may indeed be strewn with hazards. But a word of caution; we still do not know enough. All that we know is that Lise appears to have some familial connection with the powerful Medici family."

"What would you recommend that I do now, Joaquim?" Isolde asked, helplessly.

"I think that you need to delve more deeply into the history of the Medici family. Find out, if you can, more about Lise and her possible connection with the family. Find out the extent of the power that they may still wield, especially in banking and other financial services. Find out with whom they are connected; for example, is there any continuing connection with the Vatican? And find out if there is any possible connection with VolksBankBern, outside of Lise. I have gone a step further for you, Isolde. I have tracked down the international expert on the Medicis. Make a note of this; Professor Piero Rossi of *Università degli Studi di Firenze*; that is known in English as the University of Florence. They are located at Piazza San Marco in Florence. Professor Rossi is a renowned member of the Faculty of History. I would highly recommend that you meet with him and see how he can satisfy your questions about the Medicis. But whatever you do, do not reveal to Professor Rossi the true purpose of your interview. I would simply tell him that you are a free-lance journalist working on an article about the Medici family. It's a relatively short ride by train from Bern to Florence. Contact me when you get back."

"Joaquim, I cannot thank you enough. I will pursue that route ASAP. Bye."

As soon as Isolde hung up the phone, she cupped her hands over her face. She suddenly felt as if a sheet of ice had run through her whole body. What is it that she is getting into? She thought of what the Medicis had done to Savonarola. If they could have done that to a leader of the Dominican friars, a man of God, what would they do to her? Or perhaps the question is better posed as: What would they not do to her?

CHAPTER NINE

THREE O'CLOCK on the afternoon of the following day found Isolde exiting the train at Stazione di Santa Maria Novella in Florence. It was a short walk from the train station to *Università degli Studi di Firenze*. She entered the Administration Building, and asked for Professor Rossi; she had an appointment for three-thirty. When she phoned him early this morning, he seemed extremely willing to help; to talk about his life's work, the Medicis. The Professor had not arrived as yet; but should be there shortly. Kindly have a seat.

Professor Rossi arrived at about three-fifteen. He was a short, bespectacled man in his sixties. Behind the thick lenses of his glasses, she could just barely discern the colour of his eyes. Remarkably, the right eye appeared to be pewter grey, and the left a sort of indigo. His tie was twisted, under his patch-armed jacket, which looked as if in need of a good pressing. He had a bundle of papers emanating from both hands, pressed tightly against his chest. Isolde thought that he fit perfectly the typical picture of the absent-minded professor. With his head, he simply acknowledged her presence, and beckoned to her to follow him. He led her down a long, narrow corridor, into an office, which at first glance seemed as disorganized as he was. He sat down; invited her to have a seat; pulled out his pipe, the bulb of which he stuffed full of a sweet-smelling tobacco; and then set about lighting his pipe. Finally, looking out the window on his right side, he actually opened his mouth and spoke.

"Signora Bruni," he started. "Pleasure to meet you." He had a strong Italian accent. Isolde could not help but smile at the way he rolled the 'r' in 'Bruni'.

"Thank you, Professor, for seeing me on such short notice."

"So, you want to talk about the Medicis?" he asked, his arms extended wide to emphasize the ambit of the question. It was clear that he also spoke with his hands.

"Professor, I am a freelance journalist. I am working on an article entitled 'The Medicis: Past and Present'. Of course, you are the renowned expert on the Medici family. I am willing to pay you for your assistance." The professor smiled, reveling in the compliment. The offer of compensation also helped.

"I am at your service, Signora Bruni. I have written several books on the Medicis. What questions do you have for me?"

"I understand that for over three hundred years the Medici family was extremely powerful in Italy."

"Not only Italy," he interjected, "but the whole of western Europe."

"Did this power extend as far as the Holy See, the Vatican?"

"Definitely. You must appreciate that the Medicis created their own bank, *Banco dei Medici*. Highly successful. They became the leading experts in financial matters. Combine with that the fact that they produced four Popes. Can you believe it? One family producing four Popes! Pope Leo X, Pope Clement VII, Pope Pius IV, and Pope Leo XI. It was then only natural that the Vatican would develop close contacts with the Medici Bank, or vice versa. Even though the Medici Bank in itself had not prospered as much after the end of the 17th century as it had in the prior three hundred years, successive generations of the Medici family continued to influence the finances of the Holy See. Did you know that the Roman Catholic Church, through the Vatican, is today one of the richest corporations in the world? I think that its assets are estimated as having a net worth of over €4,000,000,000. Astounding!"

"Are there many of the Medici family descendants alive today?"

"That depends on how you define 'many'. Let's put it this way: there are a number of descendants of the powerful Medici family of Florence still living today. Some of them are in Rome, some in Florence, some in Switzerland, some in France; believe me, they are alive and well, the Medicis. This is a family that has been a boon to mankind. As you likely know, they were the driving force behind the Renaissance. Had it not been for the Medicis, the world of art, architecture, music, and culture would not be what it is today." At this, he rolled his grey right eye, but his left indigo eye remained as still as a corpse.

"Are there any Medicis living in Bern?" Isolde was trying to eke out something, anything, about the Brunners of Bern. The professor looked at her quizzically.

"Why Bern? I can understand if you ask about Florence; but Bern?" His question was very incisive. She cannot afford to let him get wise as to precisely what she is seeking.

"I just wondered how far the descendants of the Medicis have gone. Bern seems like a good example, being so close to Italy." The response seemed to satisfy him.

"My understanding is that a branch of the Medici family did settle in Bern."

"Can you provide me with any names?" From the Professor's body language, she had obviously gone too far. He bristled, and rolled his dominant right eye. The dead left eye showed no movement whatsoever.

"Signora Bruni, there are certain ethical standards that I must maintain," he sneered. "While I can talk about the Medici family from the historical, financial, political, and sociological perspectives, I cannot intrude upon the privacy of living members of the Medicis." His response was decisive. She had gone as far as she could in determining whether Lise Brunner was in fact a Medici.

"My apologies, Professor Rossi. I understand the privacy issue. My next question has to do with Catherine de' Medici." This brought on a short burst of laughter. The professor took a few seconds time-out to relight his pipe.

"Inevitably, everyone asks me about Catherine de' Medici. Of all the Medicis, she is the one that seems to draw the most questions. I suspect this largely stems from her fascination with poisons Do you know that at Château de Blois, about one hundred and sixty kms. south-west of Paris, there is a room that is devoted to cabinets which had been reserved for Catherine's numerous poisons and her 'research papers'? It is known as *The Chamber of Secrets;* but there are those who think a better name would be *The Chamber of Horrors*. Her collection of poisons has long disappeared. But her "research papers" still exist. The woman is so reviled, it's terrible. In my view, she simply had a hobby of investigating all the different types of poisons. Not one person has ever proven that she had ever used any of her collection of poisons nefariously. If there was ever a person that should have had the sympathy of students of history, it is Catherine de' Medici. She was married at a very early age to Henry, son of King Francis I of France. Henry became King of France, King Henry II. But then, there appeared on the scene another woman. Yes, "the other woman". Have you ever heard of Diane de Poitiers? She became the mistress of Henry II. For some years, Diane de Poitiers asserted significant control over Henry II. She was quite a woman. She seemed to have an obsession with her breasts. There are paintings of her showing both breasts revealed in all their sexuality. It had been reported that at times she had been seen swimming in the River Loire, completely naked; yes, not a stitch on." He stopped, and leaned forward, his dominant right eye looking Isolde squarely in the face, as if expecting some reaction of shock, his dead left eye just going along for the ride. Isolde cleared her throat, trying not to laugh at the weird antics of the professor's eyes. She declined to comment on the picture painted of Diane de Poitiers swimming publicly in the buff.

"In any event," the professor continued, "Diane de Poitiers wielded far more control over Henry than his wife, Catherine de' Medici. Diane even influenced Henry in the design of the royal emblem. She seemed to have a fascination with crescents." At the mention of crescents, Isolde felt a chill run through her bones. This was eerie. Without any prompting from her, the professor was volunteering information about the crescents. "The design of the emblem adopted by Henry II has been attributed to Diane de Poitiers. It is a work of genius. On the left, there is a capital "D"; on the right, there is a reversed capital "D"; the arcs of each "D", are like "crescents"; and they intersect each other. Finally, a straight line is drawn from the post of the "D" to the left, through the intersecting crescents, to finally touch the post of the reversed "D". So, what do you have? You have the letter "D", the initial of the name "Diane"; and the same with the reversed "D". You have the initial "H", for the name "Henry". And, last but not least, you have two crescents, most important to Diane." The professor opened one of his books, and turning to a page containing a photograph of the emblem of Henry II, showed it to Isolde. My God, thought Isolde, as she was reminded of the sketch from Fred's desk drawer, the gold lapel spin worn by Rapini, and Lise's beautiful gold ring with black onyx crown, inlaid with mother of pearl. This is vital information in my quest. We are really on to something here. The professor continued: "Now, I put the question to you; which of these two women deserves our sympathy? Catherine or Diane? In my book, Catherine was the aggrieved wife; Diane was the transgressor, a concubine, so to speak." He looked enquiringly into Isolde's eyes, as if begging for approval of his conclusion. Isolde's cat's eyes were fixated on his grey right eye, the good one. They were peering into the depths of his mind.

"I get your point, Professor Rossi. History eventually becomes the judge of all things." Isolde marveled at her own philosophical perspective. She felt proud of herself. She was also, in her own mind, congratulating herself on what she had unearthed so far about the 'intersecting crescents', which were now playing a dominant role in her investigation. Fred's sketch of the three intersecting crescents; Rapini's gold lapel pin with the three intersecting crescents; Lise's gold ring with the three mother of pearl intersecting crescents; and now Diane de Poitiers' design of Henry II's emblem depicting two intersecting crescents. This knowledge whetted her appetite for more.

"What more can you tell me about the intersecting crescents?" She asked. "Have you ever seen a design--- whether it be for an emblem, for a crest, or for anything--- of three intersecting crescents?" The professor's face lit up. He immediately turned to another page in his book.

"Yes. Take a look at this crest of the 'Knights of the Crescent'. You see the three intersecting crescents in the centre? Beautiful, isn't it? Diane de Poitiers claimed that three intersecting crescents design as her own. Also, take a look at the figures at the bottom left and the bottom right of the crest. You can see the dominant display of a woman's breasts. Most consistent with Diane de Poitiers." Isolde marveled at the beauty of the three intersecting crescents. The design of the crest was exactly as depicted on the sketch from Fred's desk drawer, Rapini's gold pin, and Lise's gold ring with the inlaid mother of pearl.

"Was this crest designed by Diane de Poitiers?"

"There are conflicting views on this aspect. But, in my mind, the crest bears all the markings of Diane de Poitiers."

"Incidentally, what do the Latin words '**IMPLEAT ORBEM DONEC TOTUM**' mean?" She pointed to the words on the crest.

"The English translation is 'UNTIL IT FILLS THE WHOLE WORLD'. What does this mean? It means until the glory of the King fills the world like the crescent moon does when it becomes full."

"What ever happened to the three main characters you have just told me about? Henry II of France? Catherine de' Medici? And Diane de Poitiers?"

"The first to die was Henry II. He died from injuries suffered in a jousting tournament; they say that the lance went right through one eye, into his head. Ouch! What a horrible fate! After his death, Catherine tightened control over his assets and accessibility to him, and Diane's power went into decline. Catherine died some years later. There is a school of thought that Diane de Poitiers' influence on Henry II had been so significant that she had, somewhat secretly, but with Henry's approbation, established a loyal band of followers. Her followers were well schooled in financial matters. They infiltrated the upper echelons of the business world, extending even into the inner sanctum of the Vatican. So, even while the Medici family in essence managed the financial assets of the Vatican, Diane's secret society wielded their own influence. A shadow, so to speak. While I do not have any proof of this, some experts opine that Diane's secret band of followers are alive and well in the world today."

"When did Diane de Poitiers die?"

"I cannot recall the precise date off the top of my head," he responded, apologetically. "But according to my best recollection, sometime in the 1560's."

"But, Professor Rossi," she persevered. "Tell me, seeing that it has been over four hundred years since the death of Diane de Poitiers, how could her secret band survive down to this day?"

"Well," replied the Professor, as he puffed away at his pipe, "to explain this, you have to go back to a Medici known as Gian Gastone de' Medici. Ever heard of him?"

"Nope. What was his claim to fame?'

"Not fame. Notoriety. He was the 'black sheep' of the Medicis. They prefer not to talk about him. He was the son of Cosimo III, and the last of the Medicis to hold the title of Grand Duke of Tuscany. Gian Gastone swung both ways, if you get my drift. He gradually entered upon a life of moral decay. His right-hand man, Giuliano Dami, assembled a team of young men called the Ruspanti, who were used to satisfy the sexual desires of Gian Gastone. As time went by, Gian Gastone sank deeper and deeper into depression, and wasted away more and more from a number of diseases, including syphilis. Some scholars have noted that Dami and the Ruspanti gained more and more power as Gian Gastone became weaker and weaker, and that they developed a bond with the secret society that had been formed by none other than Diane de Poitiers. After Gian Gastone died in 1737, the secret society, strengthened through Dami and the Ruspanti, grew even stronger in power, and survived until today, under the shadow of the Medicis. It is recorded that this secret society performed the tasks that were too dirty for the Medicis; and, in this way, their survival has been guaranteed, the Medicis turning a blind eye to their misdeeds. Now, unfortunately, I have to end our interview; I have another appointment."

"You have been a fountain of information, Professor Rossi. How much do I owe you?"

"€200, please." Isolde was prepared. She handed him €200 in cash. It was well worth it, she thought to herself.

"Oh, Professor Rossi. Can you recommend to me the name of an expert in the field of poisons, especially those that had been in *The Chamber of Secrets* of Catherine de' Medici?" she asked, as they both rose from their chairs.

"Definitely," he replied, as he pulled a small black book from one of the drawers of his desk. "Professor Jean Rappaport of the *Faculté des Sciences de Sorbonne Université*. He is renowned world-wide for his knowledge of the individual poisons in Catherine's secret chamber."

"Thank you, Professor Rossi. Have a good day."

Leaving the university, she headed for *Galleria degli Uffizi*, located next to Piazza della Signoria. The *Uffizi* had been a creation of the Medici family, and Isolde felt that she should be able to crawl under the skin of the Medicis through the numerous paintings that adorned its walls. At the very least, it would be an enriching cultural experience for her. Although she and Fred had been to Florence before, they had never found the time to tour the *Uffizi*. Her visit to the gallery was not disappointing. The wide array of paintings vividly transported her back to the period of over three hundred years when the Medicis ruled Tuscany.

After the *Uffizi*, she slid into a small café on Piazza della Signoria, where she grabbed a small pizza and an espresso, which she quickly devoured at one of the many tables in the square, as she watched the myriads of pigeons strutting about on, and fluttering in flight above, the white terrace. She then made her way back to Stazione di Santa Maria Novella to board the train for the return ride to Bern.

During the train ride from Florence to Bern, she utilized the time to organize in her mind the invaluable information that Professor Rossi had imparted to her. So, it definitely appears that there likely is a secret society, which is a shadow of the powerful Medicis, who still have significant power and influence in Italy and other parts of Europe. The secret society appears to have descended from a combination of the secret group of courtiers fostered by Diane de Poitiers, and the Ruspanti nurtured by Gian Gastone de' Medici through his henchman, Giuliano Dami. Diane's 'three intersecting crescents' appeared to play a part in the life of the secret society. If those hypotheses are true, then there would appear to be a deep connection between the emblem of the 'three intersecting crescents' depicted on Fred's sketch, the 'three intersecting crescents' engraved on Rapini's gold lapel pin, and the 'three intersecting crescents' of mother of pearl inlaid in the black onyx in the crown of Lise's gold ring. "Wow," Isolde exclaimed to herself; "there seems to be a huge power structure, a very secret one, implicated in Fred's death. And to make matters worse, it appears that there may just be some sort of connection with the Vatican; although the exact nature of the connection, if any, is still lacking." One thing was clear: Lise and Rapini were definitely important characters in the play that was unfolding. What was she lacking in completing the script? Yes. There was the matter of the suspected poison. And, as far as poisons go, considering the connection with the Medicis, *The Chamber of Secrets* of Catherine de' Medici at Château de Blois and Catherine's 'research papers' were matters of great interest. Could it be that *The Chamber of Secrets* had once housed a vial of poison that is unknown to modern science? And then, there was the question of opportunity to commit the crime; how was the poison administered? Fred had not died in Europe; he had died at his very own desk in his office on Bay Street in Toronto. Under those circumstances, the poison must have been administered to him in Toronto. Assuming that there was a nefarious secret society, how did they manage to get Fred to imbibe the poison in Toronto, especially when Fred had died at his desk in his office in Toronto, and the security videotapes showed no entry of any stranger into his office on the day or the night that he died? What else is lacking? There is the matter of motive. Isolde suspected that the motive was to shut Fred down in his investigation of his client VolksBankBern; and his quest to unclothe the identity of 'our mutual client'. But a mere suspicion would not get to first base in a court of law. She needed to get to the bottom of ascertaining the identity of 'our mutual client', and then determining the motive for silencing Fred. The prudent course to follow was to meet with Fankhauser back in Bern and chart the course forward. As soon as she had settled back in Room 205 at Best Western Plus Hotel Bern, she picked up the telephone and dialed Fankhauser's number. As usual, he answered on the first ring.

"Fankhauser," came the now familiar voice from the other end of the line.

"Hi, Joaquim," Isolde said excitedly, "I have just returned from speaking with Professor Rossi in Florence. Very knowledgeable. I need to get together with you to bring you up-to-date, and to decide on the next step forward."

"How about dinner tomorrow, Isolde? I will reserve a table at *Restaurant zum Zähringer*. It's here in Old Bern, overlooking the River Aare. I guarantee you will love the food; not to mention the ambience. I will meet you in the lobby of your hotel at seven, for dinner at eight. It's a short walk from your hotel." That's Joaquim, Isolde thought to herself; a true epicurean.

"It's a date, Joaquim. See you then."

The next evening, Joaquim was right on time. Isolde could not help but comment on how handsome he looked in his custom-tailored navy-blue suit, his light-blue shirt, his rich burgundy silk tie, and his long trench coat of oyster shell grey. He wore a gold pin in his lapel, which caused Isolde to do a double-take when she spotted it.

"I am happy to see that there are no intersecting crescents engraved on your lapel pin, Joaquim," she remarked, jokingly. He immediately caught the drift of her humour, and laughed heartily. He said that the lapel pin had been a personal gift from the President of Switzerland in recognition of some service that Fankhauser had performed on behalf of the Swiss Confederation. Isolde was impressed. This was almost a confirmation that she was in the right hands. As they wound their way through Old Bern toward the River Aare, he utilized the time to point out sites of historical interest. She was receiving a mini-tour of Old Bern. She surmised that this was one of the perks of being represented by the best in the business. She again had that feeling of warmth and security.

When they arrived at *Restaurant zum Zähringer*, he did not immediately take her inside. He spent a few minutes acquainting her with the architectural intricacies of the exterior of the building; with the picturesque grounds of the property; and with the pleasant sights and sounds of the waters of the beautiful blue River Aare.

They entered the restaurant at precisely eight. The hostess immediately recognized Fankhauser, and, after a greeting reserved for special guests, escorted them to their reserved table. The neck of a large bottle extended from a silver bucket full of marbles of ice. "I took the liberty of pre-ordering the beverage," he said, somewhat apologetically. I think you will love it; Franciacorta Rosé, Italy's answer to French Champagne. Have you ever had it?" Isolde said that she had not. But that she was looking forward to trying it, especially on his recommendation.

Once they were comfortably seated, the waiter appeared and opened the bottle of Franciacorta Rosé, poured some into Fankhauser's glass for tasting, and, on Fankhauser's nod of approval, poured the wine into both glasses. Fankhauser raised his glass for a toast. "Salut; here is to all the best in your quest, my dear Isolde." They clinked glasses, and she repeated "Salut." She took a sip of the Franciacorta Rosé, and smiled. "Great choice," she whispered.

"Franciacorta wines hail from the Lombardy district of Italy," Fankhauser explained. "It is made from specially selected grapes. The fermentation process takes a minimum of eighteen months. The product is simply superb. Just look at the lovely pink colour. This wine has good depth and balance; not to mention its delicate bouquet." Isolde could not believe his depth of knowledge about so many aspects of life and living; she felt lucky to have him on, and by, her side. The waiter was back to take their orders from the menu. Isolde looked at Fankhauser, and demurely asked him to order for her. She felt confident that she could trust his judgment. "You may be sorry," he commented, gracefully, "but here goes. The lady will have the Salat Zähringer, to start with. For the main course, Wienerschnitzel mit Preiselbeeren und dazu eine Prise, Pasta und Risotto; and for dessert, the Puffy Pastry filled with Berries and topped with Mascarpone Cream. For me, the same salad, the same dessert, but for my main course, Gebratenes Zanderfilet auf grünem Spargel, geschmolzen Tomaten Erdüpfeln und Safransauce. And we will both have Espressos." When the waiter left, Isolde gently asked Fankhauser: "How did you know that my favourite dish in the whole wide world is Wienerschnitzel?" "My sixth sense told me so," he complacently replied. "What main course did you order for yourself?" she asked. "Fried filet of perch on green asparagus with melted peeled tomatoes, potatoes, and saffron sauce," was his response. "Sounds yummy. Shall we discuss business now?" she asked him. "Not yet," he responded, with a smile. "Let's revel in the gastronomy first. Business can follow later."

After the consumption of the delectable meal, he ordered a second bottle of Franciacorta Rosé. Their glasses were full once again. He placed both elbows on the table, leaned forward towards her, and said: "Now let's talk business, Isolde. Tell me everything that Professor Rossi told you in Florence."

Over the next hour, Isolde repeated what the professor had told her, as best as she could recall. She emphasized the professor's comments on the vast power and influence of the Medici family, and the fact that there were still descendants of the famous Florentine family living in Italy, and other parts of Europe. She repeated his comments on their expertise in the world of finance, and the extent of their influence, even into the Vatican. And his comments on the secret society that sprang out of the mind of Diane de Poitiers, and merged with the nefarious group of courtiers that had been hatched by Gian Gastone, with no small assistance from Giuliano Dami. She quoted the professor as saying that this secret society continues to assert significant influence today, acting as a shadow of the financial advisors descended from the great house of the Medici Bank; and his comments on the emblem that had been designed by Diane de Poitiers, the three intersecting crescents. Isolde then told Fankhauser what she felt she was lacking, in her quest for 'the Holy Grail'. While she felt that she was a tad closer to establishing the identity of 'our mutual client' -----in that it seemed to somehow involve the Vatican----she still was ignorant as to the nature of the relationship between VolksBankBern and the Vatican; and, if the Vatican was involved, she had no idea as to the nature of the involvement. Further, while she suspected that one of the many poisons of Catherine de' Medici may have been used to bring about Fred's death, this was at this point just pure speculation. She lacked expert evidence as to whether or not there was a type of poison in *The Chamber of Secrets* of Catherine de' Medici at Château de Blois that fitted the bill; and, if so, who had in fact administered the poison to Fred. She also needed to get to the bottom of the involvement of Lise and Rapini, both of whom she suspected to have had parts in the tragical piece; especially considering their common bond of the emblem with the 'three intersecting crescents'. As she concluded her recitation of the facts she had garnered from the absent-minded professor, she looked enquiringly at Fankhauser. He had taken it all in. What advice did he have to offer?

Like some sort of artificial intelligence, Fankhauser had quickly grasped what Isolde had related to him, and had already computed a chart for the course forward.

"I would suggest, Isolde, that the first step is for you to interview Professor Rappaport at the Sorbonne. Is there a poison in the collection of Catherine de' Medici that is consistent with the mysterious poison that had killed Fred? What symptoms does it produce in its victim? Does it have the property of untraceability in the tissues of its victim? Can it be replicated in the laboratory? How long does it normally take for its victim to die after it has been administered? You know, questions of that nature. You should fly to Paris to meet with him; there is nothing like a face-to-face meeting on matters of this nature. The second step is to zero in on Lise and Rapini; to try and box them in; to pry from them information that they are hiding that could unmask 'our mutual client'. I already have a plan as to how we should go about boxing them in. While you are in Paris, I will take steps to have two electronic bugs planted in Lise's apartment; one hidden in a general area of her apartment; the other implanted in her telephone. I should have no difficulty doing this. On your return, you will phone Lise; I will tell you what to say to her.

The net objective is to have her running scared; running to Rapini for help. We will tape her telephone conversations with Rapini; and with anyone else that may be involved; hopefully, someone in the higher echelons of the secret society. How's that for a plan?"

"Joaquim, you are a genius. Tomorrow morning, I will phone Professor Rappaport for an appointment. As soon as that is confirmed, I will fly to Paris."

"No genius here, Isolde. It's all in a day's work. Sweat, perseverance, and common sense. Sooner or later, one way or another, I promise you that we will get to the bottom of this. As Shakespeare said through one of his characters in *Merchant of Venice*, '*Truth will out*'. We just have to press on and on, even against all odds. We have to have what I call '*sticktivity*'. It means tenaciously sticking to the task at hand until the very end. You know, like a bulldog. *Sticktivity*, my dear Isolde, is the order of the day. If you maintain *sticktivity* through thick and thin, you will prevail."

Isolde could feel that warm fuzzy feeling again, all over her body. Joaquim had that effect on her. He made her feel that together they were invincible. She thanked her lucky stars that she had him on her side.

The walk back to Isolde's Best Western Plus Hotel Bern was slow and leisurely, notwithstanding the cold air that nipped away at their bare hands, ears, and faces. The business of the day had been concluded. It was time to once again enjoy the moments of serene pleasure that life has to offer. Fankhauser pointed to the magical full moon that hovered above them in the clear night sky, surrounded by millions of tiny stars, like an endless band of ladies-in-waiting standing there to serve the queen, ready to do her bidding at her beck and call. He philosophized on the vastness of the universe; and the fact that ours is only one of several universes, which he collectively referred to as the '*multiverse*'. He was careful to say that he was not sure if the term '*multiverse*' had been his own creation; or whether he had read the term in some learned thesis on quantum physics or astronomy. Irrespective of the term's origin, he thought that it was perfect to succinctly describe the absolute vastness of the heavens and beyond.

Isolde was shocked back to reality when she entered the lobby of her hotel, and found that all the lights were out. Some kind of a power failure. But the management gave their assurance that power would be restored in an hour or two, as they handed out candles to be taken back to the rooms. No problem, she thought. She had had a divine evening with Fankhauser, and there was nothing more for her to do or ask for the time being. Back in the candle-lit Room 205, she simply dressed down to her underwear, blew out the candle, and tossed herself across the bed. Within seconds, she was fast asleep.

CHAPTER TEN

WHEN ISOLDE telephoned the office of Professor Jean Rappaport at the Sorbonne the next morning, the professor's secretary said that he was out; she had no idea as to what time he would be back; could she take a message for the professor. Isolde left her telephone number at the hotel, with a request that he phone her ASAP; it was on a critically urgent matter, emphasizing the words "critically urgent". She settled into her room for the rest of the day, ordering meals by Room Service and watching classic American movies, in German, with English subtitles.

At about four, the telephone rang. Long distance call from Professor Jean Rappaport of the Sorbonne.

"Bon jour, Madame," a high-pitched voice said, "êtes-vous Madame Bruni?" *Good day, madam. Are you Mrs. Bruni?*

"Oui, monsieur. Parlez-vous anglais?" *Yes, sir. Do you speak English?*

"Oui, Madame. How can I help you?"

"I understand that you are a world-renowned expert on poisons."

"I am not sure that that is a compliment; but I will take it as such," the professor replied, with a chuckle.

"I am a free-lance journalist. I am doing an article on the Medicis. I understand that Catherine de' Medici left a legacy of cabinets of poisons, still preserved at Château de Blois."

"Your understanding is partially correct, Madame. The cabinets are still there. They are in a room known as *The Chamber of Secrets*. But the poisons are no longer there."

"Professor Rappaport, I would like to meet with you in person to discuss this. May I have an appointment with you? The sooner, the better. I will pay you for your time and expertise."

"I have a very busy schedule. However, I can meet with you at my office at the Sorbonne tomorrow at five in the afternoon. But you are in Bern?"

"Yes; I am in Bern; but I will be there in your office at five tomorrow. Thank you very much."

Isolde was elated. As soon as she got off the phone, she dialed KLM. Can she book a return flight to Paris leaving Bern in the morning? Only Business Class? Yes; she will take it.

At five on the afternoon of the next day, she was seated in Professor Rappaport's office at the Sorbonne. Professor Rappaport was a very short man, whose girth seemed to compensate for what he lacked in height. He was not only bald on the crown of his head, but he did not have a single strand of hair on any exposed part of his body, even in the areas where his eyebrows should have been. He was a dour man, with squinting deadpan eyes, in keeping with the appearance of one who had devoted his entire life to the study of poisons. Isolde would have guessed his age at about fifty-five.

"So, you are here about Catherine's poisons," he started, which seemed to suggest that he had known the woman so well that he was on a level of familiarity with her.

"Yes, I am. Anything you can tell me about *The Chamber of Secrets* would be very much appreciated."

"Very well then. If you visit Château de Blois, you will find a room in which there are 237 small cabinets. This was a creation of Catherine's. History has it that each cabinet was there to house individual types of Catherine's poisons. The poisons are no longer there. But, when the discovery of these secret cabinets was made, they found, in each of the cabinets, records, in Catherine's own handwriting, of the properties of each poison that had presumably been kept in that particular cabinet.

The records have been removed to a more secure depository; a matter of security, I presume. Fortunately, before their removal, I was able to obtain photocopies of all the records. These records are invaluable. Catherine was indeed passionate about her 'hobby', to the point of absolute obsession. She experimented with all types of chemical elements, fauna and flora, and minerals, hell-bent on not missing one possibility of poisonous material. She was also a true alchemist; she would mix various substances in her quest to produce 'the perfect poison'. She was really extremely brilliant. If she were alive today, she quite likely would be nominated for the Nobel Prize in Chemistry. Can you believe it? Some 237 types of poison, and she became an expert on all of them! A lot of these poisons were creations of her own." The professor's shrill voice reached a high pitch of excitement. His exhilaration was contagious; Isolde could feel a blood-curdling thrill run through her veins. Her cat's eyes pierced into his spiritless eyes, as if searching for a glimmer of his soul.

"Professor Rappaport, that is so amazing. Tell me, in Catherine's collection, did you find one poison that would result in the victim foaming at the mouth?" The Professor thought about the question for a while. Then he answered.

"In actual fact, there are a handful of poisons in her collection that cause foaming at the mouth. Foaming at the mouth occurs because the victim cannot swallow his or her saliva. If the saliva cannot go down, then it has to come up; simple deduction. This is what happens with rabies."

"Among that handful of poisons, is there any that is untraceable, or almost untraceable, in human tissue?"

"Excellent question! It has been my conclusion that this was Catherine's ultimate goal. To find 'the perfect poison'; the poison that would take the life of its victim without anyone being able to find that the cause of death was poisoning. To me, this was the 'be-all and end-all' of Catherine's quest." Again, his voice became shriller with excitement. This was a man who relished his poisons, thought Isolde; forgive the pun. "There was one poison in particular that Catherine adored," he continued. "It was her own creation. She referred to it in Italian as '*Il Mio Piccolo Amico*'; in French, '*Mon Petit Ami*'; and in English it is known as '*My Little Friend*'. This was her own creation; her own little bambino." The professor looked into Isolde's eyes for her reaction. It was as he had intended; her eyes displayed the look of extremely deep interest and fascination. His trance-like delay in continuing was only brought to an end by her own coaxing.

"Is there a chemical name for *'Mon Petit Ami'*? she finally asked.

"No. There is no chemical name. You must understand, Madame Bruni, that *'Mon Petit Ami'* has slipped under the radar, so to speak. It is virtually unknown in the establishment world of chemists." He delayed again, waiting for her to ask the inevitable question. As expected, Isolde delivered.

"How does this poison work, Professor Rappaport?" He smiled, as the expected question floated in.

"You see, broadly speaking, it is a mixture of a neurotoxin known as *cobratoxin*, *arsenic*, and some other substance believed to be a mineral or combination of minerals, which Catherine named *triescrepipismite*. As the name *cobratoxin* suggests, it is the venom of the king cobra snake. It blocks what are called nicotinic acetylcholine receptors in the neurological makeup of the victim, resulting in extreme paralysis. The paralysis really results from the breakdown of cells and tissues in the victim's body; and, in turn, causes respiratory difficulty, and eventually death. Now, Catherine could not take credit for *cobratoxin*, as that is naturally produced by the king cobra snake, and has been known as a poison since time immemorial. But where Catherine's genius came in was with her experiment of combining *cobratoxin* with *arsenic*, which is, of course, another deadly poison, and with her *triescrepipismite*. As you may know, *arsenic* is, to say the least, not easily traceable; that is why it has received the alias *the king of poisons*. So, you now have the venom from the king cobra, *the king of snakes,* being mixed with *the king of poisons.* By binding the molecular properties of *cobratoxin* with the *arsenic* and the *triescrepipismite* in *the precisely right proportions*, Catherine came up with *'Mon Petit Ami'*, a poison which is untraceable in the human body. The mineral *triescrepipismite* has baffled all experts in the field of poisons. But I suspect that it sealed the untraceability feature. Legend has it that this unkown mineral was discovered by Catherine in a Tuscan cave known as *La Grotta del Vento*, located in Fornovolasco, a very small village about seventy kms. north-west of Florence. My best guess is that it is an amalgam of three substances, including crystallized bats' droppings, particles of cave stalactites, and some other mysterious substance, all coming together as one over hundreds of years. I emphasize that the mixture of *cobratoxin, arsenic,* and *triescrepipismite* must be in '*the right proportions*' in order for '*Mon Petit Ami*' to become wholly untraceable. After '*Mon Petit Ami*' enters the tissue or blood of the victim, death results in about an hour or two. In the meantime, the victim is completely paralyzed, from head to toe, except that, for some reason, the victim is still conscious and is aware of everything that is going on around him or her. A horrible death, indeed!"

"Does this mean that the victim may be sitting at his desk, completely paralyzed, and is aware that he needs help, but cannot even move his hand to dial the phone for help?" Isolde was thinking of Fred's specific case.

"Precisely," the professor responded, smiling at her as if she was a student who had just given the correct answer to a question the Professor had posed. It was all that Isolde could do to hold back the tears. What an awful period of suffering Fred must have endured in the hour or so preceding his death!

"Can you give me the formula for '*Mon Petit Ami*'?" Isolde entreated, as she pulled herself together.

"No," the professor grunted. "As part of the conditions I signed in order to obtain copies of Catherine's records, I legally agreed to never release to anyone the formula for any of Catherine's 237 poisons. These are secrets that I will have to take with me to the grave." Well, Isolde thought. That is loud and clear.

"Can '*Mon Petit Ami*' be produced in tablet form?"

"Definitely. Any poison can be produced in tablet form."

"Professor, I realize that you possess the formula for the mixture of *cobratoxin, arsenic* and *triescrepipismite,* but that you lack knowledge of the true composition of *triescrepipismite,* suspected to be some kind of combination of minerals, possibly from *La Grotta del Vento.* Are you aware of who in the world would likely possess the formula for '*Mon Petit Ami*', including the correct proportions of *cobratoxin, arsenic,* and the mysterious *triescrepipismite,* and the true composition of *triescrepipismite*?"

"As far as I know, Catherine's poisons were always under the control of the Medicis. However, there is one branch of the Medicis that formed an alliance with a secret society. That was Gian Gastone? Have you heard of him?"

"Yes; in passing." Isolde's memory rolled back to her interview with Professor Rossi.

"Some rascal he was. Have you also heard of Dami and the Ruspanti?"

"Yes; again, in passing."

"And have you heard of Diane de Poitiers, the mistress of Henry II of France?"

"Yes; again, in passing." Isolde felt that she was starting to sound like a broken record.

"Well, it appears that Gian Gastone's Ruspanti had formed an alliance with the secret society of Diane de Poitiers. This alliance developed over several years to become the shadow of the Medicis. The Medicis were the front men, so to speak. And *The Shadow* was the underground group that performed duties too dirty for the Medicis. As far as I can determine, the formulae for Catherine's 237 poisons fell into the hands of the *The Shadow*. I really do not know much about them, except that, as far as I can determine, they are still alive and well today." He looked at his watch; and then at Isolde, as if to ask if she had any more questions for him.

"Thank you very much, Professor Rappaport. You have been very helpful. How much is your bill?"

"€$250," he replied. Isolde paid him in cash, and said goodbye. She had received vital information from the professor. She was positive that she had found the type of poison that had killed Fred. It went under the very disarming name of *'Mon Petit Ami'*. She was back in Bern by ten that evening.

As soon as she entered Room 205 of Best Western Plus Hotel Bern, she picked up the phone and called Fankhauser. Once again, he answered on the first ring.

"Fankhauser." This was, in Isolde's mind, a trademark of his. Such efficiency, she thought.

"Hi, Joaquim. It's Isolde. I have just returned from Paris. I had a very fruitful meeting with Professor Jean Rappaport at the Sorbonne. I need to meet with you."

Fankhauser laughed. "You know, Isolde, we have to stop meeting like this. People will start talking." She herself laughed at his attempt at a joke. "How about an informal lunch at Bärenplatz? Do you know where that is?" he asked.

"I seem to recall seeing the name, not far from the Bundesgasse. Am I right?" she asked.

"Close enough," he responded. "It's on Spitalgasse. I will meet you there at noon. OK?"

"It's a date," she replied.

CHAPTER ELEVEN

FOR LUNCH with Fankhauser at Bärenplatz, Isolde deemed it most fitting to dress informally She wore Levi's blue jeans, a long-sleeved plaid shirt, and running shoes. While it was a bright sunny day, the outside temperature was now about 60 degrees, Fahrenheit, which, although higher than the average November temperature for Bern, was still chilly, leading to her wearing a lined jacket. It was a relatively short walk from Best Western Plus Hotel Bern to Bärenplatz, which was within close range of the *Bundeshaus*. As she entered Bärenplatz, she could see the *Zytglogge* in the distance, not far from the *Bundeshaus*. Both the *Bundeshaus* and the *Zytglogge* she remembered from her walking tour of Old Bern. Almost a Bernese, she thought, as she patted herself on the shoulder. The *Zytglogge* was tolling twelve noon. The square was overrun with people. Not surprising, Isolde thought. After all, the sun was radiant, its rays sparkling on everything piece of marble and metal. Who would not want to be outdoors on a day like this? Wafts of the smell of freshly baked bread filled Isolde's nostrils, causing her to salivate for its taste. Fankhauser, now recognized by Isolde as a slave to punctuality, was already there, seated in the square at a table for two, just outside the *Café der Baren*, a bottle of Pinot Noir and two glasses already on the table. He too had dressed down, wearing rather baggy trousers, a turtle-neck sweater, and a light windbreaker. As she approached, he rose to his feet, like a true gentleman, and moved her chair back for her to be seated.

"Welcome to Bärenplatz on market day," he greeted her, wearing his now familiar broad, engaging smile. "The crowd just multiplies on market day. It's as if it gives people an excuse to come to the square. Do you know the meaning of Bärenplatz?"

"No," Isolde confessed.

"Bären means 'bear'. The legend is that many, many years ago, almost beyond the memory of man, it was not uncommon for trained bears to be brought to this square to perform their acts. You know the old stories of the organ grinder with his trained bear performing acts for the audience. It was only natural, I suppose, that this place would be eventually named Bärenplatz; or Bear Square. And as you can see, we are eating under the auspices of *Café der Baren*, or, in English, *Café of the Bears*. So, my dear Isolde, that is your history lesson for today." He then poured the wine, and signaled to the waiter that he was ready to order lunch. "A plate of assorted cheeses; some freshly baked bread; some chocolate dessert; and two cups of Espresso." He then turned to Isolde and said: "Now, my dear Isolde, let's talk business. What did you unearth in Paris?"

"Mon Petit Ami" was all that Isolde started with, as she looked into Fankhauser's eyes, a foxy smile on her face.

"My Little Friend," mouthed Fankhauser. "I know that I am your friend; but at my height, you can hardly call me "little". Please explain, my dear Isolde."

"I have found the poison, Joaquim. The poison that likely killed Fred," she blurted out, excitedly. "It's called *'Mon Petit Ami'*. It was the favourite of Catherine de' Medici's poisons. She concocted it herself; her own creation, as if it came out of her womb. A concoction of *cobratoxin*, *arsenic*, and an unknown combination of minerals which Catherine named *triescrepipismite*. It's a poison unknown to the world, except for a very select group, including Professor Rappaport, who had to sign a pact of secrecy. All three ingredients, mixed together *in precisely the right proportions* ---also unknown to everyone, except a very select group --- produce a poison which is untraceable in the human body. Can you believe it, Joaquim?"

"Hard to believe, Isolde. Excellent progress, my dear. That's a key piece in the puzzle. *'Mon Petit Ami'*. How absolutely disarming!" Fankhauser observed, his eyes huge in astonishment. Isolde was quick to continue.

"And *'Mon Petit Ami'* can be produced in tablet form, as long as the manufacturer has the precise formula created by Catherine. Do you remember that I told you that Professor Rossi of the University of Florence had given me a history lesson involving Catherine de' Medici, Diane de Poitiers, and Gian Gastone de Medici? And the secret societies that had been formed by Diane de Poitiers and by Gian Gastone, which merged under Gian Gastone? Professor Rappaport confirmed this *shadow* of the Medicis, which he said is alive and well today. He believes that *The* Shadow, as he calls it, has access to the formulae of Catherine's 237 poisons." Fankhauser's jaw dropped as he listened to Isolde. "The plot thickens," he remarked, as he took it all in.

"So, my dear Joaquim," Isolde went on, "from all that I have garnered from Professor Rossi and Professor Rappaport, the bottom line in a nutshell is that there is a secret society, *The Shadow*, of the powerful Medicis; that *The Shadow* has access to the secret formula of Catherine's *'Mon Petit Ami'*; that *'Mon Petit Ami'* is a very potent poison that is untraceable in the human body; that one of the symptoms of ingestion of *'Mon Petit Ami'* is foaming at the mouth, which results from the extreme paralysis that cripples its victim; that *'Mon Petit Ami'* is consistent with the Underlying Cause of death of my late husband, Fred; that the emblem of the 'three intersecting crescents' is most likely the current emblem of *The Shadow;* and that the tentacles of *The Shadow* may even extend into the Vatican. You and I are convinced that both Lise and Rapini are as thick as thieves in the plot, and are somehow connected to *The Shadow,* although we currently are missing the vital chain of evidence to lock them in inextricably to *The Shadow*. We also believe that *The Shadow*, in some way or the other, through VolksBankBern, may be connected with some arm of the Vatican, most likely in relation to investments on behalf of the Vatican. Based on what I have related from my interviews with both professors, and from what you and I otherwise know, don't you think that is a good summary of where we currently stand?"

"I could not have put it better than that myself, Isolde," Fankhauser complimented. "Permit me to bring you up-to-date on what I have done while you were in beautiful Paris. The electronic bugs have been planted in Lise's apartment; one in the living room; that will pick up all sounds within the general areas of the apartment. The other electronic bug is in the telephone. Both devices will relay all voices and other sounds that they may happen to pick up to a recording device in my office. For your own good, that's all you need to know. You will remember that

I once told you that I got the basic information about Lise because I have friends in high places. Let's just say that I got the electronic bugs planted in Lise's apartment, without Lise knowing, because I also have friends in low places." Isolde's cat's eyes twinkled with satisfaction. Fankhauser had accomplished what he had promised to do. She could not have asked for better service.

"Now, Isolde, the next steps will be for you to take. Here is what you need to do. You should phone Lise. Talk to her as if you are old friends. Tell her how much you are enjoying Bern. Tell her that you are saddened by the fact that you have to leave Bern shortly. Once she has let her guard down, you are to then proceed in attack mode with the first zinger; a real shock attack. Such as a reference to *'Mon Petit Ami'*. Let her know that you have found the poison that killed Fred; but do not give her any details, such as the source of your information. You simply want to shock her with that news. Before she can recover from that assault, proceed with the second zinger. Tell her that you are aware of *The Shadow* founded in the days of power of the Medici family; and that you know that the formula for *'Mon Petit Ami'* is in their hands. By this time, she will be convinced that you are hot on her trail. You will then proceed with the third zinger. Tell her that you are aware of the fact that she and Rapini are in cahoots; that they are in bed with *The Shadow*. My guess is that she will then be anxious to terminate the conversation. But before she does so, try and get in the fourth 'zinger', the blatant fact that you know that she and Rapini were deeply involved in Fred's death. This phone conversation should drive her to seek assistance from Rapini, or whomever. It should flush her out, scared of the consequences of being charged with murdering Fred. That's when my electronic bug implanted in her telephone will be proven to be worth its salt. You must keep in mind that you will have only one shot at this. After you complete the assaults of the 'zingers', you will not have a snowball's chance in hell of speaking with Lise again, whether by phone or otherwise. Can you make the phone call this evening?"

"Yes; by all means. How about at seven?"

"That's fine with me. I have my electronic recording device running 24/7, all set up and ready to go. It is my prized assistant. As dependable as the good old Eveready battery. Now, let's make the best of a sunny afternoon. How about another bottle of Pinot Noir?"

"I would love that, Joaquim. I have nowhere to go; nothing to do---until seven, of course." With a snap of the finger, Fankhauser ordered another bottle of Pinot Noir. Once again, she had that warm fuzzy feeling, always brought on by Fankhauser. He was simply amazing; a true professional. When he worked, he was very focused on the subject at hand, and worked hard, not leaving a stone unturned. At the same time, when he took his leisure time, he enjoyed it immensely, unfettered by even the thought of that yoke called work. As they sat there at Bärenplatz, basking in the sunshine, and listening to the sweet notes of Johann Strauss' *Geschichten aus dem Wienerwald,* known in English as *Tales from the Vienna Woods,* floating pleasingly across the square, Isolde was on cloud nine, fully captivated by the sights and sounds that belong to the medieval city of Old Bern. The waiter returned with the Pinot Noir, and filled both glasses. "Salut", Fankhauser and Isolde said to each other, as they clinked glasses.

"So, tell me, Isolde," Fankhauser asked, "what historic sites have you seen of Old Bern?"

"Do you have the whole day, Joaquim?"

"Yes, I do," Fankhauser responded, jokingly.

"Well, to start with, I have visited the *Münster Kirche*, the *Bundeshaus* and the *Zytglogge*. Remarkable structures. And then there are the fountains; so many fountains, in 'the City of Fountains'; I have seen the *Läuferbrunnen*; the *Kindlifresserbrunnen*—a cruel fountain, I must say; imagine, an ogre devouring little children; the *Mosesbrunnen*; the *Pfeiferbrunnen*; the *Anna-Seiler-Brunnen*; and the *Zähringerbrunnen*. Very impressive. So many sites of such great historical significance and beauty in such a small area. There you have a bird's-eye view of what I have taken in; not to mention, of course, the sites that you yourself have pointed out to me."

"You mean 'cat's eye view', do you not, Isolde?" Fankhauser jested, poking fun at her amber eyes. Isolde grasped the play on words immediately.

"Don't make fun of my fascinating eyes, Joaquim," she chortled. "Men have gone to hell for less than that." At this, they both howled in laughter.

"I am so pleased that you have had an opportunity to see the brighter side of our ancient city," Fankhauser remarked, with a sense of pride.

"Were you born here, Joaquim?" Isolde asked, with some degree of reservation, as she did not want to appear to be prying into Fankhauser's private life.

"Yes; I was born and raised here, a genuine Bernese. Although you would not have guessed this from my first name. 'Joaquim' is really a Portuguese name, imported by my father. He had a very close Portuguese friend, and adopted his first name 'Joaquim' for me." The answer flowed so easily that she felt that she could possibly venture into other private territory.

"I do not want to be too personal, Joaquim. But, is there a Frau Fankhauser?" She tried to put the question as mildly as she could.

"Yes, indeed. There is a Frau Fankhauser. She is seventy-five; alive and well. She lives with me." Isolde was floored by this response. Joaquim is only about thirty-eight or so. Is Joaquim's wife about thirty-seven years his senior? Had he married a woman almost twice her age? How could that have happened? Of course, there are men who marry women much older than themselves, motivated by money. The wealthy woman syndrome. But Fankhauser did not appear to be that type. Surely, he was no gigolo? And why did he have to mention that she was living with him? Is that not what most wives do? Fankhauser studied the expressions on her face, as she tried to compute this latest revelation.

"I can see the wheels of your mind working," he rejoined, with a broad smile. "You are wondering how it was that I married a woman so much older than I am. The answer is simple: Frau Fankhauser is not my wife; she is my mother. I have remained a bachelor all my life. Never married; too busy working and enjoying life, I suppose." Isolde giggled. How silly of her to have not recognized that the reference to "Frau Fankhauser" could have included his mother. So much for personal questions, she concluded, and changed the conversation to the weather. Warmed by the sunshine and more bottles of Pinot Noir, they chatted about a myriad of far-ranging topics, including the position of armed neutrality of Switzerland during the Great War and during the Second World War, the reputation of Switzerland for its chocolate and its Swiss cheese, and the famous peaks of Switzerland, such as the Matterhorn, the Monte Rosa, and the Jungfrau.

Fankhauser escorted Isolde back to Best Western Plus Hotel Bern. All along the way, he took every opportunity that presented itself to praise the virtues of Old Bern. The buildings. The cobblestone streets. The people. The cuisine. Arriving at the front of the hotel, he took her right hand into his, kissed it gently and gracefully, and thanked her for a wonderful afternoon. She could hear the bells of the *Zytglogge* in the distance, announcing that it was seven. As Fankhauser melted into the darkness, she scurried into the hotel, up to Room 205. There was a very pressing task that she had to perform. Perhaps the most important phone call of her life.

CHAPTER TWELVE

PERHAPS for the first time in Isolde's life her hands were clammy from nervous perspiration. As she dialed Lise's telephone number, Fankhauser's words of caution were forefront in her mind. "You must keep in mind that you will have only one shot at this." The phone rang a number of times at Lise's, but there was no answer. If at first you don't succeed try and try again, she thought to herself. What was that word that Fankhauser had invented in his vocabulary? Yes; *sticktivity*; defined as the ability to stick to the task at hand until success is achieved. She redialed Lise's number every ten minutes. Eventually, success. Isolde looked at her watch. It was seven-twenty.

"Guten Abend." *Good evening.* It was Lise's voice at the other end of the line. Isolde cleared her throat. Her act had to be flawless.

"Hi, Lise. This is Isolde."

"Oh, hi Isolde. You are still in Bern?" Lise cooed, nonchalantly.

"Yes; I am still in Bern, Lise. What a beautiful city! I have already visited so many famous sites in Old Bern; the *Münster Kirche,* the *Bundeshaus*; the *Zytglogge.* Not to mention all the beautiful fountains. I am sure it would take me at least a month to visit all the wonderful sites of your beautiful *Altstadt.*"

"I am so happy for you, Isolde," Lise remarked, "that you have been able to see so much of Bern. I wish I had the time to escort you around, but unfortunately my schedule is too tight at this time."

"That's OK, Lise. I am doing fine on my own. My stay in Bern is drawing to a close. I want to tell you how much of a pleasure it was for me to have met you. You are a lovely person. You should come and visit with me in Canada at some time in the future. *Mi casa es su casa.*"

"How sweet of you to say that, Isolde. It would be my pleasure to do so. I have never been to Canada." Yes, Isolde thought to herself. Lise sounds so relaxed; she has completely let her guard down. Time for 'zinger #1', to use Fankhauser's terminology. Here goes.

"Lise, I must tell you this. I have been doing some reading on the life of Catherine de' Medici. You, of course, know who she was?'

"I have heard the name mentioned. She lived some centuries ago?" Isolde identified this response as a gross understatement. Mendacity of the first order.

"Yes; that's right. The fascinating thing about her life was her obsession with poisons. Have you ever heard of *'Mon Petit Ami'*?" Isolde thought she heard Lise gasp. This was followed by a few seconds of silence.

"I think that's French for *'My Little Friend'*. No; I have never heard of it." Another lie, thought Isolde.

"Well, what I found out was that Catherine's favourite poison was called *'Mon Petit Ami'*. An amazing poison. Its victim dies from extreme paralysis; and there is no known way of finding a trace of the poison in the victim's body." Isolde then stopped; she waited for a response from Lise. No response was forthcoming. So far, so good. Isolde had shot the quiver nicknamed 'zinger #1', and it had hit its target. Let's move on to 'zinger #2', before Lise has a chance to recover.

"This is really riveting, Lise. One thing leads to another. My interest in Catherine de' Medici led me naturally into reading up on the Medici family in general. Did you know that Catherine's husband, Henry II of France, had a mistress by the name of Diane de Poitiers? And that Diane de Poitiers asserted significant control and influence over Henry? And that she even went as far as creating her own secret band of courtiers? Well, it even gets steamier. Have you heard of Gian Gastone de' Medici, the last Duke of Lombardy in the Medici family? He himself had his own team of pawns, known as the Ruspanti. Eventually, under Gian Gastone, Diane's secret band of courtiers coalesced with his Ruspanti, and the merged teams became some sort of a *'shadow'* to the official advisors to the Vatican, who were mainly from the Medici family." Continued stony silence from the other end of the line. 'Zinger #2' had struck its mark. On to 'zinger #3' before it's too late.

"You know, Lise; I must confess that I cannot escape the feeling that you and Herr Rapini are in cahoots; that you both are together involved with the secret society known as *The Shadow*. I have noticed the emblem of three intersecting crescents that is engraved on Herr Rapini 's gold lapel pin; and the same three intersecting crescents on your gold ring, the one with the black onyx crown in which mother of pearl is inlaid." Still no response from Lise. Isolde must now shoot 'zinger #4' before it is too late.

"From all that, Lise, I have concluded that you and Herr Rapini are responsible for Fred's death."

There. Isolde had done it. All four zingers had been shot, and each had struck its mark. The telephone line suddenly went dead, after an audible click. Lise had terminated the conversation. Isolde had done as Fankhauser had advised. She no longer had any pathway of communication to Lise. She phoned Fankhauser at home. She told him of the telephone conversation. She described to him exactly as it had unfolded, word for word.

"Nice going, Isolde," he complimented her. "The trap has been set. I have my recording device set up here at home. It should be interesting. I will listen carefully to hear whom she phones and what is said. Hopefully, our trap will catch a rat or two. You see, I don't call you 'cat's eyes' for nothing."

"Very, very funny, Joaquim!" Isolde gibed.

"I will let you know as soon as I have something," Fankhauser continued. "In the meantime. Stay close to your phone."

Isolde settled in for the evening in Room 205. She changed into her pajamas, and ordered dinner through Room Service. As she waited, she surfed the TV for a good movie. She found an old Hitchcock thriller *The Rear Window*, starring Jimmy Stewart and Grace Kelly; again, the spoken dialogue converted into German, with English subtitles. As she watched the movie, which she had seen several times before, she thought of the life of Grace Kelly, who had married Prince Rainier of Monaco, to become Princess Grace of Monaco. It had been a story that fairy tales are made of. But then, just about two months ago, there had been a very tragic ending to the fairy tale. Princess Grace had plunged about one hundred and fifty feet down a steep embankment while driving her Rover sportscar through a mountain in the south of France, where the road coiled like a snake. It happened on "a blind curve", the reports said. She succumbed to her injuries. Her daughter, Stephanie, was a passenger in the ill-fated vehicle; but she miraculously survived. Like Fred, Princess Grace had everything to live for. And, also like Fred, all the illusory trappings of life mean absolutely nothing, once life is taken away. There was a knock on the door; it was Room Service. Once the bellhop left, she returned to the movie, snacking away at the bowl of fresh shrimp that she had ordered. But within five minutes, at the point where the Jimmy Stewart character had concluded that there had been a murder, there was another interruption. The telephone rang. It was Fankhauser.

"Isolde, I will get right to the point. You must check out of Best Western Plus Hotel Bern as soon as we hang up. Not only is Lise's life in danger, but so is yours." At these words, Isolde felt a queasy feeling in her stomach; so much for her appetite. "Immediately after Lise hung up the phone from speaking with you, she phoned Rapini. We were dead right; forgive the pun. They are in this thing together; as deep and thick as quicksand. Lise was in a state of panic when she spoke with Rapini; I will let you hear the tape later. Rapini told Lise to remain in her apartment; he will contact 'Rome'. 'Rome' will get back to her immediately; she should stay close to her phone. Within ten minutes, there was a phone call to Lise, presumably from 'Rome'. The male voice on the other end of the line identified itself only as 'Rome'. He was there to help, he assured her. Lise should remain there in her apartment. Under no circumstances should she leave. He would fly to Bern immediately. He should be in Bern within a couple hours. He would then tell her what to do. He also asked Lise for your full name; and if she knew what hotel you were staying at. Lise told him you are at Best Western Plus Hotel Bern on Zeughausgasse. Quick deduction tells me that 'Rome' wants both you and Lise dead. After all, you both know too much; and, as the old saying goes, *Dead men tell no tales*. We have to act quickly. I will pick you up in my car in front of your hotel in about fifteen minutes. When you check out, tell the Front Desk that you are flying back to Toronto tonight. However, you will in fact be staying at my apartment here in Bern; but under no circumstances should you tell them that. Once we have you tucked away safely at my home, I will have to keep an eye on Lise's apartment. We don't want to lose her. Besides, I need to know who 'Rome' is. Hurry, Isolde. See you in about fifteen minutes. Isolde quickly dressed, packed, turned the TV and lights off, and exited Room 205 for the last time, leaving most of her shrimp dinner behind. After a quick check-out, she found Fankhauser waiting in his black Mercedes-Benz in front of the hotel.

The drive to Fankhauser's address was short. Fankhauser pulled into the underground parking lot of the old walk-up apartment building on Kramgasse, in the centre of the Old City, not far from the *Zytglogge*. Isolde was amazed; she had been to the *Zytglogge*, but had not had a clue that her knight in shining armour had his abode only a few steps from where she had walked. The apartment building was like a fortress, with security measures in place at every turn. All it lacked was a moat, she thought. She could not believe her eyes when she walked into the luxury of Fankhauser's apartment. It had been modernized, but gracefully so, with obvious care having been taken to preserve the ambience of antiquity so characteristic of buildings that are hundreds of years old. The furnishings were exquisite, but not nouveau riche. Frau Fankhauser was there to greet her.

"Welcome to our humble abode, Isolde. Joaquim has told me so many good things about you." The words of welcome were warm and genuine.

"Frau Fankhauser, it is my pleasure to meet you. Thanks for permitting me to stay here. Hopefully, it will not be for too long."

"No problem at all, my dear; the company is good for me," Frau Fankhauser remarked, graciously. "And please call me Renée. It makes me feel so much younger. Golden girls like me have to grasp at whatever straws we can to keep us feeling young." Isolde liked that. Renée had a true sense of humour.

Fankhauser stood there with a smile of satisfaction on his face, as he observed how well Isolde and his mother were getting along together. There were three bedrooms; one for Renée; one for Fankhauser; and the guest room. Fankhauser carted Isolde's luggage into the guest room, while Renée gave Isolde a brief tour of her new surroundings. Fankhauser then took his leave of the two women. He had a very important mission to undertake, and it all had to do with saving Lise's life. If his instinct proved to be correct, tonight was a night for saving lives.

CHAPTER THIRTEEN

FANKHAUSER drove his black Mercedes-Benz to Spitalgasse, and parked within a block or so of 29, Lise's apartment building. It was then about nine and dark. He had with him a pair of infrared binoculars, with an attached telephoto camera; state-of-the-art technology, especially suited for the work of a private investigator. In the darkness, he simply settled back in the comfort of his car, as he awaited the arrival of the mysterious 'Rome' at Lise's apartment building. This kind of surveillance work was one of the reasons he always chooses black as the colour of his cars. He himself was dressed in a black fall coat and a dark grey hat, which allowed him, like his car, to blend into the shadows of the night.

He did not have long to wait. At about nine-thirty, a winter-white Opel pulled up and parked on the street, in front of Lise's apartment building. Fankhauser made a note of the licence plate number; it was a Hertz rental. A man, wearing a beige overcoat and a dark-grey hat, both appearing to be Italian-style, exited the car, and entered the building. Fankhauser took some photographs of the mysterious man. Within ten minutes, the man exited the building, hurriedly climbed into the Opel, and sped away. Fankhauser had another opportunity to take another series of photographs. No time to waste now, Fankhauser said to himself; he must move as swiftly as possible. Undoubtedly, there was a life to be saved. He started his motor, and quickly pulled up directly in front of the apartment building. He rushed into the building, and headed directly to Lise's apartment on the second floor. The door was closed, but unlocked. Without knocking, he entered the apartment. He found Lise flat on her back on her bed, apparently unable to move, foaming at the mouth, and gasping for breath. Jumping into action, he immediately dialed 144, the number of the *Sanitätsnotruf*, or Swiss Medical Emergency, and reported a woman on the verge of death from poisoning, at Spitalgasse 29, apartment 02. He declined to identify himself. Before he left the apartment, he removed the two electronic bugs that he had planted; the one from the living room; and the other from the telephone. He then exited the building, and moved his car to his previous vantage point, to observe what would transpire from then on. Within five minutes, the ambulance was there. Not long after, he saw the paramedics wheeling Lise's listless body out of the building and into the back of the ambulance, an oxygen mask over her face.

Arriving back at his apartment at about ten, he went straight to his dark room, which was a walk-in closet within his home office, and developed the photographs that he had taken. Success. He now had ten photographs of the mysterious man he knew only as 'Rome', which clearly displayed the face and body of his subject. He immediately retained his colleague, Alberto Fettucini, in Rome, faxing him all ten photographs, with a request to seek information ASAP from the Rome police and other law enforcement bodies as to the identity of the mysterious man he knew only as 'Rome'.

Following his dispatch to Fettucini, he telephoned his friend, Simon Hartmann, a *Polizeikommissar*, or police inspector, at the *Kantonspolizei*, or Bern Cantonal Police, at his home.

"Hi, Simon," he started. "Sorry to bother you at home; but I need an urgent favour."

"No problem at all, Joaquim. What can I do for you?"

"Some guy from Rome about an hour or so ago tried to murder a woman here in Bern."

"I am all ears, Joaquim. Murder is right up my alley," Hartmann said, jokingly.

"The woman's name is Lise Brunner. She lives at Spitalgasse 29. I had the building under surveillance; I saw the man enter. After he came out about ten minutes later, I rushed in, and found the victim on the brink of death. I immediately called Medical Emergency for an ambulance, and saw the paramedics wheel her out, apparently still alive. I am on the trail of something big. Can you find out for me if the victim is still alive? If so, arrange with the hospital to not reveal that she is still alive;

I want the perp and others associated with the crime to believe that she is dead. Further, can you arrange with the hospital to keep her there as a patient for the next couple of days or so? When I have more time, I will give you the full scoop."

"Happy to do that for you, Joaquim. I trust you implicitly. Over the many years that I have known you, you have never once misled me."

"Thanks a lot, Simon. You are a true friend." There. Fankhauser was on top of his game. He had everything moving in the right direction. Having gone as far as he could for now, he joined Isolde and his mother in the living room, where they were both enjoying Johann Strauss' famous waltz, *An der schönen blauen Donau*, so well-known in English as *The Blue Danube,* with a bottle of Roter Riesling, and a platter full of dainty sweet Swiss chocolate delights.

"How nice of you to join us, Joaquim," Renée quipped, jokingly. Now I know where Joaquim got his sense of humour from, thought Isolde. Fankhauser smiled broadly, and responded to his mother: "Business is business, Mama. As you know, my clients come first; and then my pleasures follow." These were very comforting words for Isolde. He then turned to face Isolde. "Tomorrow morning, Isolde, I will bring you up-to-date on all that I have heard, seen and done this evening. Tonight, we must enjoy the wine and the music, and I must relish the pleasure of the company of you two beautiful ladies." What a silver-tongued charmer, Isolde thought to herself.

"I take it that that is the Fankhauser Family Crest?" Isolde asked, looking at an emblazoned plaque on the wall.

"Yes," replied Renée, with a touch of nostalgia in her voice. "The Ancient Coat of Arms of the Fankhausers. Their symbol of power. Can you see the lion wearing the crown, with the eagle to its left? The Fankhausers had rather humble beginnings. But have risen up and spread their wings over the centuries. The Fankhausers have their origins in the south of Germany. In their very early days, the family made the right connections. They declared loyalty to a number of princes and other nobles, and served them well in their regional conflicts. Fortunately, they were on the right side of history. They trace their ancestry back to a knight named 'Funke'. Now how is that for a name? He lived in Rüdesheim, back in about 1280, over seven centuries ago. My late husband's grandfather was the first Fankhauser to live in Bern. Do you know what the name 'Fankhauser' means? Well, in German, a *Fankhaus* is a building or enclosure in which wild animals are kept, after being captured on a hunt; literally, it is 'a capture house'. And so, a 'Fankhauser' is the keeper of 'a capture house'. I keep joking with Joaquim that he is a true 'Fankhauser'; that this apartment is his *Fankhaus*; and that I am the wild animal under his guard." She hesitated, looking at both Isolde and her son, as if expecting a laugh at the joke she had just delivered. She appeared gratified when both Isolde and her son laughed. She then continued: "But I am boring you, Isolde, with all this wild Fankhauser family history."

"Not at all, Renée; I find it very interesting," replied Isolde, very politely. "In Canada, being such a young country, we lack the colourful history that blesses places like Bern." Joaquim looked at his watch. It was now ten-thirty. He looked at Isolde, who was by this time showing signs of drowsiness. Decisively, he dictated the next scene.

"Mama, would you please show Isolde to her room? I need to have her bright and alert tomorrow morning." So, that was it. The pleasure interlude was over. Fankhauser was already looking to the business of the next day. Taking her cue, Renée beckoned to Isolde to come with her, and the two disappeared into the guest room. But before Fankhauser turned himself in, he picked up the phone and called Best Western Plus Hotel Bern. The Front Desk answered.

"Guten Abend," he started, without identifying himself. *Good evening.* "You have a guest named Isolde Bruni?"

"Frau Bruni has checked out," came the response.

"Do you know where she has gone?"

"She told me that she was heading for the airport; flying back to Canada tonight."

"Oh, no. My friend had planned on meeting her there at the hotel. Have you seen him?"

"Yes; he arrived here at about ten-fifteen; but she had already left."

"So that I can be sure that it was my friend you were speaking with, how was he dressed?"

"I recall clearly. He was dressed in a beige overcoat and a dark-grey hat."

"That sounds like him," remarked Fankhauser. "Did he speak to you in Italian?"

"Yes; but I do not speak Italian. So, he spoke in English. A very strong Italian accent."

"Thank you. You have been very helpful. Have a good night."

Yes; he was right; 'Rome' was after Isolde. If Isolde had not checked out when she did, she would most likely have been forced to ingest *'Mon Petit Ami'*; just like Lise. Fankhauser had saved Isolde's life. It reinforced in his mind that he always had to be on top of his game. He always had to stay one step ahead. Hopefully, Lise was also still alive. He would find out from his friend Simon Hartmann in the morning.

CHAPTER FOURTEEN

AS THE BELLS of the *Zytglogge* pealed across the *Altstadt* heralding six the next morning, Fankhauser was already at work in his home office. Like a man obsessed, he played and replayed his tape of the telephone conversations secretly recorded the evening before. He listened attentively to Isolde's phone discussion with Lise, putting himself into Lise's shoes in order to fully appreciate how Lise had received the shocking words that came from Isolde. He listened more intently to Lise's phone conversation with Rapini, which immediately followed Isolde's phone call. Lise certainly had wasted no time in contacting Rapini. Her voice was shrill from fear and anguish, and her sentences were disjointed, sometimes almost incoherent. It was as if Rapini was her only lifeline. Fankhauser listened even more carefully to the phone call from 'Rome' to Lise, in which 'Rome', in a strong Italian accent, told her to remain where she was, and that he would be there at her apartment in Bern in a couple of hours.

Like her son, Renée was an early riser. It was not long before she was in the kitchen doing scrambled eggs, ham, Swiss hard-dough bread, and Swiss hot chocolate for Isolde and Fankhauser. The noise of the activity around her finally awakened Isolde, who quickly got dressed and joined Renée in the kitchen.

"That smells so good!" exclaimed Isolde complimentarily to Renée.

"Nothing but the best at the *Fankhaus*!" she remarked, proudly. "I have made hot chocolate. But if you prefer coffee, just say the word, and Presto! it will be here before you."

"I love hot chocolate," Isolde replied, gratefully. Renée called to her son to come for breakfast.

"He works so hard," she muttered, "sometimes he forgets to eat."

A couple minutes later, Fankhauser was there at the kitchen table, with his mother and Isolde. He turned to Isolde.

"Let's eat quickly, Isolde. I want you to listen to the tapes. And then there is a lot for me to do."

"There you go again, Joaquim. Business; business; business. All the time, business."

"It's my job, Mama. That's why I am the best at what I do."

"I know you are the best, Joaquim. But you must always remember, life flies by before you know it. You must take time to smell the roses. Besides, keep in mind the old adage *All work and no play makes Jack a dull boy.*" Isolde listened and observed. She had a slightly different take on Fankhauser; in her mind, he worked hard, but he also played hard. In Renée's mind, he was all work, work, work, and no play. Whichever view was correct, Isolde was more than happy to have Fankhauser working for her. As soon as the ham and eggs were gobbled down, Fankhauser touched Isolde gently on the arm and said: "Grab your hot chocolate, and come with me. I want you to hear the tapes." Isolde looked at Renée, appreciatively said "Thank you, Renée", picked up her mug of hot chocolate, and followed Fankhauser into his home office. Within a few seconds, she was listening to a replay of her conversation with Lise. She relished the compliment that Fankhauser paid her, that she had performed excellently. "Could not have been any better," he observed. Then Isolde heard Lise's frantic phone call to Rapini. The tape showed that it was at seven-thirty-five.

"I-I-I just spoke with her, Herr Rapini," Lise blurted out.

"Spoke with whom?" demanded Rapini.

"With that woman from Canada, I-I-Isolde Bruni. You know, Fred's wife. Sh-sh-she is on to me.

What am I going to do?

"Take a deep breath, Lise. You must control yourself. What do you mean 'she is on to you'?"

"She knows—she knows—she knows everything. She knows about the poison. *'Mon Petit Ami'*. She knows about the company. She even calls it *The Shadow*. She knows the connection with Catherine de' Medici; with Diane de Poitiers; and with Gian Gastone de' Medici. She knows that *The Shadow* has the formula for *'Mon Petit Ami'*. She knows about my relationship with you She said that the giveaway was the emblem of the three intersecting crescents. She had seen your gold lapel pin. She had seen my gold ring with the crown of black onyx inlaid with mother of pearl in the shape of the three intersecting crescents. What is there that she does not know? I am telling you, Herr Rapini; she is on to me. She knows that I murdered Fred. Oh my God! What am I going to do? What the hell am I going to do? I don't want to spend the rest of my life rotting away in some stinking prison! Help me, please! Help me! For God's sake, help me!" Her loud sobs resonated from the tape. She was a desperate woman, in fear of losing her freedom. Rapini remained as calm as a block of ice. He realized that there was a situation that had to be dealt with immediately.

"Are you at your apartment, Lise?" he queried.

"Yes; yes; I am at my apartment," she replied, sobbing more hysterically than ever. It was as if she was having a complete mental meltdown.

"Just to confirm, your address is Spitalgasse 29, apartment 02?"

"Yes. Please help me. What shall I do?" she pleaded, like a woman who had received a death sentence and was desperately begging for a reprieve.

"Just remain where you are. Do not leave. I will get hold of 'Rome'. 'Rome' will contact you, likely in a few minutes. In the meantime, do not speak with anyone else about this."

According to the tape, Lise's phone rang at seven-fifty. The male voice identified itself as 'Rome'. It ordered Lise to remain where she was; there in her apartment. The caller would immediately fly by private plane to Bern. He should be there in less than two hours.

The tape of sounds from the electronic bug in the general areas of Lise's apartment revealed happenings in Lise's apartment starting at nine-thirty-five. There was a knock on the door. The door was opened, and a male voice asked: "Are you Lise Brunner?" The accent was clearly

Italian. Lise responded: "Yes; I am Lise Brunner". The footsteps of the man could be heard as he entered the apartment, as if he was in full control of the space.

"I am from Rome. For privacy, may we step into the bedroom?" Within a few minutes, Lise's frantic voice could be heard saying: "What are you doing? Please don't." To this, the man calmly responded: "This is only a sedative. It will settle your nerves." The sounds that followed were consistent with a brief struggle. Shortly after, the man's footsteps could be heard as he walked to the front door. And then there was the slamming of the door, followed by complete silence. Within a few minutes, the sound of the door opening again was picked up on the tape.

Fankhauser explained: "The rest of that tape is of me entering the apartment, and going into Lise's bedroom. And then, on the other tape, picked up by the electronic bug in the telephone, my phone call to the *Sanitätsnotruf*."

Isolde's mouth was open wide in awe. She would not have believed it if she had not heard it all with her own ears. You just can't make this up, she thought. There it was. Her instinct had proven to be correct. Fred had been murdered. He had not committed suicide.

"That's it. We have them," Isolde said to Fankhauser.

"Not so fast," he cautioned. "We still have a long way to go. We really have nothing to prove motive; and that is a must. We also are lacking in relation to the evidence re opportunity. And the good evidence we have would likely be thrown out of court. As you know, the electronic bugs were illegally placed in Lise's apartment. We did not have a warrant to authorize the invasion of her privacy." Isolde's look of elation dissipated as fast as dew in the morning sun. She gently massaged the front of her neck, wondering what next. They had gone to all those extremes, and, according to Fankhauser, they still had very little. While Fankhauser was explaining to Isolde the shortcomings in their evidence, the phone rang. It was Simon Hartmann, his friend, the *Politzeikommissar* at *Kantonspolizei Bern*.

"Joaquim," Hartmann started, "I have some good news for you. Lise Brunner is still alive. When you phoned in, you apparently used the word 'poisoning". So, at the hospital, they immediately pumped her stomach out, and administered a broad-spectrum antidote, even though the blood tests did not disclose any trace of a poisonous agent. Both measures seemed to do the trick. She is still alive and kicking. They say that she is in a state of shock. She seems to be emotionally perturbed, although they have not been able to put their finger on what the problem really is. She is at *Spital Tiefenau*, over on Tiefenaustrasse, Room 315."

"Someday I will explain it all to you, Simon. May I ask two more favours of you, my friend? Number one, would you instruct the hospital to not release news of her recovery to anyone? And number two, would you ask them to hold her for a couple days?"

"Yes. As a matter of fact, I have already issued those orders to them. As far as the rest of the world is concerned, she did not recover from whatever had been inflicted on her. And further, I have instructed them that she should not be released without my approval. And one more thing, Joaquim; I have spoken with the hospital administrator. He will allow you full access to whatever you need, when it comes to Lise Brunner. The path has been paved for you, my friend."

Fankhauser breathed a sigh of relief. He had saved not one life, but two lives.

"Thanks, Simon. You are so great at your job. I owe you a huge debt of gratitude," Fankhauser exclaimed.

"The only thing that you owe me is the pleasure of your company in putting away a keg of Bavarian beer," Hatmann chortled. "Incidentally, how will you provide for her safety?" Fankhauser thought about the question. He had to decide in a split second whether or not to reveal to anyone whatsoever the fact that Lise would be at the *Fankhaus*.

"She will be under my protection at my apartment," he replied. If he could not trust his friend Simon Hartmann, then who in the whole wide world could he trust? Besides, look at what Hartmann had just done for him. "I will be away in Rome for a few days," Fankhauser added.

So far, so good, thought Fankhauser. With the assistance of Hartmann, he would now have Lise in his custody. And the rest of the world, notably *The Shadow*, would not have an inkling that she had survived the ingestion of *'Mon Petit Ami'*. "But there is still a lot of work for me to do," he told Isolde, as he sat there with her in his home office. "We must now prepare the path forward." He stressed the importance of planning not only strategy, but also the tactics necessary to achieve the strategic goals.

"From a practical perspective, Isolde, the first thing for me to do is to visit Lise in the hospital. The reasons are two-fold. Firstly, to impress upon her the fact that 'Rome' had tried to take her life. In this way, she will be in my custody, on the promise that I will protect her. If 'Rome' learns that she is still alive, they will make other attempts on her life. Thank God for Hartmann, he had already paved the way for me at the hospital. Secondly, once Lise has trust and confidence in me, hopefully she will confess to partaking in Fred's murder, on the promise that I will do everything in my power for the law to go lightly on her in return for providing evidence against the real instigators." He looked into Isolde's eyes, as if to ask if she had anything to add.

"I back everything that you do, Joaquim; I have every trust and confidence in you. Just lead the way, and I will follow."

The telephone rang. It was Fettucini, Fankhauser's man in Rome. Fankhauser put the phone on speaker, so that Lise could hear the conversation.

"Fank," Fettucini started, using the old familiar nickname with which he had labelled Fankhauser when they had been in college together. "I must say that 'when you go, you sure go big'. You've got a tiger by the tail, my friend."

"OK, Alberto. Forget the histrionics. Just give me the bad news."

"The man in your photographs is Bernardo Agimo. He is a notorious king-pin in the mobster world. His rap sheet is as long as my arm. It includes such crimes as racketeering, drug trafficking, prostitution, money-laundering, you name it. He even has the reputation of being a 'hit-man', but the police have never been able to get the murder charges to stick. Strangely enough, nothing is shown of any convictions, or even charges, over the past seven years. In fact, my further investigation reveals that he now has an aura of respectability about him, commensurate with his extreme wealth; that he has been keeping his nose clean; even considered in some circles to have ties with the Vatican. Can you believe it? He seems to have made a complete U-turn in his life. It's like an overnight conversion from evil to good. You must keep in mind, Joaquim, that, judging from his past, this man is a very dangerous man. With his record, I just don't buy this crap that he has suddenly found God."

"That's *great* news, Alberto," Fankhauser remarked, somewhat sarcastically. Any idea as to his regular hangouts? Night clubs? Restaurants?"

"I understand that he is a regular patron of *Ristorante dei Santi*; it's over on Via de Porta Cavallegeri, not far from the Vatican. My sources tell me that he goes there for dinner every Thursday evening. Usually about eight. Always with a group of about nine or ten."

"You have done well, Alberto. You may send me your invoice for what you have done so far. But I will likely require your services further. I plan on being in Rome in about a day or so. Will you be around?"

"Yes, Joaquim. I will be here. Just phone me when you need me. But---please be careful; very careful. Agimo is a very dangerous man. A real viper."

"Thanks for the warning, Alberto. See you in Rome!" Fankhauser looked at Isolde. Her face was ashen. They were now confronted by a professional 'hitman'. And, to make things worse, a 'hit-man' who was a wolf dressed in sheep's clothing. A professional 'hit-man' who had tried to snuff Lise's life out, acting as calmly as putting out the flame of a candle. A 'hit-man' who had been hot on her own trail, in order to also take her life. Had it not been for the swift actions of Fankhauser, Agimo would have claimed two lives last night.

"The plot thickens," Fankhauser remarked to Isolde. "Right now, I have to go and see Lise at the hospital. You remain here with Mama. You are safe here. There is no way that Agimo or any of his nefarious cohorts can penetrate the *Fankhaus*. I do not bear the Fankhauser name for nothing."

"I feel very safe in your *Fankhaus*, Joaquim," Isolde said, with a smile, which disguised her true emotion, the trepidation that she was feeling within her breast.

CHAPTER FIFTEEN

SPITAL TIEFENAU, the hospital that Lise was in, was well known to Fankhauser. And Fankhauser was well known to most of the hospital staff. His late father had been a patient there, for several weeks before he passed away. That had been only a couple of years before. But that was not all. Over the years, his professional accomplishments had propelled him into the stratosphere of heroes of Bern; crowned by the fact that the President of Switzerland had personally presented him with a gold lapel pin in recognition of his sublime service. The gold pin carried with it no formal honours or title, as those are prohibited under the Swiss Constitution. But once presented by the Swiss President as a personal gift, the gold pin swept Fankhauser away in a rising tide of popular acclaim.

Approaching the Nurses' Station on the third floor, he simply asked to see Lise Brunner in Room 315. He did not even need to identify himself. "Sure, Herr Fankhauser," the head-nurse responded. She was a good-looking brunette with entrancing emerald-green eyes, and a body to die for. He looked at her name tag. It read 'Lorena Meyer'. I will just tuck that away for future reference, he thought to himself. As soon as he saw her eyes, he identified a common bond with her. He also had green eyes. As he looked at her, a warm flush ran through his cheeks. "Just follow me, please, Herr Fankhauser," Head-Nurse Meyer invited him, with a captivating smile. Within a few seconds, he was standing beside Head-Nurse Meyer in Lise's room. He imbibed the delicate scent of her eau de cologne, and could not take his eyes off her pretty face. Lise was fast asleep. "I don't mind waiting," he told the head-nurse. "I will leave you with her, Herr Fankhauser. You will know where to find me, if you need me." Fankhauser watched every movement of her alluring body, as she left the room. He sat on a chair, next to the bed. He looked down at Lise, as she slept peacefully and serenely. He wondered if she had any idea of how close she had come to being cut down by the Grim Reaper. He felt a sense of accomplishment. This was a life that he had saved.

After about twenty minutes, Lise opened her eyes. At first, she was oblivious to Fankhauser's presence. As she yawned and looked around, she suddenly became aware of someone sitting there. She did a double-take. She immediately sat up in the bed.

"Who are you?" she asked, rather sharply. He handed her his business card.

"Lise, my name is Joaquim Fankhauser. I am a private investigator here in Bern."

"The name seems to ring a bell with me. Did you not receive a gold lapel pin from the President of Switzerland two or three years ago? You are something of a national hero," she remarked, rather amiably. "Why are you here?" she asked, quizzically.

"It is somewhat of a long story. But let me ask you this: Do you know why *you* are here?"

"I remember being in my apartment on Spitalgasse. I remember a man coming into my apartment. I remember him forcing a pill down my throat. I remember being paralyzed, unable to move, unable to speak, unable to scream. I remember the paramedics strapping me to a gurney, and taking me away. That's as much as I remember. When I awoke, the doctor told me that I had ingested poison; that they had flushed my stomach out; and that they had administered some sort of antidote."

"Did you know who the man was that forced the pill down your throat?" he asked. She froze in silence for a minute or two. Fankhauser could guess as to what she was thinking. If she revealed too much, then she could be sealing her own fate. She could be facing a lengthy prison term, for the murder of Fred Bruni.

"Why are you asking me all this?" she demanded, as she fidgeted with a lock of her hair. "Fair question," he responded. "You should know first of all that I saved your life. I was the person that phoned 144 for an emergency ambulance. They managed to get to you in the nick of time."

"That may be so. But how was it that you became involved in the first place?"

"That is part of the long story. Let's just say that the man whom Herr Rapini described to you only as 'Rome' is a man named Bernardo Agimo. He has a record of notoriety. A very dangerous man, this Agimo, as you can see from the fact that he tried to kill you. Do you know the name of the poison that he forced down your throat?" Once again, Lise did not respond.

"Well, I'll tell you," Fankhauser continued. "It is called *'Mon Petit Ami'*. Had you ever heard of a poison with that name?" Once again, silence. Fankhauser continued: "Lise, you must trust me. Your life is still in danger. If Agimo and his cohorts learn that you are still alive, they will move heaven and earth to kill you. They want you silenced, permanently. And they will stop at nothing to achieve their goal. They feel that you know too much about the death of Fred Bruni; and dead men tell no tales." Lise was shaking visibly; she felt sick to her stomach. She knew that what Fankhauser was saying was true; her life was still at stake. The people whom she had trusted—Rapini at VolksBankBern, and the man known as 'Rome', who had a connection with Rapini, but now identified as Bernardo Agimo--- were her lethal enemies. She needed to find refuge from them and their henchmen. She broke down and started to sob. Fankhauser offered her his clean, white handkerchief to wipe away her tears.

"Do you know about 'the secret society'? she asked, her eyes piercing as sharp as knives into his.

"Yes; I know about 'the secret society', *The Shadow.* I know its whole history. I know of the emblem that is a sign of the common bond among its members, the emblem of the three intersecting crescents." Lise came to the stark realization that the jig was up; Fankhauser knew almost everything he needed to know. It served no purpose for her to rebuff his efforts at this time. He was there to protect her; to save her life, for the second time.

"What do you now require of me?" she asked, her voice in obvious anguish. He had succeeded. She was now putting her life in his hands. What did she stand to lose? Fankhauser smiled. The rest should be easy.

"You should know that Agimo intended to murder not only you, but also Isolde Bruni." There was a gasp from Lise.

"You know Isolde Bruni?"

"Yes. In fact, she was the person that hired me. I removed her from Best Western Plus Hotel Bern just in the nick of time. After the attempt on your life by Agimo, he went directly to Isolde's hotel, and his purpose was not to have a social drink with her. It was clearly to try and force *'Mon Petit Ami'* down her throat. Obviously, *'Mon Petit Ami'* is his weapon of choice."

"What do you want me to do?" Lise asked, pleadingly.

"We need to get you out of here as soon as possible. Arrangements have been made with the hospital to not disclose to anyone that you are still alive. Agimo and his gang are likely under the impression that you are dead. But if they ever learn that you are still alive, they will be after you again."

"Where would I go?" she asked, in desperation.

"The safest place is my apartment here in Bern; in the Old Town. The place is like a fortress. The best in security. Isolde is already closeted there. We have room for you, if you don't mind sharing a room with Isolde?" A puzzled look crept over her face. This is very interesting, Lise thought. She would be sharing a room with the widow of the man that she had not only killed, but also had slept with on numerous occasions. God certainly has a sense of humour.

"From what you have told me, I really have no choice. I will do as you say, Herr Fankhauser," she said, resignedly.

"Do you feel well enough to leave the hospital?" Fankhauser asked.

"Yes; I feel well enough to leave here." At this, Fankhauser pulled his mobile phone from his pocket, and dialed the number of Polizeikommissar Hartmann.

"Hi, Simon. Joaquim here. I am at the hospital with Lise Brunner. She is on board with my plans for her safety. She feels well enough to leave. As previously mentioned to you, I am going to take her to my apartment, for her own safety. Would you please arrange with the hospital for her discharge into my care?"

"By all means, Joaquim. It's as good as done. I will phone the hospital administrator immediately. Take care now."

Turning to Lise, he told her to get dressed, and be ready to leave in ten minutes. In the meantime, he will step outside the room and have a cup of coffee. When he returned to the room, she was fully dressed. He had her checked out at the Nurses' Station, where he admired Head-Nurse Meyer once again. He had the uncanny feeling that Head-Nurse Meyer also could not take her eyes off him.

Within a few minutes, Fankhauser and Lise were in his black Mercedes-Benz, driving along Tiefenaustrasse, well on their way to the safety of the *Fankhaus*. Fankhauser had a deep feeling of satisfaction within his chest. He had pulled it off. He now had Lise under his control. Beyond that, he had her on his side. She was so desperate to keep on living that she would do anything that he suggested to her. As they drove toward his apartment, he thought he should make good use of the time. There were questions that she would be able to answer. No time like the present. He surreptitiously put his hand into his coat pocket, and quietly activated the small recording device he was carrying.

"Tell me, Lise. How did you administer *'Mon Petit Ami'* to Fred?" She thought about the question for a few seconds.

"It had all been orchestrated for me. Herr Rapini knew that Fred was coming to Bern. And he knew that Fred would stay with me in Bern. After all, Fred always did. Herr Rapini told me that he had his orders from 'Rome'; 'Rome' had delivered into his hands a small vial of the poison in tablet form; *'Mon Petit Ami'*, as he called it. Some months prior to this, he had asked me if Fred took any prescription pills. I had told him yes; that Fred took Cafergot to control his migraines. You know, the little round tablets, light-brown in colour. Herr Rapini came to my apartment shortly before Fred's last visit. He gave me a single tablet. It was small and light-brown. He said it was *'Mon Petit Ami'*. He said that 'Rome' had ordered that I slip this one tablet into the vial containing Fred's Cafergot pills; that it was as simple as that." She snapped her fingers as if to show how easy Rapini had said it would be. "At some point in time," she continued, "Fred would take *'Mon Petit Ami'*, mistaking it for Cafergot. That's all there was to it, Herr Rapini told me. If I followed 'Rome' orders, I would be rewarded handsomely; CHF1,000,000 would be deposited into my account at VolksBankBern.

On the other hand, if I failed to obey the orders from 'Rome', I would be killed. Kaput. I ask you, Herr Fankhauser, what choice did I really have?" For a minute or so, Fankhauser did not respond. Great, he thought. Let's press on to find out more.

"I really don't think you had a choice, Lise. It was a matter of Fred's life or yours. You know, we human beings—as a matter of fact, all animals—are wired for self-preservation. Survival. It's ingrained in all of us. You did what was necessary for your survival. But tell me about 'Rome'. I know that the man that had previously been referred to as 'Rome' is really Bernardo Agimo. But Agimo is only a representative of a larger group, is he not? Who, or what, is the real 'Rome'?" She sat there, silent, thinking as to how she should respond.

"If *they* find out that I am telling you all this, I will be a dead duck for sure before we know it." She was looking at Fankhauser, hoping he would understand.

"Look, Lise. As I see it, they want you dead anyway. I am your only protector. You need to come clean with me." At this, she was now looking out the window to her right, likely seeing blank. All she could hear was the oozy whir of the tires of Fankhauser's black Mercedes-Benz as they bit into the moist pavement. Eventually, she spoke.

"The man you call Bernardo Agimo is a big deal in my life. But he himself is only a small cog in the huge secret machine known as *'OMBRA SEGRETA DELLA FORZA DI FIRENZE'*. Have you ever heard the name?"

"Can't say that I have. My knowledge of Italian tells me that it means the *'SECRET SHADOW OF THE FORCE OF FLORENCE'*. Is that correct?"

"Dead on," she replied. "Commonly referred to among its members as *'The Shadow.* Do you know what *The Shadow* is?"

"I am all ears, Lise. Please fill me in."

"One should never underestimate the power of *The Shadow.* It has the ability to survive, just like the cockroach. It has not only survived, but has also flourished, for centuries. And talk about power? *The Shadow* has tentacles like an octopus, stretching everywhere. And when I say everywhere, I mean *everywhere*. There is no place on earth that is not touched by a tentacle of *The Shadow*. Always ready to crush its foes to death, *The Shadow* has as its mantra the principle advocated by Machiavelli, *'The end justifies the means'*. That, Herr Fankhauser, is, in a nutshell, what we are up against." She then coughed a number of times, as if she had something stuck in her throat. Sheer fear, thought Fankhauser.

"What is the *'Forza di Firenze'*?"

"As you likely recognize, that means *'The Force of Florence'*. What is *'The Force of Florence'*? The question is better phrased as *Who* is *'The Force of Florence'*? Well, first and foremost, the noble Medici family, of course. When you talk about power, the Medici family is synonymous with the word. *The Shadow* has its origins in at least one of the Medicis; Gian Gastone de' Medici. But then there is another side, the part that springs from Diane de Poitiers, who was the mistress of Henry II of France, who was married to Catherine de' Medici. The Medicis had built a strong and honourable reputation in the world of finance; and, even after the decline of the Medici Bank in Florence, the Medicis continued to be dominant in financial affairs, even continuing down to current times to be active in handling the finances of the Vatican. While the Medicis, aka *'The Force of Florence'*, are the good guys in financial matters, *The Shadow* is a group of bad actors that perform the services that the good actors refuse to touch." That was indeed a mouthful, thought Fankhauser. He had struck gold. It was just as Isolde had described, after her interview with Professor Rossi. He was now drawing close to his apartment building. He slowed his speed. He needed answers to two or three more questions.

"How did you get drawn into *The Shadow*, Lise? In other words, what's a nice girl like you doing in a place like this?"

"The answer is simple. I am a Medici. *The Shadow* is attracted to the Medici name, like a bear to honey. Before approaching me, Herr Rapini had conducted an in-depth study of me. He obtained reports as to how I lived; how much money I owed; the night clubs that I visited; et cetera, et cetera. They knew that my lifestyle was beyond my means; and that I suffer from the cardinal sin of greed. Herr Rapini made me an offer that I could not refuse. And so, I was inducted into the secret society known as the *'The Secret Shadow of the Force of Florence'*. I took their oath of allegiance, which included a statement that, if I breached their rules,

I would suffer the supreme penalty, death. Like Faust, I sold my soul to the Devil. And the Devil has now come to demand it." At this, she sniffled, as if holding back tears.

"Two more questions, Lise. Is *The Shadow* connected to the Vatican? And, if so, how?"

"Those questions I am unable to answer; because I just do not know. They have kept secret from me the financial and other affairs of *The Shadow*. Herr Rapini would know about such things. But he has never revealed anything of the sort to me. He never revealed to me more than he felt I needed to know."

Fankhauser pulled into the underground parking garage of his apartment building. Lise had made his work so much easier. There is so much that he has learned from what she had unloaded on him. There was a symbiosis. She obviously trusted him implicitly. And he had won her over as a true convert to his team, loaded with vital information about the infamous organization known as *The Shadow*. How could the day have gone any better?

When Fankhauser entered his apartment, with Lise in tow, he found his mother and Isolde sitting at the dining table, playing gin rummy. Isolde looked up. Her eyes and Lise's eyes met one another instantly. Isolde was paralyzed at the sight of Lise. Lise was right there in the *Fankhaus*! Isolde's mind immediately went back to Fred. This is the woman who had slept with her husband. Not once. Not twice. But on innumerable occasions. Likely on every occasion he had come to Bern on business. This is the woman who, like the black widow spider, the species known as *Latrodectus hesperus*, had engaged in sexual cannibalism on her lover. This is the woman who, following her sexual relationship with Fred, had cannibalized him, chewed him up, and ingested him, leaving not one live scrap of him to be returned to his wife, to his children. Although she had heard Fankhauser tell Hartmann that Lise would be under his protection in his apartment, now that Lise was actually in the *Fankhaus,* she was having great difficulty coming to grips with her presence there.

"How are the two dominant women in my life?" Fankhauser asked, referring to Renée and Isolde. Renée laughed. Isolde just glared at him, speechless.

"We were doing just fine at our game of gin rummy," Renée responded, jokingly, "until you came in and put a stop to it. Who is your friend?"

"Mama, I would like you to meet Lise Brunner. Lise was just discharged from *Spital Tiefenau*, and she has no place to go. She will be a guest of the Fankhausers for a short time." The stark realization that she would be sharing close quarters with the woman who had not only screwed her husband, but had also taken his life, hit Isolde like a ton of bricks. This was the woman who had robbed her of her husband, and Emil and Sophie of their father. And there is only one guest room in the *Fankhaus*. So, where is Lise going to sleep? Undoubtedly, in the same room as her, Isolde. And, as a member of *The Shadow*, is Lise not a dangerous woman? Fankhauser himself had told her, Isolde, that 'Rome' had in fact gone to her hotel, Best Western Plus Hotel Bern, with the intention of killing her. What would have changed on the part of *The Shadow?* So many unanswered questions.

"Welcome, Lise," said Renée, already on her feet and walking toward Lise, her arms outstretched toward her. "Our home is your home. Do you know Isolde?" Isolde, still confused, rose to her feet and said, offhandedly: "We've met."

"What a small world!" Renée exclaimed. "The mobility of these modern times astounds me. I am not sure if it's a good thing, or a bad thing. I guess I will just have to go with the flow." She held hands with Lise, leading her to the dining table. "May I get you anything, Lise? Coffee? Hot chocolate? Wine?"

"A glass of red wine would be great, if you have it. Thanks." Lise sat down beside Isolde, who was still in a quandary as to how she should receive Lise's presence in the *Fankhaus*. "How are you doing, Isolde?" Lise politely asked, trying to make conversation.

"I am not doing badly, considering what happened to my husband," Isolde snapped. The sarcasm was as plain as day. "But, more to the point, how are *you?*"

"At least, I am still alive," Lise responded. "I take it that Herr Fankhauser told you what had happened to me?"

"Yes. He did." So, the two women were exchanging civil words. But deep down, Isolde was still bothered by the presence of Lise in the *Fankhaus*. She needed some answers. And the only person that could provide those answers was Fankhauser, who had disappeared into his home office. "Excuse me for a few minutes, Lise," Isolde said, as she rose from the table. She made a bee-line for Fankhauser's office. She knocked on the door softly, entered, and shut the door behind her. Fankhauser welcomed her with a faint smile, and told her to have a seat. It was as if he had been expecting her.

"Joaquim, I must tell you that I am sick to my stomach from having to share living quarters with Lise Brunner. I originally thought that I could cope with it, when I heard you telling Hartmann that she would be residing here. But the sight of her and the thought of living with her are driving me nuts. Do you understand where I am coming from?"

"Fair question," he replied. "I have not had an opportunity to fill you in." He got up, went to the door, and locked it. As soon as he returned to his chair, he pressed the 'Play' button of his portable recording device, which sat on his desk. "Just listen to this," he said, as he leaned back in his chair, both arms behind his head. Isolde was all ears, as she listened to the recorded conversation between Fankhauser and Lise on the drive from *Spital Tiefenau* to the *Fankhaus*. By the end of the playback of the recording, she appeared to be a sea of calm. She was pleased that Fankhauser had received all that invaluable information from Lise. But she still had some concerns.

"OK, Joaquim. All well and good. But how do you see this playing out in the future? How can you trust this woman, this murderess?"

"I have no choice but to keep her here. If she were on the loose, her life would not be worth a plug nickel. *The Shadow* would kill her in the blink of an eye, and would likely get away with it, no questions asked. I have got her to the point where she is deathly scared of *The Shadow*. She wants to live. She is far too young to die; and she knows it. What else could I do, Isolde? I had to bring her to the *Fankhaus*. This is the only place where she can be safe. Preserved, so to speak, as a source of evidence for you in seeking justice for Fred's death. Lise is not the main villain in the piece. She is not the one we are really after. She is only an amanuensis; an instrument; a tool used by the master-mind. We are after the big enchilada. In my opinion, Lise is now with us, the good guys. She realizes how closely her connection with *The Shadow* came to taking her through death's door. She would be foolish to run back into the arms of the grizzly bear that came within an inch of taking her life. In any event, it is too late to let her leave the *Fankhaus*. She knows where you are. If *The Shadow* procures that information, you can bid farewell to your life. They would stop at absolutely nothing to get at you. Got the point?" As Isolde thought about it, she knew deep down that Fankhauser was right. And he was the professional. She had to keep trusting him.

"Thanks for filling me in, Joaquim. I am with you one hundred per cent. I will try my best to live with Lise. Peaceful coexistence, so to speak. But one more question: Where is she going to sleep? You have only one guest room." Once again, a faint smile crept across Fankhauser's face.

"I was thinking that she could sleep on one of the twin beds in the guest room. Would that be OK with you?" Isolde was not at all pleased with this arrangement. She would be sharing a bedroom with the woman who had, to say the least, murdered her husband.

"Do I have a choice?" she quipped, knowing that the question was rhetorical.

"The only alternatives would be for her to share my bed, and that is a complete *no-no*; completely *verboten*, as we say in German. Or, to share Mama's bed. But I could not ask that of an elderly lady. So, in answer to your question, you have no choice. But look at it this way. I will be away for two or three days; going to Rome on business, which, incidentally, will be on behalf of a lovely lady client of mine from Canada. I will be leaving by plane early tomorrow morning. During my absence, you will be welcome to sleep in my bed." Fankhauser looked into Isolde's cat's eyes, inviting from her a purr of approval. She nodded, not uttering a sound. After all, as Fankhauser had put it, she had no choice.

"Why are you going to Rome?" she asked.

"In order to get at the big enchilada, I have to find out more about Bernardo Agimo. More about *The Shadow.* And, last but not least, more about the involvement, if any, of the Vatican." Again, Isolde nodded. She understood fully, and approved.

Fankhauser and Lise then rejoined Renée and Lise at the dining table. "OK," he announced loudly. "We have a full house. Let's all play a few games of Five Card Stud. Here is a box of chips. I am giving an equal amount to each player. Everybody on board?" Before anyone could respond, he was already dividing the chips equally among all four players. For the next two or three hours, they were all fully absorbed in the poker game. The game ended when Renée said she had to prepare dinner, at which time Fankhauser asked her to step into his office for a couple minutes. He closed the door behind them.

"Mama," he started, "I know that it is an imposition on you for me to have brought both Isolde and Lise into the *Fankhaus*. I just want to say how much I really appreciate your grace and kindness. You have hosted them as if they were family; no questions asked."

"Anything for you, my dear Joaquim. That's what mothers are for."

"I will be leaving for Rome in the morning. While I am away, Isolde will occupy my bedroom. Without giving you the full history, you should know that Isolde is my client, and that Lise was responsible—at least in part—for the death of Isolde's husband. But there is a much bigger picture. Lise is a member of a very large and dangerous secret society known as *'Ombra Segreta della Forza di Firenze'*. I am sure you have never heard of them?"

"Nope. Never. My Italian tells me that that translates to *'Secret Shadow of the Force of Florence'*. What is *'The Force of Florence'*?"

"Your Italian tells you correctly. *'The Force of Florence'* is the Medici family of Florence, who, you will likely recall, was a leading light in Florence, and the rest of Italy, for over three hundred years; and who were very successful in the world of finance, even creating their own bank, *Banco dei Medici*. Well, to put it simply, *The Shadow* emanated in part from the Medicis and in part from another historical figure, one Diane de Poitiers. Have you ever heard of her?"

"Was she not the mistress of Catherine de' Medici's husband, Henry II of France; the one that was obsessed with her own breasts?"

"You have hit it right on the head, Mama. Your knowledge of history overwhelms me," Fankhauser remarked. Renée laughed.

"Well, at least my years at *Universität Bern* were not entirely wasted," she said. Fankhauser laughed.

"*The Shadow* executes the nefarious acts that the Medicis and their colleagues would never dream of stooping to," he continued. "They are true disciples of Machiavelli, in whatever they do. They follow blindly the principle *The end justifies the means.* In following this Machiavellian mantra, there is nothing in the world to which they would not condescend. That makes them very, very dangerous. That, my dear Mama, is what we are dealing with."

"If Lise is a member of such a dangerous group, what is she doing here in the *Fankhaus*?"

"The answer is simple, Mama. In short, she has changed sides. *The Shadow* made an attempt on her life. Tried to poison her. I saved her from the jaws of death." Renée roared with laughter. Fankhauser just looked at her, wondering why she found that funny.

"What you have lost sight of, my dear Joaquim, is that Lise is a woman. Need I say more?" Fankhauser thought about this response. Renée was correct. Sure, there are all the old cliches about women, such as *It is a woman's prerogative to change her mind.* But it was different this time. Lise was a convert; and it would not be in her best interests to betray him.

"Thanks for the caution, Mama. This leads me to my next point." He opened one of his desk drawers. He picked up an object wrapped in a shopping bag. From the shopping bag, he removed a small pistol.

"Ah!" Renée exclaimed, with a knowing look. "Now things are getting lively!" There was a touch of raw sarcasm in her voice.

"Mama, this is the state of the art in pistols. It is called a Glock G43x. Produced in Austria. Would you believe that this is the first year of its production and release? Perfect size for ladies, don't you think? A great feature is that it's a semi-automatic."

"Thank you very much, Joaquim, for the crash course in weaponry. But, what has that got to do with me?"

"I bought it for your protection, Mama."

"For my protection!" she exclaimed, with another sarcastic laugh. "Why in the name of Christ would I need protection?"

"Well, you see, Mama, I never like to take chances. I never leave anything to luck, so to speak. As explained to you, Isolde and I are up against a very dangerous group, the size and identity of which I cannot begin to fathom, except to say that it could be very large, and, of course we know, very dangerous. While I am away in Rome over the next two or three days, I want you to guard the *Fankhaus*. I know that the *Fankhaus* is very safe, with all the security features we could possibly desire. But I think it would be prudent for you to have this Glock semi-automatic while I am away."

"Some job for a seventy-five-year-old mother!" she gibed, as she gingerly picked up the pistol. "Perfect fit," she observed, as she clasped the grip in her right hand, placed her index finger on the trigger. Then, in a moment of fun, she pointed the muzzle at her son. "Pow!" she uttered, almost under her breath.

"Careful, Mama. Don't ever point a pistol at someone, unless you are willing to use it."

"Who says I am not willing to use it?' she laughed, breaking herself up from her own joke. And then, with a serious look, she said: "You know, my dear son, that I will do anything for you. Putting the frivolity aside, thanks for this small gift. But, pray tell, Herr Kapitan, under what circumstances should I use it?"

"In very extreme circumstances, Mama. Number one, if the *Fankhaus* is under siege, or is penetrated by any member of *The Shadow*. You do not know what the enemy looks like. But believe me, Mama, you will recognize him when you see him. Just shoot to kill. Number two, if Lise tries to leave the *Fankhaus*, point the Glock at her, and try to persuade her to remain here. But, if she persists, shoot her. Under no circumstances is she to be permitted to leave the *Fankhaus*. You, my dear Mama, must prevent her from leaving, at all costs."

"Oh my God! But I thought you trusted Lise!" Renée said, sarcastically. She rolled her eyes in bewilderment.

"I trust her, Mama," Fankhauser reaffirmed. "But I do not take chances, unless the odds are overwhelmingly in my favour."

"That's what makes you a good PI," she complimented.

"One more thing, Mama. While I am away in Rome, I do not want Lise to have any contact whatsoever with the outside world. Her whole world must be the *Fankhaus*. So, I have disconnected the phone. If she asks, just tell her that the phone is out of service; that the repairman will be here in a couple of days. And, by the way, keep the Glock semi-automatic out of her sight and reach. I am locking it away in my desk drawer; and I will leave the door to my office locked. But you will have both keys."

Renée stood at attention; saluted; and said: "Ahoy, mein Käpitan. Oberleutnant Renée Fankhauser at your service. Your wish is my command, mein Käpitan." At this, they both laughed heartily, as they rejoined Lise sitting alone at the dining table, stroking a glass of red wine. Isolde was sitting on her bed in the guest room, thumbing through a 1979 issue of the German fashion magazine *Der Glanz*.

"Sorry to have left you here all by yourself," Fankhauser said to Lise, somewhat apologetically.

"No problem at all, Herr Fankhauser," Lise responded.

After a few minutes of small-talk with Lise, Fankhauser excused himself to go to his room. He wasted no time in packing his luggage for his trip to Rome.

"Dinner will be ready in twenty minutes!" Renée shouted. I am keeping it simple. But you will all love it, I guarantee. I hope you are hungry?" No-one responded. Fankhauser was too busy packing. Isolde was thumbing through the outdated fashion magazine. Lise was lost in reverie.

CHAPTER SIXTEEN

ROME was not Fankhauser's favourite city. Not by any stretch of the imagination. He found it overcrowded, bustling, and, except for the places that tourists flocked to, grungy. Give him the peace, quiet, and cleanliness of Old Bern anytime. Perhaps not the fault of Rome, he would tell himself. Maybe he was too much of a creature of habit, a lover of the natural order of the universe and all things in it. In any event, here he was, once again, in the overcrowded, bustling, grungy city of Rome.

He checked into *Palazzo Cardinal Cesi* on Via Conciliazione. From this hotel, it was only a short walk to *St. Peter's Square,* which he could actually see from his room. What a view, he said to himself. The Palazzo's proximity from the Vatican was the main reason why he chose it; the magnificent view was only a fringe benefit. After all, a major reason for his visit to Rome involved the Vatican. He had to find out the truth. Was Rapini's bank, VolksBankBern, and '*Ombra Segreta della Forza di Firenze*', aka *The Shadow,* tied in somehow with the financial activities of the Vatican? The choice of a hotel so close to Vatican City was, in his mind, a tactical move.

As soon as he settled into his room, he phoned his colleague, Alberto Fettucini.

"Hi, Alberto. Joaquim here. I am in your overcrowded, bustling, grungy city."

"Thanks for your complimentary words about my city, Joaquim. I will return the compliment the next time I am in Bern. Dove abiti, tu paesano?" *Where are you staying, you peasant?*

"I am at *Palazzo Cardinal Cesi* on Via della Conciliazione. Yes. I know it's expensive. But I need to be near the Vatican. Can you make time for lunch? Yes. In the hotel dining room here should be fine. See you at noon. Ciao."

The next telephone call that he made was to *Degli Studi di Roma la Sapienza*, known in English as the *University of Rome at Sapienza*. He was doing a study of the Vatican. He was seeking the leading expert on the Vatican. Professor Angelo Barricardi? Yes. May I speak with him? Within a few minutes, he was speaking with Professor Barricardi.

"Professor Barricardi, my name is Vincenzo Barone. I am doing a study of the Vatican. No; not for academic purposes. Just pure fascination. I am studying this state within a state. Can you spend a few minutes with me to discuss the topic? I am willing to pay you for your time. Yes; five today would be fine. I am staying at *Palazzo Cardinal Cesi*, over on Via Conciliazione. You will be here? Great. Perhaps we can dine together? Great. I will meet you in the lobby. You will be wearing a blue suit with a gold vest? See you then. Ciao."

When Fankhauser met his colleague Fettucini at noon in *La Cucina Caffetteria*, the cafeteria in *Palazzo Cardinal Cesi*, it was like old friends meeting at a university homecoming weekend.

"Buongiorno, Fank," Fettucini said to Fankhauser, using the old familiar nickname that he had so long ago created for Fankhauser, as he warmly embraced his friend and colleague. "Benvenuti a Roma!" *Good morning, Fank. Welcome to Rome!*

"Great to see you Alberto," Fankhauser responded. "How are the beautiful women of Rome?" he asked, with a knowing twinkle in his eyes.

"They are as beautiful as ever," exclaimed Fettucini, as he gestured with outstretched arms that made a downward swoop denoting the curves of a woman's body. "So, Fank, you are in chase of *The Shadow*?"

"Exactly. That's why I am here."

"All that I can say is be very, very cautious, Fank. You are now in dangerous territory. You are like a Christian in the Roman Coliseum, ill prepared to face the hungry lions. They will kill you, chew you up, and then spit you out. I can guarantee that you have never ever had to face such a powerful malevolent force in your lifetime. And likely, if you are lucky enough to survive, never ever will again in the future."

"Thanks for the friendly advice, Alberto. But you know me. I am from a long and glorious line of gladiators known as the Fankhausers. Fear is not a word in our vocabulary. I have a client to serve; and I will serve her to my utmost as long as there is breath in this body of mine. But why are we talking business so early into our luncheon date? I am dying to consume the delicious foods of Rome." With that, he snapped his fingers, summoning a waiter.

"Una bottiglia di Chianti, per favore," he ordered. *A bottle of Chianti, please.* While they waited for the wine, they talked about the weather in Rome. After the wine arrived and was poured, they said "Salut" to each other, and talked about everything under the sun, except business. The changes that had taken place in Rome since Fankhauser was last there. The vacations that Fettucini had taken over the years, including his trip to Fiji, his visit to Easter Island, and his expedition to Antarctica. The vacations that Fankhauser had taken over the years, such as his excursion to Egypt, his junket to Rio de Janeiro, and his safari in Africa. By the time the waiter came to take their orders, they were feeling no pain. Fankhauser ordered Italian wedding soup, a club sandwich, and an espresso. Fettucini ordered a plate of Fettuccine Alfredo, which caused Fankhauser to laugh out loud.

"You are aptly named, Alberto,' Fankhauser remarked. "Why would I marvel at a man called 'Fettucini' ordering a plate of Fettuccine?" Picking up on the joke, Fettucini responded: "It's a family tradition, you know. It goes a long way back. There always is a relationship between a man and his name. For example, take the name 'Fankhauser'. I remember you telling me that it means 'keeper of the 'Fankhaus'; undoubtedly referring to what one, or a number, of your ancestors did for a living. Another example is the English name 'Percy'. I remember my history teacher in high school teaching that it had its origin in the Norman conquest of England in 1066. At the Battle of Hastings, one of the English soldiers had the misfortune of receiving an arrow in one of his eyes. Put the eye right out. From then on, he was called 'Pierced Eye', which eventually devolved into the name 'Percy'. In any event, you should note that my name is spelled 'F-E-T-T-U-C-I-N-I'; the dish is spelled 'F-E-T-T-U-C-C-I-N-E. A distinct difference." Fankhauser chuckled. "The spelling makes no difference. And people having the handle 'Percy' do not keep piercing out their eyes!" Fankhauser exclaimed, as he wallowed in a wave of laughter. "How is it that people named 'Fettucini' love to eat Fettuccine? And why did your parents not name you 'Alfredo' instead of 'Alberto'? If they had, you would have had the classic name of 'Alfredo Fettucini'!" By now, both men were howling with laughter.

After about an hour of drinking and eating, Fankhauser, ever in control, looked directly into the eyes of Fettucini, and said; "Now, let's talk business."

"Alberto," he continued. "I understand how much you have cautioned me as to the dangers of pursuing *'Ombra Segreta della Forza di Firenze'*. And I am sure you understand my position. But I need the help of a partner while I am here in Rome; not only as a consultant, but also as an active participant in what I am about to undertake. It is completely optional. You may decline the mission now. But, once you commit to me, you cannot then walk away. I will explain to you in a few minutes the proposed undertaking. You can then say 'Aye; I am in", or "Nay; I am out." For your participation, you will be very well paid. Is that clear, Alberto?"

"As clear as mud," Fettucini said, jestingly. "Go on, Fank. Let's hear it." Fankhauser then proceeded to give Fettucini details of how he intended to pursue *The Shadow.*

When he finished, he asked Fettucini: "Well, Alberto? Are you 'in' or are you 'out'?" Fettucini was absorbed with playing with the empty wine glass in front of him, as if he was in some kind of a sexual act with a woman. First, he lovingly embraced the foot of the glass with the fingers of both hands. Then, he moved his fingers upward, gently stroking the long, slender stem, as he would a woman's legs. Then, he caressed the bowl of the glass, as if massaging the woman's breasts. And, finally, moving further upward, he lovingly rubbed his fingers around the rim, as if reveling in every nook and cranny of the woman's sensuous lips. His metaphoric acts of love completed, he responded to Fankhauser's all-important question.

"Yes, Fank. Aye, I am in. Hook, line, and sinker."

"Excellent," Fankhauser remarked. "Welcome aboard! There are two other things you can do for me, Alberto. Firstly, find out the days and times that a vehicle bearing the name 'VOLKSBANKBERN' arrives at the Vatican; the point at which it enters the Vatican; and where it goes once it is on the Vatican's grounds. The second thing is to find me a local man to act as my driver. He must understand that the mission will be highly confidential and must be the best-kept secret; and that there is some danger involved in the operation, but he will be paid danger-pay."

"I will get back to you within the next twelve hours," Fettucini replied.

"Thanks, Alberto. Until we meet again in the very near future, my friend," Fankhauser said, as he rose and shook hands with Fettucini.

"Ciao, Fank," Fettucini responded. *Bye, Fank.* "Death to *'Ombra Segreta della Forza di Firenze'*!" They both snickered, and parted ways.

Fankhauser returned to his room. He made a reservation at *La Scala da Pranzo*, the hotel dining room, for two at five. After freshening up, he went to the lobby to meet Professor Barricardi. Barricardi was there at five on the dot, dressed in his blue suit and gold vest. Not bad, thought Fankhauser. He always thought of professors as never being punctual. Barricardi seemed to puncture the balloon of that myth. As they shook hands, Fankhauser complimented Barricardi on his punctuality, which immediately put the professor at ease.

Once seated in *La Scala da Pranzo*, Fankhauser ordered a bottle of Valpolicella. Nothing like some good Italian wine to loosen the professor's tongue.

"How much time do you have, Professor Barricardi?" asked Fankhauser.

"I am at your service for the next two hours," Barricardi politely responded.

"Good. Let's enjoy the fine cuisine of your country. And then we can talk business. I try to avoid mixing business with pleasure."

"A man after my own heart," Barricardi remarked. Fankhauser was liking him more and more. The waiter was now at the table, waiting for the orders from the menu. Fankhauser deferred to Barricardi, inviting him to order first.

"Per l'antipasto, Zuppa Minestrone, per favore. Per il corso principale, Saltimbocca all Romana." The main course dish was veal medallions with a fine layer of the Italian dry-cured ham known as Prosciutto. The waiter turned to Fankhauser.

"Per l'antipasto, Zuppa Garmugia, per favore. Per il corso principale, Coda alla Vaccinara sulla Pasta." When the professor heard what Fankhauser had ordered for his main course, he raised his eyebrows and smiled. It was an oxtail and vegetable stew, made from the *quinta quarta*, or the 'fifth-fourth', the 'leftover' parts of the animal; the parts of the cow that would normally be discarded, and fed to the pigs. While the dish is very popular among Italians, foreigners normally shy away from it.

For a full hour, Fankhauser and Barricardi chatted about everything under the sun but the business at hand, while they savoured the fine cuisine of *La Scala da Pranzo*. Their palates gratified, Fankauser did a U-turn, and said to the professor and said: "Now, Professor Barricardi, I need to pick your brain."

"My brain is at your disposal, Signor Fankhauser," the professor acceded, his body slouched in his chair, a vision of relaxation and composure.

"Tell me," Fankhauser opened, "is Vatican City really a 'tax-free zone', as I have often heard it described?"

"When we talk of 'Vatican City', we are talking of *Stato della Città del Vaticano*, or the State of the City of the Vatican. So, it is a full-fledged 'state', as fully independent as Luxembourg or Lichtenstein. And its territory is fully encompassed within the City of Rome. So, in effect, it is a city within a city. Vatican City state is not to be confused with the Holy See, which is the religious entity. The Pope is the sovereign of Vatican City, while the Pontifical Commission holds the legislative authority. The President of that Commission exercises Executive power. In the final analysis, the Pope has full and absolute Executive, Legislative and Judicial power in Vatican City State, which makes him the only absolute monarch in the whole of Europe. I am giving you this background as it is important, in answering your question, to have you appreciate how unique Vatican City State is. Vatican City answers to no-one. It conducts its own financial activities, and this is even on an international basis.

Do you know that the Vatican even has its own bank? It is known as *Instituto per le Opere di Religione*; in English, *Vatican Bank.*

"Just like the Medicis?" Fankhauser interjected.

"Yes; just like the Medicis did in Florence many centuries ago. *Banco dei Medici.* And I must say that the Medicis and their descendants have proven to be very helpful in imparting their financial wisdom and acumen to the Vatican Bank over hundreds of years. In that role, they have been involved in the Administrative Branch of the Vatican. Vatican Bank has proven to be extremely good for the Vatican. Do you know the estimated current net financial worth of the Vatican worldwide? This is not public knowledge, but I would hazard a guess that it is in the vicinity of €$5,000,000,000!

"Now, back to your original question. Yes; one can say that Vatican City is a 'tax-free zone'. Let me clarify. No taxes whatsoever are payable in Vatican City. There are no customs or excise duties; no duties on goods that one buys in Vatican City. There are no income taxes paid by employees of the Vatican. And no income or other taxes payable on gains from investments made by Vatican Bank."

Fankhauser interjected: "Does that 'tax-free' feature not give rise to the potential for money-laundering?"

"Yes; it does. But one has to trust the integrity of the cardinals and the administrative staff."

"But, is it not open to the possibility of one of the cardinals, or one member of the administrative staff, turning a blind eye to some financial misdeeds being performed by some other agents not directly connected to the Vatican?" With a perplexed look, the professor stared into the eyes of Fankhauser, before responding, as if trying to figure him out.

"Yes; it is possible," he replied eventually, although somewhat hesitantly. "I suppose that not all cardinals and members of the administrative staff are without sin."

"Precisely," Fankhauser commented. "But let us assume that almost all the cardinals and the administrative staff are without reproach; including the advisory body on financial matters, which group includes descendants of the Medicis; but that some other group, not as clean and not as visible, infiltrated the Vatican and, albeit without the knowledge of the cardinals, directed some activities through Vatican Bank, that one could not in good conscience describe as 'above board', is that not possible, without visibly tarnishing the reputation of the 'good guys', so to speak?"

"Yes," the professor responded, again somewhat hesitantly, his brows raised. "A mere possibility, I suppose." Fankhauser was puzzled by the introduction of the word "mere". Why the sudden hedging?

"And so, Professor Barricardi, you agree that the possibility exists that the Vatican Bank could conceivably be used as a channel for laundering money obtained through nefarious means?" There was a noticeable change in the expression on the professor's face. Previously calm, smooth and confident, his face had suddenly become wizened and twisted for some reason that Fankhauser could only guess at. It was a remarkably abrupt and drastic transformation, like Dr. Jekyll being transformed instantaneously into the evil Mr. Hyde. The prolonged silence that followed was unsettling.

"Yes. I agree. But highly unlikely." The professor's voice was so low, it was almost inaudible. He fidgeted with his chin, and then his tie, and then his napkin. Fankhauser got the feeling that the professor was, to put it mildly, not comfortable with the line of questioning. This could be one of those situations where more is revealed from what is not said than from what is said. Fankhauser decided to go for the jugular.

"Professor Barricardi, have you ever heard of '*Ombra Segreta della Forza di Firenze*'?" asked Fankhauser. At this poignant question, the professor fell completely silent. He started to breathe heavily, as if suffering an asthmatic attack. Fankhauser could hear the professor's feet shuffling nervously on the floor. The professor was fidgeting with his fingers, as if they wanted to hide, with no place of refuge in sight. Fankhauser had struck his mark; albeit not in the manner he had intended when the conversation started.

"I am referring to *The Shadow,* Professor Barricardi," Fankhauser persevered boldly, as he observed closely every facial expression, every body language exhibited by Barricardi. A bead of perspiration fell from the professor's forehead, notwithstanding the air conditioning in *La Scala da Pranzo*. He looked and acted like a prisoner who had just received the death sentence. Fankhauser took this as confirmation that there was indeed an entity known as '*Omba Segreta della Forza di*

Firenze'. Yes; indeed, *The Shadow* must be extremely dangerous, just like Fettucini had warned. The very mention of the name had put the fear of God into the professor.

"Are you OK?" asked Fankhauser, giving the professor an opportunity to come clean. This simple question caused an expression of rage on Barricardi's face.

"Why the hell do you ask such inane questions? Who do you think I am? Do you think I am a damn fool? This whole thing is a big joke. I need to leave immediately." Before Fankhauser could say another word, Barricardi got up and scurried away, like a badly wounded dog, out of *La Scala da Pranzo*, into the lobby of *Palazzo Cardinal Cesi*, and onto the Via della Conciliazione, where he merged anonymously into the huge crowd. Left alone at the table in the dining room, Fankhauser was putting two and two together. He had struck a raw nerve in Professor Barricardi. He was now fully convinced that he was on the right track.

At about ten the next morning, there was a telephone call from Fettucini.

"Hi, Fank," Fettucini started. "I have the schedule for you. The VolksBankBern vehicle enters Vatican City at two, twice a week; on Tuesdays and Fridays. It is a turquoise-coloured van with a big sign on its front doors: VOLKSBANKBERN. On Tuesdays, it does a delivery; on Fridays, it does a pickup. My sources could not give me any more details. As for a van and driver for you, your man is Giuseppe Cipola."

"Are you kidding me, Alberto? Cipola? Does that not mean 'onion' in English?' Fankhauser bellowed, with laughter.

"Yes; it does. But he does not stink. He comes highly recommended. Take him or leave him, Fank." Fettucini was having difficulty controlling his own laughter. There goes Fank again, he thought. Finds humour in everything.

"OK, Alberto. I will take your 'Joe Onion'. Please have him pick me up in front of my hotel at one-fifteen tomorrow, Tuesday. Incidentally, can you assist him to affix a fake business sign on the front doors of his van? Perhaps '**SERVIZIO PULIZIA DI BENNY**'? He will be working for 'BENNY'S CLEANING SERVICE'."

"As good as done, Fank. Good luck, my friend."

CHAPTER SEVENTEEN

AT ONE-FIFTEEN in the afternoon of the next day, Fankhauser, a large paper bag in his hand, was standing on Via della Conciliazione, in front of the Palazzo, awaiting the arrival of Giuseppe Cipola in his van. One-twenty went by, and no Cipola. One-twenty-five went by, and still no Cipola. This stinks as badly as a rotten onion, Fankhauser thought to himself. The guy is well named.

Finally, at about one-thirty, a canary-yellow Fiat hatchback pulled up slowly in front of the Palazzo, the business sign **SERVIZIO PULIZIA DI BENNY** prominent in bright red on the front doors. A chill ran through Fankhauser's bones as he stared at what must be the smallest 'van' ever made. To add to Fankhauser's apprehension, Cipola appeared to be in no hurry. It was as if he had all the time in the world. His teeth flashed like white Carrara marble in the sunlight, made more prominent by his broad smile and the dark backdrop of his swarthy complexion. He did not come quietly. Between smiles, he was singing loudly at the top of his voice. Fankhauser recognized the piece. It was one of his favourites, the ever popular *La donna è mobile* from Verdi's *Rigoletto*. What a scene, thought Fankhauser. An ordinary Roman, named 'Joe Onion', belting out an opera piece, in a good, full voice, right in the middle of Via della Conciliazione. Only in Rome, thought Fankhauser. And one could easily have been fooled into thinking that Cipola was a famous tenor. Spotting Fankhauser, Cipola waved him into his van, without even taking the time to ensure that this stranger that entered his van at his invitation was indeed Fankhauser.

"Buon pomeriggio, Giuseppe," Fankhauser said, as he entered the small van. *Good afternoon, Giuseppe.* Cipola just kept on singing, without even acknowledging Fankhauser's presence. Still parked in front of the Palazzo, he was fully immersed in the rapture of his own vocal music. This 'Joe Onion' is a real card, thought Fankhauser, as he sat there listening to his host belting out the famous aria. Obviously, time meant nothing to Cipola. Fankhauser looked at his watch, hoping that Cipola would get the point. But this act was lost on Cipola. He had to finish his rendition of the Verdi piece, come hell or high water. Once it was ended, he turned to Fankhauser.

"Ciao, Signore. Come sta?" *Hello, sir. How goes it?*

"Bene, grazie," Fankhauser responded, a ring of impatience in his voice. "Lei parla inglese?" *Fine, thank you. Do you speak English?*

"Poco poco," Cipola replied with a sheepish smile. *A little bit.*

"Good. We must hurry. Put on these coveralls." Fankhauser extracted a pair of coveralls from his paper bag, and handed them to Cipola. Then he pulled out a pair for himself. There was not enough room to don the coveralls in the tiny Fiat hatchback, and so they had to exit the vehicle and put them on in the middle of the bustling crowd on Via della Conciliazione. Cipola's coveralls were a couple sizes too large; he ended up with about three extra inches of material hanging loose around the waist, and about two inches extra length hanging beneath his heels. They were now in workmen's garb, although Cipola looked more like a clown than a workman; all that he was lacking were the balloon-shaped red nose and the frizzly orange hair.

"We are going to the Vatican," Fankhauser announced as soon as they were back inside the van. "Look for the service entrance. But do not enter. I will tell you when to enter." At this, Cipola took off like a speeding bullet. Within a few minutes, his canary van was parked in plain sight of the service entrance to the Vatican. There, they sat and waited; Fankhauser was waiting for the turquoise VolksBankBern van; Cipola had no clue as to what he was waiting for.

"Tell me about your family," Fankhauser asked, to kill time while they waited. Cipola's face lit up. It pleased him that Fankhauser would take an interest in his family.

"I have wife," Cipola replied. "Bellissima. From Napoli. And bambino." No sooner had he said that than Fankhauser observed a turquoise van, with **VOLKSBANKBERN** imprinted in white on the front doors. Two men were seated in the cab section. The VolksBankBern van drove slowly through the service entrance, onto the grounds of the Vatican.

"Now, Giuseppe!" Fankhauser ordered. "Follow that van, but don't let them see us." Within seconds, Cipola's canary-yellow van was also on the grounds of the Vatican. The guard at the entrance had simply looked at the words **SERVIZIO PULIZIA DI BENNY** emblazoned in red on the doors of the Fiat hatchback, and waved it on. The VolksBankBern van was in plain sight, parked at the main back door of the Administrative Building; the two occupants had entered the building. Fankhauser instructed Cipola to park in front of the service entrance to the building. As they watched, they saw the two men exit the VolksBankBern van, from the back of which they removed two large canvas bags, which they carried into the building. "Wait here, Giuseppe," Fankauser instructed. "If you see me heading in the other direction, away from the VolksBankBern van, do not wait for me. For your own safety, you should then leave immediately. It would be every man for himself." As he exited the hatchback, he could hear Cipola starting into *Aprite un po' quegli occhi*, the well-loved aria from Mozart's *Le Nozze di Figaro*, known in English as *The Marriage of Figaro*. What a guy! thought Fankhauser. Of all the times to sing opera! Fankhauser stealthily approached the VolksBankBern van. He tried the back door of the vehicle; by some stroke of luck, it had been left unlocked. Three canvas bags were in full sight, and within his reach. He quickly opened one bag. Whammo! There it was. A bag full of cash. But what was amazing was that the cash was not in one denomination only; some notes were in French francs; some in German marks; some in Austrian schillings; and on and on. Just as he was about to close the back door of the van, he heard the voices of the two VolksBankBern men as they were about to exit the building. He dodged them by moving around their van. As soon as they reached the van, they saw the open back door, and realized that someone had accessed the back of the van. Looking around, they saw Cipola sitting there in his canary-yellow Fiat hatchback, singing away to himself. With pistols drawn, they headed for Cipola. Fankhauser made a clean getaway in the opposite direction, heading towards the rear of the *St. Peter's Basilica* complex. It did not make sense for him to go back to Cipola's vehicle at this stage, he reasoned. As he had warned Cipola, it was now 'every man for himself.' Hopefully, Cipola will follow his warning. But if Cipola was apprehended, what's the worst that can happen to him? A fine for loitering? As he distanced himself from Cipola, he suddenly heard a 'pop', as if a pistol had been discharged. While he feared for the worst, he quickly dismissed it from his mind. Surely, they would not shoot Cipola for simply sitting there in his hatchback. Exercising caution for himself, he entered the service entrance of *St. Peter's Basilica*, still wearing his workman coveralls. Once inside, he made his way to the public area, and into a rest room, where he removed his coveralls, which he dumped into a trash can. Now a member of the site-seeing public in the Basilica, he blended into the crowd of visitors, worked his way forward to the front of the Basilica, and finally slipped out into the throng of people gathered in *St.Peter's Square*. From *St.Peter's Square*, he entered Via della Conciliazione, and made a hasty retreat into *Palazzo Cardinal Cesi*. As he sat there in his room at the Palazzo, his overwhelming concern was as to the fate of Giuseppe Cipola. He picked up the phone, and dialed the number of his colleague, Alberto Fettucini.

"Alberto," Fankhauser started, "I am concerned about Cipola?"

"What do you mean, Fank, that you are concerned about Cipola?" Fankhauser then related to Fettucini what had happened at the Vatican; that he, Fankhauser, had to make a quick getaway; and that, while he was making a break for it, he heard a 'pop', like the sound of a pistol having been discharged.

"Does not sound good, Fank. Sounds to me that they shot Cipola. Hopefully, I am wrong. But you will remember that I warned you that *The Shadow* is a very venomous viper."

"Can you find out, Alberto? Do you have any source at the Vatican Police?"

"Yes; I do. Give me a few minutes. I will get back to you at your hotel room."

While he waited, Fankhauser wondered about Cipola's wife, the girl from "Napoli", whom he had described as "bellisima". And about Cipola's "bambino". And about how he, Fankhauser, had never even had a chance to ask Cipola how old his child was, or whether it was a boy or a girl. If Cipola is dead, how would his wife and child survive? Thoughts of Cipola and his family kept racing through his head. Eventually, the telephone rang. It was Fettucini.

'Fank, I am afraid that the news is bad," Fettucini groaned. Fankhauser had a sinking feeling. "Cipola was shot in the head by the VolksBankBern men. They said that he was trying to rob the VolksBankBern van. He died instantly. When the Police arrived, they found a pistol and a small wad of cash on the passenger seat of Cipola's van."

"Oh, no!" Fankhauser cried out. "Those sons of a bitch! They killed the man for just sitting there in his vehicle. They staged it so that it would look like he had robbed the VolksBankBern van." He was distraught. He could not help but feel that he bore some responsibility for Cipola's early demise.

"Don't let it get to you, Fank. I had warned Cipola that it was a dangerous assignment. He accepted the risks. In our profession, it's all in a day's work." This did not make Fankhauser feel any better. Cipola was an endearing man, in his own way. A lover of classical music. A man with a voice which could have propelled him into the heavens, to be one of the celestial stars. A husband. A father. And now all that his family, his friends, the whole world would have that remained of him were memories.

"I know, Alberto. I have to move on. I will need your assistance for my next steps forward. Give me a couple hours to collect my thoughts. I will call you back shortly." Fankhauser was more than ever convinced that he was on the right path. VolksBankBern was tied in thick with *The Shadow*. *The Shadow* was somehow funneling ill-gotten gains through the Vatican Bank. *The Shadow* was indeed very, very dangerous. In true Machiavellian style, *The Shadow* would stop at nothing whatsoever in order to achieve their goals, as evidenced by the murder of Fred Bruni through ingestion of *'Mon Petit Ami'*, the attempted murder of Lise Brunner by forcing her to ingest *'Mon Petit Ami'*, the foiled attempt to find Isolde Bruni to murder her, and the cold-blooded murder of poor Giuseppe Cipola by a gunshot wound to the head in broad daylight. Cognizant of the very dangerous nature of *The Shadow,* Fankhauser swore that he would bring them to justice, sooner or later, even if it was the last thing he did on earth. But the plans had to be well laid, every step being taken with extreme caution. Sitting there in his room at the Palazzo, he would now prepare to penetrate the inner recesses of the labyrinth of this hideous monster; this Hydra; this huge, multi-headed snake, whose immortal head is ever protected by the other deadly snakes, each snake ready to kill with its poisonous venom. The overriding feature of the monster was that one of its nine heads had regenerative powers. In his mind, Fankhauser went through the various scenarios he could undertake. After intense concentration for about an hour, he picked up the telephone and called Fettucini.

"Alberto," he said, "I have devised a plan to trap the beast. You are a necessary part of my plan. You will recall telling me that Agimo dines at *Ristorante dei Santi* over on Via de Porta Cavallegeri every Thursday evening. Are you available for Thursday evening at about ten?"

"Yes, Fank. I am free for ten. How long would you need me for?"

"Possibly about four or five hours."

"I will be at your service, Fank. Please tell me more."

At this, Fankhauser described in detail, step by step, the plan that he had devised to entrap the dangerous hitman, Bernardo Agimo, now masquerading as a respectable citizen of Rome. He stressed to Fettucini the importance of following to a tee every aspect of the plan, and the critical requirement of punctuality. If one small detail of the scheme was not adhered to, it could easily become a matter of life or death, for either Fankhauser, or Fettucini, or both. There was absolutely no room for error. "Remember what happened to Giuseppe Cipola" were the last words that Fankhauser spoke to Fettucini before they hung up.

CHAPTER EIGHTEEN

ON THURSDAY MORNING, back in the Old City of Bern, Renée Fankhauser was doing her darndest to keep the two 'animals' in the *Fankhaus* from going at each other's throat. While Isolde realized that what Fankhauser had done in bringing Lise into the *Fankhaus* was in her, Isolde's, best interests, nevertheless, as a woman governed largely by her emotions, she could not dispel the thought from her mind that Lise had not only had an affair with her husband, but had in fact murdered him. At the same time, Lise, while realizing that she had been brought to the *Fankhaus* for her own safety, felt not only that she was an animal in captivity, having lost the freedom that she had so highly valued, but also that there was another animal in the *Fankhaus* who, at the drop of a button, would most likely rip her heart from her breast, and, to add insult to injury, eat it raw, blood and all. In this scenario, Renée inwardly complimented herself on having kept peace in the *Fankhaus*, at least for the past few days. If only she knew when Joaquim would be returning home; but, with the telephone having been disconnected, she was completely incommunicado.

In her usual kind and efficient manner, Renée was busy in the kitchen whipping up some pancakes and fried eggs for breakfast. There was a knock on the front door. Renée looked at the clock. It was only nine-fifteen. Far too early for an unannounced visitor, she thought. Besides, why had the visitor not buzzed her on the security system intercom at the front entrance of the building? She smelled a rat. She looked at Isolde and Lise, who were both sitting at the dining table, Isolde with a cup of coffee and Lise with a cup of hot chocolate. Instinctively, Isolde and Lise looked back at Renée. They all sniffed trouble. Renée put her right index finger over her lips, as if to say "Shh". They all remained absolutely still and quiet, while the knocking continued. After about ten minutes of non-stop knocking, it finally ended.

"Something stinks to high heaven!" exclaimed Renée as she left the kitchen and headed for her bedroom, where she grabbed the keys to her son's office and his desk drawers. Without losing any time, she retrieved the Glock G43x from the desk drawer, and placed it in the pocket of her housecoat.

"The vermin will be back," she told Isolde and Lise, not mentioning the weapon that she now had on her person. "Remain where you are. Nobody is to answer the door. Nobody is to open the door, under any circumstance." No doubt as to who was in charge of the *Fankhaus*. After all, this is what Fankhausers are trained to do, and she was a 'Fankhauser'; albeit not by birth, but by association. It is a trait that runs in the blood of the Fankhausers, a natural disposition evolved over many centuries. Darwin would have had a field day in a study of the evolution of this phenomenal characteristic of the Fankhausers. Renée returned to her common household chore of making pancakes and frying eggs, as if nothing had happened. She had to feed the animals in the *Fankhaus*; that is part of the duties of a Fankhauser.

Everything remained unremarkable for about an hour. And then it happened. Suddenly, the fire alarm system for the whole building went off. Once again, all three women, seated at the dining table, looked at one another. Isolde and Lise were seeking guidance from Renée as to what to do now. "Remain where you are!" Renée ordered. "The vermin is back." From the apartment, they could hear the voices and footsteps of other occupants as they exited the floor, heading for the safety of the street. After about five minutes, there was heavy knocking on the front door to the apartment. Once again, Renée signaled to Isolde and Lise to remain quiet; and then she quietly crossed the floor, and took up a position immediately behind the door, which, for someone entering, normally opened from left to right. A male voice at the door kept shouting in German: "Das Gebäude brennt! Raus jetzt!' and then in English: *The building is on fire! Get out now!* No-one moved in the *Fankhaus*. And then, utterly unexpectedly, there were two shots fired from the hallway into the door-lock, and a man rushed in, his Luger pistol pointed at Lise and Isolde, who were both still seated at the dining table. This is when Renée acted without hesitation. She pulled the trigger of her Glock G43x semi-automatic, firing three shots, each bullet, in rapid succession, into the back of this vicious intruder. The man fell face-down on the floor, his Luger beside him. Renée, unperturbed, checked for a pulse. The man was dead. She returned her Glock G43x to the pocket of her housecoat. She then grabbed the corpse by its arms, pulled it wholly into the apartment, and shut the door, the lock of which was now shattered. As Isolde and Lise, both petrified, watched all this horror unfold before their eyes, their jaws dropped. They were not only stunned that Renée had a pistol, but, even more so, that she had the gumption to use it. This woman was a true Fankhauser.

The fire alarm was no longer ringing. The occupants were returning to their apartments. After all that, it was only a false alarm. Some of the residents could be heard saying that someone had obviously played a childish prank, by activating the fire alarm. One woman, as she was passing the front door of the Fankhauser apartment, noticed the damage to the door-lock, and called out to Renée, asking if everything was OK in there; to which Renée shouted back that there had been a small mishap with the door-lock, but everything was fine. By now, both Isolde and Lise were standing beside Renée, all three looking down at the corpse of the intruder, which was oozing blood all over the parquet floor. One thing immediately struck Isolde's eyes; they were drawn as if by a magnet to the gold ring that was on the dead man's right middle finger. She had seen that ring, or one like it, before. It bore the emblem of the three intersecting crescents. It was the emblem of *The Shadow*. The same emblem she had seen on Rapini's gold lapel pin. The same emblem on the beautiful gold ring on Lisc's finger, with its crown of black onyx inlaid with the three intersecting crescents. Instinctively, Isolde looked down to see if Lise was still wearing the ring, the sign of *The Shadow*. The ring was still there on Lise's finger. Isolde thought it best not to draw anyone's attention to the ring on the dead man's finger. She went to her room, and returned with her camera. She took some pictures of the corpse, being sure to get some clear shots of the gold ring bearing the emblem of the three intersecting crescents. There was a slight rebuke from Renée for doing this. "No time for picture-taking, Isolde. We have some clean-up work to do."

"Are we not going to call the police?" Lise asked.

"For the time being, I prefer to have Joaquim make that decision. He should be back by Friday. In the meantime, we have to wrap and 'store' the body; and clean up this messy floor." With that, she fetched a scatter rug from her bedroom, and, with help from the other two women, rolled the corpse into the rug. All three women then carried the corpse, wrapped in the rug, and deposited it under the window in the guest bedroom. "There," remarked Renée, with a cackle, "I now have three guests in the *Fankhaus*. We should put up a sign **AUSGEBUCHT DAS FANKHAUS IST VOLL**. This means in English NO VACANCY. THE FANKHAUS IS FULL." She offered this small taste of humour in an effort to thaw the ice-sheet of tension in the apartment. She then got a pail, filled it with water mixed with bleach, and returned to the locus delicti with the pail and a mop. All three women then took turns at swabbing the floor, until not a single drop of blood could be seen. Renée placed a chair behind the door-knob of the front door, hoping that it would help to forestall the entry of any other intruder.

When it was all over, Renée poured some Pinot Noir for all three of them. As she took her first sip, Isolde said: "Let's all say a prayer for Joaquim's early return from Rome." "Ditto", said Renée. "Ditto," echoed Lise. They drank away the time, as if nothing had happened. But deep down, they were all terrified. Renée kept her Glock G43x in the pocket of her housecoat. After all, she could not be sure that the full stream of unwanted intruders had run its course. Only time will tell.

CHAPTER NINETEEN

THURSDAY EVENING found Fankhauser priming himself for his grand appearance at *Ristorante dei Santi* on Via de Porta Cavallegeri, not far from the Palazzo. Over and over, he reviewed in his mind the plan that he had engendered to snare the notorious hitman, Bernardo Agimo, whom he viewed as his gateway to *The Shadow*. His performance had to be fool-proof. He could not afford a single error. He dressed meticulously in his rented black tuxedo. From what he had learned from his colleague Fettucini, *Ristorante dei Santi* was a high-class restaurant, a fine dining establishment frequented by cardinals from the Vatican and political and religious envoys from all over the world. He had to look his best in order to fit in. Nothing should be permitted to reveal Fankhauser's true identity to Agimo, until Fankhauser decided to do so. Any failure could mean instant death.

As he straightened his black bowtie, he glanced at his watch. It was now seven-thirty. From what Fettucini had reported, Agimo and his cohorts would likely be at the restaurant at about eight. Fankhauser had previously scouted the joint. There was only one table large enough to accommodate ten diners. That had to be Agimo's table. He booked a table for two as close as possible to Agimo's table. The last thing he did before he left his room was to pack his revolver, the old reliable Russian Nagant M1895, which he buried in his waist.

When he entered the hotel lobby, his date was already there, waiting serenely for his arrival. It was not hard to spot her. She was a striking strawberry blonde, perhaps about twenty-five, with hazel eyes that now and again revealed traces of blue, at other times traces of green, all depending on the type and angle of the light that hit them. Her body was the perfect specimen, with its well-defined protruding breasts and exquisitely shaped buttocks, both accentuated by a slender waist and long legs. The type of beauty that turns heads whenever she enters a room. Fankhauser had rented her for the evening from a high-class Rome escort service known as *Le Migliori Donne*. He chuckled as he recalled his conversation with the 'booking agent'. Fankhauser had told him that at the prices they charged the rental had better be A-one in order to live up to the agency's name, in English, *The Best Women*. In response, the agent swore that "la merce è la migliore", meaning "*the merchandise is the very best*"; that he would personally guarantee that the 'rental' would meet with Fankhauser's satisfaction; and that, if for any reason Fankhauser was dissatisfied, a full refund would be made, no questions asked. As he approached the young lady, he could not help but think "no refund will be necessary". From first sight, she seemed to fit the bill completely. She rose from her chair to greet him, wearing a bewitching smile and laughing eyes that completely captivated their subject.

"Good evening, sir," she purred, in perfect English. This had been one of his specifications. The 'rental' must speak perfect English.

"Good evening, Paola. Call me Joaquim. It is my pleasure to meet you. Shall we go? We have a table at *Ristorante dei Santi*."

"The pleasure is mine, Joaquim. I can see you like nothing but the best," she said, complimentarily. That could be an excellent triple entendre, Fankhauser thought to himself. Yes; good taste in hotels; good taste in restaurants; and, above all, good taste in women, with her being the perfect example. The woman is smart. A good start for an evening of intrigue. She slipped her left hand under his right arm, and they stepped out onto Via della Conciliazione, where they could easily have been mistaken for husband and wife, or a man and his fiancée.

They arrived at *Ristorante dei Santi* after a short walk. It was now eight-o-five. The maître d' welcomed them as if they were celebrities, and escorted them to their table, set for a party of two. Fankhauser sat where he could have a full view of the large round table reserved for Agimo. He tipped the maître d' handsomely. There was no-one seated at Agimo's table. Fankhauser ordered a bottle of Franciacorta. "I just adore Franciacorta," Paola remarked, thereby revealing that she was accustomed to *la dolce vita*. As they sipped their wine and waited,

Fankhauser engaged Paola in chit chat. "Who is Paola?" he asked. She explained that she was born in the small, walled medieval Tuscan town of San Gimignano, located about one hundred and seventeen kms. from Bologna. She was a graduate student at *Università di Bologna*, where she was pursuing her Master's degree in Psychology. She worked for *Le Migliori Donne* because she needed the money, in order to achieve her goals. And so, she had organized her schedule so that she would have every Thursday afternoon and Friday free of classes, permitting her to travel by train from Bologna to Rome on Thursday afternoon, ply her trade in the large metropolis of Rome for three nights, and return by train to Bologna on Sunday afternoon. The amount of money that she would earn at some pedestrian job, such as waiting on tables in some busy restaurant, or cataloguing books in some dull library, paled in comparison to the huge amount that she rolled in through the escort service. "In a way, I guess, that makes me Machiavellian in my outlook," she confessed. "But, at the same time, you must admit, very enterprising," she remarked, with a wink and a sense of deep pride. He looked at his watch. It was now eight-fifteen. Agimo and his group were nowhere in sight. Fankhauser took a few minutes to brief Paola on some 'do's and don'ts' for the evening.

"Now, Paola, I would like you to listen very carefully. First rule: You must speak in English only. As far as people in this restaurant are concerned, you and I do not speak Italian. Second rule: Apart from ordering food through the waiter, you are to speak with no-one in the restaurant, except me, of course. If anyone tries to engage you in conversation, you must just simply smile and never answer. Third rule: When I say it's time to leave, you must follow me immediately. And the fourth and final rule: Once we are outside, we will part ways. I will walk to the right towards Via di Madonna, the narrow side street to the right of the restaurant. You will walk quickly to the left until you are about fifty feet from *Ristorante dei Santi,* and then hail a cab. Your services will then no longer be required." He slipped a gratuity of USD100 into her hand. "Do you understand those instructions?' he asked. "Yes, I do," she replied, very happy to be receiving the gratuity before her services were even completed.

At about eight-thirty, there was some sort of commotion at the Reception Desk at *Ristorante dei Santi*. A small crowd of patrons had made their entry. It is not an understatement to say that they did not enter quietly. They were talking in Italian, at the top of their voices, as if they owned the establishment. Without even looking to see who these patrons were, Fankhauser opined to himself: "Agimo is here." Sure enough, a group of about eight, led by no other than Bernardo Agimo himself, were escorted to Agimo's table. The first thing that Agimo did after he was seated was to survey his surroundings. It was as if he had to be aware of who else was in the restaurant, and what they were doing. Fankhauser watched discreetly as Agimo's eyes eventually centred on him, which caused Fankhauser to look away. Fankhauser got the uncanny feeling that Agimo was aware of who Fankhauser was. You know, that scintilla of recognition that causes one to do a double-take. Strange, thought Fankhauser; he had seen Agimo back in Bern, entering and leaving Lise's apartment building. In fact, he had photographs of Agimo. But how in the world could Agimo ever have recognized the stranger by the name of Fankhauser sitting opposite him? This bothered Fankhauser. He had made every effort to cover his tracks in his quest for the dangerous Agimo. His mind was now working at full speed. His colleague Fettucini knew that he, Fankhauser, was in Rome, and was in hot pursuit of Agimo. But he trusted Fettucini. Fettucini would never let him down. His friend, Simon Hartmann, at the Bern Police Department, knew that he was in Rome. But Simon did not know that Fankhauser was chasing Agimo. Besides, Simon was his friend of many years. The occupants of the *Fankhaus* knew that he, Fankhauser, was in Rome. But, except for Isolde, they did not know what the nature of his business was in Rome. There was absolutely no doubt that he could trust his mother and Isolde. And as for Lise, she was incommunicado in the *Fankhaus*, where she was a guest, not only for her own safety, but as a person in captivity. Don't be paranoid, Fankhauser, he thought to himself. Let's get back to the business at hand.

When the waiter came to his table to take the orders for meals, he made a point of asking the waiter at the top of his voice to translate into English the Italian items on the menu. In other words, he was disguising the fact that both he and Paola understood Italian. Throughout dinner, Fankhauser was eavesdropping on the conversations at the Agimo table. He found that Agimo was suspiciously quiet, and did not join in the animated discussions that permeated that table. From what Fankhauser was able to garner, the dinner was a weekly event to celebrate the successes of the past week, and to briefly review the events over that time period. Wine flowed freely, and tongues were naturally loosened, as time drifted on. One topic of conversation was the shooting at the Vatican. They celebrated the death of poor Giuseppe Cipola as a victory. It was evidence of the invincibility of *The Shadow,* and their position of power. In other words, no-one, absolutely no-one, messes with *The Shadow,* which they referred to as *l'Ombra.* Fankhauser could not keep count of the number of times he heard the mention of *l'Ombra.* Another topic of conversation centred on *le spedizioni,* or 'the shipments'. Did *'la spedizione'* from Croatia arrive? How about the one from the Ukraine? And the one from Bangkok? And from Baghdad? It was clear that shipments were being received from numerous countries. And, two or three times, there actually was mention of *'riciclaggio di denaro'.* That was really bold, thought Fankhauser. They actually 'called a spade a spade'. They actually used the term 'money laundering' to describe their activity. Buried deep in the pants pocket of Fankhauser's tuxedo was his trusted friend, a small cassette recorder, recording every word that was spoken at the Agimo table, for whatever it was worth.

By about ten, the meals had been fully consumed, not only at Fankhauser's table, but also at the table of *The Shadow.* It was now time for wine, mirth, and frivolity. The waiter brought bottles of expensive wine to both tables, "Cortesia della Direzione". *Courtesy of the Management.* Agimo got up and left the dining room, presumably for the rest room. Within five minutes, he was headed back to his table, but took a route directly by Fankhauser's table. He stopped beside Paola, looked her over admiringly, and said: "Buona serata, signorina. Da che parte d'Italia vieni?" Both Paola and Fankhauser understood fully well what he had said. *Good evening, miss. What part of Italy are you from?* But Paola remembered the first rule that Fankhauser had established. Speak English only. "I'm sorry; but I do not speak Italian," she replied, demurely. "I'm sorry, too," remarked Agimo. "You look like a beautiful woman I used to know in Tuscany." He then looked at Fankhauser, nodded, and went back to his table. So, concluded Fankhauser, the hunted is about to hunt the hunter. Agimo, the hunted, was trying to get some insight into Fankhauser, the hunter. Fankhauser was aware that it is not difficult for roles to be reversed, where Agimo becomes the hunter and Fankhauser the hunted.

At about ten-forty-five, Fankhauser looked at his watch. Time to get into action. He motioned to Paola that they should now leave. If he played his cards right, Agimo would follow him. This is what Fankhauser wanted. He took his time in paying the bill, as he thanked the waiter for the excellent service. He got up, assisted Paola from her chair, and, arm in arm, they headed toward the coat room at the Reception Desk. He was aware of Agimo's eyes following every move that he made. As he and Paola stepped out onto Via de Porta Cavallegeri, he released Paola from his grasp, and veered her in the direction to the left. Slowly, as if waiting for someone, he took a few steps to the right. As he heard the front door of the restaurant open, he moved more quickly away from the bright lights of Via de Porta Cavallegeri towards the darkness of Via di Madonna. He was now enshrouded in the blackness of the abandoned side street, where he walked slowly, as if enjoying the fresh air. The die was cast. In his efforts to ensnare the dangerous Agimo, he had crossed the Rubicon. No turning back now. He heard footsteps behind him. If his hunch was right, it was Agimo following him, with only one purpose in mind; to dispatch his soul to the dark unknowns of purgatory. The footsteps got louder and louder, until his pursuer was right upon him. Fankhauser could suddenly feel the muzzle of a pistol in his back. No sooner had this happened than another player entered the game. It was Fettucini. He himself was upon Agimo, a pistol in Agimo's back. 'Lasciarlo cadere!', Fettucini ordered. *Drop it!* "O muori." *Or die.* Fankhauser breathed a sigh of relief, as he heard Fettucini's voice. Faced with a choice of life or death, Agimo chose life. He let his Luger fall to the pavement. Fankhauser picked up Agimo's pistol, and pointed it at Agimo's head. Agimo was now a captured animal. Fettucini's pistol was in his back, his own Luger at his head. In true style of the ancient tradition of the Fankhauser family, all that they needed now was a 'Fankhaus', to hold the captured animal in captivity. Within a few minutes, an olive-green Mercedes-Benz car pulled up behind them. Fettucini and Fankhauser forced the trapped Agimo into the back seat, Fettucini on one side and Fankhauser on the other. Fettucini gagged Agimo, and affixed a blindfold over his eyes. "Andiamo, Giovanni," Fettucini ordered. *Let's go, Giovanni.* The car sped off toward its secret destination. So far, so good, thought Fankhauser. It was working exactly as he had planned. He now had within the palms of his hands a member, if not the king-pin, of the *'Ombra Segreta della Forza di Firenze'*, the mysterious and extremely dangerous organization known in English as *The Shadow.*

CHAPTER TWENTY

GIOVANNI knew exactly where to go. Crossing the River Tiber by way of Ponte Cavour, he headed easterly on Via Tomacelli, and then northerly on Via del Corso. He pulled into a nondescript, old, narrow building on an unnamed alley that emanated from Via del Corso. Considering its Lilliputian size, it was difficult to fathom the raison d'être of the odd-looking building. Perhaps, thought Fankhauser, the purpose that its builders had in mind when it was constructed, likely over a century ago, was that for which it was going to be used tonight. If not, then the only reasonable conclusion was that it was someone's folly; a structure constructed simply because the owner of the land decided to put a building there. Once the Mercedes-Benz entered, the door of the small building was shut tight and locked, leaving hardly any room for movement outside the vehicle. Just a few feet ahead, a solitary light bulb hung from the ceiling. Beneath the light bulb was an old wooden chair, the arms of which had been removed. A perfect interrogation room, thought Fankhauser. With difficulty, Fettucini squeezed the portly Agimo into the narrow space between the car and the wall, like someone forcing an elephant into a small cage.

Fettucini sat Agimo down on the chair, the light from the single bulb highlighting his balding head. Giovanni fetched from the trunk of the Mercedes-Benz some pieces of twine, a roll of duct-tape, a video camera, a recording machine, and a closed steel box. The closed steel box was Giovanni's 'instrument of torture', affectionately referred to by him as *lo shock delle palle*, or *the balls-shocker.* The feet and hands of the captured Agimo were quickly tied to the chair. The blindfold was removed from his eyes, which quickly darted from face to face to face, as he studied all three of his captors. He was undoubtedly marking the faces well, for a day of vengeance yet to come. His nostrils quivered, as he snorted like an angry bull, and his breathing became rapid and heavy. This is not how he had planned it while at *Ristorante dei Santi*. Back there, it all seemed like a cinch to him. He would stealthily follow Fankhauser as he left the restaurant, and, if the opportunity presented itself, would quickly dispatch Fankhauser's spirit from his body in some dark alley off Via de Porta Cavallegeri. But he had underestimated Fankhauser. Little had he thought that Fankhauser had simply set himself up as a honey pot, a bait for none other than Agimo himself. Instead of Agimo being the hunter, he was now like a beaten bear whose paw was trapped in the powerful grip of a snare, from which there was no escape. Now, he was about to undergo an intense interrogation by Fankhauser and company. Standing about a foot or two from his captive, Fankhauser looked him squarely in the eyes. At the hands of Fettucini, the video camera and the recording machine were now running. Giovanni, wearing a broad smile, had Agimo's Luger point-blank at Agimo's head.

"You are Bernardo Agimo?" Fankhauser demanded, although he had no doubt as to who his captive was.

"Vai all'inferno!" came the defiant retort. *Go to hell!*

Fankhauser laughed, sarcastically, and said: "You, my friend, may be in hell before you know it, if you do not answer my questions. Are you a member of the organization known as *'Ombra Segreta della Forza di Firenze'*, more commonly known as *The Shadow*?"

"Vai all'inferno!" Agimo sneered. As Fankhauser looked Agimo over, his eagle eyes centred on the gold ring that adorned Agimo's right index finger. It bore the emblem of the three intersecting crescents. Yes. No doubt about it. Agimo was a member of *The Shadow*. But Fankhauser wanted it from Agimo's own mouth.

"OK, Signor Agimo. If that's the way you wish to play the game, let's play it your way." He nodded at Giovanni. Giovanni handed Agimo's Luger to Fankhauser. He then unbuckled the belt of Agimo's trousers, and pulled down both his trousers and underwear below his knees. Agimo's eyes were darting about wildly. What the hell was going on? Giovanni then pulled the ends of two electric cords from his metal box, his *balls-shocker*. One end of one cord he attached to Agimo's testicles. One end of the other electric cord he plugged into a wall receptacle. The other end of each cord was buried within the metal box. Agimo was now petrified. He could guess as to what was about to happen to him. Sweat ran down his podgy face. Without another word being spoken by anyone, Giovanni lifted the lid of the metal box, and pressed a button. Agimo let out a hellish scream, as a sudden surge of electricity ran through his testicles.

"Now, do you want us to do that again?" inquired the deadly serious Fankhauser. "You know, after three of those shocks, you may as well bid farewell to your sex life. Your sexual organs will be so permanently damaged that both your wife and your mistress will be saying 'Ciao, ciao, uccellino!' as they leave you for virile studs. *Bye, bye, birdie!*" Agimo remained defiant. Giovanni released another surge of electricity. Again, the piercing scream. Agimo nodded his head. He was now willing to talk. Fankhauser repeated the two questions that Agimo had refused to answer. To each question, he now responded with a flaccid "Yes".

"OK, Bernardo. We are on the right track. But I warn you. If you lie to me just once, I have a special procedure for you that will make you wish you had never been born. You will curse your own mother for having brought you into this world. Do you understand me?" Agimo looked ahead with a vacant stare. "I will take that as a 'yes'," Fankhauser scoffed.

"Did you know Fred Bruni?" Fankhauser asked.

"Yes"

"Do you know that he is dead?'

"Yes."

"Do you know Lise Brunner?"

"Yes."

"Do you know Constantino Rapini?"

"Yes."

"Do you know how Fred Bruni died?" Agimo simply looked up at the ceiling. He gave no response. Fankhauser repeated the question. Still no response.

"OK, Bernardo. I do not have all night to play your silly game. I am going to ratchet up the stakes. We are going to picture this garage as a casino

as a casino. The game will be roulette. Russian roulette, to be precise." He pulled out his Russian Nagant revolver from his waist. It had seven chambers. He emptied six chambers of bullets, leaving only a single round, inside one chamber. He instructed Giovanni to untie the cord that bound Agimo's right hand. "Every time that you refuse to answer my question, or that you give me the wrong answer, Giovanni here is going to place the muzzle of my revolver within your mouth, and you yourself are going to pull the trigger. But I am going to increase the odds for you, my dear Bernardo. I am going to re-spin the cylinder after each trigger pull. This means that, instead of your odds diminishing, they will remain constant at a one in seven chance that you will blow your brains out. That's far more than you allowed Fred Bruni. So, the game is on. Do you know how Fred Bruni died?" Still, Agimo did not respond, although he had worked himself into a state of severe agitation, and sweat was washing his whole body. "Do your thing, Giovanni," Fankhauser instructed. Giovanni untied Agimo's right hand. Then he took the revolver from Fankhauser, and placed the grip carefully within the palm of Agimo's right hand. He twisted the hand around so that the muzzle was inserted within Agimo's mouth. He put Agimo's right index finger on the trigger. He cocked the hammer partially. And then, as the final blow, he pressed Agimo's right index finger harder against the trigger, until the hammer came down abruptly against the chamber that was aligned with it. The hammer hit the chamber with a thud. Agimo was lucky, this time. It was an empty chamber. Agimo was now frozen with fear. He had by now expelled enough sweat to cause the River Tiber to overflow its banks.

"As you can see, Bernardo. I am very serious. This is a deadly game. The only person that can lose is you. I ask you again: How did Fred Bruni die?"

"By poisoning," Agimo admitted in desperation. He was now as soaking wet as a pig that had just rolled around in its sty after a heavy rainfall.

"Good answer. What was the name of the poison?"

"It's known as *'Mon Petit Ami'*."

"Who administered *'Mon Petit Ami'*?"

"Lise Brunner."

"Why did *The Shadow* want Fred Bruni dead?"

"He was asking too many questions."

"Too many questions about what?"

"Too many questions about *'Ombra Segreta della Forza di Firenze'*."

"Has *The Shadow* been involved in illegal activities?" At this question, a look of sheer panic crept over Agimo's face.

"Yes."

"What sort of illegal activities?"

"Drug trafficking, prostitution, human trafficking; you name it."

"And money laundering?"

"Yes."

"Is that money laundering operation through VolksBankBern, for example?"

"Yes."

"Is the Vatican involved?"

"Unwittingly."

"What do you mean "unwittingly"?"

"We planted a man on the inside that launders for us."

"Are you confirming that the cardinals and their administrative staff are clean?"

"Yes. Our whole operation depends on our undercover man. He works alone behind the scenes."

"Did you make an attempt on Lise Brunner's life?"

"Yes. It was not an attempt. By now, she is dead."

"You would not know this, but she was rushed to the hospital and survived."

"I know that she survived the poison. But she should by now be dead." This response floored Fankhauser. How could Agimo possibly know that Lise Brunner survived? Apart from Isolde and Renée, the only other person that knew was his friend, Inspector Simon Hartmann. And what does he mean by the words "But she should by now be dead"?

"How did you learn that Lise Brunner had survived the poison?"

"I have my sources." At this refusal to answer, Fankhauser signaled to Giovanni to proceed with the next spin of the roulette wheel, the magical cylinder of his Russian Nagant revolver. But before Giovanni could get moving, Agimo hollered a response. "Inspector Simon Hartmann of the Bern Police." This floored Fankhauser. His friend Simon had betrayed him?

"What do you mean that "she should by now be dead"?" For the first time, Agimo smiled, a smile which was more of a smirk indicative of the dark evil that lurked in the inners of this man.

"While you are away in Rome, Simon was to finish the job. He was to enter your apartment in Bern and kill everyone in sight. Lise Brunner, Isolde Bruni, and your mother." It was as if Agimo had plunged a sharp blade into Fankhauser's chest. The feeling that overcame Fankhauser was, to say the least, devastating. It was a sensation of utter helplessness. Here he was in Rome, over three hundred and forty kms. from Bern, chasing down Agimo. Meanwhile, back in Bern, the *Fankhaus* was to be, or possibly has been, invaded by his very own friend Simon Hartmann, a wolf dressed in sheep's clothing, with the intention of killing all inhabitants of the *Fankhaus*, every man Jack, including his, Fankhauser's, own mother. And he could not even phone home, as the *Fankhaus* was completely incommunicado, the telephone having been disconnected by his own decision. The tables are turned, he thought. He was now the one that was terrified. He could not help but feel that, with this one statement, Agimo had wholly disabled him. And he could not even phone the Bern Police to have them check on the welfare of the inhabitants of the *Fankhaus* . If he could not trust his own friend, Inspector Simon Hartmann of the Bern Police, then who in this world could he trust? He certainly could not trust anyone at the Police Department, of which Hartmann was a senior officer. The only solution was to get back to Bern, post haste. The brutal words of Bernardo Agimo had their desired effect. They took Fankhauser's mind away from his interrogation of Agimo. Fankhauser now wanted to leave Rome and head back to Bern as soon as possible. Agimo fiendishly studied the change in Fankhauser's demeanour, as he watched beads of sweat now trickle down Fankhauser's face. He had taken his captor by surprise, and succeeded in dulling the incisive interrogation that Fankhauser had so shrewdly planned. He now wore a diabolic smirk, satisfied with how he had sidewinded Fankhauser. Fankhauser had to think fast. He already had video and voice recordings of Agimo with certain damning admissions. The admissions fell short of what he had intended. But at least they were incriminating. Of course, in a court of law, Agimo 's lawyers would likely seek to throw that evidence out on the basis that the admissions were not given voluntarily. The only solution, Fankhauser reasoned, was to turn Agimo and the recorded evidence over to the proper authorities, and have them pick up where Fankhauser had left off. The authorities would then interrogate Agimo intensely, and thereby themselves obtain admissions that could survive the tests for admission of evidence in court. Leaving Giovanni to guard the captive Agimo, Fankhauser beckoned to Fettucini to step outside with him for a few minutes.

"You heard what he said, Alberto? That inspector Simon Hartmann of the Bern Police, a man in whom I had placed my complete trust, is in fact a member of *The Shadow*? And that Hartmann has been instructed to eliminate Lise Brunner, Isolde Bruni, and my mother?"

"I heard it all, Fank. You need to get back to Bern ASAP."

"My feeling precisely. Here is what I think. I am going to fly back to Bern as soon as I get out of here. I am leaving you in charge. You should make sure that the videotape and voice recordings contain no hint of any acts of torture. In other words, delete anything that could give clues that we have utilized what Giovanni referred to endearingly as *lo shock delle palle*; and that we engaged Agimo in my deadly game of Russian roulette. Make eight copies of the abridged videotape and the abridged voice recording. Hold Agimo here until daybreak. Do you have any trustworthy high-ranking contact at the *Guardia di Finanza*, the Italian Financial Police?"

"Yes. I know Colonel Antonio Caruso very well. As a matter of fact, he was the best man at my wedding."

"And at the *Carabinieri*?"

"Yes; Inspector Sergio Grasso. We have a very good rapport."

"And at the *Polizia di Stato*, the Italian State Police?"

"Yes. I know Pietro Lombardi, who has been there for many years."

"Excellent. At the break of dawn, I want you and Giovanni to deliver Agimo, copies of the abridged videotape, and copies of the abridged voice recording into the hands of all three. The *Guardia di Finanza* will be very interested because of the money laundering aspect. The *Polizia di Stato*, because of the organized crime aspect. And the *Carabinieri*, because of the attempt made by Agimo in Rome to take my life. My guess is that, on the basis of the videotape and the voice recording, they will ensure that Agimo is held in custody. Before I fly out of Rome, I will telephone my contact, Stefano Conglari, at *INTERPOL*, and fill him in. Because of the transnational nature of the crimes of *The Shadow*, *INTERPOL* will be most interested. I would not be surprised to learn that they already have an open file on *The Shadow*, including one on Agimo personally. I will have them contact you for copies of the videotape and the voice recording. And one more thing: Send me by same day courier four copies of each of the videotape and the voice recording. Is that all clear, Alberto?"

"Yes, Fank. I will do the best I can. I sincerely hope that your mother is OK. Not to mention Isolde Bruni and Lise Brunner."

"Only time will tell, my dear Alberto. I cannot be back in Bern soon enough. I will be in touch with you as soon as I can. Thanks for the yeoman work that you are doing on this case. I will ensure that you and Giovanni are well compensated."

"How will you get back to the Palazzo?"

"I will walk from here to Via del Corso. It's a main thoroughfare. I will hail down a taxi-cab there."

Fankhauser and Fettucini re-entered the building. Agimo, with a knowing smirk still on his face, looked at Fankhauser. It was a look of evil satisfaction. With one short statement, he had completely curtailed the aggressive interrogation that Fankhauser had been engaged in, and had almost completely decimated Fankhauser emotionally. Fankhauser got the feeling that Agimo was saying to him "Don't mess with me. I am the wrong man to cross." Fankhauser retrieved his Russian Nagant revolver from Giovanni. In a fit of anger, Fankhauser spun the chambers and pointed the muzzle point-blank at the head of Agimo, who immediately closed his eyes, and uttered the words "Ave, Maria, piena di grazia, abbi pietà dell'anima mia." *Hail, Mary, full of grace, have mercy on my soul.* Agimo could have sworn it was going to be his last words on earth. Fankhauser pulled the trigger. Fortunately, for Agimo, and also for Fankhauser, the hammer came down on an empty chamber. But Agimo had got the message. Fankhauser had just responded "Don't mess with me either." Fankhauser loaded six more bullets in the seven-round cylinder, and returned his revolver to his waist.

Shaking hands with Fettucini and Giovanni, he disappeared despondently into the desolate darkness of the nameless alley, and was soon standing on Via del Corsi, where he waved down a taxi-cab. *"Palazzo Carxinal Cesi!* E calpestalo!" he ordered the driver. *Palazzo Cardinal Cesi! And step on it!* As the taxi-cab sped along at breakneck speed, Fankhauser kept mumbling to himself "Oh, God. Please let them be alive."

CHAPTER TWENTY-ONE

AS SOON AS he returned to his room at the Palazzo, Fankhauser picked up his telephone and dialed the home number of his friend, Stefano Conglari, a police official at the *INTERPOL National Central Bureau* in Italy.

"Ciao. Chi sta chiamando a quest'ora empia della notte?" *Hello. Who is calling at this ungodly time of night?* It was Conglari. It was obvious that he was not the least bit amused that his sleep had been disturbed.

"Hi, Stefan. This is Joaquim Fankhauser from Bern."

"What's the problem, Joaquim. Can't you sleep? Are you calling from Bern?"

"No. I am in Rome. But only for another couple of hours. I am flying back to Bern shortly. Got to get back ASAP because of an emergency. No time to fill you in on details now. I will do so later. Have you ever heard of an organization called *'Ombra Segreta della Forza di Firenze'*?"

"I sure have. That's the one known as *The Shadow*?"

"Yes. They have a king-pin by the name of Bernardo Agimo. Have you heard of him?"

"Can't say that I have. But we do have a file on *The Shadow*. A rather thick file, as a matter of fact."

"I am working on a case with my colleague, Alberto Fettucini. Agimo was about to shoot me in a dark alley off Via de Porta Cavallegeri. Fettucini saved my life. We whisked Agimo off to an unknown destination, where I interrogated him. It's all on videotape and voice recording. He made admissions of the involvement of *The Shadow* in transnational crimes. Drug trafficking; human trafficking; prostitution; you name it. I got involved in this case because of the death of a Toronto lawyer. Agimo admitted that *The Shadow* was responsible for the death. It was pure murder. They used a secret poison. I have the woman who administered the poison."

"Wow!" exclaimed Conglari. "You have been a real busy-body, Joaquim. You have sure perked my interest."

"Fettucini will be delivering Agimo into the custody of the *Giuardia di Finanza*, the *Polizia di Stato*, and the *Carabinieri* at the break of dawn. You should contact Fettucini. He will get copies of the videotape and the voice recording into your hands. You should also contact my friend Colonel Antonio Caruso at the *Guardia di Finanza*. Once he meets with Fettucini, he can make sure that you are in the loop of investigators. Sorry I can't stay to take part. But *The Shadow* has ordered the murder of some individuals back in Bern, including my own mother."

"Gesù santo!" Conglari swore. *Holy Jesus!* "They are much more dangerous than I had ever imagined."

"You just would not believe how dangerous they are, Stefano. You've heard of the mythical monster known as the Hydra? Well, *The Shadow* is the real-life version of the Hydra."

"Well, that's what *INTERPOL* is here for. To trap international monsters for the individual states to prosecute. I really pray that your mother is fine, Joaquim."

"Thanks, Stefano. Will be in touch later."

"You are welcome, my friend. And thank you for the information and the leads. We will follow up ASAP. Have a safe flight back to Bern."

"Ciao, Stefano. Sorry to have awoken you."

Fankhauser then phoned Alitalia. He needed the next flight out of Rome for Bern. The next flight to Bern was scheduled to leave at six a.m. This would put him back in Bern by about seven-thirty. Perfect. He then packed his suitcase, checked out of the Palazzo, and grabbed a taxi-cab to the Rome Airport.

Once boarded on the Alitalia flight, Fankhauser made good use of the ninety-minute flight time to Bern. He tried to put out of his mind his fears as to the safety, or lack thereof, of his mother, Isolde and Lise back at the *Fankhaus*. Instead, he concentrated on his whole encounter with Agimo back in Rome. How was it that Agimo had been able to recognize him at *Ristorante dei Santi*? He had known what Agimo looked like, from the photographs which he had taken of him entering and leaving Lise's apartment building on Spitalgasse. But how did Agimo know what Fankhauser looked like? It must have been through Simon Hartmann, he concluded. Yes. Hartmann would have had a number of photographs of Fankhauser. After all, Fankhauser had been photographed at many social events they had attended together. He must have provided photographs to Agimo. And so, while Fankhauser had intended that he would be incognito while at *Ristorante dei Santi*, Agimo all that time knew full well who he was. In the long run, that really did not pose a problem, as it had been Fankhauser's goal to eventually attract Agimo's attention in order to have him follow Fankhauser into the dark alley off Via de Porta Cavallegeri. The whole encounter had been very fruitful. He had picked the low-lying fruit from the tree of *The Shadow*. Agimo had admitted to the involvement of *The Shadow*, and of himself personally, and of Lise Brunner in the murder by poisoning of Fred Bruni. He had also admitted to the attempted murder by poisoning of Lise Brunner, to the involvement of *The Shadow* in international racketeering, and to the conspiracy with Simon Hartmann to kill all occupants of the *Fankhaus*, including Fankhauser's own mother, Renée Fankhauser. Fettucini and Giovanni heard all these admissions. Hopefully, Isolde, Lise, and Renée are still alive, failing which the conspiracy charges would turn into murder charges. And Fettucini had the physical evidence, the videotape and the voice recording. These pieces of physical evidence may, or *likely* would, not stand up in court, but they do provide the authorities---the *Guardia di Finanza*, the *Polizia di Stato*, the *Carabinieri*, and *INTERPOL*---with leads to pursue investigations which would yield the higher-hanging fruit. They would obtain evidence that was wholly admissible in court. With the evidence that she already has, Isolde should be able to meet the standard of proof required in a civil case for damages; that is, proof on the balance of the probabilities. What was this body of evidence? The evidence of Professor Rossi of the *Università degli Studi di Firenze* in relation to the origin and existence of *'Ombra Segreta della Forza di Firenze'*. The evidence of Professor Rappaport of *Faculté des Sciences de Sorbonne Université* in relation to the secret poisons of Catherine de' Medici, with special reference to *'Mon Petit Ami'*. The evidence of Lise as to the planting of one tablet of *'Mon Petit Ami'* among Fred's Cafergot pills. The evidence of Fettucini and Giovanni, together with the videotape and the voice recording, all as to the admissions made by Agimo. The evidence of himself, Fankhauser. And, last but not least, the evidence of Isolde Bruni herself. The evidence yet to be obtained by the authorities should hopefully be enough to prove the guilt of Agimo and his cohorts in crime based on the criminal standard, that is, proof beyond a reasonable doubt. Not only for the murder of Fred Bruni, but also for international racketeering. He felt a sense of satisfaction in the fact that he had served his client, Isolde Bruni, to the best of his ability, even putting his own life in extreme danger in doing so. Luckily, he was still alive. Hopefully, Isolde, Lise, and Renée were also still alive. "Dear God," he prayed, "let it be so." In looking ahead, the major concern that he had was for the safety of all three. He can never lose sight of the fact that *The Shadow* was an incontrovertible monster, the Hydra, with a head of many poisonous snakes, and the ability to regenerate itself. There is so much more planning that he still needs to do in the matter. He will do so as soon as he learns of the status of the residents of the *Fankhaus*.

As he approached the front door of his apartment on Kramgasse in Old Bern, his heart was doing flutters like the wings of a dozen butterflies, and he had goosebumps all over his body. "Oh, my God!" he kept repeating to himself, "let them all be alive." With each step, his legs felt weaker and weaker. He knew that he had to prepare himself for the worst. But he just was unable to accept such a catastrophe. Finally, the door was standing there before him. He quickly noticed that the lock had been damaged, obviously from gunshots. He felt as if he was being swallowed up by the floor on which he stood. Yes. Obviously, *The Shadow* had been there. And most likely in the form of the man he had thought to have been his very close friend, Simon Hartmann. He tried to open the door. But even though the lock had been shot away, the door would not budge. This was a good sign, he thought to himself. Someone within the apartment must have placed some furniture behind the door to prevent it from being opened from the outside. That meant that someone had survived the attack. He knocked three times on the door. There was no response from within. He felt that, if this is what purgatory is like, he wants to have no part of it. He then shouted "Mama! Mama! Are you there? This is Joaquim. Please open the door." Within seconds, the furniture behind the door was moved, and there standing before him in living colour was his mother. She fell into his arms, embracing him tightly, her Glock semi-automatic pistol in her hand. "You may put the pistol away now, Mama," Joaquim joked. "Unless you intend to shoot me."

"Oh, Joaquim; Joaquim," she sobbed. "It is so good to see you."

"I was worried about you, Mama. And Isolde; and Lise. How are they?"

"We are all OK, Joaquim. God has been good to us. But let's block the door again. And then I will tell you the whole story. You will find it incredible." Fankhauser put the furniture back against the closed door. He looked across the room, and saw both Isolde and Lise sitting at the dining table. Thank God they were all alive and well. He walked over to Isolde and Lise, and gave each of them a hug.

"I feared that you were all in danger," he said, looking at Isolde, then Lise, and then Renée.

"We were," remarked Renée, a faint smile of relief on her face.

"Well, at least you are all alive and well," he commented. From the look on each of the three faces, he could tell that there was something very important that they had not yet told him. But that was to be expected, he thought. There obviously had been an intruder, and the women had not as yet had time to give him the details.

"What is that smell?" Fankhauser inquired curiously, his nose raised toward the ceiling. "It smells like death." This drew a quick guffaw from Renée.

"We have another guest," Renée ventured.

"You mean you *had* another guest," Fankhauser retorted, emphasizing the past tense.

"No, Joaquim. We still have him. He is here with us in the *Fankhaus.*"

"Where is he, Mama?" her son demanded, as he pulled out his Russian Nagant revolver, and looked around the room. "We do not want anyone stinking up the *Fankhaus.*" He was trying to lighten up the dour atmosphere with a touch of humour.

"He is in the guest room," Renée replied. At this, Fankhauser's countenance changed back to a look of deep concern. He rushed into the guest room, his revolver still in his hand.

"There is no-one here," he observed, looking at Renée, Isolde and Lise, all of whom had followed him in.

"He is lying on the floor, Joaquim. Look down, over by the window," Renée said. A few seconds of silence followed, as Fankhauser approached the window.

"Holy mackerel!" boomed Fankhauser's voice in shock and amazement. A few more seconds of silence, as he opened up the make-shift shroud to reveal the corpse. "Jumping Jehoshaphat!" roared Fankhauser's voice again. He had just recognized the face of the dead man as Simon Hartmann. This all made sense to him. Agimo had warned him that there was a hit out on the lives of the occupants of the Fankhauser *Fankhaus*. And that Hartmann would be the hitman. Truer words had never been spoken.

"Take a look at the gold ring on his right middle finger, Joaquim," Isolde whispered to Fankhauser. Fankhauser pulled up the right hand of the corpse, toward his face. Rigor mortis had not as yet set in. "Yikes!" Fankhauser's voice bellowed for a third time. This was his day for words of shock and amazement. "Yes," he continued, loudly "I see the mark of the Beast; the three intersecting crescents. There is our confirmation that Hartmann was a member of *The Shadow.* You just never know about people! And for all those years I had thought that he had been one of my closest friends!" This remark caused Lise to impulsively put her right hand behind her back in order to conceal the beautiful, expensive gold ring that adorned her middle finger; the ring with its crown of black onyx inlaid with mother of pearl in the shape of three intersecting crescents. She loved this ring, notwithstanding the emblem that it bore. After Fankhauser rewrapped the corpse in its make-shift shroud, he and the three women retreated to the dining table.

"And to think that I called that man my friend," he sighed. "It is said that there is a special place of torture reserved in Hell for traitors. You can read about this special place that exists in the bowels of Hell in *The Divine Comedy.* You know, Dante's masterpiece. It is pictured as a place where its inhabitants exist as frozen blocks of ice, never ever to be thawed. They are condemned to remain frozen throughout eternity. Well, all I can say is that Hartmann deserves a special spot in that special place of torture. There is none on earth worse than one who betrays his friend." Isolde nodded her head in agreement. Renée looked at her son, shaking her head disapprovingly, as she believed in the Christian concept of forgiveness. Lise showed no emotion, one way or another.

"So, we have a corpse on our hands," remarked Fankhauser, nonchalantly. "I take it that he succumbed to your Glock pistol, Mama?"

"Yes," Renée replied, glumly. "Thank God that I had it! He broke in, gun in hand. I stood behind the door, and, when I saw the drawn pistol, I fired three shots. He fell down, dead. It was a petrifying experience for all three of us. Especially for me! I had never before in my long life killed someone. You know me, Joaquim. I believe in the sanctity of life for all God's creatures. I am sure I will be punished by my Maker for what I have now done." Her tone was remorseful.

"Good work, Mama. You are a true Fankhauser. You guarded the *Fankhaus* well, Mama," Fankhauser deflected. "When did all this happen?"

"Yesterday morning. He first knocked on the door. We refused to answer. He then triggered a false fire alarm. We held our ground. We refused to abandon ship. He then fired his pistol into the lock, and gained entry. That's when I shot him dead."

"Have the police been notified?"

"No. We did not know what to do. We decided to wait for your return. Thank God you came back this morning, Joaquim! As you know, the corpse is starting to smell. And poor Lise has had to share the guest room with it! And with you being back, Isolde will have to give up your room, and move back into the guest room, with Lise and the stinking corpse."

"I am glad you waited. You see, Simon Hartmann was a senior inspector in the Bern Police Department. Heaven knows how they would have received the news that you killed one of their own. And a senior one at that!" There were expressions of shock on the faces of the three women. Renée had killed a cop! "But do not worry about it. I will get us over that hurdle," Fankhauser assured them, wearing a look of utter confidence. "First things first. We need to reconnect the telephone system. And we need to replace the lock. Stay here until I get back. I am going downstairs for a few minutes."

Within a short time, the telephone was back in service. When Fankhauser returned, he took photographs of the damage to the door lock, both from inside and outside the apartment. He then phoned the building superintendent, Dmitri Arkelov, to request the replacement of the broken lock. Within a few minutes, Dmitri appeared, a toolbox in his hand. While Dmitri replaced the lock, Fankhauser engaged him in conversation.

"I was away in Rome for a few days. Anything exciting happened in Bern during my absence?" he asked.

"Same oold, same oold," Dmitri replied, in a strong Russian accent, rolling all his "r's". "Firre alarrm vent ooff vesterrday morrning. False alarrm. I vonder who is prranksterr. Headline in morrning *Berner Zeitung*. Just finished reading newspaperr. Man from Berrn Police vent missing. Some inspectorr named Harrtmann, Oone of higherr-ups. Left Headquarrterrs Prrecinct yesterrday morrning; don't say vherre going. Hasn't rreturned. Can't rreach him. Just disappearred frrom face of earrth; POOF! Likely in arrms of mistrress, I say. But who am I to say? Just poorr Rrussian immigrant." Dmitri guffawed at his own attempt at a joke. Most likely in the arms of Satan, Fankhauser thought to himself. Most people have difficulty understanding Dmitri's broken English. But Fankhauser had become used to it, after several years of being subjected to it. He understood Dmitri perfectly. Suddenly, Dmitri raised his nose slightly, and started sniffing away.

'Vot smells in 'erre? He asked curiously. "Prroblems vith toilet?"

"No problem, Dmitri. That's just my dirty laundry. I was away for three days, you know."

"You know vere laundry rroom is," commented Dmitri, dryly.

As soon as Dmitri left, Fankhauser locked the door, and sat down with the three women to discuss 'the case of the unwanted guest'. In other words, how to dispose of the corpse, which, if the story was not fully known, one may be tempted to describe as a 'corpus delicti'.

Fankhauser, the mastermind, was at work. He had the three women fill him in on everything that had happened, from the first knock on the door on the Thursday morning, up until the placing of the shroud-wrapped body in the guest room. Every little detail. Key to the whole scenario was that Hartmann had violently broken into the apartment, his pistol drawn and pointed at Isolde and Lise. There was the question of motive. What motive did he have? one would naturally ask. This is where the videotape and voice recording of Agimo taken in Rome would play an essential role; at least initially, until the authorities could elicit their own admissions from Agimo himself. And then, of course, there is the evidence of Lise as to the common bond linking the members of *The Shadow* together, the emblem with the three intersecting crescents. In Fankhauser's mind, it had been a clear case of self-defence. The delay in calling the Bern Police could be explained by the fact that the intended victims were three petrified women, who were confused, and justifiably had waited until the man of the house returned home. It should be an open and shut case of self-defence. But care had to be taken in the course of action to be pursued. After all, the deceased had been a senior member of the Bern Police Department. It was not uncommon for the police, no matter what country they are in, to protect their own. To close ranks, so to speak, and go on the offensive. Like a pack of wolves, they are bound together by the pack mentality of extreme devotion and loyalty to one another. They stand as one cohesive unit, dead-set against an enemy who poses a threat to a member of the pack. Fankhauser excused himself from the three women, and disappeared into the quietude of his home office. He needed time to think. Had to sort out his thoughts. Had to play his hand right. No room for errors. His mother's future, her freedom, depended on it.

He picked up the telephone and dialed Fettucini's number.

"Hello, Fank," Fettucini answered. "How is your mother?"

"Thank God, everyone is safe and sound. How are things in Rome?"

"Everything is running smoothly here in Rome. I have already met with the authorities. Copies of the tape and the voice recording are now in their hands. They thanked me for bringing this to their attention. The *Carabiniei* have taken Agimo into custody. To put it mildly, he is not a cool customer. When I last saw him, he was raging like a madman. Very, very dangerous man, this Agimo. I just pray that they keep him in custody. How are things up there in Bern?"

"Agimo was right. There was a hit ordered on my mother, Isolde, and Lise. The hitman was my old friend, Simon Hartmann. He was a senior inspector at the Bern Police Department. Broke into my apartment, pistol in hand. Ready to kill. Fortunately, my mother shot him dead. We now have to decide how to proceed with the corpse. Hence, the reason for my call. You know the four copies of the videotape and of the voice recording I had asked you to send me by same-day courier? Can you be sure to dispatch them to me immediately? I will need this evidence when I speak with the Bern Police."

"I will get them off to you within an hour," Fettucini replied. But remember, the beast is not dead; only slightly wounded. As Shakespeare said through one of his characters in *Macbeth, 'We have scotch'd the snake, not kill'd it'*. Watch out for your safety; and the safety of your charges in the *Fankhaus*."

"Thanks, Alberto. Ciao." *Bye.*

Fankhauser decided that it was best to have the copies of the videotape and of the voice recording of his interrogation of Agimo before alerting the Bern Police Department as to the death of Inspector Simon Hartmann. As soon as he receives this vital evidence, he will then phone the Bern Police and report the shooting of Hartmann. It would then be a slam-dunk conclusion that the apartment would, within a short time after, be swarming with policemen and investigators from the Bern Police, like maggots all over a corpse. His mother would admit that she was the one who had shot Hartmann, but that it was a matter of self-defence; Hartmann had violently broken into the apartment, pistol drawn, with the intention of killing his mother, Isolde, and Lise. The police would likely take his mother into custody, and require that he, Isolde and Lise also attend at the headquarters precinct for interrogation and signed statements. At that time, he would produce the videotape and the voice recording, and provide details of the activities of *The Shadow*, of which Hartmann had been a secret member. If he was correct in his evaluation of how events should unfold, his mother would likely be released on the condition that she remain in Bern until the investigation was over. Isolde and Lise would be cautioned to also remain in Bern. One tacky question was as to whether or not he should at this time engage legal counsel for his mother. What advocated against that was that it may give the perception that she needed protection, because the evidence against her was so strong. On the other side of the coin, if she was interrogated without the assistance of legal counsel, it would likely send the message that she had nothing to hide. After all, what she had done was a simple act of self-defence. There was strong evidence to corroborate this. Besides, he, Fankhauser, would be there to assist her. He made the decision to not engage legal counsel for her at this time. There, he said to himself; in a nutshell, that is the plan. All he had to do now was to await the delivery of the videotape and the voice recording. He returned to the dining table, where all three women were seated, each nursing a hot beverage, while the smell of the rotting corpse became more and more overpowering. "At least we are all alive," Reneé consoled the others.

"OK, ladies," Fankhauser started, professorially, "I would like you all to get dressed. You all have a couple of dates. Firstly, you will be meeting here with a team of cops and investigators from the Bern Police. If my instinct serves me right, we will all then go to the Headquarters Precinct of the Bern Police for in-depth interrogation. As you know, what Mama did in shooting Hartmann was an act of self-defence. We will all maintain that position. Are we all in agreement on this?" Each of Renée, Isolde, and Lise nodded. "OK," Fankhauser continued. "I am expecting a rush courier delivery from Rome within the next couple of hours. As soon as that arrives, I will phone the Bern Police, and report the death of Simon Hartmann. From then on, the course forward will be largely out of our hands." All three ladies then rose from the table, and went to their rooms to get dressed for the upcoming inquisitorial events.

CHAPTER TWENTY-TWO

FEDEX delivered the package from Fettucini at twelve-thirty in the afternoon. Fankhauser now had in his hands the vital evidence that he needed. It was time to help the Bern Police solve 'the case of the missing police inspector'. He checked on Renée, Isolde, and Lise. They were all dressed and ready to go. He picked up the telephone, and dialed the number of the Headquarters Precinct of the Bern Police, and asked for 'Homicide'. Within seconds, he had a senior officer on the line.

"Inspektor Gabriel Schneider spricht." *Inspector Gabriel Schneider speaking.*

"Hello, Inspector. I am Joaquim Fankhauser."

"The great Fankhauser, the private investigator?" Schneider asked, complimentarily, having recognized the name, likely from the gift of the gold pin which the President of Switzerland had made to Fankhauser a few years before. The whole world seemed to have known about it.

"You may say that," Fankhauser replied, jestingly. He had to find a delicate balance between conveying the gravity of his phone call on the one hand and making light of it on the other. "I would like to report a homicide." For a few seconds, there was deafening silence at the other end of the line.

"Who killed whom?" Schneider asked.

"The victim is Inspector Simon Hartmann. His body is at my apartment, Kramgasse 15."

"My God!' Schneider bellowed out. "Simon is dead?'

"Yes. I knew him well. No doubt as to who it is."

"Are you there now, in your apartment?"

"Yes; I am here."

"Don't leave. We will be there in fifteen minutes."

"I will be here."

Within twelve minutes, the apartment building was swarming with police, both uniformed and plainclothes, led by Schneider himself. They moved the shrouded corpse from the guest room to the living room, carefully unfolding the rug, in which it had been wrapped, to reveal the dead Simon Hartman. Rigor mortis had by now set in.

"That's Simon, alright," Schneider remarked, looking curiously at Fankhauser. "OK. Who shot him?" Renée, Isolde, and Lise were sitting at the dining table, all leaving it up to Fankhauser to answer the questions. Renée was looking down at her hands, her fingers intertwined perplexedly.

"Would you mind if we discussed this in my office?" Fankhauser asked him, pointing in the direction of his office.

"No problem," Schneider replied, obligingly. "Let's go."

Fankhauser led him into the office, and offered him a seat.

"I was in Rome at the time it happened. It's a long story, but I will give you the capsule version now. Then, at your discretion, my mother, Renée, my client, Isolde Bruni, the other lady Lise Brunner, and I will provide the full details. The long and the short of it is that Simon broke into my apartment yesterday morning, his pistol drawn, with the intention of killing all three women. Before he could pull the trigger, my mother shot him with her Glock semi-automatic pistol. You may now wish to question my mother, Renée Fankhauser." Schneider nodded in agreement, and said "Let's hear what she has to say." Fankhauser called out to his mother to come into his office. As she entered, Schneider rose from his seat.

"Frau Fankhauser, please tell me exactly what happened," he asked, courteously. Renée straightened her shoulders in preparation.

"Yesterday morning at about nine-fifteen, someone knocked on the door. I refused to answer. At about ten-fifteen, the building's fire alarm went off. Someone knocked on the door again. Shouted to us that the building was on fire. Told us to get out immediately. I smelled a rat. We all remained in the apartment. At about ten-twenty, this man, who we now know to be Simon Hartmann, fired two shots into the door-lock, and entered, with gun drawn and pointed at the other two ladies, Isolde and Lise. Fortunately, I was standing behind the door with my Glock G43x semi-automatic. In self-defence, I fired three shots into him, and killed him. It was a case of self defence." Tears were filling her orbital sockets.

"Did you know who this man was, Frau Fankhauser?"

"Never seen him before in my life. I learned later that he had been a good friend of my son Joaquim." Schneider looked at Joaquim inquiringly.

"Yes. I had known Simon for several years," Fankhauser chirped in. "I had considered him to be one of my closest friends."

"Frau Fankhauser, what happened after you shot him?"

"Seeing that he was dead, we were confused. Didn't know what to do. We decided to wrap his body in the rug and wait for Joaquim to return from Rome."

"Frau Fankhauser, do you have any idea as to what his motive was in attempting to kill you and the other two women?"

"This is where the long story starts," Fankhauser intercepted. "Have you ever heard of an organization called 'Ombra Segreta della Forza di Firenze'?" Schneider gave out a faint laugh.

"Herr Fankhauser, I am here to ask the questions. Not to answer your questions." He winked at Fankhauser.

"Of course, I know that. But I thought it would save time if I knew how much you know about this organization, more commonly known as The Shadow. In any event, The Shadow is a very powerful and dangerous group involved in international organized crime. Drug trafficking, human trafficking, prostitution, money laundering. You name it, and they are in it. They are so powerful they have infiltrated the Vatican." Schneider raised his eyebrows in surprise.

"Tell me more, Herr Fankhauser."

"Frau Isolde Bruni is one of the women seated at the dining table. She is the widow of a Toronto lawyer named Fred Bruni. Fred Bruni died in Toronto after a business visit to Bern several weeks ago. He was poisoned. The other woman seated at the dining table is Fraulein Lise Brunner. She lives here in Bern. Believe it or not, Fraulein Brunner has admitted to planting the poison pill that Fred Bruni took in Toronto, causing his death in Toronto. She admits to having been a member of *The Shadow*. When *The Shadow* learned that Frau Bruni had been speaking with Fraulein Brunner, and that Fraulein Brunner was running scared that she may be put away for murder and was likely to spill the beans, they ordered a hit on both Fraulein Brunner and Frau Bruni. They administered poison to Fraulein Brunner. But I rescued her in the nick of time. They went to Frau Bruni's hotel to kill her, but I had already arranged for her to check out of the hotel. I took both Frau Bruni and Fraulein Brunner into my apartment here, to provide for their safety and protection. Before I left for Rome to investigate *The Shadow*, I purchased the Glock G43x semi-automatic for my mother. Thank God I had done that!" Fankhauser breathed a deep sigh of relief.

"That's quite a tale, Herr Fankhauser," Schneider commented. "But how did Simon Hartmann fit into all this?"

"Simon Hartmann was a member of *The Shadow*." At this, Fankhauser gave Schneider the videotape and the voice recording of his interrogation of Agimo.

"In Rome, I interrogated a man by the name of Bernardo Agimo. He had tried to kill me in a dark alley last night, but we foiled his attempt. Agimo admitted the existence of *The Shadow*, the murder of Fred Bruni and Fraulein Brunner's role in it, the membership of Simon Hartmann in *The Shadow,* and the involvement of *The Shadow* in international racketeering. And, believe it or not, Agimo mockingly alerted me to the fact that there was a hit out on the lives of all three women here in my apartment. It's all there on the videotape and the voice recording. This caused me to cut short my interrogation of Agimo in Rome, and hightail it back to Bern, where, as you can see, I found that he was correct in what he had told me. You will also note on Hartmann's right middle finger a gold ring bearing an emblem of three intersecting crescents. That emblem is worn, in some form or the other, by all members of *The*

Shadow. You will note the same emblem on a ring which sits on one of the fingers of Fraulein Brunner. And you have to ask yourself this: If not to do harm to one or more of the three women, why else would Hartmann destroy the door-lock and enter the apartment, pistol in hand, and point the pistol at Fraulein Brunner and Frau Bruni?"

"Are any other authorities involved in investigating the activities of *The Shadow*?"

"Definitely. First of all, the *Giuardia di Finanza* of Italy is involved. The contact there is Signor Antonio Caruso. The *Polizia di Stato* of Italy is involved. Signor Sergio Grasso is the one to speak with there. And the *Carabinieri* is involved. Just speak with Signor Pietro Lombardi there. Oh, yes; and last, but not least, Signor Stefano Conglari of *INTERPOL* is also on the case."

"I am impressed," Schneider remarked, admiringly. "It's no wonder they call you 'the great Fankhauser'. Frau Fankhauser, may I have the Glock G43x semi-automatic, please? We will need it as evidence. When the file is closed, we will return it to you."

"By all means," Fankhauser interceded, looking to his mother to turn the weapon over to Schneider. Without saying a word, Renée reached into her pocket, took out the pistol, and delivered it into the gloved hands of the inspector, who immediately deposited it into a plastic bag.

"As you understand, Herr Fankhauser," the inspector advised, "we have to declare the whole apartment a crime scene. Is there some other place where you can all stay until the investigation is concluded?"

"I suppose we can stay at a hotel. How long do you estimate that would be?"

"Only a couple of days," Schneider replied.

"No problem." Fankhauser picked up the phone and reserved a three-bedroom suite at *Hotel Ricardo*, over on Spitalgasse.

"One more thing, Herr Fankhauser. I would like you and the three women to go to the station where I will meet with you for written statements. Can you be there in about an hour?"

"Would that be at *Headquarters Waisenhaus* over at Waisenhausplatz?" Fankhauser asked.

"Yes; Waisenhausplatz 32."

"We'll be there."

Schneider then exited the apartment, taking with him the videotape, the voice recording, and the plastic bag containing Renée's Glock G43x. Fankhauser and his mother rejoined Isolde and Lise at the dining table.

"OK, ladies," he said, with a smile. "As expected, we have to go to Police Headquarters. They need written statements from us."

Within twenty minutes, Fankhauser, Isolde, Lise, and Renée were out of the apartment, overnight bags in hand, leaving behind a small army of investigators, who were fully engaged in taking photographs, lifting fingerprints, searching for other clues, and performing such other activities as they normally engage in in reconstructing a crime scene. Before Fankhauser left, he buried his Luger Pistole Parabellum semi-automatic in his waist, and gave his Russian Nagant revolver to Renée to put in her purse. "Never can tell when these will be needed", he whispered to Renée. In the parking lot down below, they climbed into Fankhauser's black Mercedes-Benz, Fankhauser himself in the driver's seat, Isolde in the passenger seat beside him, Lise in the passenger seat behind him, and Renée in the passenger seat to the right of Lise. This seating arrangement had been dictated by Fankhauser. In this way, he, with his Luger Pistole Parabellum semi-automatic, could protect the driver's side of the vehicle, and, Renée, with the Russian Nagant revolver, could protect the other side, just in the event that *The Shadow* reared its ugly head and made another attempt on their lives. At this point, Fankhauser was not considering anything whatsoever as being beyond the long octopal reach of *The Shadow*. And he was just not leaving anything to chance. Before he pulled out of the parking space, he looked around to see if there was anyone else around. Anyone who could be another hitman of *The Shadow*. The coast was clear. So far, so good. As the Mercedes-Benz exited the building, he spotted a volcanic-ash-grey Opel parked on the south side of Kramgasse, within eye-sight range of number 15. It was not far from the *Zytglogge*. There were two men seated in the front seats. Red flags loomed high within his head. Need to keep a watch on them, he thought to himself.

He turned to go easterly on Kramgasse, toward Kreuzgasse, peering in his rearview mirror. He was watching like a hawk for the volcanic-ash-grey Opel. A sigh of relief. It had not moved from its parking spot close to the *Zytglogge*. Fankhauser turned left, onto Kreuzgasse, and then left onto Rathausgasse. As he drove westerly on Rathausgasse, he noticed, in his rearview mirror, a navy-blue Citroen overtaking him. This could be the start of trouble, he mumbled. "Mama," he cautioned Renée, "take out the revolver, and hold it in your right hand, your finger on the trigger. Be prepared to use it, if and when I give the word." In a jiffy, the Russian Nagant revolver was in Renée's right hand, her index finger wrapped around the trigger. As Fankhauser approached the lighted intersection of Rathausgasse and Brunngasse, the navy-blue Citroen, with a single occupant, dashed ahead of him, and, swerving into his own lane, stopped for the red light. Glancing into his rearview mirror, he could now see the volcanic-ash-grey Opel approaching at a high rate of speed behind him. Before he fully realized what was happening, the navy-blue Citroen suddenly backed up, smashing into the front grill of his Mercedes-Benz. "Nobody is to leave this car!" he commanded. "Isolde! Lise! Lower your heads to your knees, and stay there! Mama, take down anyone that approaches your side of the car." As he shouted those orders, he held his Luger in his hand. The passenger door of the Opel opened, and the passenger, a man with a Lenin-type beard, hurriedly approached Renée's side of the car, a pistol in his hand. "Here he comes, Mama; on your side; and he is armed. Take him down, Mama, no questions asked!" When the intruder reached the Mercedes-Benz, Renée simply pointed the cocked revolver into his face, and shot him point-blank. He fell to the pavement. She looked behind to keep an eye on the driver of the Opel. He was still sitting in the driver's seat, likely frozen from the inhospitable welcome that his cohort had received. For a minute or so, there was a Mexican standoff. And then, another car, a milk-white Porsche, appeared on the scene, directly behind the Opel. The driver, the lone occupant, got out of his car to simply ask why the cars ahead of him were standing still at the intersection, notwithstanding that the light was green. As he approached the driver of the Opel, there was a sudden 'pop', and he fell to the pavement. The driver had shot him dead. The driver then hurriedly got out of the Opel, and rushed toward Fankhauser's Mercedes-Benz, shooting blindly at the rear window, and then through the open side window. Fankhauser heard one of the women in the rear scream in angony. She had obviously taken a bullet. He quickly turned around to confront the raging assailant, and, with a barrage of bullets from his Luger Pistole Parabellum semi-automatic, eliminated him. The Citroen then turned the corner onto Brunngasse, and sped away from the deadly scene. Fankhauser checked in on the women in the rear seats. One of them had been shot. Was it his mother? Or was it Lise?

"Lise has been shot!" Renée yelled. "But she is still breathing." Just then, another car turned left from Brunngasse onto Rathausgasse. As soon as the driver saw the gory scene, he called the *Kantonspolizei.* Within minutes, two police cars and an ambulance were there. The ambulance whisked Lise off to *Spital Tiefenau,* her old hospital over on Tiefenaustrasse. The officer in charge impounded Fankhauser's Luger semi-automatic, and the Nagant revolver that had been used by Renée. Fankhauser told the officer in charge that he and the three women had an appointment to meet with Inspector Gabriel Schneider at Police Headquarters, for which they were already late. The officer took Fankhauser to his police car, got Inspector Gabriel Schneider on his car radio, and left Fankhauser alone to speak with Schneider.

"Inspector Schneider," Fankhauser started, "this is Joaquim Fankhauser. I would like to report two more homicides."

"Dammit, Herr Fankhauser. Have we not been through this scenario before?" Schneider retorted, somewhat jokingly. "I am waiting here for you. What the hell happened?"

"We were en route to meet with you at Police Headquarters. Would you believe we were ambushed by *The Shadow?"*

'No. I can't believe it," Schneider retorted, with an earsplitting horselaugh.

"Well, we were! Fortunately, we were prepared, and got the better of them. Two of them dead. One shot by my mother, and the other by me. Lise Brunner is injured. She has just left by ambulance for the hospital. Oh, yes; I should also mention that one of the hitmen shot an innocent driver dead. Do you still want my mother, Isolde Bruni, and I to meet with you today?"

"So," Schneider replied, "instead of one homicide for me to investigate, there are now four. You must tell your mother to stay away from guns, Herr Fankhauser," he guffawed, at his own joke. Fankhauser was not amused. "You know, Herr Fankhauser; up until now, we had averaged about three homicides a year here in Bern. Now, between you and Frau Fankhauser, we have in one fell swoop exceeded our quota." Again, he laughed at his shrewd observation. Again, Fankhauser was not amused. "I think we better cancel today's appointment,' Schneider continued. "I need to get up to speed with these latest homicides before we meet. How about tomorrow morning at eleven?"

"That's fine with me. See you then." Fankhauser was relieved.

"Please tell the officer in charge at the scene of today's homicides I would like to speak with him on the police radio."

Once the officer in charge had spoken with Schneider, he told Fankhauser that, as was to be expected, the area of the shootings and Fankhauser's Mercedes-Benz, the rear seats of which were covered in Lise's blood, had become crime scenes. This of course meant that Fankhauser would temporarily lose the use of his Mercedes-Benz. At his request, the officer contacted Hertz Rent-a-Car for rental of a vehicle for him. Fankhauser requested a Mercedes-Benz. It would be there at the scene in about thirty minutes. Fankhauser rejoined his mother and Isolde, who were both standing outside Fankhauser's black Mercedes-Benz. Renée appeared distressed, and Isolde was still shaking from the horrid experience.

"A rental car will be here in about thirty minutes," Fankhauser started. "First, we will have to go to the Hertz office over on Casinoplatz to sign the rental contract. Then we must go see Lise at *Spital Tiefenau* as soon as possible. No problem with the appointment at Police Headquarters. It has been rescheduled to eleven tomorrow morning."

"Before we go," Isolde said surprisingly to Fankhauser, "there is something I need to see."

"What is that?" Fankhauser asked, with furrowed brows.

"Are the two dead hit-men wearing the emblem of the three intersecting crescents?"

"Good point, Isolde. But the police will not let us wander through the crime scene." He signaled to the officer in charge that there was something he needed to ask him. "Would you kindly check for me as to whether or not any of the dead men is wearing a gold ring with an emblem of three intersecting crescents?" The officer was willing to oblige. He walked over to each corpse, and checked the hands.

"Yes," he shouted out to Fankhauser. "Each of the two men shot by you and your mother has a gold ring with three intersecting crescents."

"One more favour, please. Would you have your photographer take pictures of each of the two rings for me, and identify each photograph with the name of each wearer?" The officer was willing to oblige. He said that the photographs would be available the next day at *Headquarters Waisenhaus.* "Perfect," responded Fankhauser. On schedule, a rental Mercedes-Benz from Hertz arrived, and Fankhauser and the two women were whisked off to the Hertz office on Casinoplatz. Once the requisite papers were signed and the deposit paid, they piled into the rented Mercedes-Benz, and were soon on their way to *Stipal Tiefenau* to see how the injured Lise was doing.

"Mama," he chortled to Renée, "you are getting good at using a pistol."

"What do you mean "getting"?" Renée asked, indignantly. They both laughed.

"No doubt about it", exclaimed Fankhauser. "This monster has many heads. This thing called *The Shadow* is a real Hydra. You cut off one head, and it simply regenerates itself. We sure have our work cut out for us."

"Poor Lise," Renée murmured, sadly. "I think she took a bullet in the spine."

At *Stipal Tiefenau,* Lise was in surgery. The bullet that she had taken had shattered two cervical vertebrae, and, with them, a portion of her spinal cord. The surgery was long and delicate. Estimated seven hours. And that was only to save her life. There was only one prognosis. She would never be able to walk again.

"What will become of her?" Renée asked, pitifully "She has no husband to care for her."

"Remember, Mama. She is a Medici. The Medicis are true survivors. Someone, somewhere, will care for her. Well, I guess we better head to our hotel. As you know, the *Fankhaus* is under lockdown as a crime scene. It will not be available to us for a couple days."

As he drove along the route to *Hotel Ricardo*, Fankhauser, for the first time in umpteen years, felt naked. He was completely unarmed.

Renée's Glock G43x semi-automatic was in the possession of the Bern Police as critical evidence in the shooting of Simon Hartmann. His Luger semi-automatic was in the possession of the Bern Police as critical evidence in the shooting of one of the two assailants at the intersection of Rathausgasse and Brunngasse. And his Nagant revolver, which Renée had used to plug the second assailant at the intersection, was also in the possession of the Bern Police as critical evidence. This would not do. Knowing that *The Shadow* was hunting them down, he had to re-arm without delay. As he drove along Kramgasse, he caught sight of *Waffen Depot*, a retail store that specialized in selling small arms. Leaving his mother and Lise locked in the rental Mercedes-Benz, he rushed into the store. Within ten minutes flat, he purchased two handguns, together with ammunition for each. One handgun was a DWM Luger semi-automatic, with an eight-round magazine, the 'DWM' meaning it had been manufactured in Germany. The other was a W+F Bern Swiss Luger, with a blood-red handle that he knew his mother would love. The purchases made, he scurried out of the store and back into the driver's seat of the car. He turned around and handed the W+F Swiss Luger to his mother.

"Mama," he said, with a broad smile, "I knew you would love this. Just look at the beautiful blood-red handle."

"Joaquim, you are a bad boy. You want me to kill again? Are the two that I whacked not enough?" she asked him, as she fitted the blood-red handle in the palm of her right hand. "Perfect fit," she commented. "And I just love red!"

Being armed once more gave Fankhauser a good feeling. He was no longer running around in the buff. He was once again one of King Arthur's knights, dressed in a suit of armour, and, above all, fully fortified, ready to take on the world, especially *The Shadow.*

CHAPTER TWENTY-THREE

HOTEL RICARDO, on Spitalgasse in Old Bern, was not exactly what you would call 'the Ritz'. In fact, it scored pretty low down as far as hotel ratings go, usually shown as two and one-half stars out of a possible five. But Fankhauser had to take stock of the fact that it was Isolde's money he was spending, not his. At the end of the day, his client Isolde would have to reimburse him for all expenses incurred by him in relation to her case. The expenses were piling up. He had not as yet received an invoice from his colleague Fettucini, who had put a significant amount of time into the case, and, of course, would have had to pay his assistant, Giovanni. Then there were Fankhauser's travel expenses, to and from Rome. His hotel expenses at the Palazzo in Rome. His meal expenses, not only at the Palazzo, but also at the expensive *Ristorante dei Santi*. The invoice of the escort service *Le Migliori Donne* for the 'rental' of the young woman Paola, the strawberry blonde from Tuscany. and so on. This already adds up to a tidy sum, and it did not include a penny for his own services. It therefore made sense for him not to go hog-wild on this emergency accommodation, originally planned for four, but, with Lise's condition, now for three. Considering all this, *Hotel Ricardo* was a perfect choice.

Their suite, Number 665, was on the third floor, not far from the elevator. Sure glad it's not '666', thought Fankhauser, as they exited the elevator. That would be a bad omen. *'The mark of the Beast'*, otherwise known as *'The sign of the Antichrist'*. He had read about it in the *Book of Revelation* when he was a boy and his mother had forced him to read the Bible. The last thing that he needed now was to have to deal with superstitions and prophesies. He already had enough on his plate.

Entering the suite, he was taken aback by not only the spaciousness, but also by the artistic designs that adorned the ceilings and the walls. He could have sworn that he had just stepped into some place like the *Cappella Sistina* back in Rome, displaying the magnificent frescoes of Michelangelo. There were angels with outstretched hands reaching up to archangels above them. There were what appeared to be cherubim and seraphim. There were nude mortals beneath the angels, their eyes raised to the heavens in the hope of achieving salvation. These images were in every room. "Signs of the age of this hotel," Fankhauser commented to Renée and Isolde. "Quite likely dating from the times of the Medicis. It's amazing what modern refurbishing can do."

They spent the next hour or so freshening up, and settling into their new environment.

"This is not what I would call home," commented Renée, sarcastically. "Give me the *Fankhaus* any day."

"I know, Mama. But remember the words that St. Paul wrote to the Philippians: *'I have learned the secret of being content in any and every situation. I can do everything through Him who gives me strength.'* Have you forgotten those words that you taught me as a boy, Mama?"

"Oh, Joaquim. Don't throw the scriptures back at me." But deep in her heart, Renée was proud of her boy. He had ingrained within him a certain amount of spirituality. He was a good man.

They were now all seated in what served as the living room of their new abode. Fankhauser was scrolling the TV screen with the remote, trying to find some movie that would take their minds off the hair-raising experience of the day. He found a rerun of the classic 1942 film *Casablanca*, starring Humphrey Bogart and Ingrid Bergman, picking up at the scene in *Rick's Café Americain*, in which Ilsa speaks that legendary line to Sam, the piano player. The movie was the English version, with German subtitles. Great choice, mused Fankhauser. The sentimental scene should instantly transport the two ladies out of the traumatic experience that they had to endure earlier in the day. When the movie was over, he read from the room menu the main dishes that were available in the hotel. Taking each order, he phoned down to Room Service and placed the orders, including four bottles of Pinot Noir. 'Good," he said, as he hung up the phone, "dinner will be here within an hour." How about another movie?" The next movie on the same channel was another Bogie movie, *The Maltese Falcon*, starring Humphrey Bogart and Mary Astor, with other memorable actors such as Peter Lorre and Sydney Greenstreet. "I love Bogie movies," exclaimed Renée, nostalgically. Isolde nodded her head in agreement. "OK," Fankhauser interjected, "You won't find any objection from me there. This is the film in which Bogie plays a San Francisco private investigator. Right up my alley! Maybe I'll pick up a pointer or two from the great Bogie." Thirty-five minutes into the movie, dinner arrived. As the bell-hop wheeled in the cart laden on top with food and wine, Fankhauser kept a close eye on him. After their experiences with *The Shadow*, every stranger was suspect, especially Italians, until cleared by Fankhauser's eagle eyes. "Buona serata, signor e signore," the bell-hop said, very courteously. *Good evening, sir and ladies.* The Italian words made Fankhauser all the more wary. Chances are that a hitman from *The Shadow* would be an Italian, he thought to himself. He caught the bell-hop unawares when he ordered him to sit for a minute and take a tasting of every food on the plates. The poor bell-hop was non-plussed. Once Fankhauser concluded that the food was safe to eat, he tipped the bell-hop handsomely and sent him on his way. Fankhauser then bent down, lifted the linen tablecloth that covered the cart, and examined the underside of the cart to ensure that there was no bomb planted there. "It's clean," he concluded, with a sigh of relief. They were all famished, and dived right into the wine, the gourmet dishes, and more wine. And that is how they spent the rest of the evening. Complete relaxation. Good wine. Good food. And more good wine. And good movies. Isolde was by now fully familiar with Fankhauser's style. His modus operandi, his philosophy of work on the one hand and play on the other. There is a time for work; and there is a time for pleasure. Like two competing forces, they must be kept completely separate and apart; and 'ne'er the twain shall meet'. Tonight, Epicureanism, with a touch of bacchanalianism, prevails in Suite 665 at *Hotel Ricardo.*

CHAPTER TWENTY-FOUR

LAST NIGHT was a synonym for relaxation; today is a day of work, thought Fankhauser, as he roused himself from sleep before the break of dawn the next morning. He immediately got dressed, and went to the living room. Renée was already up, and had made coffee. The Fankhausers have always been early risers.

"Guten Morgen, Joaquim," she said to her son, as she placed a cup of piping hot coffee before him. *Good morning, Joaquim.*

"Guten Morgen, Mama," he responded. *Good morning, Mama.* "Thanks for the coffee."

His first concern was as to the condition of Lise Brunner following her lengthy surgery yesterday. He picked up the telephone and called *Spital Tiefenau.* He asked for Head-Nurse Lorena Meyer. Within a few seconds, she was on the other end of the line.

"Guten Morgen," came the pleasant voice. "Das ist Oberschwester Lorena Meyer." *Good morning. This is Head-Nurse Lorena Meyer.* At the sound of her voice, an overwhelming wave of euphoria swept him away, and his heart started to pound.

"Good morning, Lorena," he ventured, using a stroke of familiarity. "This is Joaquim Fankhauser."

"Oh, yes, Herr Fankhauser. How can I help you?" Good. There was instant recognition. This should pave the way forward.

"Please call me Joaquim," he said. "You remember your old patient, Lise Brunner?"

"Ah, Lise. She is back with us. On this floor. She was shot. Recovering from surgery. Poor girl!"

"I was just calling to see how she is doing. I take it that the surgery was successful?"

"Yes; and no, Joaquim. The surgery went well, in that it saved her life. But she has irreversible damage to her spine. The prognosis is bleak. She will likely never be able to use any of her limbs again. But at least she is still alive. I guess we have to thank God for small blessings."

"Is she able to have visitors?"

"They say only close relatives. But, Joaquim, for you, I make an exception. Just make sure you come when I am on duty. Today, I leave at five." Fankhauser could not believe how accommodating she was.

"Thank you very much, Lorena. I will likely be there about three."

"See you then, Joaquim. I look forward to seeing you again. Bye for now."

He then dialed the number of his colleague Fetuccini in Rome. Fetuccini answered.

"Hi, Alberto. Fank here."

"Hi, Fank. How are you doing up there in beautiful Bern?"

"Alberto, you will never believe this. On our way to *Headquarters Waisenhaus* yesterday, we were ambushed. Two cars boxed us in. I shot one of the assailants. Mama shot another. Both are stone cold dead. Would you believe that the dead men were wearing gold rings with emblems of three intersecting crescents on them?"

"Yes, I can believe it. Remember what I told you, Fank? *The Shadow* is very, very dangerous. You cannot let your guard down for a minute, not even a second."

"Sound advice, Alberto. Believe me, we were ready for them. Unfortunately, they plugged Lise Brunner. Hit her in the cervical spine; shattered two vertebrae. She will likely never be able to use any of her limbs again."

"Those sons of a bitch," Fetuccini uttered.

"How are the investigations going in Rome?" asked Fankhauser.

"As well as can be expected. I understand that Agimo is still in custody. The authorities are all over him, like flies on a pile of *you know what*. They say that this was the break they had been looking for. Of course, the investigations will take some time."

"That's good news, Alberto. Nice work. Keep me advised of any further developments. We're going to Police Headquarters this morning. I don't think there should be a problem. In each of the two incidents, a clear case of self defence. Talk with you later, my friend."

"Good luck, Fank. Ciao."

Fankhauser reminded his mother and Isolde that they had an appointment with Inspector Schneider at Police Headquarters at eleven that morning. Once the women were dressed, he escorted them down to *Café Galleria* on the main floor of *Hotel Ricardo*. After a quick breakfast, they were off in the rental Mercedes-Benz to *Headquarters Waisenhaus*. Fankhauser parked in a tiered parking lot, within walking distance of Police Headquarters. Before he allowed anyone to leave the car, his eagle eyes surveyed the scene, looking for any activity whatsoever on the parking level he was on. Satisfied that there was no sign of *The Shadow* in sight, he exited the car, and then told the two women that it was safe to step out. Throughout all this time, he had his DWM Luger tucked away in his waist, and Renée had her F+W Swiss Luger discreetly hidden in her purse, both within easy reach in the event of an emergency. They were in the waiting area of Inspector Schneider's office at eleven sharp.

Schneider came out to greet them personally. "I appreciate your punctuality," he complimented them. "Have you all recovered from the turmoil of yesterday?"

"We are all holding our own," Fankhauser responded, grimly. "Thanks for asking." Schneider led them into a conference room, which was equipped with electronic recording devices. He sat on one side of the long table, with Fankhauser directly opposite him. Renée sat on the right of Fankhauser, and Isolde on his left.

"I have reviewed my notes of the oral statements that you had all given me back at Fankhauser Haus," Schneider started, "together with the report of the officer in charge of the shootings at the intersection of Rathausgasse and Brunngasse. I have also reviewed the videotape and voice recording of Bernardo Agimo's admissions. I have spoken personally with *Guardia di Finanza,* the *Polizia di Stato*, the *Carabinieri,* and *INTERPOL*. No doubt about it; this mysterious organization known as *The Shadow* is one of the most corrupt and dangerous racketeering mobs on the face of the earth. You are all very lucky to be alive today. Too bad that my late colleague Simon Hartmann somehow got tied up with them. My conclusion is that the death of Hartmann was a clear case of self-defence. The same with the deaths of the two assailants at Rathausgasse and Brunngasse. Also, each a clear case of self-defence."

"We are relieved to hear that, Inspector Schneider. I was confident that you would reach that conclusion," Fankhauser remarked. Renée breathed a sigh of relief. A faint smile crept across Isolde's face.

"As a matter of formality, I need signed written statements from all three of you. For this, you will be split up into three separate rooms, each with an interrogating officer. Your answers will be transcribed into written statements, which you will be required to sign. Once you have signed, you are free to go. But I warn you: be very cautious, as *The Shadow* is everywhere, and they want all three of you eliminated, not to mention Lise Brunner. They feel you know too much. You all are a clear and present danger to them. And so, they have given the order. They want you 'kaput'. They will try to get at you when you least expect it."

"Thanks for the warning; but it is nothing that we didn't already know. Machiavelli could not have been prouder of any of his students."

"Well spoken," Schneider chuckled.

"A few questions, Inspector," Fankhauser started. "First, is my apartment still designated a crime scene?"

"No. You are free to move back in."

"May I have my pistols back?"

"No problem. As long as you keep pistols away from Frau Fankhauser," he replied, jokingly. Fankhauser and Isolde laughed. Renée was not amused.

"May I also have my car back now?"

"Definitely. I will have an officer accompany you to where we have it, and he will release it to you. But what a bloody mess in the back seat! And, as you know, the rear window is shattered."

"I know that it will need some work. Any recommendations for the repair work?"

"Yes. Fricker's. The best in the business. Here is their card." Fankhauser took the business card, which read *Autoreparaturen von Fricker.* In English, *Fricker's Auto Repairs.* They were located only a block or so away.

"Thank you," Fankhauser said, gratefully. "Please lead the way for the written statements." At this, Schneider led each of Fankhauser, Renée and Isolde into separate rooms, each with an interrogating officer. The interrogations lasted about an hour, following which they each signed two typed statements, one in relation to the shooting at the *Fankhaus,* and the other re the shootings at the intersection of Rathausgasse and Brunngasse. At about twelve-thirty, Schneider appeared. He gave Fankhauser all three pistols: Renée's Glock G43x semi-automatic, which had been used in the shooting of Simon Hartmann; and Fankhauser's Luger Pistole Parabellum and Russian Nagant revolver, which had been the instruments causing the deaths of the two assailants at the intersection of Rathausgasse and Brunngasse. He also delivered to Fankhauser an envelope containing the photographs of the gold rings on the fingers of the two dead assailants, each ring adorned with the emblem of the three intersecting crescents. These were the photographs Fankhauser had requested back at the scene of the shootings at Rathausgasse and Brunngasse.

"You are all free to go," Schneider advised Fankhauser and the two ladies. He then looked directly into Renée's eyes. "Frau Fankhauser," he cautioned, jocularly, "for heaven's sake, no more shootings, please! We just cannot deal with any more corpses." Renée looked away from him, and grunted. She was not amused. Schneider instructed an officer to accompany them to Fankhauser's black Mercedes-Benz, and to release it to Fankhauser. When they got there, Fankhauser gave Renée the keys to his black Mercedes-Benz, and told her to take Isolde with her and follow him to Fricker's. He then climbed into the driver's seat of the rental car, and drove off to Fricker's, Renée following close behind. At Fricker's, he ordered the repairs, which involved the replacement of the rear window and the cleaning of the back seats. The whole process took only ninety minutes. "The old girl looks as good as new," Fankhauser beamed, as Renée and Isolde climbed in, with Fankhauser in the driver's seat of the rental. Soon, they were off to the Hertz Rent-a-Car office over on Casinoplatz to return the rental. Next stop was *Hotel Ricardo*, where they proceeded to check out. There was one more stop to make before moving back into the *Fankhaus*. They had to visit Lise at *Spital Tiefenau* over on Tiefenaustrasse. When they approached the Nurses' Station at the hospital, it was now three-thirty. Pretty Head-Nurse Lorena Meyer beamed as she saw Fankhauser approaching. They were looking each other directly in the eye. "Something between you two?" Renée observed jokingly to her son, while they were still out of earshot. "That's none of your business, Mama," Fankhauser chuckled. "It's certainly my business, *if* she comes to live in the *Fankhaus*!" Renée remarked.

"Hi, Joaquim," Lorena greeted Fankhauser, with a broad, engaging smile. "Lise is awake in her room. I told her that you would be visiting her. Fankhauser introduced his mother to Lorena. "I can see where he got his good looks," Lorena remarked, complimentarily. Fankhauser then introduced Isolde to Lorena, commenting that she was from the cold northern land of the Eskimos called Canada. "I've been to Canada," Lorena remarked. "As a matter of fact, my late husband and I honeymooned in Montreal. It was the year of Expo. You may go and see Lise, Joaquim. Room 350. Your mother and Isolde will have to wait here." She beckoned them to the nearby waiting area.

Lise smiled as she saw Fankhauser enter her room. That's a good sign, thought Fankhauser.

"Hi, Lise. Are they treating you well here?" he asked.

"Not too badly, as far as hospitals go." She sounded somewhat groggy, undoubtedly from the anesthesia and painkillers.

"How do you feel?"

"Like a rotten egg that has just been cracked open. I hurt badly and I stink!"

"Did the doctors give you the prognosis?"

"Yes. The whole damn spiel. They say I will never be able to walk or use my arms again. That I am lucky that I can even move my head. They say I am quadriplegic. Something like that."

"Is there anything I can do for you, Lise?" This caused her to laugh out loudly, almost in a sort of sneer.

"Yes. There is. Give me back the use of my arms and legs!" There was deep sarcasm in her voice. Fankhauser looked around the room, as if searching for the right words to utter.

"I am deeply sorry, Lise, that you are in this state."

"Not your fault, Joaquim. I brought this upon myself. I had sold my soul to the Devil and he has been trying to take possession of it." Somehow, thought Fankhauser, it just did not seem right that Lise heaped all the blame upon herself.

"I want you to know that I will never abandon you, Lise."

"Danke schön, Herr Fankhauser." *Thank you very much, Herr Fankhauser.* "How is your mother?"

"Fine," he responded.

"And Isolde?"

"She is fine also. I expect that she will be returning to Canada fairly soon. Mama and Isolde are waiting outside; down by the Nurses' Station. They would only permit me to see you. I will bring them back some day when you can have more visitors."

"Thanks again, Joaquim." Her hands lay limp at her sides. She was still wearing the gold ring with the crest of the emblem of three intersecting crescents. I wonder, Fankhauser asked himself, is she still loyal to *The Shadow?* He immediately dismissed that thought as crazy.

"Auf Wiedersehen für jetzt, meine Fräulein." *Goodbye for now, my lady.*

Rejoining his mother and Isolde, he could not help but notice that Lorena was beside herself at his presence. No doubt about it, she seemed to enjoy his company.

"How did it go?" she asked.

"Not badly, considering the circumstances," he replied.

"When will you be back?" she persevered, almost plaintively.

"In another couple of days," he replied. "I will call you first."

"Good. I will be waiting for you," she promised. Her face was flushed to the shade of a red rose.

"Please do. I would like that very much."

This interchange of words was not lost on Renée, who gave her son a knowing look, as if to say: "Aha! Cupid has fired the first arrow from his quiver. I know what you and the Head-Nurse are both up to, my son." Isolde watched the whole interplay with interest.

As she stepped back into the *Fankhaus*, Renée made a deep sigh of disgust. This was not the home that she had previously taken such great pride in. Mind you, the furniture was all back in place, and nothing was missing. But she felt that something had been lost, something she just could not put her finger on. Truth be known, the feeling she had was natural. After all, her whole realm of privacy had been violated, like a woman who has just been raped. She now had to work hard to restore the virtuosity of her home.

"Mama," Fankhauser said to Renée, "here is your good old Glock G43z semi-automatic. I know how much you love this small pistol. Keep this handy, just in case the occasion arises for its use again. Give me the W+F Swiss Luger. I will store that away in my desk." He handed the Glock pistol to her, and she gave him the W+F Swiss Luger.

"Happy to get this little devil back," she remarked, as she fitted the Glock into the palm of her right hand. "Just like the good old days. Someday, I will write a book entitled '*My Son Taught Me How to Kill*'. She laughed at her own joke. Fankhauser simply stared at her.

Fankhauser opened a bottle of Cabernet Sauvignon, and poured three glasses for the two women and himself. "Mama," he said, "please excuse Isolde and me for an hour or so. We will be talking business in my office." With that, he and Isolde withdrew to his office. Renée played a Vienna Symphony Orchestra recording of Beethoven's *Concerto for Violin and Orchestra* while she madly scrubbed away at everything in sight. She was on a mission to restore the *Fankhaus* to its former state of privacy, propriety, and inviolability.

Fankhauser was behind his desk in his office, Isolde sitting on the other side. Isolde waited, as Fankhauser put away the Luger Pistole Parabellum, the Russian Nagant M1895, and the German DWM Luger in a drawer of his desk. "I feel like an arms dealer," he commented, jokingly.

"Isolde," he continued, *"The time has come, the Walrus said, to talk of many things."* Isolde laughed at this quote from Lewis Carroll's *Alice in Wonderland,* and quickly chirped in "Da-da-da-da-da-da-da-da, *'And whether pigs have wings.'* I hope to high heaven that my case is not down to determining whether pigs have wings!" Fankhauser laughed admiringly at her exhibition of both literacy and humour.

"No, Isolde. I am satisfied with what we have achieved in your case. We need to take a close look at where we are, and the path forward. You retained me to assist you in the investigation of Fred's death, as you were not satisfied with suicide being shown as the cause of death. The evidence we have unearthed shows overwhelmingly that Fred was murdered, and that the cause of death was Catherine de' Medici's favourite poison lovingly referred to as *'Mon Petit Ami'*. This poison was encapsulated in a single pill, disguised to look like a Cafergot pill. Lise secretly deposited the single pill into Fred's bottle of Cafergot pills, used for treatment of his migraines. Lise's own evidence admits to this. Thank God, Lise is still alive. Bernardo Agimo's taped interrogation also admits to the involvement of *The Shadow* in the plot, including Constantino Rapini and his VolksBankBern. Not to mention such other evidence that the authorities may unearth in their investigation of *The Shadow.* Good background evidence in relation to *'Mon Petit Ami'* and the possession of its secret formula by *The Shadow* is provided by the eminent scientist, Professor Jean Rappaport of the *Faculté des Sciences de Sorbonne Université.* Good background evidence of the evolution and existence of *The Shadow* is provided by Professor Piero Rossi of the *Universita degli Studi di Firenze.* We also have to remember that the Coroner's Office in Toronto had already determined that the cause of Fred's death was poisoning; but that where they went wrong was in concluding that the poison had been purposely self-administered. Of course, I will be available to testify on your behalf.

"The net conclusion is that, while I am not a lawyer, I believe that you should have a good cause of action for a huge award of damages for wrongful death against the organization known as *The Shadow;* against its individual members, including Agimo and Rapini; and against VolksBankBern. You also have a right of action against Lise, although you will undoubtedly waive any claim for damages against her in return for her cooperation and evidence. We do not appear to have any evidence which implicates the Vatican in any way whatsoever in the plot to kill Fred. In other words, the Vatican is as clean as a whistle.

"As far as the criminal activities of *The Shadow* and its members and associates are concerned, those are under investigation by the Italian *Guardia di Finanza,* the Italian *Polizia di Stato,* the Italian *Carabinieri,* and *INTERPOL.* These criminal activities will focus on the international racketeering of *The Shadow,* including drug trafficking, human trafficking, prostitution, money laundering, and the like. *INTERPOL,* in conjunction with the *Bern Kriminalpolizei,* will investigate Fred's murder, with a view to bringing the perpetrators to justice. My expectation is that they will go lightly on Lise, in light of her cooperation, her current condition brought about by *The Shadow,* and the fact that the main perpetrators were *The Shadow,* its members, and its associates.

"That leads me to my conclusion in relation to the criminal aspects. This is in essence a matter between the various states and the perpetrators. Inasmuch as you would wish to see the perpetrators of Fred's murder punished criminally, it is my opinion that you should not go further down that rabbit-hole. You must keep in mind that the individual states have almost endless public resources behind them; whereas you have limited resources.

"So, my dear Isolde, where does that lead us? In plain and simple language, it's time for you to go back home to Toronto. Your next step is to find competent legal counsel in Toronto to commence an action for damages for wrongful death. Do you have any questions?" Lise had a look of disappointment on her face. She searched for the words to express herself, without offending Fankhauser.

"You know, Joaquim, that I have the utmost confidence in you, and that I trust you implicitly. I must say that I am somewhat disappointed in not being able to see *The Shadow,* VolksBankBern and their members and associates receive the maximum penalties permitted by law for having brought about the death of my husband. I know that you have done everything within your power to date to bring them to justice. Deep down, I know that your counsel to me is wise. With that in mind, I must follow your recommendations. If I cannot trust 'the great Fankhauser', who else can I trust?" This brought a broad smile to Fankhauser's face. He was basking in the sunshine of the compliment.

"Danke schön, Frau Bruni," he said with a smile. *Thank you very much, Mrs. Bruni.* "I will put together an invoice for you. You will, of course, be credited with the money retainer you had paid me. Any idea as to when you will leave? You are free to stay in the *Fankhaus* as long as you wish---within reason, of course."

"I miss my kids," she replied. "They must think that I have abandoned them. I would like to see Lise before I go. And then I will book the first available flight to Toronto."

"How about if I try to get special permission for you to see Lise at *Spital Tiefenau* tomorrow afternoon? And then you can fly out the following day?"

"With your connections at the Nurses' Station, I do not doubt that you can get us into Lise's room very quickly," she said, giving him a knowing wink as she said this. Fankhauser laughed uneasily. What's this thing with his mother and Isolde about his relationship with Head-Nurse Lorena Meyer? Fankhauser picked up the telephone and dialed *Spital Tiefenau.*

"May I speak with Oberschwester Lorena Meyer at the Nurses' Station on the third floor, please/" Within couple minutes, he had Head-Nurse Lorena Meyer on the other end of the line.

"Hi, Lorena. This is Joaquim."

"Hi, Joaquim. I was hoping I would hear from you." At the sound of her voice, he was tongue-tied.

"I am phoning on business, Lorena," he managed to blurt out.

"Shucks! I was hoping that you were phoning to ask me to dinner. Well, I guess it's just not my day!"

"Sorry to disappoint you, Lorena. But would it be any at all possible for Isolde Brunner and I to visit Lise tomorrow?"

"I cannot see a problem with that, provided Lise is willing to see you. Do you want me to check with her?"

"Not necessary. She will see us. You can tell her that Isolde will be returning to Canada on the day after tomorrow. We will be there at about two tomorrow. Will you be on duty then?"

"Yes. I will be here, Joaquim. Look forward to seeing you again."

"Oh, by the way, would you like to have dinner with me next Friday evening?" Fankhauser could hear Lorena gasp for breath. This took her completely by surprise.

"I certainly would," she replied, almost breathlessly.

"Good. I will make the reservations and get back to you."

Isolde smiled at Fankhauser, as she took all this in. 'The great Fankhauser' has been snared into a trap by a woman's lure. "I wonder if Lorena will try and keep you in *her* 'Fankhaus'?" she asked Fankhauser, jokingly. He simply looked at her and smiled back.

Isolde immediately got on the phone with KLM. Was a seat available on a KLM flight directly from Bern to Toronto on the day after tomorrow? No direct flight. But she could fly SwissAir Flight 088 from Bern to Charles de Gaulle Airport in Paris, leaving Bern at three in the afternoon, and then connect with KLM Flight 057 from Charles de Gaulle to Pearson International Airport in Toronto. Perfect. She booked the flights. She felt as if she was already on her way home. She then phoned her sister-in-law, Margot Baumann, in Toronto.

"Hi, Margot. How are you holding up with the kids?"

"Hi, Isolde. It is so good to hear from you. I was starting to fear the worst. Are you OK?"

"I am fine. But you will never believe the hair-raising experiences that I had here in Bern. I will tell you all about it when I return. How are Emil and Sophie?"

"They are fine. Real troopers, I tell you. But they started to wonder if you would ever come back to them."

"My business is finished here in Bern. Quite successful. For now, you should know that Fred did not die by his own hand. He was murdered. I will be arriving at Pearson at about eight o'clock in the evening, Toronto time, the day after tomorrow. KLM Flight 057 from Paris. I will just grab the airport limo when I get there. I will phone you as soon as I am back at the house. Would you please phone Yvonne at her home and let her know. Her number is in the phone directory. Tell her I will phone her when I get back."

"Good job, Isolde. As I always told you, I never ever felt that Fred had committed suicide. He was just not the type. Besides, he had the world by the tail. No reason whatsoever to kill himself. I will let Emil and Sophie know that you will be here within the next couple of days. And for sure I will phone Yvonne for you."

"Thanks, Margot. You are a great sister-in-law, and a fantastic friend. Bye for now."

Fankhauser, Renée and Isolde spent the rest of the day in complete relaxation, playing gin rummy, listening to classical music, such as Verdi's *Rigoletto* and Mozart's *Le Nozze di Figaro,* and knocking back a number of bottles of Spätburgunder, more commonly known in other regions of the world as Pinot Noir. Fankhauser was true to his mantra. Never mix business with pleasure. When you work, work hard. When you play, play hard. The rest of this day was dedicated to pleasing the senses.

CHAPTER TWENTY-FIVE

AS FANKHAUSER drove toward *Spital Tiefenau*, Isolde in the front passenger seat and his mother in the rear, he was ever on the lookout for any suspicious activities that may arise. Knowing the nature of the beast, the many-headed Hydra known as *The Shadow*, the one thing he knew was that it was not over. In fact, it would likely never be over, until both Lise and Isolde, and perhaps even he himself, were dead, or, hope beyond all hope, *The Shadow* destroyed.

A speeding avocado-green BMW rapidly approached from behind. He felt for his Luger Pistole Parabellum. Yes; it was still there, tucked away securely in his waist. "Mama," he called out to Renée, 'is your Glock in your purse?" "Yup," she replied. "I don't leave home without it." It was an attempt at a witty takeoff from the well-known tagline of the old American Express commercial. Both Fankhauser and Isolde laughed, somewhat patronizingly. "Good," Fankhauser remarked, his eyes focused on the rapidly approaching BMW, "always be ready to use it." Having to have the last word, Renée said: "Don't worry. I am like the Energizer Bunny. I am always energized to kill." A reference to another well-known commercial. The BMW passed Fankhauser's Mercedes-Benz, and kept speeding ahead, until it was out of sight. "We can relax now," Fankhauser said, with a sense of relief.

Oberschwester Lorena Meyer spotted Fankhauser, and with him Renée and Isolde, some fifty feet away, as they walked toward the Nurses' Station. She had been on the lookout for Fankhauser. Her smile was like the radiant sun, lighting up the dimples in her cheeks. Up until then, Fankhauser had not been conscious of her dimples. As he adored her beauty, he could feel butterflies fluttering around in his stomach.

"Welcome back to my parlour, Joaquim," Lorena said coyly to Fankhauser, completely ignoring the two women in his company. Her emerald eyes gleamed with ecstasy as she stared into his. "Lise is prepared to meet with you and Isolde. You may go to her room. Frau Fankhauser can remain here." Renée was astonished at the rapid pace at which Lorena was ensnaring her son. Of course, she did not know that there was a planned dinner date for Friday evening, nor that the physical attraction was mutual.

When Fankhauser and Isolde entered Lise's room, Lise was all smiles. Isolde shuddered at the sight of the once vibrant Lise now laying there in bed as limp as a rag doll. There was a wheelchair sitting in a corner of the room.

"Hi, Lise," both Fankhauser and Isolde said, at the same time, which caused Lise to respond: "Was that line rehearsed?" Both Fankhauser and Isolde laughed. At least Lise still had a sense of humour.

"I understand that you leave for Canada tomorrow?" Lise said to Isolde.

"Yes. My kids need me. They are starting to feel that I abandoned them."

"Thanks for making the effort to see me before you go. Means a lot to me, Isolde. Especially after all the misery I have caused you."

"These things happen in life, Lise. We can never understand them. When God put us here on earth, he likely said that there are some things that will be revealed to us; and there are other things that will never be revealed to us. The true reason why God permitted you to be involved in what happened to Fred is one of those things which will never be revealed to us. Such are the designs made by the hands of destiny." Isolde's philosophical remarks gave some comfort to Lise; but Lise was still overcome with guilt, which brought tears to her eyes. What a heavy load to carry, especially in her current handicapped condition, Fankhauser thought to himself. His eyes centred on the wheelchair in the corner of the room.

"I see that they have brought you a carriage?" Fankhauser commented.

"Yes; my royal carriage. But no white horses, and no footmen. They have not wasted any time in trying to adapt me to this roadster. They want me out of here as soon as possible. This is an active hospital, they tell me; not a convalescent home. As soon as I am mobile, they will whisk me out of here."

"Do you have any relatives to assist in your care until you regain your independence?" Isolde asked.

"As I once told Joaquim, I am sprung from that noble lineage known as the Medicis. There are Medicis all over Europe, especially in Italy and Switzerland. We tend to travel incognito. It's because I am a Medici that *The Shadow* sought me out in the first place, thanks to Herr Rapini. Somehow, they are really attracted to the Medicis. It must be the long historical connection. Or it could be that they associate the name 'Medici' with power and influence. Or it could be a combination of both. That attraction of *The Shadow* to the name 'Medici' has proved to be my affliction. But, on the plus side, I have numerous relatives, all on the good and decent side of the fence. Sisters and brothers, uncles and aunts, cousins, nephews and nieces, a host of relatives of various degrees of consanguinity. If there is one thing about a Medici, he or she never starves. Do not be concerned as to how I will manage. The Medici clan will care for me." Fankhauser and Isolde were pleased to hear this. Lise would not just be tossed out like yesterday's garbage. She will survive.

"Well, Lise," Isolde offered, "if there is anything at all that I can do for you, just let me know. You can get in touch with me through Joaquim." Fankhauser could not believe his ears. These two women, who had every reason in the world to hate each other, now seemed as close as twin sisters. It must be the magic of the *Fankhaus*, he reasoned to himself. The thought struck him that he should prepare Lise for the fact that she would be needed as a witness in the litigation to be brought by Isolde in Canada for damages for wrongful death. But, the more he thought about it, the more he decided not to broach that subject. This was just not the time nor the place. And, as Solomon said in the Book of Ecclesiastes, '*To everything there is a season, and a time to every purpose under heaven*'.

"Lise, I had previously left my business card for you. In case it has been misplaced, here is another. When you are discharged from the hospital, please call me and let me know that you have, along with where you will be staying." Fankhauser placed his business card on the small table beside the bed.

"By all means, Joaquim," she responded, acquiescently.

"We must leave now, Lise," Joaquim said, looking at his watch. "Be sure to do what the doctor orders."

"Doctors," she corrected him. "I have a team of about six doctors, each in a different specialty. I have a neurosurgeon, an orthopedic surgeon, a rehabilitation specialist, an occupational specialist, my family practitioner, and, would you believe, even a shrink---as if my head needs shrinking!"

"You are in good hands, then," Fankhauser commented, with a reassuring smile. "Auf Wiedersehen, meine Fräulein." *Goodbye, my lady.*

"Auf Wiedersehen, Lise," Isolde said, as she bent down and hugged her.

"Auf Wiedersehen," Lise returned.

Back at the Nurses' Station, Fankhauser and Isolde found Lorena sitting beside Renée, engaged in animated conversation.

"What are you two ladies conspiring about?" Fankhauser chortled.

"You," retorted Lorena, a broad smile on her attractive dimpled face. "I got your full history from Frau Fankhauser."

"Lorena is doing a special project on you, Joaquim," commented Renée. "A word of warning: don't lower your guard." At this, everybody laughed.

When Lorena returned to the Nurses' Station, Fankhauser approached her, and quietly asked her to write down for him her home address and telephone number on the back of his business card, which she did and returned the card to him. He would call her soon to firm up plans for the dinner date.

"One last thing, Lorena," he said to her in a hushed tone, "as you know, two attempts have already been made on Lise's life. There may be others. Is there any added protection the hospital can offer?"

"By all means, Joaquim. I can have her room guarded, day and night. I will give instructions that, outside of medical and nursing staff, no one is to enter her room without my pre-approval. Of course, the hospital will have to bill you for this service."

"Have them send the invoice to me. If anything unusual happens as far as Lise is concerned, would you immediately let me know? Here is my business card, with my mobile phone number."

"Ohne Zweifel, mein Schatz!" *Without a doubt, my sweetheart.* At this touch of familiarity, Fankhauser was floating on air.

"You are a perfect gem, Lorena." She beamed at this compliment. He could not have said anything better to her. From the small waiting area, Renée and Isolde observed this interaction between Fankhauser and Lorena. They could put two and two together. They knew the dynamics of exactly what was going on. Within a few minutes, Fankhauser, Renée and Isolde said "Auf Wiedersehen" to Lorena, exited the hospital, and were on their way back to the *Fankhaus*.

Back at the *Fankhaus*, Isolde packed her luggage in preparation for her departure the following day, and soon joined Fankhauser and Renée in the living room.

"Isolde," Fankhauser said to Isolde, "we cannot let you leave without one final feast of the divine Swiss foods that the *Altstadt* has to offer. I have reserved a table for three for dinner at seven at *Gourmanderie Moléson*. It's an old restaurant on Aabergasse, in the centre of the Old Town, not far from the *Bundeshaus*. Within walking distance from here. The cuisine is to die for."

It was a nice, leisurely walk for Fankhauser, Renée and Isolde from the *Fankhaus* to *Gourmanderie Moléson*, taking only about fifteen minutes. The *Moléson* started catering to customers in about 1865, making it one of the oldest dining establishments in Old Bern. Isolde was visibly impressed with the ornate mirrors, the nostalgic lighting, and the beautiful windows with their colourful stained glass panes. It was like walking back through the ages, all the way back into the preceding century. From the time they entered until a few minutes after they were seated, Fankhauser studied the surroundings. He scrutinized the faces of the other diners, especially those in juxtaposition to his table. You never can tell where and when *The Shadow* will extend its tentacles and strike again. He must always be on his toes. The waiter brought the menus.

"You will note that the dominant theme of the cuisine in the *Moléson* is *à la française,*" Fankhauser volunteered to Isolde. "The multicultural feature of Switzerland is a real plus. You have the German, you have the Italian, and you have the French, all very evident in Swiss cuisine. Tonight, we are going to dine *à la française*. With that fare, we need to drink French wine." He ordered a bottle of Bordeaux wine, the 1979 Château Lafleur Pomerol, a sweet, full-bodied red wine, which would pair well with the top feature on the menu, the Charolais beef. He also ordered a large starter dish of Salmon Tartare for all three of them to share. When the waiter came to take their orders, Renée turned to her son and said: "Joaquim, I defer to your expertise on beef. You know what I like. What would you recommend for me?"

"Madame Fankhauser will have the Tournedos de Boeuf du Charolais Poêle with Béarnaise sauce, assorted Vegetables, and Mashed Potatoes." The waiter looked at Isolde. Isolde was having difficulty making up her mind. She was tempted by the Veal Cordon Bleu; and by the Emmental Rack of Lamb; and by the French Poultry, which tonight was Guinea Hen; and by the Scottish Salmon. They all seemed so enticing, so mouthwatering. But Fankhauser had said that the specialty of the house was the Boeuf Charolais. That's it, she decided. *When in Rome, do as the Romans do.*

"I will have the Filet de Boeuf Charolais prepared with Morel Mushrooms and Sauvignon Vino Sauce, together with Roasted Potato." The waiter looked at Fankhauser.

"I will have the Tournedos de Boeuf du Charolais Poêle, just as I ordered for Madame."

As the waiter left their table, Fankhauser's eyes settled on a young man, about twenty-eight, sitting alone at a table, not more than eight feet away. He was obviously Italian, having the same swarthy complexion as the unfortunate Giuseppe Cipola, and black hair that was brushed straight back and clearly waxed in too much pomade, giving him that suave look of Rudolf Valentino, star of the 1920's silent films He was wearing an Italian suit, likely manufactured somewhere in the Calabria region of southern Italy, commonly referred to as 'the toe of Italy's boot'; or, perhaps in Sicily, Calabria's island-neighbour to the west, commonly called 'the ball to Italy's boot'. There was a gold ring on his ring finger, but, from where he sat, Fankhauser could not discern whether or not it bore the notorious emblem of the three intersecting crescents. Every now and then, between erratic gulps of wine, the man furtively glanced at Fankhauser and his two female protégés. When his foxy attention

226

was not aimed at Fankhauser's table, his eyes were wandering around the rest of the dining room, as if he was on the verge of committing some heinous crime, or, on the other side of the coin, was frightened to death. Fankhauser's hand automatically settled upon his Luger Pistole Parabellum, buried in his waist. Yes; it was still there. He leaned across to Renée and whispered in her ear. "Mama, do you have your Glock semi-automatic in your purse?" "As I previously told you, Joaquim, I don't leave home without it," she whispered back, humorously. "Good," he warned, "be prepared to use it, if and when I give the word." "Who do you think I am," she asked jokingly in a very low voice, "your hired gun?" Fankhauser snickered, patronizingly. Isolde wondered what in the world was going on. The mystery of the Italian stranger did not last long. Suddenly, there was a commotion at the front entrance of the *Moléson*, and, in the blink of an eye, there were six members of the *Kantonspolizei* rushing toward the lone young Italian, who was by now on his feet. Fankhauser fingered his Luger semi-automatic, and ordered his mother "Be ready, Mama!" Renée's right hand was already in her purse, grasping the handle of her Glock semi-automatic. Isolde sat there, frozen. In no time at all, the police handcuffed the Italian dandy, and escorted him out of the building.

"Thank God for that, whatever that was. False alarm," commented Fankhauser, relievedly. "Let's forget the whole thing, and enjoy ourselves. Eat, drink and be merry; for tomorrow we die."

"I hope not," commented Renée, saucily, "about the 'dying' part." Good old Renée. Never without her sense of humour.

The rest of the evening was uninterrupted delight. After the main meal, Fankhauser and the two women enjoyed desserts of Tarte Flambée, straight from the oven, with shots of Cognac.

"Thanks, Joaquim. I can honestly say that this was one of the most delightful dinners that I have ever had," Isolde complimented, her hands gently stroking her abdomen.

"Even with the drama thrown in?" asked Fankhauser, with a wink of his right eye.

"The drama simply added to the excitement," Isolde replied.

They lingered on at the *Moléson*, enjoying a couple more bottles of Bordeaux, until about eleven, when the waiter told them it was closing time. Fankhauser asked the waiter what the commotion involving the Italian stranger had been about.

"Un membre de la Mafia italienne, monsieur," the waiter replied, offhandedly. *Some member of the Italian Mafia, sir.*

The walk back to the *Fankhaus* was more leisurely, and even more delightful, than the walk to the *Moléson*. The full moon was a giant silver orb that reigned as queen of the night. It was so close Isolde could have sworn she could touch it. She heard the vagrant fallen leaves of autumn shuffling across the deserted street. To her, the Old Town had taken on a special nostalgic glow, reminiscent of Paris at midnight along the banks of the Seine. Besides, she was feeling no pain. She felt as if she had enough alcohol in her blood to sink a battleship. As they ambled along disconcertedly, Renée recounted tales of the glory and innocence of her childhood, spent, like a child in wonderland, in Old Bern. "Now, here I am," she confessed, "a damn killer, responsible for the death of two men. So much for the days of innocence! May God have mercy on my soul!" Fankhauser was quick to brighten up her thoughts. "Mama," he cajoled, "why don't you just breathe in the fresh air of the Old Town, and enjoy the moonlit night?" He then wandered on about the idyllic life that he had spent there as a child and as a young man.

"Just think," he said, "a world war raging around Switzerland, and we never had to fire a shot. That's armed neutrality for you."

"And you had to go and spoil it by becoming a private investigator!" snapped Renée, jokingly. "Now look at what it has done to your poor mother! Made a hitman of me! A good Christian girl turned into a vicious killer!"

"But, remember, Mama. You have only killed in self-defence," Fankhauser laughed.

"But think of the Ten Commandments," she responded quickly. The Fifth Commandment says 'THOU SHALL NOT KILL'. Show me where it says 'EXCEPT IN CASES OF SELF-DEFENCE'!" Fankhauser laughed. He could try and argue with her that some Bible translations read 'THOU SHALL NOT MURDER'. But he knew that such an argument would be useless; as his mother always has the last word, when it comes to the Bible. Wisely, he quickly changed the subject.

As they entered the *Fankhaus*, they could hear the bells of the *Zytglogge*. It was now midnight. Fankhauser pulled out a bottle of German Himbeergeist Schnapps, which, with three Scnapps glasses, he placed on the dining table.

"In true Swiss-German tradition, we cannot let you leave the *Fankhaus*, Isolde, without knocking off a bottle of Schnapps."

Renée put on a recording of Chopin's *Tristesse, Étude Opus 10, No.3*; also known as his *Farewell* piano solo. Most appropriate for the occasion, she felt. She had grown attached to Isolde, and will be sad to see her leave. With this music in the background, Fankhauser and the two women set about to imbibing the whole bottle of Schnapps. It was a perfect way to wind up the evening and Isolde's stay at the *Fankhaus*.

CHAPTER TWENTY-SIX

EARLY THE NEXT MORNING, Fankhauser picked up his copy of the weekly *Wochen Zeitung* left at the front door of the *Fankhaus*. As he walked into his home office, he opened up the newspaper. He gasped as he read the headline: **DREI ERSCHOSSEN TOT IN BERN.** *THREE SHOT DEAD IN BERN.* Steadying himself in his chair, he read and reread the article. It contained all the nitty-gritty details of the shootout at the intersection of Rathausgasse and Brunngasse. The photographs of the bodies of the dead men were graphic. The skull of one corpse had been blown apart, the shattered fragments, washed in tinges of blood, littering the light-grey-white sidewalk. Fanhauser surmised that Renée's bullet from the Russian Nagant revolver had done this damage, while the barrage of bullets from his Luger Pistole Parabellum had struck the torso of the other assailant, ripping his abdomen into so many shreds you could see his entrails. What a marksman my Mama is, marveled Fankhauser. The body of the innocent driver was also shown, a trail of blood running down from his heart, his eyes still wide open in shock. Fankhauser was appalled by the prominence that the article had given to Lise. It described the condition of the injured woman as critical, and prognosticated that she would never ever walk again. Her blood relationship in the prominent Medici family was by no means understated. In fact, it occupied over one-half of the article. It bothered Fankhauser that Lise's current whereabouts were even revealed; that she was a patient in *Spital Tiefenau*. This is reckless journalism, Fankhauser concluded, agonizingly. Now, not only does *The Shadow* know that Lise Brunner is still alive, but they are aware of the fact that she is a sitting duck at *Spital Tiefenau*. Fortunately, he had arranged with Head-Nurse

Meyer for a security guard to be posted outside her room. Let's hope that works.

Fankhauser made the decision to not show the *Wochen Zeitung* article to Isolde. There was no worthwhile purpose that could be served by her reading it. If she read it, a natural consequence would likely be a resurgence of traumatic memories, and paralysis from fear. At breakfast, he offered to drive Isolde to Bern International Airport to catch her SwissAir flight to Paris.

After an emotional parting in which both Isolde and Renée broke down in tears, Isolde and Fankhauser left the *Fankhaus* at about noon on their way to the airport in the black Merfcedes-Benz. Isolde was in an upbeat mood, and was thanking Fankhauser profusely for all that he had done for her, when Fankhauser's mobile telephone rang.

"Hallo. Fankhauser hier." *Hello. Fankhauser here.*

"Oh, Joaquim." It was the voice of Lorena Meyer. Joaquim's heart fell. Was she calling to cancel their dinner date? "I am so glad I got hold of you," she continued. "You asked that I immediately let you know if there are any unusual activities involving Lise Brunner. Well, about an hour ago, a well-dressed woman appeared at the Nurses' Station, with a bouquet of red roses in her hands. She identified herself as one Valentina de' Medici. She said that she was Lise's cousin from Florence. She asked for Lise's room number; she wanted to take the roses to Lise and pay her a brief visit. Not taking any chances, I told her to wait there for a minute, while I spoke with Lise. I could see her flinch at this. She persisted that it would only be a very short visit. Ignoring this, I went to Lise's room. I asked her if she had a cousin from Florence known as Valentina de' Medici. She said "no". By the time I got back to the Nurses' Station, the mysterious woman was gone, roses and all."

"Good work, Lorena. Keep it up, my dear. See you later for dinner." Fankhauser was relieved on two fronts. Firstly, Lorena had not canceled their dinner date. Secondly, she had most likely foiled another potential attempt by *The Shadow* on Lise's life.

While Fankhauser was relating to Isolde what Lorena had conveyed to him, Isolde's mobile phone rang. It was Margot calling from Toronto.

"Isolde, my darling. I am so relieved to have gotten hold of you!" Her voice was quivering, obviously from fear. She sounded almost breathless.

'What's the matter, Margot? Is it the kids? Are Emil and Sophie OK?' It was all that Isolde could do to get those words out. She felt a vacuous feeling in the pit of her stomach.

"They are fine, at least for now," Margot assured her. "But I thought I should let you know about a mysterious phone call I just received." She stopped as if to take a breath.

"What do you mean 'at least for now'? Are they in any danger?"

"The phone had rung. I picked it up. And then I received this cryptic message. 'Sag Frau Bruni: Schau auf die Kinder.' The caller then hung up."

"What does that mean, Margot? You know that I don't speak German." She could hear Margot now sobbing. There was a short delay, as Margot tried to compose herself.

"I hate to tell you this, Isolde. But in English, it means: *Tell Mrs. Bruni: Look to the children.*" There was an audible gasp from Isolde. She was suddenly gripped with fear. Her breathing became fast and shallow. She felt as if she was about to pass out. Sensing that Isolde was having problems, Fankhauser pulled off onto the shoulder of the highway.

"Isolde? Isolde?" Margot kept repeating. "Are you there?" Fankhauser took the mobile phone out of Isolde's hands.

"Hi, Margot. This is Joaquim Fankhauser, PI. I think Isolde is in shock. Would you mind just holding for a couple of minutes?" Margot was relieved. Isolde seemed to be in good hands.

"No problem at all. I will be here."

Fankhauser looked into Isolde's eyes. They had rolled over, reminiscent of someone who is apoplectic. He pulled out from his glove compartment a small bottle of Cognac. His elixir, he called it. He opened the bottle and put it to her lips, forcing its contents into her mouth. Almost instantly, Isolde was back. She stared into Fankhauser's eyes, pleadingly.

"Margot received a mysterious phone call. *Tell Mrs. Bruni: Look to the children,* the voice told her in German. Oh, Joaquim, if anything happens to either Emil or Sophie, I just would not be able to forgive myself! What am I to do?" she implored, desperately, her face still blanched from the sudden attack that had afflicted her.

"First things first, Isolde. Margot is still on the phone. You should speak with her again. Assure her that you are OK. Tell her to hire security guards to provide the children with round-the-clock protection. And thank her for letting you know so speedily about the mysterious phone call. You will see her when you arrive in Toronto." He handed the mobile phone back to Isolde.

"Hi, Margot. Sorry about that, sweetheart. The news was too much for me. But I am OK now. My private investigator Joaquim Fankhauser recommends that we hire security guards to provide round-the-clock protection for Emil and Sophie. Can you do that for me? All at my expense, of course."

"Oh, Isolde. You had me worried for a minute. I am so relieved that you are fine! No problem at all with the security guard thing. Anything else I can do?"

"Nope. Just keep safe. See you when I get back." Isolde then turned to Fankhauser, her hands still shaking from the shock of the message relayed by Margot. "Sorry about that, Joaquim. I guess I had a dizzy spell."

"Only natural, Isolde. A veiled threat like that would send anyone into a daze. Especially when it comes from an organization as nefarious as *The Shadow.* But you have to pull yourself together. Fear is a very negative force. It causes one to worry, and that is not only counter-productive, but it is also destructive. You have taken the practical course of action, by arranging for security guards to be hired to protect the children. Now, you *must* pull yourself together. Or else you will be no good to anyone, including yourself."

"I know you are right, Joaquim. But your words are easier said than done. There is no greater love than a mother's love for her infant child. The maternal instinct is pervasive throughout all types of life. What would I ever do if I lost Emil or Sophie?" she sniveled, tears running down her tautened cheeks. She looked questioningly at Fankhauser, as if she expected an answer. Fankhauser remained silent. He had already imparted his advice. Eventually, Isolde looked at her watch and said: "Let's get to the airport, Joaquim. I don't want to be late for my flight check-in."

When they got to the airport, Fankhauser helped Isolde with her luggage, putting it in the hands of a porter. He could see that her nerves were still frazzled. She extended her right hand into his to bid him farewell. Instead of shaking hands, he pulled her into his arms, and gave her a warm bear-hug. "Auf Wiedershen, Frau Bruni," he whispered. "Don't worry, Isolde. We will slay this monster called *The Shadow*. But a word of caution: Do not speak to strangers on the flights or at the airports."

Fankhauser watched as Isolde walked circumspectly into the Airport Terminal. She was noticeably agitated, her head turning rapidly from side to side, as if half-expecting *The Shadow* to suddenly emerge, like a bogeyman, out of nowhere.

CHAPTER TWENTY-SEVEN

KLM FLIGHT 057 from Paris touched down at Pearson International Airport at eight ten in the evening, Toronto time. Isolde was overcome by a tremendous feeling of relief at being back safely on Canadian soil. She had no regrets at having spent the time she did in Bern, Florence and Paris. Yes, her quest had been successful. She, with the able assistance of Fankhauser, had solved the mystery of Fred's death. It lifted a huge weight from her head to know that Fred had not committed suicide, as tragic as it was that he had been murdered. She would now be able to look Emil and Sophie in the eyes, when they were old enough to understand, and tell them that their father had not died by his own hand. And she knew whom to blame for the murder. But there were experiences that she had had in Bern that she would never want to repeat themselves. More specifically, the violent intrusion of Simon Hartmann into the *Fankhaus*, and the resultant shooting that caused his immediate demise, not to mention having had to share the *Fankhaus* with his corpse. And then the shootout at the intersection of Rathausgasse and Brunngasse, which left two of the three attackers and an innocent driver stone cold dead, and Lise quadriplegic, to be confined to a wheelchair for the rest of her life. Not to mention the fact that *The Shadow* had issued a death warrant for Isolde's own demise, which, thanks to Fankhauser's adroitness, was never executed. But the most disturbing aspect of all was the veiled threat which *The Shadow* had imparted to her in that cryptic telephone call to Margot. The words still resounded in Isolde's ears. *Tell Mrs. Bruni: Look to the children.* She broke out in a cold sweat every time she pondered those words. All very scary experiences, which, prior thereto, she had only read about in crime and mystery novels, or seen on the silver screen. I could write my own novel about all this, she thought to herself. But that's for another day down the road. For now, she had her hands full with reorganizing her life, with protecting her children and herself, and with pursuing remedies for wrongful death on behalf of Emil and Sophie and herself.

She felt her heart go pitter-patter as the airport limo pulled into the driveway of her Saddlers Court mansion. At long last, she was home. She wasted no time in phoning Margot, who was waiting anxiously for her call, the two children already packed and ready to return to the home they knew and loved so dearly.

"Hi, Margot. I am now home. I will come and get the kids."

"Don't be foolish," Margot countered. "You must be dead beat. Jet lag, and all that jazz. Stay where you are. I will just whisk them over to you myself. I will have the security guard accompany me, and I will introduce him to you. See you in ten minutes."

Isolde heard the welcome soft buzz of the motor of Margot's peacock-blue Alpha Romeo as it rolled down the driveway and pulled up in front of the Saddlers Court mansion. In no time at all, Emil and Sophie came rushing in, headed straight for their waiting mother. "Mommy! Mommy!" they both shouted, as they folded themselves into her outstretched arms.

"Mommy," Emil bubbled. "We thought we would never see you again." This brought tears of joy to Isolde's eyes, as she immediately thought of how closely that fear had come to being realized. After all, she had at least thrice been only a whisker away from being eliminated back in Bern. Margot stood a few feet away, watching this joyful family reunion. Isolde and the two children chatted for a few minutes. Then, Isolde told them to go to their rooms, unpack their bags, and get ready for bed. She would tuck them in later. Once the children left, Isolde and Margot hugged, tears streaming down their cheeks.

"How about some coffee, Margot?" Isolde asked.

"Better yet, how about some wine, Isolde?" Margot responded, with a twinkle in her eyes. "But first I must introduce you to Miguel, the children's 'guardian angel'. Come with me for a minute. He is outside in his car." She took Isolde by the hand and led her outside. Miguel was leaning against his 1969 battleship-grey Ford Bronco SUV, which was parked behind the Alpha Romeo, his arms and legs crossed. The whiteness of his teeth was accentuated by its contrast with his chocolate complexion and his jet-black hair. He was a giant of a man, standing at least six feet seven. He straightened up to stand erect as Margot and Isolde approached.

"Miguel," Margot started, "this is Mrs. Bruni."

"Glad to meet you, Mrs. Bruni. I just love your children," Miguel greeted Isolde, his English tinged with a Spanish accent.

"Thanks for helping us," Isolde responded, amicably. "Do I detect a Spanish accent?"

"Yes, ma'am. I was born in Cuba. I was a captain in President Batista's army when the government was overthrown by Castro's revolutionary forces in 1959. I fled to the United States, and eventually worked my way to Canada. I have been in the personal security business since then."

"Good for you, Miguel," Isolde complimented, with a charming smile. "I look forward to working with you." Miguel glowed.

"Miguel is on duty around the clock, Isolde. I gave him a room in my house. I expect that you will do the same."

"Absolutely, Miguel. Just follow me."

Back inside the house, Isolde assigned to Miguel a room in close proximity to the children's rooms. She then rejoined Margot, who was now in the kitchen. She fetched a bottle of Cabernet Sauvignon and two wine glasses. The two women sat down at the kitchen table and started into the wine.

"OK, Isolde. Tell me all about Bern. I am all ears."

"Are you sure you are ready for all this?" asked Isolde, an impish smile on her face.

"After Fred's death, I am ready for anything and everything."

"Ok. Fasten your seatbelt. Here we go. Had I told you that, before Fred died, I knew absolutely nothing about Fred's law practice; nor about our financial affairs? Absolutely zilch?"

"I cannot recall you telling me that. Why? Were there surprises?"

"I would not call them surprises; but shocks. Fred essentially had only one client." Margot raised her eyebrows. "Through this one client, he had an income of $2,000,000-$3,000,000 a year. Can you believe that?"

"Incredible, Margot commented, dryly. "I knew he must have had a good income. But only from one client! Who was this client?"

"The files were opened in the name of VolksBankBern, a bank in the *Altstadt*. Run by a guy named Constantino Rapini. Apparently VolksBankBern was acting in a trustee capacity, for an undisclosed principal. Rapini told me that under banking rules he was not at liberty to disclose the name of the principal. So, with him, I ran into a brick wall."

"Very interesting. Go on," Margot prompted. Isolde took a big gulp of Cabernet, before continuing.

"Can you believe that Fred had a girl-friend in Bern?" At this, Margot took a big gulp of Cabernet.

"You gotta be kiddin' me!" Margot choked, in astonishment.

"Yes. He had. Her name is Lise Brunner. Born and bred in Bern. Well, this thing between Fred and Lise went on for some time. Fred would stay at her place whenever he was in Bern. She admitted the affair to me. Lise was the one that got Fred connected to VolksBankBern. She is very well connected. She is a Medici. You must have heard of the Medicis?"

"Do you mean the Italian Medicis that were part of the Renaissance?" Margot asked, her bottom jaw dropping almost down to her breast.

"The very same ones".

"I read about them in my history courses back at U of T. But, are you kiddin' me? Fred's girl-friend was from that remarkable family?"

"She was, Margot."

"Well, that son-of-a-bitch brother of mine. When he screwed around, he sure plucked the fruit from the most productive family trees! Go on, Isolde."

"To get to the bottom of things, I hired a private investigator in Bern. Joaquim Fankhauser."

"That's the fellow I spoke with when I phoned you about the cryptic phone call I had received?"

"Yup. The very same one. Expensive; but the best money I ever spent. I also consulted with a Professor Rossi at the University of Florence. He gave me a brief history of the Medicis. But it turned out that it was not the Medicis that were involved with VolksBankBern. But rather a nefarious outfit known as *'Ombra Segreta della Forza di Firenze'*."

"You've got me there. I can only tell that that is Italian. Please translate for me, Isolde."

"That fancy term translates to *'The Secret Shadow of the Force of Florence'*. In more common parlance, the organization is called *The Shadow*," Isolde explained.

"Wow! Right out of a mystery novel! So, who is *'The Force of Florence'?*"

"That, my dear Margot, is a reference to the noble Medici family. Did you know that the Medicis produced four Popes? Did you know that the Medicis were whizzes at finance, and even started their own bank in Florence, *Banco dei Medici*, which they successfully ran for decades and decades? Did you know that there are reports that there are descendants of the Medicis who are very influential in acting as financial advisors to the Vatican?"

"My answer to each of your questions is No."

"While the Medicis were generally honourable in their dealings," Isolde continued, "the group known as *The Shadow* sprang up as a nefarious group to sponge off the good character of the Medicis. They live in the shadow of the Medicis. *The Shadow* is an extremely dangerous and corrupt organization. Its members are truly Machiavellian. They will stop at nothing in the pursuit of their goals. They are involved in international drug trafficking, human trafficking, prostitution, money laundering, and the like. You name an illegal activity, and somewhere in the world *The Shadow* is likely involved in it." Isolde stopped to take a sip of Cabernet. "Incidentally, the members of *The Shadow* are identified by a common bond. It is an emblem that came down over the past four hundred years from a woman named Diane de Poitiers. Have you ever heard of her?"

"Can't say that I have. Who was this Diane woman?"

"Believe it or not, her claim to fame was that she was the mistress of Henry II of France, while he was married to Catherine de' Medici. Diane pretty well controlled Henry, until he suffered a horrific head injury while jousting. From then on, Catherine cut off Diane's access to the ailing Henry. Another thing about Diane; she had an obsession with her own boobs."

"You mean that she had a fetish for her own knockers?"

"That's precisely what I mean. She was fixated on her own breasts."

"Wow! This is out of this world. This is surely what great novels are made from."

"So, the emblem that came down from Diane was her own design; a simple but ingenious design. Three intersecting crescents. This emblem was adopted by *The Shadow*, which was an amalgamation of Diane's secret force with a group called the Ruspanti, which had sprung up under the morally corrupt Gian Gastone de' Medici. Gian Gastone was the last Medici to hold the title Grand Duke of Tuscany."

"The plot gets thicker. But, what has all this got to do with Fred's death?" asked Margot.

"Fred had started asking too many questions about the identity of his client. He needed to know the true identity of the principal for which VolksBankBern was acting. That was the reason for his business trip to Bern a few weeks ago. This resulted in *The Shadow* decreeing his death. He was asking too many questions, the answers to which could expose *The Shadow* in their money laundering schemes, which is what Fred, unknowingly, had been participating in for *The Shadow* here in Toronto."

"But the Death Certificate showed that Fred died from poisoning here in Toronto?"

"The scheme devised by *The Shadow* to eliminate Fred was really ingenious. Central in this plot is the legacy of Catherine de' Medici. She had a big role in history as one of the main sponsors of the Renaissance. Well, good old Catherine had a rather interesting hobby. She became an expert on poisons. If you get the opportunity, visit Château de Blois in France, not far from Paris. The guides will show you Catherine's little

Chamber of Secrets; some people call it her *Chamber of Horrors.* This is the room with cabinets in which she used to store her poisons. Catherine was always experimenting with poisons. There was one poison which was her own personal creation. She dubbed it *'Mon Petit Ami'.* As you know, this is French for *'My Little Friend'.* I consulted with a Professor Rappaport at the Sorbonne University. He is a renowned international expert on poisons. He confirmed that *'Mon Petit Ami'* is completely untraceable in human tissues and cells. The formula is known to less than a handful of people. But he was able to confirm that the formula was in the hands of *The Shadow.* And that the formula could be replicated in tablet form."

"Fascinating," commented Margot, excitedly. "I am anxious to hear the rest."

"Having determined that Fred *must* die, *The Shadow*, through Rapini, engaged Lise to plant a single tablet of *'Mon Petit Ami'* in the bottle containing Fred's Cafergot pills, which, as you know, Fred took for his migraines. The single tablet of *'Mon Petit Ami'* was manufactured to be indistinguishable in appearance from the Cafergot pills. Lise planted the single tablet of *'Mon Petit Ami'* in Fred's Cafergot bottle. Back in Toronto, Fred, removed from the bottle a pill which he thought to be Cafergot, but which in reality was *'Mon Petit Ami'.* He swallowed *'Mon Petit Ami'* while working late at his law office, and you know the rest."

"Holy Maloney!" uttered Margot, wide-eyed, as she took another gulp of Cabernet. "That is incredible! Poor Fred!"

"When *The Shadow* learned through Rapini that Lise was running scared as a result of my investigation, they decided to kill both Lise and me. Fortunately, Fankhauser was ahead of the game, and saved Lise's life, after they attempted to murder her by forcing *'Mon Petit Ami'* down her throat. They also had a hit out on my life. Fankhauser had me leave my hotel and move into his apartment, which he shares with his mother, Renée, and which they both call the *Fankhaus.* When Lise was released from the hospital, he also had her move into the *Fankhaus.* So, there we were, all four of us, sharing the *Fankhaus.* Things got way out of hand while Fankhauser was away in Rome tracking down *The Shadow.* A Bern police inspector, one Simon Hartmann, whom Fankhauser had called his friend, but who was a secret member of *The Shadow,* broke into the *Fankhaus,* pistol in hand, ready to kill Lise, Renée and me.

Fortunately, Fankhauser, again ahead of the game, had left Renée armed with a pistol. She was ready for him. She shot him dead."

"Oh my God! You went through all this?" Margot gasped.

"You have not heard the end of it yet. We rolled the body into a rug, and carried it into the guest bedroom, then occupied by Lise, until Fankhauser returned from Rome. When he came home, he reported the shooting to the Bern Police, who declared the *Fankhaus* a crime scene. The police inspector questioned us, and made an appointment for us to go to the Police Headquarters the next day to give written statements. You would never believe what happened the next day on our drive to the Police Headquarters?"

"Go on. I cannot wait!"

"We were slowing down to stop for a red light at an intersection. Suddenly, a speeding car overtook us, moved into our lane, and then backed up into Fankhauser's Mercedes-Benz. Just immediately prior to that, another car had come up behind us. We were completely boxed in. The long and the short of it is that one of the two men in the car behind us got out and approached our car with pistol drawn. We were under siege. Renée shot him dead. Bang! Blew his damned head off! The other occupant of that car then came at us, firing wildly into Fankhauser's Mercedes-Benz. Fankhauser was ready for him, and shot him dead, with a barrage of bullets that ripped his abdomen to shreds. Oh, yes; I should mention that an innocent driver came upon the scene, and the surviving assailant shot him dead, poor guy."

"This is the sort of thing that one sees only in movies!" exclaimed Margot. "And to think that my sister-in-law was in the middle of all this action!"

"Unfortunately, Lise took a bullet in her upper spine. She is now permanently a quadriplegic." Isolde took another mouthful of Cabernet. "When we eventually got to Police Headquarters the next day, we were further interrogated. We signed statements, and were free to go. In both situations, a clear case of self-defence."

"Sounds like self-defence to me, too. Is that the end of it?"

"No. What I am about to tell you is what Fankhauser related to me as to his exploits in Rome. He suspected that *The Shadow* had some sort of connection with the Vatican, and that VolksBankbern was tied in with this connection. So, he hired a driver, an Italian named Giuseppe Cipola, which translates into English as 'Joe Onion'. Can you believe that handle?" Both women erupted into hilarious laughter. "Joe Onion was to turn up with a van. Instead, what he was driving was a canary-yellow Fiat hatchback. Hardly the type of vehicle used by servicemen! A make-shift sign on the doors was in the Italian for 'BENNY'S CLEANING SERVICE'. Joe Onion, with Fankhauser in the passenger seat, followed a VolksBankBern van onto the grounds of the Vatican. While the two guards from the VolksBankBern van were inside the Administrative Building, Fankhauser left Joe Onion sitting in his canary-yellow Fiat hatchback, and went to inspect some bags in the back of the VolksBankBern van. Suddenly, the two guards reappeared. Fankhauser took off in the direction of the *Basilica*, leaving Joe Onion sitting in his Fiat hatchback. Would you believe that the guards shot Joe Onion dead?"

"My dear Isolde," Margot responded, "nothing in this whole wide world would surprise me after all that you just told me."

"Well, that's what they did. And then they apparently planted evidence in his Fiat hatchback to point to poor Joe Onion as just having robbed their van. Fankhauser escaped unscathed. At least he now knew that VolksBankBern was delivering to the Vatican Bank huge amounts of money in a number of different currencies. The obvious conclusion was that money of different currencies was being passed on by VolksBankBern as part of a money laundering scheme." Isolde poured the last portion of Cabernet from the bottle into Margot's glass. "Another dead soldier," she commented, and went to find another bottle of Cabernet Sauvignon. She soon returned with a full bottle, opened it, poured some into her glass, and continued her tale.

"So, in hot pursuit of *The Shadow*, Fankhauser, a professional escort on his arm, went to a top-notch restaurant for dinner at a time when he knew that a man named Bernardo Agimo would be there. Agimo was a member of *The Shadow*. He was the one who had made an attempt on Lise's life by forcing *'Mon Petit Ami'* down her throat. With the assistance of a Rome colleague, a P.I. named Alberto Fettucini, Fankhauser entrapped Agimo, and had him whisked off to an unknown location." Margot was laughing uncontrollably.

"You must mean 'Alfredo Fettucini', my dear Isolde!"

"No. Fankhauser told me 'Alberto'." They were now both rolling in laughter. First, a man named 'Joe Cipola'. And now a man named 'Alberto Fettucini'.

"The Italians must love their food so much they even adopt the names of foods for their own names," Margot commented, still howling in laughter.

"By one means or another, Fankhauser got Agimo to admit everything. Fred's murder by the poisoning agent *'Mon Petit Ami'*. The existence of *The Shadow*. The huge money laundering scheme, including the involvement of VolksBankBern; and the involvement of one accomplice planted by *The Shadow* at the Vatican Bank. The admissions were all recorded on videotape and voice recording. As an aside, Fankhauser and Fettucini had their driver, Giovanni, use an instrument of torture on Agimo. You will laugh when you hear what it is called."

"I am waiting with baited breath."

"Fankhauser said that Giovanni called it his *'balls-shocker'*.

"Ouch!" screamed Margot. "Does it really shock *'balls'*? That would hurt! You can spare me the details of how it works! Sounds like a good tool for women to use to keep their men in line." Once more, they both burst out into laughter, until tears streamed down their cheeks.

"One more thing. When Fankhauser decided to speed up the interrogation, he pulled out a revolver, put one bullet in it, had the muzzle inserted into Agimo's mouth, and for every question that he asked to which he did not receive an answer, or received an unsuitable answer, he had Agimo pull the trigger."

"A game of Russian roulette! But with only one player. That would be sure to speed things up!" Margot was fully immersed into the strange story that Isolde was telling her.

"Fankhauser told me that he had arranged for Fettucini to turn Agimo, the videotape, and the voice recording over to the various law enforcement authorities, including *INTERPOL*. He recommended to me that I pursue an action in the civil courts here in Ontario for damages for wrongful death in relation to Fred's murder, and that I leave it up to the law enforcement agencies to pursue the perpetrators criminally. I decided to follow his advice."

"You are a real Trojan, Isolde. And that Fankhauser seems to be 'a man for all seasons'."

"That's putting it mildly, Margot, your words about Fankhauser. I really lucked into him."

"So, what are your next steps forward, Isolde?"

"First, with Fred's income coming to a dead stop, I have to liquidate some of our assets. Would you and Heinz be interested in buying our chalet in St. Moritz? If so, I will let you have it at the appraised price less fifteen percent. Discuss it with Heinz and let me know within the next week. The same with our condo on Jupiter Island, and, of course, our luxury superyacht *Isle of Capri*. I know that you and Heinz do not need another car; but Fred's Rolls-Royce is also for sale. I will try to hang on to this house and our summer house in Muskoka Lakes. The sale of the St. Moritz chalet, the Jupiter Island condo, our yacht *Isle of Capri*, and Fred's Rolls-Royce should provide enough cash to keep me and the kids afloat for a while."

"I will speak with Heinz about this ASAP. You should know our decision within the next couple of days."

"The second thing on my agenda is the civil action. I need to get into the hands of a top-notch civil litigator to start the action for damages for wrongful death. Would you ask Heinz for me if he knows of anyone that can fit the bill?"

"I certainly will, Isolde," Margot replied, as she looked at her watch. It was now eleven thirty. "I didn't realize it was so late. Your poor kids! They were so anxious to have you back. I'd better go." She got up, and was already on her way to the front door.

"Thanks for listening, Margot."

"No; thank *you*, Isolde, for all that you have done. It is such a load off my mind to know that Fred did not die by his own hand." Margot then disappeared into the darkness of the night, as Isolde went to check on Emil and Sophie, who, by now, were both fast asleep in their rooms. Resolutely, she vowed to herself that over the coming months and years she would spend quality time with her fatherless children.

CHAPTER TWENTY-EIGHT

CHRISTMAS was upon Isolde before she knew it. At the Christmas eve service at the Lutheran Reformed Church of Switzerland, Isolde, with both Emil and Sophie seated beside her, gave special thanks to God that He had protected her throughout her trials and tribulations in Bern; had spared her life so that she could return to her dear children, who had already lost one parent; had revealed to her, mainly through the able assistance of 'the great Fankhauser', the answers to the mysteries surrounding Fred's demise; and, last but not least, had kept Emil and Sophie safe and sound. She prayed for inner strength in the battle that she had yet to face; the legal action against the perpetrators that had brought about the death of her husband, the father of her two young children. A war that she had resolved to wage, notwithstanding the veiled threat of *The Shadow*. She recalled Fankhauser's description of *The Shadow* as the Hydra, the many-headed monster that had the capability of regenerating itself. She fully realized that, especially with the commencement of the legal action, *The Shadow* would likely pursue her to the death. Yes. *We have scotch'd the snake, not kill'd it.* It will be the fight *of* her life, and *for* her life. And Fankhauser, her Sir Galahad, is thousands of miles away in Bern.

As she, Emil and Sophie left the church, followed by the hawk-like eyes of Miguel, it was pure heaven to hear the chimes of the church bells pealing out old familiar Christmas pieces, like *Away in a Manger* and *O Little Town of Bethlehem*. The only thing missing was Fred. But this state of bliss was now her utopia. She had to take what she could get, and she had to keep it that way. She had to plan ahead for survival of the children and herself. Knowing what she knew about *The Shadow*, about the dangers that she still faced, and about Fankhauser, what would

Fankhauser do under the circumstances? she asked herself, quizzingly. Her mind drifted back to what Fankhauser had done to protect the three women in the *Fankhaus* before he left for Rome. He had purchased a pistol for his mother, her beloved Glock G43x semi-automatic. The Glock had in fact saved their lives. Had Renée not been armed with it when Hartmann broke into the *Fankhaus*, then all three women—Renée, Lise and Isolde -- would have been stone cold dead. Absolutely no doubt about it. Of course, she and the children enjoyed the protective services of Miguel. But was there nothing more that she should be doing? There and then, following a lovely service, in the midst of wishing peace and goodwill to all mankind, she resolved that she would purchase a Glock G43x semi-automatic pistol, just like Renée's, only to be used, of course, for the defence of her and her two children.

Returning home from church after the Christmas eve service, she decided to phone Yvonne at her apartment to catch up on news at Fred's office, to make arrangements to pay her salary, which was now well past due, and to wish her Merry Christmas and a Happy New Year. She had to leave a message on voicemail for Yvonne to return her call. Yvonne returned her phone call two days later. Her voice was in the low range of the musical scale. She sounded groggy and distant.

"Hi, Yvonne," Isolde started, chirpily. "You sound as if you were out celebrating late last night." There was silence on the other end of the line.

"Oh, hi, Isolde. How was Bern?" Yvonne eventually asked, lethargically.

"Very successful. Anything new at the office?"

"Nope. Same old, same old."

"I owe you some money for salary? Can you tell me how much? I will mail you a cheque."

"How about $1,000? Does that sound fair?"

"Fine with me. I will mail you a cheque. Also, Merry Christmas and a Very Happy New Year."

"Thanks, Isolde. Same to you. See you sometime." Strange, Isolde mused. that was not the same ebullient Yvonne that she had always known. Yvonne had somehow lost the effervescence in her voice. It must be from too much partying. Isolde immediately wrote Yvonne a cheque for $1,000, and mailed it to her.

Once Christmas had come and gone, Isolde now had the time to move ahead with her plans to reorganize her life and pursue *The Shadow* and the other perpetrators through the courts. Margot had got back to her and told her that she and Heinz would take the Jupiter Island condo, the *Isle of Capri* super-yacht, and the St. Moritz chalet off her hands; the terms were perfect. Isolde should set about to obtain appraisals. They would close the deals ASAP. Margot said that she had asked Heinz if he could recommend a litigation lawyer, and that Heinz had recommended that Isolde seek the advice of Barney Ratskeller on that aspect.

Isolde phoned Barney Ratskeller. She briefly explained that she felt she had enough evidence for an action for damages for wrongful death. Which litigation lawyer in Toronto would he recommend for the case? Right off the cuff, Barney said: "Ben Higginbottom. No doubt about it. The best goddamn counsel for wrongful death." "That's good enough for me, Barney. Can you pave the way for me before I call him?" "Absolutely, Isolde. I will call him immediately."

She then checked the Toronto Yellow Pages for gun shops and for gun safety courses. She visited *A-One Gun Store* on Bathurst Street, and told them that she was interested in acquiring a Glock G43x semi-automatic pistol. They had none in stock, but could order one from a dealer in the United States. She would need a Firearms Licence before she could conclude the purchase. The order was placed; and within three days she had taken the requisite course and obtained the licence. Three days later she concluded the purchase. She was now armed in exactly the same manner as Renée had been during Fankhauser's absence in Rome. She thought of herself as 'a second Renée', 'an armed killer'.

Ben Higginbottom's office was perched like an aerie on the twenty-sixth floor of the Richmond-Adelaide Centre on Adelaide Street West in the heart of the Toronto financial district. From that height, the pedestrians looked like swarms of ants, as they scurried around penguinlike here, there and everywhere, most of them with briefcase in hand, their status symbol, many a briefcase containing nothing but today's lunch. Isolde was zoomed by the elevator to the twenty-sixth floor. The sign on the door to Higginbottom's office read **BYCUFF AND HIGGINBOTTOM, Barristers-at-Law.** Higginbottom's senior partner, Jonathan Bycuff, had kicked the bucket twelve years ago. He had suffered a massive heart attack while working in the office one Saturday morning. His body was not discovered until the following Monday, long after rigor mortis had set in. Out of respect for the memory of his deceased partner, Higginbottom chose to leave the firm under the old name **'BYCUFF AND HIGGINBOTTOM'**. The receptionist, an elderly matron with a mop of ashen hair that Isolde swore was a wig, made Isolde comfortable, taking her winter coat and offering her a cup of coffee. Isolde made herself at home, leafing through the latest issue of *MONEY* magazine, which was all Greek to her.

"Mrs. Bruni?" a loud, commanding voice bellowed in the reception area. Isolde looked up, expecting to see a Colossus of a man standing before her. Instead, what she saw was what she would call 'a shrimp of a man', a man of slight stature, standing no more than five two, and weighing no more than ten stones. The pate of his head showed no signs of hair, but at each temple a tiny puff of grey outcropping appeared, which could easily have been mistaken as ear-muffs. Rimless spectacles rested on the bridge of his prominent, bulbous nose; if you did not see the earpieces sweeping back to the ears, you would bet that you were looking at a pince-nez. This is not what she had expected Higginbottom to look like. This must be his paralegal, she thought to herself.

"I am here to see Mr. Higginbottom," she said firmly, in order to avoid any misunderstanding.

"You are looking at him," Higginbottom replied, with a faint smile. "Please follow me to my office." As she entered his office, she was immediately struck by the Picasso painting that hung on the wall behind his desk.

"Forgive me for asking," she started, 'but is that an original Picasso?" His smile immediately broadened to reveal the most perfect set of teeth God had ever created.

"Yup. Done by Pablo himself," he responded, proudly.

"You speak as if you knew him."

"Yes. I had the pleasure of meeting the great man about twenty years ago. As a matter of fact, I was a guest in his house in Madrid. This painting was a gift from him. Are you a student of art, Mrs. Bruni?"

"I studied Art as one if my undergraduate courses. But, to be honest, I would be lying to describe myself as 'a student of art'."

"Well, this painting was done by Pablo in 1909. It was during his African Period."

"What a gift! It must be worth a couple of millions today?"

"Let's put it this way. It's not for sale. Not at any price." Isolde was impressed. She stared at the feet of this little man sitting in his huge executive chair about four feet behind his desk. They were dangling in the air, unable to touch the floor. But there was nothing dwarfish about him. She was already looking at him as a true giant. Just from this. The Picasso thing. Because of what he had said, she was looking up to Mr. Higginbottom. "So, Mrs. Bruni. You are not here to discuss art. Let me first say that I knew your late husband, Fred. He was a good guy. You know, in life, and especially in the legal profession, there are 'good guys' and there are 'bad guys'. As a famous judge once told me, 'In every case that comes before me, there is'---and please forgive my French, but these were his exact words---'a *fuckor* and there is a *fuckee*; the bad guy and the good guy. My first task is to find out who is the *fuckor* and who is the *fuckee*. I then tailor my decision so that the good guy wins. Justice is as simple as that.' I can wholeheartedly say that Fred was one of the 'good guys'. I have never really believed that he died by his own hand." Isolde was a taken aback by the bluntness in the remarks of the little man, almost approaching crudeness, especially when spoken to a woman. But his words had been delivered with great finesse, and were very complimentary of Fred.

"I am glad to hear you say that of Fred, Mr. Higginbottom."

"Please. Call me Ben."

"OK, Ben. And please call me Isolde." She felt wholly connected to Higginbottom.

"Now, Isolde, please assume that I know nothing whatsoever about your case. I want you to outline all the pertinent facts, and, at the same time, give me copies of all relevant documents in your possession."

Isolde spent the next three and one-half hours relating all the facts to Higginbottom, giving him each and every relevant document as she moved forward in her description of events. He was all ears, taking copious notes, and never interrupting her, except in the rare circumstance that some clarification was needed. When she was finished, he asked her some specific questions, which she readily answered.

"OK. I have a good grasp of the facts, from what you have told me and shown me. On a preliminary basis only, it is my opinion that you have a good case for substantial damages for wrongful death against the organization known as *'Ombra Segreta della Forza di Firenze'*, aka *The Shadow,* against the individual members of *The Shadow*, against VolksBankBern, its manager Constantino Rapini, and against Lise Brunner. From what you have told me, I see no case against the Vatican, aka 'the Holy See', or any of its cardinals. Unless the authorities such as *INTERPOL* come up with something to implicate them in Fred's death, you can just forget about them for the purposes of this action here in Ontario."

"I will not be seeking any damages against Lise Brunner," Isolde said decisively.

"I understand, Isolde. But she will be a necessary witness to prove your case at trial. Will she be available?'

"I strongly believe so. *The Shadow* has already made three attempts on her life, leaving her without the use of her arms and legs. She is on our side."

"Good. You will also need to bring other witnesses from Switzerland, Italy, and France, such as Joaquim Fankhauser, Alberto Fettucini, Professor Rossi, Professor Rappaport, and some officers from the law enforcement agencies. There will likely be a jurisdictional challenge, on the argument that the proper forum and law is that of Switzerland. But I think that we can overcome that. Although the pill *'Mon Petit Ami'* was planted in Fred's Cafergot pill bottle in Bern, it was not ingested until Fred was back here in Toronto and Fred's death took place here in Toronto. Moreover, you will have a number of witnesses who reside here in Toronto, such as Fred's secretary Yvonne Becker, the investigating officers from the Toronto Police Department, the pathologist, and numerous witnesses to prove the quantum of damages. We will seek judgment here in Ontario, and the defendants will have to defend here. Once we obtain judgment, we will have to bring other actions in Switzerland and Italy to enforce the judgment. As far as the amount of our claim is concerned, considering that Fred's income was

$2,000,000- $3,000,000 per year and considering his age, my current thinking is that we claim $60,000,000. Because of the complexity of the litigation and its trans-national nature, the litigation costs will be enormous. I would need a cash retainer of $50,000.00 to begin with. Can you provide that?" Isolde was thrilled with what she had just heard, about the quantum of damages. She was having difficulty even picturing such a huge sum as $60,000,000.

"It is a lot of money, Ben. But I can manage it."

"Good. I will have my secretary prepare a Retainer Agreement for you to sign."

Higginbottom left to instruct his secretary. As Isolde sat alone in his office, her eyes naturally circled the room, looking to see what other *objets d'art* lay therein that could possibly rival the Picasso masterpiece. On one wall, she spotted what appeared to be a Van Gogh. I wonder, she asked herself whimsically if that was 'a gift from Vincent'? After the story of the 'gift from Pablo', she would not even think of denying that possibility, had it not been that Vincent had departed this earth in 1890, long before Higginbottom was even born. On the other wall which was not a window, her eyes landed on a group of seven paintings, clearly depicting Canadian landscape sceneries. No doubt paintings done by the famous Canadian painters who became known as 'The Group of Seven'. Higginbottom was back with the Retainer Agreement, which he reviewed with Isolde, paragraph by paragraph. They both signed the document, and she delivered into his hands a cheque for $50,000. "I promise that you will be well served, Isolde. I will commence the litigation without delay. In the meantime, considering what you have told me about the ubiquitous nature of *The Shadow*, are you taking any precautions for your safety?" She assured him that she was ever conscious of the danger which she faced from her Hydra-like adversary, and that she had indeed taken some steps toward self-preservation of herself and protection of the children. As she stepped out of the Richmond-Adelaide Centre to become lost amid the bustling throng of penguin-type pedestrians on Adelaide Street West, she had a good feeling about Higginbottom. She was convinced that she was in the right hands, as physically tiny as they were.

CHAPTER TWENTY-NINE

FOR THE FIRST TIME in her life, Isolde felt overwhelmed by legal matters. It had all been so easy when Fred was alive. She had been all too happy to leave everything of that nature up to him. With the pressures of the administration of Fred's estate, including winding up his now dormant law practice, she started to wonder why she had ever studied law in the first place, especially considering how pedantic legal procedures now appeared to her. Yes. Why had she decided to become a lawyer? As to whether or not her parents had exerted undue influence on her in the selection of law as a career, the jury was still out. She may as well forget about it, as, in any event, the jury would likely be a hung jury, and forever remain so.

She was all too pleased to pile the whole shebang on the shoulders of Barney Ratskeller. Good old Barney. He was very willing to take it on. Yvonne Becker worked alongside Barney in formally closing the office down, disposing of mountains of documents, and surrendering the vacant office to the building management.

"Isolde," Barney said, when he phoned her to tell her that the administration had been completed, "I just want to add that that young lady Yvonne Becker has been a tremendous help throughout. She could not have been any more helpful. I told her that if she needs a job there will be one waiting for her at my office."

"That's great to hear, Barney. Fred thought the world of her. And in the short time that I have worked with her, I have found her to be very loyal and efficient. What did she say about working for you?"

"Surprisingly, she said that she had other irons in the fire. She would take it under advisement, and get back to me. I thought she would have grabbed at the opportunity to work for Barney Ratskeller."

"I am puzzled by that response. She must have other options. Or maybe she does not find you that good looking, Barney?"

"Very funny, Isolde. I am splitting with laughter."

As soon as Isolde hung up the phone from speaking with Barney, she dialed Yvonne's number. The phone rang a number of times before Yvonne answered.

"Hi, Isolde," Yvonne answered in a low, rather gruff voice. "What's up?"

"Hi, Yvonne. Thanks for assisting Barney Ratskeller in the winding-up of Fred's estate. He spoke very highly of you."

"Thanks. All in a day's work."

"How much extra do I owe you for all that work?"

"Not a dime. I received compensation from Barney out of estate funds."

"He told me he offered you a job." Isolde was fishing to try and get some clues as to what Yvonne was up to, without asking her directly. There were a few seconds silence on the other end of the line.

"Well, to be honest, Isolde," Yvonne finally replied, "I am not sure that I want to continue being a legal secretary." Isolde was shocked at this response. She had always had the impression that Yvonne had loved what she had been doing for so many years.

"But how will you live?"

"Well, that is something for me to figure out, isn't it?" Isolde was taken aback by such a curt, sharp response. Yvonne must be in a bad mood today, she thought to herself. Better change the subject.

"Yvonne, I will likely need your help at some time in the future. I have a case pending here in Ontario against VolksBankBern and a number of other parties. I have a number of witnesses who will be coming in from Europe. One of them is a lady named Lise Brunner. She is a quadriplegic; confined to a wheelchair. Can I ask you to assist my lawyer and me in managing one or more of these witnesses? Transportation, accommodation, etc.?" Another few seconds of silence.

"May I think about it and get back to you?" Isolde was baffled. What was there to think about?

"If you cannot handle it, just let me know, and I will make other arrangements. I just thought that you would be perfect for the task."

"I will get back to you sometime tomorrow. OK?"

As she hung up the telephone, Isolde just could not figure out what had come over Yvonne. She wrote it down to a bad hair day. We all have days like that. Obviously, Yvonne was having one of those days. Isolde spent the rest of the day thinking through potential arrangements for transportation and accommodation for her European witnesses. No problem with transportation from Pearson. She would simply make arrangements with the airport limousine service to pick up Fankhauser, Renée, and Lise at the airport. As for accommodation for Fankhauser and Renée, she had ample room in her house to comfortably accommodate them. Her main problem was Lise. The house on Saddlers Court was not designed for accessibility for the handicapped. This meant that she had to find accessible accommodation for her, likely in a nursing home. But there was plenty of time for that.

When Yvonne phoned the following evening, Isolde again found her to be somewhat aloof. This was not the former animated soul that Isolde had become accustomed to. It appeared to Isolde that Yvonne's personality had taken a one hundred and eighty degree turn for the worse.

"Hi, Isolde," Yvonne started, "I will do this thing for you." Isolde was stunned. First of all, the reference to "this thing" left her with an empty feeling in her stomach. It was such an impersonal approach. And then the words "for you" made it sound as if Yvonne was doing her such a great favour, one that would undoubtedly result in a huge debt of gratitude in return. Isolde decided to overlook the semantics and the tone of voice. After all, she must be reading too much into mere spoken words.

"Thanks, Yvonne. I will be in touch with you once the witnesses are scheduled to arrive. In the meantime, take care of yourself."

"Don't worry about me. I always do." As she hung up the telephone, these words resonated within the recesses of Isolde's ears, like an echo which kept coming back again and again at you. She wondered if Yvonne had suffered some type of a breakdown which had completely changed her personality. Isolde much preferred the old Yvonne, and prayed to God that she was all right.

CHAPTER THIRTY

EIGHT MONTHS had passed since Isolde had met with Higginbottom in his office at the Richmond-Adelaide Centre. For his part, Higginbottom had not let any grass grow under his feet. The action was well on its way. As Higginbottom had predicted, one of the defendants, VolksBankBern, made a motion for dismissal of the action, on the basis that Ontario was not the proper jurisdiction. They argued that the proper jurisdiction was Switzerland and that the governing law was that of Switzerland.

Isolde was on pins and needles as she sat there, in the front row of the gallery, waiting for the judge to enter the courtroom on University Avenue in Toronto. Strange, she thought to herself, she had been a lawyer for umpteen years, and throughout all that time she had never once set foot into a courtroom. Once she decided to marry Fred, she ditched all the plans she had ever made to practise law. She found it even more strange that she, with all her legal education and training, would have goose bumps running all over her body, just from being in a courtroom. A subtle smile crept across her face, as she became amused by her own attempt at a joke, not spoken but simply thought of. At least, she mused, she had not peed her pants. But then, the day had just begun. Higginbottom was already there, seated in front of her at the counsel table, looking as impressive as he could look, considering his height, or lack thereof. His long black gown of silk reached down to his ankles. He'd better be careful, she thought, lest he trip over his own gown, taking her case down with him.

When the judge entered the courtroom, she heard the clerk shout "All rise!", and observed both counsel stand, and, as the judge took his seat, bow with an obsequiousness which reminded her of a figurine she had once seen of the Dickens character Uriah Heep, whose name had, since the publication of the novel *David Copperfield*, become synonymous with servility and groveling. If the degree of fawning was a factor in the determination of the winner and the loser of the motion, then, she thought, she would surely win, as her counsel, when he got into the act, was so short that his head was almost touching the floor. The judge, a young man with handsome features and a contagious grin, was attired in a copious garment of flowing silk, which comprised differently coloured pieces, one piece in black, another piece in white, and another piece in red, reminiscent of an actor dressed for a Shakespearian play. She eyed the white anachronistic collar and its two-pronged emanations, and seemed to recall being told, back in law school, that the emanations had had their origin from the dinners in the English Inns of Court, where the barristers wore white bibs, to protect their shirts from falling morsels that missed their mouths. It must be quite a chore, she thought to herself, for the judge to dress for court, what with all the different accoutrements that he had to be strapped into.

As the judge listened to the argument of counsel for VolksBankBern, something suddenly caught Isolde's eye. The bright light from the ceiling directly above the judge's dais struck something which caused the object to glisten. Peering at it from where she sat, she discerned that it was a gold ring on his right middle finger. But it was not just a band. It actually had a crown, which bore some sort of an emblem. She became panic-stricken. Could it be that the emblem depicted the three intersecting crescents, the brand of the infamous defendant, *The Shadow*? Had the tentacles of *The Shadow* stretched so far as to corrupt a judge in Ontario, thousands of miles from its enclave in Rome? She slipped a note to Higginbottom; 'Ben, I think the judge is wearing a gold ring with the emblem of *The Shadow*. You know, the three intersecting crescents. Perhaps he should recuse himself from our case?' Higginbottom read and discreetly secluded the note. When the opportunity presented itself, he asked for permission for counsel to approach the bench for a brief discussion with the judge. During that discussion, he took a close look at the emblem on the crown of the judge's gold ring. It was the emblem of a secret society known as the *Benevolent and Protective Order of Elks*, which had as its emblem the horns of an elk, easily mistaken from a distance to be crescents. Well, so much for a wild goose chase, he thought to himself. When they broke for lunch before Higginbottom presented his argument to the court, he explained to Isolde that the emblem on the ring was that of a secret society, but not of *The Shadow*. Isolde felt like a fool. She pinched herself, and resolved to be not so paranoid in the future. After Higginbottom presented his argument in response to the motion and counsel for VolksBankBern gave his reply argument, the judge reserved his ruling. Ten days later, he issued his written Ruling. He held that Ontario had jurisdiction to hear the case and that the governing law was that of Ontario. Isolde was tickled pink. First round for the good guys. This was a good psychological victory for Isolde. David had scored his first point against Goliath. But that was only one battle. In fact, a mere skirmish. The war had yet to be won.

While the litigation dragged on in pre-trial procedures, Isolde kept abreast as to what was happening on the other side of the Atlantic. Her bills for phone calls to and from Fankhauser in Bern were already running into thousands of dollars. The news of developments in Bern and Rome was good. The authorities were deep into their investigations of *The Shadow*, and had already laid a number of very serious charges against *The Shadow*, VolksBankBern, and various members of both entities, including Agimo and Rapini, both of whom were now being held in jail without bail. Fankhauser anticipated that the trials of all the accused would be held in the very near future. He also informed Isolde that he was in constant contact with Lise, and that she had come to stoically accept her condition of paraplegia. He was ensuring that she was in a secure environment, where the long tentacles of *The Shadow* could not reach her.

"Joaquim," Isolde informed Fankhauser in a telephone conversation in February of 1984, "my lawyer just told me that my case will be tried sometime next month; and that we need to start making arrangements for the attendance of our witnesses. He estimates that the trial will last about three weeks. Of course, I would like you to be with me throughout the liability phase of the trial. Will you be available for about two weeks in March?" She crossed her fingers and her legs, praying that he would say yes.

"For you, Isolde, I will make sure that I am available. Just let me know when you want me there." Isolde breathed a sigh of relief.

"Thanks, Joaquim. I don't know what I would do without you. You can stay at my house while you are here. My lawyer tells me that we should also have Renée as a witness. Would you kindly check on her availability? She would not have to stay as long as you."

"No problem with Mama," he replied, with an air of confidence. "You can rest assured that she will be there. She can fly to Toronto with me, and fly back to Bern as soon as she has testified."

"That's good to know. And then, of course, Lise will be a vital witness. Do you think that between you and Renée you can get her here? She can also leave as soon as she has testified. She and Renée can then fly back to Bern together."

"Leave that with me. I will get Lise there." That warm, fuzzy feeling once again crept through Isolde's body. Fankhauser came through once again. Like Hercules in his Twelve Labours, nothing seemed to be beyond his capability.

"Because of her accessibility needs, I will make arrangements for her to be accommodated in a nursing home. I have already enlisted the assistance of Fred's former legal secretary."

"Sounds good, Isolde. I will let Lise know."

"Then there are Professor Rossi and Professor Rappaport. I will contact them directly to arrange for their attendance. My lawyer tells me that he can arrange with the court to have them testify as soon as they are here, and they can leave as soon as they have testified. He will contact them directly at the appropriate time to make the necessary arrangements. He will also make similar arrangements for the attendance of the reps of the various law enforcement agencies."

"Nice going, Isolde. It seems that you and your lawyer have everything under control."

"I will keep in touch with you, Joaquim, as to any further developments. Auf Wiedersehen."

"Auf Wiedersehen, Isolde."

As she hung up the telephone, there was a broad smile of satisfaction on her face. The great Fankhauser had done it again. He had caused problems to diminish in size, if not to magically vanish into thin air.

CHAPTER THIRTY-ONE

ISOLDE suddenly jumped out of bed. Within two seconds flat, she was standing in the middle of her pitch-black bedroom, her fingers wrapped around her Glock G43x semi-automatic, her eyes shooting like darts around the room, as if expecting to find an intruder. "Show your face, you cowardly bastard!" she shouted. She had just roused herself out of the clutches of another one of those horrible nightmares she had been experiencing periodically since the series of violent attacks that had been made in the Old Town of Bern, first at the *Fankhaus*, and then at the intersection of Rathausgasse and Brunngasse. She had not talked to anyone about them, hoping that they would just go away. It was always the same. A scene from the *Fankhaus*, alive with the sound of gunshots, and one dead body walking around like a zombie, with a savage face intent on devouring her. Or a scene at Rathausgasse and Brunngasse, vibrant with a barrage of gunshots, and two zombies instead of one. Always, she would wake up in a cold sweat, frozen in fear.

Her voice had awoken Miguel. He knocked softly on the door to her bedroom. "Señora Bruni, are you OK?" he asked. Isolde slipped into her housecoat, and opened the door. Miguel was standing there in his pajamas, his Colt Commander Parabellum in his hand.

"Everything is fine, Miguel," she replied. "I just had a bad dream. Please go back to bed."

Scared stiff of *The Shadow*, she took some comfort in knowing that thousands of miles separated her from that monster. Thank God for small blessings, she would say to herself. But from all that she and Fankhauser had been able to unearth about the blood-curdling beast, it may matter little that you are on the opposite side of the world from its lair. You are never ever fully beyond the menacing reach of its long, octopal tentacles. The fact that, except for the veiled telephone threat about the children, *The Shadow* had not triggered any violence since the second attack in Bern was, at least to Isolde, no reason to be complacent. This period of inaction may have been just a ploy to clothe her in a shroud of false security. For this reason, her Glock G43x semi-automatic was never more that an arm's length away from her. If she had learned one lesson from Fankhauser, it was ever to be *en garde*; ever to be *semper paratus.* To be incessantly *on guard;* to be *always prepared.*

Now fully awake, she ambled downstairs to the kitchen, her faithful Glock still in her hand. As she set about making a pot of coffee, the grandfather clock in the front hall chimed three. As had always happened after each of those nightmares, she was now in for the long haul. Goodbye to sleep for the rest of the night. No use even trying. She sat there, contemplating nightmares. She had once read a German fable which had been illustrated with an ugly demon riding a mare, which came down crushingly on the victim as she lay prostrate in bed. They called it a *NachtMahr,* the word 'Nacht' meaning 'night', and the word 'Mahr' meaning 'mare'. Hence the word 'nightmare'. Could this be what was happening to her? She quickly shook herself out of this train of thought. But then started thinking that she must be losing her mind. Perhaps, she thought, she should see a shrink. As she sipped away at cup after cup of Jamaica Blue Mountain coffee, she dispelled these negative thoughts, resolving instead to beat *The Shadow*, both physically and mentally. For this, she would muster all her inner strength. No need for any shrink to screw around with her head.

Before she knew it, it was six-thirty. Time to make sure that Emil and Sophie were dressed for school, and to prepare breakfast for them. When she went to Emil's room to wake him up, he was already wide awake.

"Mommy," he said, "I had a horrible dream last night. I dreamt that you had left Sophie and me again. But that this time you were never coming back to us." Isolde stared into his flummoxed eyes, not knowing how to respond. Then, instinctively, she hugged him in a tight embrace, and responded.

"Oh, my darling Emil. You don't have to worry. Mommy will never leave you and Sophie." She kissed him on his forehead, and continued.

"Now let's get a move on. You need to get ready for school." She yawned from lack of sleep, as she headed into Sophie's room to awake her from a solid sleep. She could not dispel from her mind the extent to which *The Shadow* had altered the course of the lives of her and her family. It was a tragedy of the first order, she groaned.

Miguel drove Emil and Sophie to school. For the rest of the morning, Isolde just dragged her tail around the house, being in a sleep-deprived state. Immediately after lunch, she flung herself down on the sofa in the family room, and drifted off to sleep. Not long after, she was awoken by the doorbell. It was as if someone had a finger glued to the button.

"All right; all right; I am coming," she blurted out, disgusted with the impatience of the caller.

When she got to the front door, she looked through the peephole, and saw a man dressed in a shirt bearing a logo which read **ENBRIDGE GAS.**

"Who is it?" she asked, without opening the door. She felt the right pocket of her slacks. Yes; the Glock semi-automatic was still there.

"Enbridge Gas," a voice responded.

"What do you want?"

"We have a gas leak in the neighbourhood. I need to check your gas appliances." Red flags of suspicion suddenly rose in her head.

"What is your name?"

"Jim Colbeck," he replied.

"Allow me about five minutes to phone Enbridge." She wheeled around, went to the telephone, and phoned Enbridge. The response was swift. No, there was no report of a gas leak in her neighbourhood. No, there was no Enbridge employee by the name of 'Jim Colbeck'. If you open the door to this stranger, you do so at your own risk. Isolde returned to the front door, her Glock semi-automatic drawn, her right index finger on the trigger. But there was no-one there. The man had vanished into thin air. Undoubtedly, she thought, he was from *The Shadow*. She breathed a sigh of relief that she had just foiled a plot aimed at her. But she still felt trepidation from the realization that the many-headed Hydra seemed to be closing in on her.

She phoned Fankhauser in Bern. It was important for her to pass the news of the 'foiled plot' on to him, and seek his sagely advice.

"Fankhauser here," he answered, in his usual style, immediately after the first ring.

"Hi, Joaquim. Isolde here. I have to tell you this." She then proceeded to tell him of the incident of the 'Enbridge man'.

"Good thinking, Isolde," he responded. "That's exactly the sort of thing I would expect from *The Shadow*. If you had let him in, chances are you would be a dead duck by now."

"Not if I nailed him first. I had my Glock semi-automatic primed and ready to go," she said, with bravado in her voice. Fankhauser laughed.

"You must have learnt too much from Mama," he joked. "In any event, you did well. Remember, always be vigilant. You can never tell when the monster may strike. You are a prime target. Without you, the litigation would possibly die. Any word on a trial date?"

"I am glad you ask. My lawyer tells me that the trial will start on March 15. I will fax you a schedule for you, Renée and Lise, as to when you should be here, and for how long."

"Thanks, Isolde. Auf Wiedersehen."

When Miguel returned with Emil and Sophie at the end of the school day, his whole demeanour had changed. This was not the calm, confident security guard that had left the house with the children earlier that day. Instead, what Isolde saw standing before her in her den was a trembling, scared mouse of a man drenched in cold sweat.

"Señora," he spluttered, "I cannot continue." His frightened eyes were flitting all around the room.

"What's wrong, Miguel. What do you mean you 'cannot continue'?" a bewildered Isolde asked.

"Look at this, Señora!" he replied, shoving a typed note into her hands. The note was written in Spanish:

Deja a los niños Bruni ahora. Si no, lo enviaremos de regresso a Castro..

"I do not speak Spanish, Miguel. What is it in English?"

"It says '*Leave the Bruni children now. If not, we will ship you back to Castro*'. I don't know who wrote the note and left it on the windshield of my car. But I cannot take the chance of being shipped back to Cuba. If that happens, I will be shot dead by a firing squad in the public square in Havana." His emotions were now fear mixed with despondency. Isolde was caught unawares. She was speechless. Miguel looked into her eyes, as if for answers.

"Who or what are we dealing with, Señora Bruni? I never did ask Señora Baumann." Isolde rolled her eyes. She never expected to have to deal with something of this nature. Where does she start?

"It's a long story, Miguel," she started. "But the abridged version is that we are dealing with an international organization called *The Shadow*. Have you ever heard of them?"

"No. But I can't take the chance of ending up back in Cuba, Señora Bruni. I am quitting now." Isolde could see that his mind had been made up. She paid him what he was owed, and he scampered off like the coward that he was.

Isolde sat with her head in her hands. She no longer had security for Emil and Sophie. The more she thought about it, the more she was convinced that this note was another scare tactic from *The Shadow*. If *The Shadow* were really after Emil and Sophie, they likely could have nailed them by now, security guard or not. The real purpose of the note, as with the telephone message to Margot, was to put the fear of God in Isolde so that she would abandon the pursuit of *The Shadow*. Now more than ever, she resolved to complete her mission.

CHAPTER THIRTY-TWO

LISE COWERED in apprehension as she was wheeled by Yvonne out of the Terminal Building at Pearson, onto the broad, concrete sidewalk, to wait for the airport limousine that would transport her, Fankhauser and Renée to their places of accommodation, wherever those might happen to be. As she sat there in her wheelchair, with a helpless expression on her face, she looked like a scared, defenceless, cornered rabbit, staring into the barrel of the hunter's shotgun, with nowhere to turn, and, through no choice of its own, only waiting for the inevitable deafening crack from the discharge of the fatal bullet. She was a helpless stranger in a strange land. And, for a woman who had always prided herself on her independence, she now found herself totally dependent on virtual strangers, without the familial care and support that she had received from her Medici relatives back in Bern. She winced as a sudden blast of subzero wind cut sharply into her face. She quickly turned her head away in order to avoid a repeat attack. She was cognizant of the fact that, in the eyes of *The Shadow,* of all the billions of people on the planet, she was its primary persona non grata. They had already made three attempts to eliminate her from the face of the earth, one of which had left her totally infirm. Why not a fourth? Knowing the inner workings of *The Shadow*, she was ever conscious of its vampirical lust for blood, and its macabre reputation for the ferocity and tenacity of a pit bull in its Machiavellian pursuits. She could never rest assured that she was beyond the reach of its long tentacles.

"Careful; careful now; easy does it," she heard Fankhauser say, as he supervised the loading of Lise and her wheelchair by Yvonne and the limo driver into the black stretch limo. The sound of his voice was reassuring. She trusted him implicitly. And that was the only reason why she had agreed to come voluntarily all the way from Bern to testify on Isolde 's behalf. Had it not been for him, there was not a snowball's chance in hell that she would have agreed to come. Whenever she felt any misgiving about coming to Toronto to testify, she simply thought of Fankhauser, and the thought of him would regenerate her belief that everything would be OK. As her hobbled body was wiggled this way and that for her in an attempt to settle her into the posh leather seat of the limousine, she suddenly became conscious of the fact that Isolde was not there.

"Where is Isolde?" she asked Fankhauser, quizzingly.

"She told me that she would not be here," Fankhauser replied. "She sent Yvonne to assist you. Yvonne had been Fred's trusted legal secretary for years. Isolde has hired Yvonne to assist you throughout your stay. If you ever need anything, just ask Yvonne." Lise looked at Yvonne; Yvonne looked at Lise. Neither uttered a sound. It was as if they were assessing each other. Fankhauser and Renée watched them both, as they looked each other over, from head to toe. Renée broke the silence.

"You know, I had always wanted to visit Canada," she blurted, looking at her son. "But I could never convince your Papa to leave Switzerland. He was such a homebody. Said all he needed in life was right there in Switzerland. Now that I am here, I am wondering if I was really missing anything. Perhaps your Papa was right." Fankhauser grinned. He recognized what his mother was up to. She was trying to ease the tension inside the limo.

"This is only your first few minutes here, Mama. Give it time. Toronto is a beautiful city. World-class, they say."

"What time am I going to have to see it, sitting around some stuffy courtroom?" Renée asked. "This is cruel and unusual punishment for a woman my age." At this quip, Fankhauser guffawed. Lise gave a knowing smile. Yvonne grunted, almost undiscernibly.

"Were you instructed as to our destinations?" Fankhauser asked the driver, as the limo merged from the Airport Road into traffic on Highway 427.

"Yes, sir," the driver responded. "First stop at the Pinkerton Convalescent Home on Bayview Drive? And then over to Saddlers Court in the Bride Path?"

"Sounds good to me," commented Fankhauser.

It was not long before the limo pulled up in front of the lobby of the Pinkerton Convalescent Home. Yvonne went in, and returned with an attendant. The heart of the already frightened Lise was palpitating rapidly. To add to her panic, she was now being carted into a strange institution, by two strange persons. And out of Fankhauser's sight. The limo driver waited for Yvonne to return with word that Lise was safely registered as a guest in the Home. Yvonne would remain there to ensure that Lise was fully settled in. She would not require a ride to her apartment, as she had her car already sitting where she had left it in the parking lot of the Home. The limo headed out onto Bayview for its final destination on Saddlers Court in the Bridle Path.

"That Yvonne is not very affable, is she, Joaquim?" Renée uttered, in a low voice. Fankhauser pondered the question for a minute or two.

"Strange woman," commented Fankhauser. "And yet, she can't be all that bad. After all, she worked for Fred throughout his entire career."

As the limo entered the Bridle Path, Renée gasped several times as she observed the opulence and majesty of the mansions on *Millionaires' Row.*

"Sure makes the *Fankhaus* look like a pauper's abode, doesn't it, Joaquim?" Renée remarked.

"Give me the *Fankhaus* any day, Mama. In life, there is only so much that one needs to live in happiness. Beyond that, there is a disconnect, which often results in isolation, misery and unhappiness," he commented, philosophically.

At 22 Saddlers Court, Isolde had the house lit up like a Christmas tree, both inside and out. She was at the door to greet her newly arrived guests. After showing them to their rooms, she invited them to go to the dining room to enjoy a gourmet meal of Rack of Lamb served with Mashed Potato under Wild Mushroom Gravy, Mixed Vegetables, and

Crusty Rolls, not to mention a couple bottles of Robert Mondavi NAPA Valley Special Cabernet Sauvignon, which she had selected from her own exquisite wine cellar.

Back at the Pinkerton Convalescent Home, once Lise seemed to be comfortable in her new surroundings, Yvonne said goodnight and left the building. She climbed into her new silver BMW and sped off to her pad in Brampton.

CHAPTER THIRTY-THREE

OUT OF THE BLUE, Isolde received the telephone call from the Pinkerton Convalescent Home. She remembered the time well. She had been disturbed from a deep sleep. It was two-thirty-five in the morning, two days before the commencement of the trial. At this ungodly hour of the morning, she thought to herself, this had better be goddamned good.

"What is it?" she rudely barked into the phone. "Do you know what time of the night it is?" These sharp questions surprised even Isolde herself, as she had always prided herself on treating everyone with the utmost courtesy.

"Is that Mrs. Bruni?" the caller asked, with an apologetic tone in her voice. "This is Pinkerton's. There has been an incident at our Home." Isolde was immediately crushed by this response. It must have to do with Lise. Lise was the only connection that Isolde had with the Pinkerton Convalescent Home. At this hour of the morning, it just cannot be good news.

"Why don't you just get to the point? Is Lise Brunner OK?" There was hesitation at the other end of the line.

"No, ma'am," the caller resumed, sombrely. "The night nurse was doing her regular rounds at about two. When she checked in on Lise, she found her gasping for air. There was a red mark around her neck, as if someone had tried to strangle her. We immediately administered oxygen, and called the police." Isolde felt the walls closing in on her; not to mention on her whole case. Lise was her most important witness.

"Is she still alive?" She had to ask the question. But she dreaded a negative reply.

"Yes, ma'am. She is alive. But she cannot speak. The injury appears to have affected her vocal cords. We are hoping that it is temporary. The doctor said that the vocal cords have been seriously damaged." Isolde's mind was working at a mile a minute, running in all directions. A rat was on the loose. *The Shadow* has struck again. It has proven that there is no place on earth to which it cannot extend the long reach of its tentacles. Was Lise now incapacitated as a witness? How will this affect the court case? Isolde had so many questions to which she needed answers.

"I will be there within an hour," Isolde told the caller. As soon as she hung up the telephone, she rushed to Fankhauser's room and knocked loudly on the door, which immediately awoke not only Fankhauser, but also Renée, Emil and Sophie.

"What's the matter, Mommy?" Emil asked, as he stood outside his room, rubbing his sleepy eyes. Sophie also stood there, looking on. "It's OK, Emil. You and Sophie just go back to bed." Fankhauser opened his door, and, immediately afterward, Renée was at his side.

"Joaquim, you won't believe this," Isolde said to Fankhauser, her voice quivering. "It's *The Shadow*. It has struck again."

"Is it Lise?" Fankhauser asked, intuitively grasping what could cause such consternation at that time of the night. Isolde nodded her head three times. "Yes, it is Lise," she replied, despondently.

"Is she alive?"

"Yes; thank God for that. But she has lost her voice. What good is a witness without a voice?"

"Mama," Fankhauser whispered, turning to Renée, who was standing there, her jaws wide open. "Isolde and I have to rush down to the Convalescent Home. Would you please look after the kids? We should be back in time for Isolde to take them to school."

"I would be pleased to do that, Joaquim."

On the short drive to Pinkerton's in Isolde's flamingo Ferrari, Fankhauser and Isolde speculated on how *The Shadow* could have accessed Lise's room without being identified by the Pinkerton staff.

"You know, there is a back door reserved for access and egress of staff," Isolde commented. "But it is not reserved for staff only. I was able to secure a key to the back door for Yvonne Brunner. This allowed her faster and easier access to Lise's room." Fankhauser suddenly swung his head around to look at Isolde.

"That may have been a mistake," he opined. "You cannot forget that *The Shadow* comes in all shapes and forms. Unlike in your courts of law, we have to consider everybody guilty until proven innocent." This did not give Isolde any comfort. After all that Fankhauser and Renée had done to stave off *The Shadow*, had she blown it all by one act of indiscretion?

"But, Joaquim, Yvonne was Fred's trusted and loyal legal secretary ever since he opened his law office. We both trusted her implicitly."

"I am just saying……" Fankhauser remarked. "Let's hope you are right."

When they arrived at Pinkerton's, the police were still there. Lise had been transferred to another room, and her old room had been cordoned off as a crime scene. Fankhauser first spoke with the receptionist at the Front Desk, Isolde standing at his side.

"Do you have a list of everyone that had access to Lise Brunner's room this evening?" he asked. The receptionist checked the Visitors' Book.

"Yes. All visitors are required to sign in and out," she replied. "Of course, staff have ready access to her room. One exception; with the permission of the resident or someone having authority to speak on behalf of the resident, certain trusted individuals are permitted to use the back door for entry and egress. This privilege was allowed to one Yvonne Brunner, as both Lise and Mrs. Bruni had permitted it." She opened the Visitors Book to today and yesterday. Although there was no signature, there was a note that a woman by the name of Marietta della Caprioni had tried to gain access at eight in the evening. She had claimed to be a cousin of Lise's visiting from Rome. But on checking with Lise, she said that she did not have a female cousin who lived in Rome. When the receptionist returned to the Front Desk, the woman was no longer there. Fankhauser and Isolde looked at each other. This is all too reminiscent of the *Spital Tiefenau* incident that had been related by phone to Fankhauser by Lorena Meyer.

Fankhauser, with Isolde still beside him, then spoke with the police detective in charge of the case, Detective James Murray, who was still on the scene. Fankhauser identified himself as a friend of Lise from Bern. While he was not himself investigating in his capacity as a P.I., as he was not licensed as such in Ontario, he was assisting Lise as a friend to come to grips with what had occurred that night. As a professional courtesy, the detective was forthcoming.

"Entry was gained from the back entrance door," Detective Murray expostulated.

"How can you be sure of that?" Fankhauser shot back.

"Because the lock was broken. Sure sign." Whew! Isolde breathed a sigh of relief. That surely rules out Yvonne as a suspect. If it had been Yvonne, the lock would not have been broken. After all, Yvonne had a key. Perhaps the mysterious Marietta della Caproni from Rome had broken the lock in order to get in through the back door, after she had been denied entry through the front door. It's good to know that she, Isolde, had not misplaced her trust in Yvonne.

"What is your initial assessment of the crime?" Fankhauser queried.

"Off the record, I think it was attempted murder. Clear strangulation marks on the neck of the victim, as red as blood. Consistent with marks left by hands. For some reason or the other, the perp could not finish the job; or thought that he or she had done the deed. Don't ask me about motive. I don't have the slightest clue. At least, not at this point."

"How about the condition of the victim?"

"She is stable. She is on a ventilator. I spoke with the Pinkerton doctor. He said that she has suffered serious damage to the vocal cords. She will need to be examined by an E.N.T. specialist. But from what he sees, he believes that nerves to the vocal cords have been significantly damaged. This cuts off communications between the vocal cords and the brain. Calls it vocal cords paralysis, which is a condition that could be permanent. Here and now, she cannot utter a single sound. Poor woman!" Egad, Isolde exclaimed to herself. What good is a witness who cannot communicate? Her stomach was tied in knots. Lise cannot speak. How will she ever be able to give her evidence. What is Higginbottom going to do without Lise's evidence? Notwithstanding its failure in its efforts to kill Lise, *The Shadow* has somehow attained its objective, to silence her. Fankhauser gave Detective Murray his business card. "If ever you are in Bern, please do not hesitate to phone me. I will show you around the beautiful Old Town of Bern." Detective Murray beamed. He thanked Fankhauser for the invitation, and said that he and his wife had always yearned to visit Europe.

On the way back to Saddlers Court, Fankhauser told Isolde to look at the brighter side. At least, Lise was still alive. Hopefully, she could still move her head, her eyes, and her lips. As long as those functions were intact, she would still be able to communicate. Good, old Fankhauser. He had evoked in Isolde that warm fuzzy, feeling all over again.

CHAPTER THIRTY-FOUR

THAT MORNING, the break of dawn found Fankhauser in the family room, the back of his head pressed tightly against the high-back chair in which he was seated, his shut eyes and furrowed brow raised toward the ceiling. Renée, seated on a love-seat not far from her son, was leafing through the March publication of *CHATELAINE*, in between furtive glances at her son. She made a habit of not disturbing Joaquim whenever he was in deep contemplation. She had seen him like that on numerous occasions; and recognized it as a sign that he just wanted time to think. This was akin to Pythagoras closing his eyes to picture the geometrical lines and angles of some enigmatic design in order to come up with a brand-new theorem to solve the problem. Isolde crept in quietly, carrying a tray laden with a pot of her beloved Jamaica Blue Mountain Coffee, with Croissants and an assortment of Cheeses, and with three coffee mugs, which she set down on the coffee table. Instinctively, like Renée, she knew that Fankhauser was engaged in deep thought, and she played by the rules. She and Renée dove into the continental breakfast, keeping their voices down. At long last, Renée caught her son with his eyes open and lowered.

"So, Joaquim," she bellowed at him. "Have you solved the problems of the world yet?" Fankhauser looked at her in a blank stare. Then he looked at Isolde. Isolde's face was twisted into a mask of curiosity, as if to say "Yes; explain yourself, great one".

"Isolde," he started, "this is Friday."

"We all know that, Joaquim." Renée laughed. "Tell us something new and exciting." Fankhauser politely ignored her, still looking at Isolde.

"Your trial starts on Monday. We have some work to do before Monday." Isolde raised both palms upwards, signifying a desire to learn more. Fankhauser was in no hurry. He cut open a Croissant and smeared some Cream Cheese on both interior sides. He then chomped down on the Croissant and Cream Cheese. Renée put her hand to the right side of her lips, to indicate to him in sign language that there was a daub of cheese on that part of his face. Still looking at Isolde, his hand moved to his face and wiped away the imperfection, while he chewed away.

"The lock; the lock. The answer lies in the lock. The broken lock at Pinkerton's. You should phone them and find out if the lock has been replaced, and, if so, who has replaced it. And get the contact info."

"I am on it!" exclaimed Isolde, as she reached for the telephone. She spoke with the receptionist at the Front Desk at Pinkerton's. Yes; the lock has been replaced. It was done by their building superintendent, Bryce Keenleyside. If you wish to speak with him, just let us know. Yes; we will have him phone you. Within fifteen minutes, the telephone rang.

"This is B-B-Bryce Keenleyside at P-P-Pinkerton Convalescent Home," a husky voice said, but with a distinct stutter. "H--How may I help you?"

"Just a minute," Isolde replied, and handed the telephone to Fankhauser, giving him the name Bryce Keekleyside. Fankhauser placed it on speaker phone.

"Bryce," Fankhauser said, "I understand that you replaced the broken lock on the back door of the Home. Is that correct?"

"Sure did. Someone did quite a job on it."

"Have you retained the broken lock?"

"Sure did. I am holding the b-b-broken lock for the p-p-police."

"Would you please take some photographs of it for me? I will pay you for them."

"Sure can. When do you need them?"

"As soon as possible today, Bryce. Will you call Mrs. Bruni when they are ready?"

"Sure will."

"Before you go, Bryce; can you tell if the lock was damaged from the outside of the door or from the inside?"

"F-F-From the inside. It was a set-up. They tried to make it look as if it was f-f-from the outside."

"Bryce, Mrs. Bruni has a case in court on Monday. Can you appear as a witness as to what you just told me? It will only take about an hour or so. How about $100 an hour for your time? We will pick you up personally."

"Yes, sir. Just let me know what time. Will I ride in Mrs. Bruni's red F-F-Ferrari?"

"Yes, Bryce. In the red Ferrari. We will pick you up at seven. Court starts at ten."

"Great! I always wanted to drive in a Ferrari."

Great is right, Fankhauser thought to himself. So, we now have two witnesses with speech problems. One, Lise, could not speak. And the other, Keenleyside, spoke with a very noticeable stutter. But to look on the brighter side, his hunch was right about the door lock. Entry to get at Lise was an inside job. But who had provided the keyed entry to the interior?

"We must talk with Yvonne immediately," Fankhauser told Isolde. Higginbottom had already subpoenaed Yvonne to appear as his first witness on Monday morning. But Fankhauser had figured that, in light of the fresh attack on Lise, it was important to learn ASAP what, if anything, Yvonne knew of what had transpired last night. "We should pay her an unannounced visit. You know. Surprise! Surprise!"

"Let's go," Isolde agreed. "I know where she lives. It's over in Brampton." Isolde and Fankhauser hopped into the Ferrari. Isolde elicited a guffaw from Fankhauser when she bellowed "Speed limit be damned!" and slammed heavily on the gas pedal of the speed machine.

In no time flat, they were entering the Meadowvale Village dated walk-up apartment building, in the basement of which Yvonne occupied a dingy studio apartment. The sounds of their heels clacking against the bare concrete of the stairs descending into the dungeon called the basement was loud enough to awaken the dead. Their nostrils were overcome by the pungent smell of curry mixed with some other strange odour that Fankhauser was unable to identify. It was as cold within the building as it was outside. Both Fankhauser and Isolde could see vapours rising from their breaths, like spirits escaping from a tundra, fleeting but real. Slowing down as they traipsed on the worn-out carpet in the dimly-lit hallway, they gave a knowing look to each other. Yes; this is what the other side of the world looks like. Isolde softly knocked on the front door of Yvonne's apartment. Fankhauser flattened his ears against the door, trying to discern any activity whatsoever within. After four sets of knocks, still no answer. Fankhauser could hear the beeping from a coffee percolator coming from the interior; and then the sound of footsteps as if someone was scurrying off to some distant part of the room.

"She's in there," he whispered to Isolde. He then took the bull by the horns. He knocked heavily on the door, causing such a disturbance that other apartment doors were now popping open, one by one, as if in planned succession, and heads were peeling out into the hallway to try and catch a glimpse of what all the mayhem was about. One elderly toothless woman, dressed only in her nightgown and a sleeping cap, crept out into the hallway and shouted: "Yvonne, why the hell don't you open the door!" Eventually, the door popped open. Yvonne had realized that she could run, but she could not hide. She was standing there in living colour, dressed in a multi-floral housecoat that had long seen better days.

"Hi, Isolde," she said, completely ignoring Fankhauser. "It would have been helpful if you had phoned first. Come in." Isolde, followed by Fankhauser, entered immediately, before there was a withdrawal of the invitation. They were met by a strong odour. The unmistakable smell of burnt marijuana pervaded the air. "Would you like some coffee?" Both Isolde and Fankhauser had already quickly observed the squalor of the small apartment, and the unwashed dishes, mugs, and cutlery piled a mile-high in the part of the room that served as a kitchen. In unison, they declined the offer.

"What can I do for you, Isolde?" Yvonne asked, nonchalantly.

"Have you heard about Lise?" Isolde asked her.

"What do you mean? Is she ill? She was fine when I left her yesterday."

"What time did you leave her yesterday?"

"Oh, must have been about five-thirty. Just before her dinner time. She was fine. What's happened?" Her voice cracked as she asked the question.

"There was an attempt on her life. Someone tried to kill her." The blood was drained from Yvonne's head. Isolde thought it was out of concern for Lise. Fankhauser, with his discerning eye, had another possible take on the reaction. Was it from shock that Lise was still alive?

"Oh my God! No. I can't believe it. Where is she now?" Tears were already welling in her eyes.

"She is still at the Home; but on a ventilator. She cannot speak," Isolde responded.

"Do they know who tried to strangle her?" Major error, thought Fankhauser. Who said anything about "strangling"? He decided not to alert Yvonne to this faux pas.

"They have no idea," Isolde continued. "The Toronto Police are conducting their investigation."

"I understand that you have a key to the back door which serves as the staff entrance?" Fankhauser asked Yvonne.

"Yes; Isolde arranged that for me. But I still have it. I have never let it out of my possession. Oh, God; poor Lise. How could anyone do that to her?" In her look of consternation, she lifted her right hand to her forehead, moved a lock of her golden hair back into place, and then kept the hand on her brow. Trying not to be obvious, Fankhauser stole glances of the beautiful ring that she wore on her right ring finger.

"Well, so much for that. But before we go, can I take a photo of you charming ladies?" Fankhauser asked. "You are just like twin sisters". Both Yvonne and Isolde agreed to pose for the photograph. Fankhauser pulled out a pocket camera from his coat. He positioned the women for proper lighting. "OK. Yvonne, please stand to the left of Isolde, and put your right arm around her shoulders. Now get ready. Say 'cheese'." Fankhauser scored about five or six good shots.

"I guess we will see you in court on Monday, Yvonne," remarked Isolde, as they walked to the front door.

"Yes. You have a great lawyer, Isolde. He has been through my evidence with me. I will do the best I can for you."

As the door shut behind them, Fankhauser remarked in a low voice to Isolde: "I can't believe that people live like that." Lise smiled, knowingly.

When they arrived back at the Saddlers Court mansion, Isolde clutched Fankhauser by the sleeve and asked: "What was all this photographs poppycock about, Joaquim? And *twin sisters*?" Fankhauser looked at her and smiled.

"You will see, my dear Isolde. You will see. God reveals all things in His own time." Renée heard this, and smiled. She knew her son.

"Are you likening yourself to God, Joaquim?" she piped in, jokingly. "You know that that's blasphemy." Fankhauser did not answer her. He just raised his eyes toward the ceiling, his white teeth exposed like the Cheshire cat that had just eaten the canary.

CHAPTER THIRTY-FIVE

MONDAY MORNING arrived far too quickly. The bells of Old City Hall, at the corner of Queen and Bay in downtown Toronto, were pealing out to signal eight. Fankhauser, with Bryce Keenleyside in tow, exited Lise's flamingo Ferrari to enter the Court House on University. His long legs moved with giant steps. Keenleyside, a runt of a man, had to take two steps for every one of Fankhauser's just to try and keep up with him. By the time they arrived in the courtroom, it was eight-o-five, and Keenleyside, who sweated profusely, was as wet as a drowned mouse. As they entered, Higginbottom approached them, his eyes centred upward on Fankhauser, whom he had never met before. To watch the five-two Higginbottom stand beside the six-three Fankhauser was like witnessing a modern-day reincarnation of the old comic strip *Mutt and Jeff*.

"You are late," Higginbottom said to Fankhauser, looking at his watch. Fankhauser extended his right hand to Higginbottom, who received it in a limp handshake.

"I am Joaquim Fankhauser."

"I gathered that," retorted Higginbottom, as he looked at the soaked Keenleyside, wondering who he was.

"This is Bryce Keenleyside," Fankhauser explained. "He is here as one of your witnesses. Is there a room where we can talk?"

"Oh, a witness of mine that I have not been aware of?" Obviously, Higginbottom found it somewhat funny, as he broke into a laughter which ended almost as soon as it started. "Just follow me," he said, as he led them out of the courtroom to a small interview room.

"OK, Joaquim. What's up?" Fankhauser was pleased. Higginbottom had addressed him by his first name. The ice was broken.

"An attempt was made very early Saturday morning to strangle Lise Brunner at the Pinkerton Convalescent Home where she is staying." Fankhauser could see Higginbottom immediately stiffen. This revelation had roused his interest. "She is still alive, but has lost her ability to speak."

"Who did this?" Higginbottom asked quizzingly, his mouth wide open.

"We don't know yet. The police are still investigating. But I have a very good idea as to who is behind it."

"Let me guess. *The Shadow?*"

"That's precisely whom I suspect. Lise had been one of them, before they tried to kill her. You know the story."

"Yes; I am somewhat acquainted with the case," Higginbottom commented, as a gross understatement. "Does Pinkerton not know who had gained entry last before the strangulation?"

"That is where this gentleman, Mr. Bryce Keenleyside, comes in. Tell Mr. Higginbottom what you know, Bryce, about the broken lock." Keenleyside, awash in sweat, chirped in, and, stuttering as he tried to express himself, pointed to the photographs of the broken lock, and explained his theory that the lock had been broken from the inside and not from the outside. It was elucidating, but frustrating for Higginbottom, who kept watching the hands of his watch as they ran a marathon while he suffered laboriously to pick up pieces of what Keenleyside was saying, in between stutters.

"Any idea who acted from the inside?" At this point, Fankhauser asked Keenleyside to step out of the interview room and wait for him in the courtroom.

"My suspicion is Yvonne Becker."

"But she is one of our witnesses. Isolde had told me that she had always been a loyal employee of Fred's."

Fankhauser then related details of his and Isolde's meeting with Yvonne at her apartment. What he told Higginbottom was a real eye-popper for the lawyer, whose brilliant mind was already processing the mechanics of using the newly-found evidence.

"Will Lise be able to testify in court?" asked Higginbottom. Fankhauser was expecting that question. He was prepared for it.

"She cannot move her limbs, and so she cannot write. She cannot speak, as her vocal cords are paralyzed. But we have a saving grace. She can move her head upward and downward; she can move her head sideward; she can move her eyelids; and she can move her lips. Take your choice. She is still able to communicate, allowing some latitude for her condition."

"I get your drift. Will she be here today?"

"Yes," Fankhauser replied. "Isolde has made arrangements for her to be transported here as soon as you give the word as to what time you can put her on the stand. Lise is anxious to get the whole thing over with. She already misses Bern. After the bumper-to-bumper traffic we encountered getting here this morning, I can't blame her for that!" Higginbottom laughed.

"Good old Don Valley!" he remarked. "I know you are not a lawyer. But how do you see the order for calling Yvonne, Lise and Keenleyside?" This pleased Fankhauser. It was a sign of respect. What amazed Higginbottom was that Fankhauser had already worked that out.

"Funny you should ask," Fanhauser said, jokingly. "I would call Yvonne first. She will think that she is being called to testify about Fred's law practice, and Fred's death. She has no clue as to the insights that I have just given you. I would then call Keenleyside as to the broken lock. And then I would call Lise. Once Lise has testified, I would then recall Yvonne, challenging her with the evidence of Keenleyside and Lise." He looked at Higginbottom for a sign of approbation.

"My thoughts exactly," Higginbottom agreed, with a broad smile. "OK. We don't have much time. Let's run through the evidence that you yourself will be giving. I already have a detailed outline from Isolde." The two men, both true professionals, huddled together in the small interview room, and quickly ran through the gist of Fankhauser's evidence.

They made it back into the courtroom in the nick of time. The court clerk was already making enquiries as to whether anyone had seen Mr. Ben Higginbottom, counsel for the plaintiff. Counsel for the defendants, Mr. Richard Hickshok, was already seated at the counsel table. As the court clerk ordered all persons in the courtroom to rise, The Honourable Justice Jaime Santiago entered and took his seat. It was a trial by judge alone. In the interests of time, Isolde had dispensed with trial by jury. In her absence, the trial of her case began. Higginbottom, with a voice that was loud enough to wake the gods from their sleep on Mount Olympus, made his opening statement. As planned, his first witness, was Yvonne Becker. She was quickly sworn, and was off and running with her evidence, just as she had reviewed it with Higginbottom in preparation for trial. She exuded an air of supreme confidence, both in carriage and in speech. She presented well, not to mention her good looks, which seemed to make an impression on the judge. Higginbottom was permitted to lead her through the preliminary stuff—her position and duties at Fred's law office; the number of years she had worked there; the nature of Fred's practice; the gruesome discovery of Fred's corpse at his desk; and what she did following that. Then Higginbottom got down to the nitty gritty.

"Have you ever heard of an organization called *'Ombra Segreta della Forza di Firenze'?*"

"No. Never."

"Have you ever heard of *The Shadow?*"

"No. Never."

"While Mrs. Bruni was away in Bern recently, there was an incident in the Bruni Law Office involving Fred's files?"

"Yes. Two men appeared at the office and served me with a copy of an Order of the court to deliver up to them all of Fred's files relating to VolksBankBern. I complied. But it turned out that the Order was a fake. I was fooled."

"Do you have the name of those two men?"

"No. It all happened so quickly. They were out of there before it struck me that I should have asked for their names."

"Where is the copy of the Order that they served on you?"

"I dumped it while cleaning up the office." The judge lowered his glasses to the tip of his nose. His eagle eyes stared at her incredulously. "But I had faxed a copy of it to Lawyer Barney Ratskeller before that. He should still have the faxed copy."

"Mrs. Bruni had recently engaged you to assist the witness Lise Brunner during her stay in Toronto?"

"Yes."

"Lise Brunner is a quadriplegic?"

"Yes."

"Ms. Brunner has been a resident at Pinkerton Convalescent Home since her arrival in Toronto?"

"Yes."

"With the permission of Mrs. Bruni, the Home gave you a key for easy access and egress through the back door of the building?"

"Yes."

"When was the last time you saw Ms. Brunner?'

"About five-thirty on Friday afternoon; just before her dinner-time."

"You entered via the staff entrance?"

"Yes."

"When you entered, there was no problem with the lock?"

"No."

"Has your key to that back door ever been out of your possession?"

"Never."

"On Friday afternoon or evening or early Saturday morning, did you open the back door to allow anyone to enter the building?"

"No."

"When you left Ms. Brunner, was there any sign whatsoever that someone had tried to strangle her?"

"No. she was in good shape….. for the shape she was in." There was a ripple of laughter from the spectators in the gallery. "You know, not being able to use her limbs," Yvonne continued.

"Have you ever heard of a woman called Marietta della Caproni?"

"Never."

"Did Mrs. Bruni and Mr. Joaquim Fankhauser pay you a surprise visit at your Meadowvale Village apartment on Saturday?"

"Yes."

"Did they inform you that Ms. Brunner had been the victim of an attack, and that she had lost her ability to speak?"

"Yes. They did."

"Was that the first time you heard of the attack?"

"Yes."

"I want you to listen carefully to this question, remembering that you are under oath. Did you ask them the following question, 'Do they know who tried to strangle her?' A blank look suddenly appeared on Yvonne's face, as her eyes turned up toward the ceiling. She winced, took a deep breath, and then replied.

"I might have."

"Ms. Becker, both Mrs. Bruni and Mr. Fankhauser will testify that you did. I repeat the question. Did you ask them the question, 'Do they know who tried to strangle her?' Please answer 'yes' or 'no'."

"Yes", Yvonne admitted.

"Tell me, Ms. Becker, if that was the first time you heard of the attack, and if the evidence of Mrs. Bruni and Mr. Fankhauser is that they had never told you that there had been a strangulation, how in the world did you know that?" This was followed by a long silence. Again, Yvonne raised her eyes toward the ceiling.

"Very simple," she eventually muttered. "Mrs. Bruni said that Lise had lost her ability to speak. I immediately put two and two together and concluded that it must have been a strangulation." Higginbottom was impressed with how Yvonne Becker had proved to be a Houdini in that little exercise. But he was just getting warmed up.

"Do you own a ring?"

"I own a number of rings."

"Did you pose with Ms. Bruni on Saturday for some photographs taken by Mr. Fankhauser?" She looked puzzled. Where was he going with this line of questioning?

"Yes. I did."

"Please look at these four photographs. Are those the photographs that were taken of you and Ms. Bruni by Mr. Fankhauser?" She studied the photographs carefully. Her eyes popped out of her head, as she stared at the ring displayed on her right ring finger in the photographs. A bead of sweat started to trickle down her forehead.

"They look like them," she mumbled, hesitantly.

"Please answer the question, 'yes' or 'no'. Are they the photographs?"

"Yes. They are," she blurted out, defiantly. Higginbottom introduced the four photographs into the record as Exhibits A-1, A-2, A-3 and A-4.

"The beautiful ring on your right ring finger, can you describe it to the court, please?"

"It is a gold ring, with an emblem on the crown."

"What is depicted in the emblem?"

"Looks like three intersecting crescents."

"What is the black stone in the crown?"

"I don't know. My guess would be onyx?"

"And what is inlaid in the onyx?"

"Again, I don't know. I would guess that it's mother of pearl?"

"How did you come by this ring?" She was very uncomfortable, twisting and turning. The fingers of her right hand scratched away feverishly at her left wrist.

"It was a gift."

"A gift from whom?" Her eyes turned upward to gaze at the bright lights beaming down like many moons from the ceiling. She now appeared to be in a type of trance, oblivious to her surroundings.

"Are you OK Ms. Becker?" Higginbottom asked.

"Yes. I'm OK," she replied, meekly.

"You said it was a gift. A gift from whom?"

"I cannot remember. I just recall that someone gave it to me years ago as a birthday gift."

"No more questions at this time, My Lord. I reserve the right to recall this witness."

"Very well, Mr. Higginbottom. Any cross-examination, Mr. Hickshok?"

"None at this time, My Lord. I reserve the right to cross-examine Ms. Becker once I am tuned in to where Mr. Higginbottom is going with this line of questions about a broken lock and a beautiful ring."

"What's good for the goose is good for the gander, I suppose," the judge remarked, a broad smile across his face. "Next witness, please."

Higginbottom's next witness was Bryce Keenleyside. Keenleyside, a cigarette sitting on his right ear, made his way to the witness box, his legs appearing to be in conflict with each other and his clothes as wet as if he had just swam across Lake Ontario in them. Higginbottom immediately motioned to him to remove the cigarette from his ear.

"State your name in full for the court, please," the Court Clerk ordered, Keenleyside's right hand on the Bible.

"B-B--Bryce Keenleyside, sir," he stuttered, his head arching back toward his spine with each stutter. The judge took a second look at him, undoubtedly thinking to himself: 'This is going to be a very, very long day.'

"Do you swear that the evidence you are about to give will be the truth, the whole truth, and nothing but the truth?"

"Sure do, sir."

"Are you the building superintendent employed by Pinkerton Convalescent Home?" asked Higginbottom.

"Sure am, sir."

"For brevity of time, Mr. Keenleyside, you can skip the 'sir' to every answer," the Judge interrupted.

"Thank you, sir," Keenleyside answered, with a deep bow. Again, there was a ripple of laughter from the spectators. The judge himself could not help but snicker.

"How long have you held that position?" Higginbottom asked.

Since I was a y-y-young lad. F-F--First job, and only job, I ever had."

"And how old are you now?"

"Too old to r-r-remember, sir," Keenleyside quipped. The judge was becoming irritated.

"Witness, please give direct answers to the questions!" he ordered.

"F-F-Fifty-two, sir."

"During that period of time, have you had any experience with repairing or replacing broken locks?"

"B-B-Both," he replied. He looked up at the judge, half expecting some sort of commendation for his brevity. The judge was looking down at his notes, which, at this time, were sparse.

"In the early morning of last Saturday, did you inspect the lock to the back door used by staff to access and egress the Home?"

"Sure did, sir." At this, the judge simply shook his head, thinking that this witness was hopeless.

"What was the condition of the lock?"

"It was b-b-broken b-b-beyond repair, sir."

"I present to you four photographs of a lock. Were these photographs taken by you?"

"Yes, sir"

"Exhibits "B-1, B-2-, B-3 and B-4, please," Higginbottom said to the court clerk, as he handed her the four photographs.

Defence counsel Hickshok objected to the line of questioning. "What does a broken lock have to do with the issues in this case?" he argued. "Absolutely irrelevant."

"The relevance will be revealed before the end of the day, My Lord. Please allow me the leeway to proceed with these questions."

"I will allow the questions," the judge ruled. "Mr. Higginbottom has never been known to trifle with the court. Please proceed."

"In your opinion," Higginbottom asked Keenleyside," was the lock broken from the outside of the door or from the inside?"

"The lock was not b-b--broken from the outside, sir. Someone standing inside the b-b-building b-b-broke the lock. And then monkeyed with the outside of the d-d-door to fake it. Make it look like it was not an inside job."

"Those are all my questions for this witness, My Lord."

"Cross-examination, Mr. Hickshok?" From his voice, it was clear that the judge, anxious to speed up the progress of the trial, was hoping that he could immediately dismiss this witness.

"As with the previous witness, My Lord, I reserve my right to cross-examine this witness once Mr. Higginbottom reveals to us what he is doing."

"Fair enough." The judge stared down at both counsel, a curious smile on his face. "I was just wondering if we will ever finish this trial within the allocated three weeks. Seems to me that at this pace it will be three months, not three weeks. Please call your next witness, Mr. Higginbottom. We are all waiting with bated breath for the grand revelation in the mysteries of the broken lock and the beautiful ring."

"I call Lise Brunner to the stand." Lise was sitting in her wheelchair in the hallway, at the main entrance to the courtroom, Isolde and a nursing attendant by her side. The judge watched with interest as she, wheelchair and all, were lifted up to the slightly raised flooring of the witness stand. An oxygen tank was strapped to the back of her wheelchair, tubes from the oxygen tank running into her nostrils. Lise was pale and drawn and looked like death frozen over. Higginbottom addressed the judge.

"As your Lordship observes, Ms. Brunner is under a severe disability. She is a quadriplegic. As her evidence will indicate, she lost the ability to speak when an attempt to take her life by strangulation was made in the very early hours of Saturday morning."

"Without the use of her arms and the use of her vocal cords, how can she possibly give evidence at this trial?" the judge interrupted, sharply.

"She can still move her head, her facial muscles, her lips, teeth, and tongue," Higginbottom responded. "We need the accommodation by the court to permit the use of an interpreter in the art of what is commonly called 'lip reading'. Ms. Claire Worthington is an expert in the field. She is able to interpret what the witness is saying by close observation of the movements of the witness' head, facial muscles, lips, teeth, and tongue."

"Any objection, Mr. Hickshok?" the judge asked.

"None whatsoever, My Lord."

"Please proceed, Mr. Higginbottom." Higginbottom then had the interpreter sworn and elicited enough from her to have her qualified as an expert in lip reading. He then had Lise sworn.

"Is your name Lise Brunner?" Lise mouthed the word "yes", which was entirely inaudible, at the same time confirming her answer with a nod of her head. The interpreter audibly said "Yes", which was then recorded by the court reporter. The process, though it worked, was slow and tedious. The judge was beside himself. First, a witness that is a reluctant witness. Then a witness that stutters. And now a witness that cannot speak. He shuddered. This is quickly becoming a comedy of errors, he thought. Or, more appropriately, a Greek tragedy.

For the protection of Lise from evidence given by her being used against her in a later civil or criminal proceeding, Higginbottom told the court that she was taking the protection of the Ontario Evidence Act and the Canada Evidence Act. He then took Lise through her life history. Born and raised in Bern, Switzerland; a descendant of the famous Medicis of old Florence. Her initiation through the defendant Constantino Rapini, manager of the defendant VolksBankBern, into the defendant organization called *'Ombra Segreta della Forza di Firenze'*, commonly known as *The Shadow*. Her role in her friend Fred Bruni obtaining VolksBankBern as a major, if not his only, client. The instructions from *The Shadow* to plant a single tablet of Catherine de' Medici's favourite poison *'Mon Petit Ami'* in the bottle containing Fred's Cafergot pills used to treat his migraine attacks. The first attempt made on her life by *The Shadow* in trying to poison her at her apartment in Bern. The second attempt made by *The Shadow* on her life and the lives of Isolde Bruni and Renée Fankhauser when Simon Hartmann invaded the *Fankhaus* with pistol drawn. The third attempt made on her life, along with the lives of Isolde, Fankhauser and his mother Renée at the intersection of Rathausgasse and Brunngasse in Bern. The judge was now thinking to himself, 'This is what good novels are made of', as his countenance changed from one of boredom to that of a reader absorbed in the unfolding of the gripping plot of a novel loaded with crime and intrigue. He was taking notes ferociously. And then Higginbottom introduced him to the recent happenings at the Pinkerton Convalescent Home.

"Ms. Brunner, did someone try to strangle you in the early morning of last Saturday?"

Lise mouthed the answer, and nodded her head. The interpreter translated "Yes."

"Can you show the court any marks left by the strangulation?" Lise raised her head, exposing the elevated red marks around her neck. "Let the record show that the witness raised her head to reveal elevated red marks around her neck."

"Do you know who did this to you?"

The interpreter translated "No", as Lise mouthed the word and swung her head from side to side. Lise went on to mouth the words "It was dark."

"I am producing to you four photographs which have been admitted into evidence as Exhibits A-1, A-2, A-3 and A-4. Do you recognize the persons in these photographs as Isolde Bruni and Yvonne Becker?" She mouthed "Yes" and nodded her head.

"Please look at the ring on the right ring finger of Ms. Becker. Do you recognize that ring?" There was an instant glint of recognition. It was as if the lost had been found. This was soon followed by a grimace.

"Is that a ring that belonged to you?"

The answer was immediate. "Yes. That is *my* ring. It was removed from my finger during the attack."

"Please describe the ring."

"Gold ring. Crown of black onyx, inlaid with three intersecting crescents of mother of pearl."

"Is that a very expensive ring?"

"Yes. It was a gift from VolksBankBern. Only one like that in the world, Herr Rapini told me. Worth thousands of Swiss francs."

"What does the emblem on the crown represent?"

"Long history. Came down from Diane de Poitiers, the mistress of Henry II. He was married to Catherine de' Medici, my ancestor who developed *'Mon Petit Ami'*."

"Diane who?" the judge interrupted, anxious to keep up with the intrigue.

"de Poitiers, My Lord," Higginbottom intercepted. "Lower case d-e-; followed by upper case P; immediately followed by lower case -o-i-t-i-e-r-s; as in Sidney Poitier, but with an 's' added at the end." The judge smiled gratuitously at this spoon-feeding by Higginbottom.

"And what is this *'Mon Petit Ami'*? What does *'My Little Friend'* have to do with this case?" the judge persevered, anxious to garner the intricacies of the plot, into which he was now totally immersed.

"It will all be revealed to you in due course, My Lord. I beg your indulgence."

"Please proceed."

"To your knowledge, does that sign on the crown of the ring mean anything to *The Shadow*?" Higginbottom continued in his questioning.

"Yes. It is their mark; their emblem. All members of *The Shadow* wear or carry that emblem. It's like 'the mark of the Beast' referred to in the *'Book of Revelation'*," she elaborated, through her interpreter. What a fascinating case, the judge thought to himself.

"Those are all my questions for Ms. Brunner, My Lord."

"Cross-examination, Mr. Hichshok?" the judge asked. Hickshok rose to his feet. He looked at the clock.

"My Lord, considering that it is now five-thirty, may I suggest that we break for the day and that I do my crops-examination tomorrow?"

"The court is adjourned for the day," the judge declared.

Back at the Saddlers Court mansion for the evening, Isolde, Fankhauser and Renée were huddled together in the family room, a bottle of Robert Mondavi California Special Cabernet Sauvignon split among them. Margot had picked Emil and Sophie up at the school, and the excitement in their voices could be heard, drifting down the stairs, as they played video games in their rooms. Isolde looked at Fankhauser with a knowing smile.

"So, I got the epiphany," Isolde said to Fankhauser. "You rascal, you purposely wanted to surprise me, Joaquim; and you sure did. You know, the evidence about the ring. You sure led Yvonne into a trap." Fankhauser smiled appreciatively.

"As I told you, God makes his revelations in his own time," he responded.

"I wish you would quit the blasphemy, Joaquim," Renée scolded him, a half-smile on her face.

"Remember, Mama, you taught me as a child that *'For everything there is a season, and a time for every purpose under heaven'*. I think that is written in the *Book of Ecclesiastes*, is it not?" he remarked, with a burst of laughter.

"Your problem, Joaquim, is that you have a memory like a sponge. You never forget anything, good or bad. My words to you come back to haunt me, like some ever-reverberating echo. Sometimes I pray to God that you would forget half of what I taught you," she groaned, taking the joke to its limit.

"Your problem, Mama, is that you are a doer, not a talker. Look at how you plugged Simon Hartmann! Wham! Plumb in the back! And look at how you took down the guy at the intersection of Rathausgasse and Brunngasse. Wham again! Dead on! Blew his brains out! You are my Annie Oakley, Mama. You never miss."

"A goddamned hitman you have made of me, my renegade son. I am sure I will pay the price for this when I meet St. Peter at the Pearly Gates!" She and Fankhauser were at the height of exhilaration whenever they bantered back and forth between themselves. It was all a game to them. Isolde sat back, watching the loving rapport between mother and son, and admired Fankhauser all the more. Fankhauser yawned; looked at his watch; and slowly rose from his chair.

"I am turning in, after all the drama of today. Tomorrow, after all, is another day. Goodnight, ladies." With that, he vanished to his room, leaving Isolde and Renée looking at each other, stunned at his abrupt departure. Enjoying each other, they killed another bottle of Robert Mondavi, and speculated about the evidence of Yvonne Becker.

CHAPTER THIRTY-SIX

WHEN COURT OPENED the next morning, Lise was back in the witness box, her hair beaming under the bright lights of the courtroom ceiling and her face highlighted by a radiant glow which made her appear almost saint-like. It was as if an angel had breathed new life into her soul, if not her body, and she was now wholly within her comfort zone. As the judge turned to ask her if she was settled in and ready to face the cross-examination, their eyes met, and he suddenly became lost within himself as he succumbed to the clutches of her captivating smile. She nodded confidently, signifying that she was ready to proceed, her lipreading interpreter standing down below, directly opposite her. Hickshok rose to cross-examine.

"Ms. Brunner, when did you first become aware of an organization called *'Ombra Segreta della Forza di Firenze'*?"

"About eighteen years ago, through Herr Rapini," she responded by mouthing, through her interpreter.

"Apart from what Mr. Rapini may have told you, did you have any contact whatsoever with what you have referred to as *The Shadow*?"

"No."

"So, you were not able to identify any members of *The Shadow,* other than Mr. Rapini?"

"That is correct."

"And you did not know of any activities of *The Shadow,* apart from what Mr. Rapini told you?"

"That is correct."

"And yet you have given this Court a tale of this ghostlike entity called *The Shadow* that produces some super-poison known by the wacko name of *'Mon Petit Ami'*?"

"I trusted Herr Rapini in his words. He had me sworn to be loyal to *The Shadow,* under penalty of death. He sealed my trust with the gift of the expensive gold ring; the one with the emblem of the three crescents. He told me that this emblem is worn by all members of *The Shadow.* I was paid One Million Swiss francs to plant the poison pill in Fred's pill bottle."

"How did you come by this information about this alleged emblem of the three intersecting crescents having its origin in some mistress of King Henry II of France, this woman called Diane de Poitiers, who lived over four hundred years ago?"

"I heard it from Isolde Bruni."

"So, would you agree with me that this is self-serving evidence garnered from the Plaintiff herself in this litigation and based on tales of historical writings?" Lise hesitated. She did not know how to respond.

"Mr. Hickshok," the judge intercepted, "that calls for a conclusion on the part of this witness. It is unfair. The evidence will speak for itself. Move on, please."

"Ms. Brunner, you have no idea as to who may have removed the ring from your finger last Saturday morning, do you?"

"That is correct."

"Are you able to identify with absolute certainty the ring shown in the photographic Exhibits as being the ring that had been removed from your finger?"

"When Herr Rapini gave me the ring, he told me that it was the only one of that type and design in the whole wide world." Hickshok then concluded his cross-examination. The judge looked at Higginbottom. Higginbottom rose to his feet.

"I would like to recall the witness Yvonne Becker to the stand, My Lord." The court clerk called out for "Yvonne Becker" to come forward. Yvonne slowly made her way to the witness box. The look on her face was the complete opposite of the radiance that glowed on Lise's face that morning. Despite the mask of heavy make-up, sullen eyes peeped out, darting back and forth, almost like some scared rabbit looking to exit its escape hole after a chase by an unrelenting hunter.

"Ms. Becker, you testified as to a fake Order that had been served on you while Mrs. Bruni was away in Bern?"

"Yes."

"And that you had thrown out that document with the trash?"

"Yes. That was a mistake on my part."

"But you had been a legal secretary for over eighteen years?"

"Yes. As I already said, it was a mistake."

"How much were you paid to turn over Fred's files, Ms. Becker?" Higginbottom's voice thundered, as he peered down at one of the small bundle of documents which he held in his hand. A stunned look captured Yvonne's face.

"I resent being asked that question!" she shouted at Higginbottom.

"The witness must answer the question," the judge ordered. "And you must control your temper."

"Would you mind repeating the question?" Yvonne asked, fighting for time to find an answer, as she stared down at the document in his hand, trying to second-guess what it was.

"How much were you paid to turn over Fred's files?" Again, he scanned the document, which was the size of a bank statement.

"Nothing," she snapped. He changed the subject, returning the bundle of documents to the front of his file.

"Ms. Becker, you heard the testimony of Ms. Brunner that the ring you were wearing when the Exhibit "A" photographs were taken was her ring that had been removed from her finger at the time of the recent attack on her?"

"Yes. I heard her say that."

"And you have claimed that the ring had been a gift to you, but you cannot recall from whom?"

"Yes. That is my evidence."

"I suggest to you that the ring had been removed from Ms. Brunner's finger and given to you in partial payment for your part in the strangulation attack?"

"That's a lie!" she shouted, causing the judge to admonish her for raising her voice.

"Ms. Becker, you heard the evidence given by the building superintendent of Pinkerton's that the lock on the back door of the building had been broken from the inside, and not from the outside?"

"Yes; but what has that to do with me?" she asked, defensively.

"It is my job to ask the questions; your job to answer them. Do you understand that?"

"Yes."

"So please answer the question."

"Yes. I heard Mr. Keenleyside say that," she answered, gruffly.

"I understand that you were the only non-staff that had a key to the back door. I am suggesting to you that you either loaned the key to someone or let that person in yourself?"

"Neither," she snorted. With the back of her right hand, she wiped away the drainage from her nostrils. Higginbottom could see the beads of sweat on her forehead, repeating their act of the previous day. Good sign, he thought; she will not withstand the pressure. He pulled out from his file the same documents that he had held in his hand when he had intimated that she had received payment for turning over Fred's files.

"Do you have a bank account with Bank of Montreal at Bay and King?" he asked, as he shuffled through the small bundle of documents in his hand, as if looking for a specific document. The tension proved too much for her. She resigned herself to the fact that the game was over. The little shrimp had her bank records, right there in his tiny prongs.

"I know, you will find a couple large deposits; but I can explain those," she blabbered. Higginbottom looked up at her, with an engaging smile. It was as if he was playing a game of 'good cop, bad cop'. That's my girl, Yvonne. Now out with it.

"The first deposit back in November was a payment of $20,000.00 from my late uncle's estate." His instinct told him that she was now outright lying. OK, let's play her little game.

"And the second?" She looked up at the ceiling. She was now completely out of it.

"The second—uhm—uhm—uhm. What the hell!" she bellowed, her face now beet red with rage. The judge raised his head, his eyes full of shock as he stared down at her. "You have the documents, anyway. Yes; I was paid the $20,000.00 to give up Fred's files. It seemed like such easy money at the time, for just a simple act of cutting the files loose. And then last week a woman approached me; said she was from Florence. I'm sure she said Florence, not Rome. She did not give me her name. She said she would deposit $100,000.00 into my bank account, and all I had to do was to give her access through the back door of the Home. I asked her why. She said Lise would be strangled. The choice was clear. If I allowed her access, I would be paid $100,000.00; but if I refused or reported her to the police, *The Shadow*, as she called it, would hunt me down, wherever I was on this earth, and kill me. Besides, she told me, Lise did not have much to lose; she was already half-dead anyway!" Tears were now flowing in torrents down her cheeks, taking the heavy cake of cosmetics with them, and revealing a gaunt, twisted outline which was her begrimed face. Her loud sobs overpowered the courtroom. The judge ordered the police sergeant on duty in the courtroom to take Yvonne into custody, and announced to counsel that he wanted to see them both in his chambers immediately. Isolde and Renée sat there, frozen like statues, their jaws dropped to the floor, in awe of the abrupt change of events. Fankhauser showed no sign of being amazed. This is exactly as I had anticipated, he smugly thought to himself. As the sergeant handcuffed and escorted the now frantic Yvonne out of the courtroom, her screaming words rebounded throughout the corridors of the solemn halls of justice. "This is not fair! Not fair! Not fair! Isolde had it all! The house in the Bridle Path; the fancy yachts; the red Ferrari; the vacations all over the world! Why her? Why not me? Why not me? Why not me?"

Once the judge, Higginbottom and Hickshok were all inside his chambers, the judge slammed the door shut, sat down, and stared at Hickshok.

"Mr. Hickshok," he said, "you must settle this damn case; and settle it now. Your guys are as guilty as sin." Hickshok could read the writing on the wall. The judge had made up his mind. Settlement was the only option. The judge returned to the courtroom, and adjourned the trial for the day. Settlement negotiations were being pursued. By eight that evening, a settlement agreement was in place. The defendants would forthwith pay to Isolde for herself and on behalf of Emil and Sophie the sum of $15,000,000.00, all in. While Isolde was thrilled with the amount of the settlement, she wanted more. She wanted to have the Death Certificate for Fred revised to remove any mention of suicide from the Manner of Death. In the Judgment pursuant to the Minutes of Settlement, the judge inserted a declaration that in the death of Friedrich Bruni the Immediate Cause of Death was Asphyxiation; the Underlying Cause of Death was Poisoning by ingestion of a poison identified as *'Mon Petit Ami';* and that the Manner of Death was Homicide. Higginbottom produced the Judgment to the Office of the Coroner, which was amenable to issuing an Amended Death Certificate. The Amended Death Certificate stated that the Immediate Cause of Death was **ASPHYXIATION;** that the Underlying Cause of Death was **POISONING BY THE INGESTION OF A POISON IDENTIFIED AS 'MON PETIT AMI'**; and that the Manner of Death was **HOMICIDE.**

Higginbottom personally delivered the Amended Death Certificate to Isolde at the Saddlers Court mansion. When she read it, she scooped the little man up in her arms, planted several kisses on the pate of his head, and wept with joy. "Thank you! Thank you! Thank you, Ben. This is what I wanted. This, above all, has made it all worthwhile," she bubbled.

CHAPTER THIRTY-SEVEN

THAT EVENING, it was party time at the Saddlers Court mansion. The diminutive Higginbottom, a crystal champagne flute in one hand and a huge magnum of Dom Pérignon in the other, was holding court, basking in the glory of his victory. He was the little man in the centre of his happy throng of admirers. Fankhauser saw him as Julius Caesar, riding into Rome on his high horse, the laurels of victory on his forehead, while the masses prostrated themselves before him and shouted "Hail Caesar! Hail Caesar! Hail Caesar!" Fankhauser, as towering as the Colossus at Rhodes, but as humble as a pious Jesuit monk, stood by his side. Isolde and Margot were amused at the sight of the little Higginbottom dwarfed by the tall Fankhauser. "A veritable scene from the well-known cartoon *Mutt and Jeff*," Margot whispered to Isolde, which evoked a chuckle from Isolde. Renée was off to the side, not unaware of the rather comedic scene. Joaquim has met his match, thought Renée to herself. Even Emil and Sophie were there, in party mode, darting around with bottles of Coke and pieces of Swiss chocolate in their hands. They did not know what they were celebrating. They only knew that there must be reason to celebrate. Fankhauser sidled up closer to Higginbottom. There was something on his mind.

"Tell me, Ben. The bundle of bank statements that you held in your hand as you cross-examined Yvonne was the straw that broke the camel's back. How were you able to obtain those bank statements in so short a time?" Higginbottom looked up at Fankhauser, a twinkle in his little eyes.

"What bank statements?" Higginbottom asked. "That was a bundle of blank pages." He winked at Fankhauser, like a magician at his audience, after performance of an outstanding piece of magic.

"Well, I'll be damned!" Fankhauser blurted out. The little man was a trickster. He had pulled off a fascinating ruse, a sleight of hand, so to speak. Suddenly, in the eyes of Fankhauser, Higginbottom had picked up another six inches in height. Better stop this, Fankhauser thought to himself; or else pretty soon this little guy will be taller than me.

It was now twelve-forty, and the end of the celebration was nowhere in sight. There were by this time five empty champagne magnum bottles sitting on the kitchen counter. Sonny and Cher were in the middle of their 1965 hit *I Got You Babe*. Margot was looking into the eyes of Isolde, mouthing the lyrics of Sonny. Isolde was responding, mouthing the lyrics of Cher. Suddenly, the telephone rang.

"Hello. May I speak with Mrs. Bruni, please?" the high-pitched voice asked.

"This is Mrs. Bruni speaking."

"Mrs. Bruni, I am sorry to have to tell you this." Isolde's heart fell. What in the world has happened? "I am calling from Pinkerton Convalescent Home. Lise Brunner passed away this evening."

"Oh, no! No! No!" Isolde's words hit the ears of the other revelers with a deafening thud. They rushed to Isolde's side. "What happened?" Isolde asked the Pinkerton caller.

"She suddenly started vomiting. She choked on her own vomit. Please get back to us later today to make arrangements for the removal of the body." With one fell swoop, the party was over. They retreated to the family room, where they all sat, just looking at one another in stunned silence. Eventually, Fankhauser opened his mouth.

"By some strange twist of faith, *The Shadow* has won its war against Lise," he said glumly, shrugging his shoulders with an air of philosophical resignation. "The relentless many-headed Hydra has brought her to her knees. In fact, to her grave. As they saw it, she had committed the ultimate sin. She had betrayed them. In their unwritten code of evil, this was unforgivable. The penalty was death."

The women wept openly for Lise. She, who had bedded down with Isolde's husband in Bern, over and over and over again. She, who had taken Fred's life in its prime, when he had everything to live for. She, who had robbed Isolde of the love and companionship of her husband. She, who had denied Emil and Sophie the nurturing of a father. And, she, who had left Margot without the society of her dear brother. She, this woman descended from the infamous alchemist Catherine de' Medici, now commanded tears that flowed down the mountainside of the weepers' souls like springtime streams stemming from the heights of Mount Olympus.

"May God have mercy on her soul!" Isolde declared, her tear-filled copper-coloured cat's eyes fixated on the floor. "She, in spite of her manifold misdeeds, may have been the greatest Medici of them all."

THE END

BOOKS BY NEVILLE JOHNSTON

*THE NAKED AND THE DAMNED (a novel) --to be released in 2022

*THE SHADOW OF THE FORCE (a novel)

*ROAD TO OBLIVION: THE GREAT WAR OF OSBIE McDONALD (a novel)

*BURDEN OF BONDAGE (a novel)

*THE CHALICE FULL: POEMS FOR THE COMMON MAN (a collection of poems)

*WILD AS WHIPPOORWILLS IN THE NIGHT (a collection of poems)

*RIMES OF PASSION (a collection of poems)

*SONGS OF MY SEASONS (a collection of poems)

ABOUT NEVILLE JOHNSTON

NEVILLE JOHNSTON is a Canadian novelist and poet who resides in Brockville, Ontario. He is the author of three published novels, BURDEN OF BONDAGE; ROAD TO OBLIVION: THE GREAT WAR OF OSBIE McDONALD; and THE SHADOW OF THE FORCE. All three novels were written and published during the Covid-19 pandemic. His fourth novel, THE NAKED AND THE DAMNED, a sequel to ROAD TO OBLIVION: THE GREAT WAR OF OSBIE McDONALD, will be released in early 2022.

He has been writing poetry since the age of twelve, and describes it as a lifelong passion. His published poetry books include SONGS OF MY SEASONS; RIMES OF PASSION; WILD AS WHIPPOORWILLS IN THE NIGHT; and THE CHALICE FULL: POEMS FOR THE COMMON MAN. He has been dubbed 'Poet of the 1,000 Islands'.

Neville was born in St. Andrew, Jamaica, and has resided in Canada since 1959. He holds a Bachelor of Arts degree (B.A.) from the University of Toronto and a Doctor Juris degree (J.D.) from Osgoode Hall Law School (York University). He is an Honourary Life Member of the Bar of Ontario, and a Member of the Bar of New York.

In 1973, he was the recipient of the 'GOVERNOR GENERAL VANIER AWARD' as one of five OUTSTANDING YOUNG PERSONS OF CANADA. Other recipients of the VANIER AWARD include former Governor General Edward Schreyer (1975) and hockey great Wayne Gretzky (1982).

He is married to Geri, his wife of fifty-seven years, with whom he resides in Brockville, Ontario, Canada. They have three children, Robin of Tallahassee, FL, Allison of Gainesville, FL, and Ryan of Palm Beach Gardens, FL, and five grandchildren, Olivia, Madison, Caden, Nico, and . DJ, all of Florida.

Readers are invited to visit Neville's website at https://nevillejohnston.com.